MW00438114

SETH CARLSON: A desperate act and a cynical journalist made him into a national hero. He hoped for redemption in the heat of battle but found instead a regard for his enemy that made it impossible to follow orders without question. . . .

COREY BRYCE: A newly commissioned officer eager for the life of an Indian fighter, he set out for New Mexico with his pretty young wife. But fate would shatter his plans and pit him against the man who had been his closest friend. . . .

JEANETTE CUNNINGHAM BRYCE: She followed the man she loved without a qualm into Indian country. But her husband soon wondered if he had made a mistake in bringing her to New Mexico—for the tribes were growing more brutal in their resistance, and he could sense the love springing up between her and his own best friend. . . .

JEMEZ GRAYEYES: His bravery and honor had become legendary among his people—as was his fear of a dishonorable death by the white man's rope. His fame among the Apache made him a target of the army, and his deeds earned him the regard of the man who was commissioned to cut him down. . . .

NAT BISCHOFF: America's most popular frontier newspaperman, he gave the people what they wanted—heroes—and whipped up the nation's frenzy for Indian blood. And total war against the Indians happened to be good for the business of certain friends. . . .

KATHLEEN BARTON: A teacher on the Mater Dolorosa Apache Reservation, she saw the bloodiest of betrayals. Still she had the courage to stand her ground and face both Jemez Grayeyes and Seth Carlson. . . .

THEY CAPTURED THE IMAGINATION OF A
COUNTRY . . .
AND FORGED THE DESTINY OF A NATION

THE UNWRITTEN ORDER

John Edward Ames

BANTAM BOOKS
NEW YORK   TORONTO   LONDON
SYDNEY   AUCKLAND

THE UNWRITTEN ORDER

A Bantam Book / March 1995

All rights reserved.
Copyright © 1995 by John Edward Ames.
Cover art copyright © 1995 by Tom Hall.
No part of this book may be reproduced or transmitted in any
form or by any means, electronic or mechanical, including
photocopying, recording, or by any information storage and
retrieval system, without permission in writing from the publisher.
For information address: Bantam Books.

If you purchased this book without a cover you should be aware
that this book is stolen property. It was reported as "unsold and
destroyed" to the publisher and neither the author nor the
publisher has received any payment for this "stripped book."

ISBN 0-553-56778-0

Published simultaneously in the United States and Canada

Bantam Books are published by Bantam Books, a division of
Bantam Doubleday Dell Publishing Group, Inc. Its trademark,
consisting of the words "Bantam Books" and the portrayal of a
rooster, is Registered in U.S. Patent and Trademark Office and in
other countries. Marca Registrada. Bantam Books, 1540 Broadway,
New York, New York 10036.

PRINTED IN THE UNITED STATES OF AMERICA

RAD   0 9 8 7 6 5 4 3 2 1

For the Bergman ladies:
Barbara, Carolyn, and Susan,
who spent a sunny Christmas with
me in New Orleans.

This is forbidden even
to God—the power to undo the past.

GREEK PROVERB

Prologue

Chimaca heard a rifle bolt slide home in the chilly darkness just outside the cave, and the old Apache woke instantly.

Silver-white moonlight slanted in through giant boulders that formed a natural rampart at the cave entrance. The dry bunchgrass mat under his blankets rustled when he sat up. The sound was amplified in the cold stillness of the cavern.

Moonwash limned the interior in a soft glow. He could just make out dim mounds where the others huddled together for warmth. One of the infants moved in its sleep, and the wicker cradle squeaked like a new saddle.

The old man's blood slowly stopped throbbing in his palms. The sound he'd heard was nothing, a memory smell from the bloody days of fighting the Pope's army. Jemez, his nephew, had searched out this stronghold high in the Dragoon Mountains because he knew the Mexican *rurales* were too lazy to come this far north. And Jemez, now there was a man who knew which way the wind sets. If he said this place—

Just then Chimaca smelled the bitter cactus-liquor smell of pulque staining the air.

A cool feather of fear tickled the bumps of his spine. A moment later he spotted the Mexican soldier.

It was a *rurale* officer. Chimaca glimpsed the familiar kepi and crossed bandoliers. He made out a beard shadow, eyes too small for the huge skull. The wrinkled pouch dangling from his pistol belt had once been a bull's scrotum. Chimaca saw that, and a heartbeat later he knew they were all about to die.

It's this cold, they spotted the smoke from the campfires earlier, didn't Jemez tell me before he went north, no more fires, old-timer, at least pretend you have more brains than a rabbit, didn't he say that?

Despite these words he heard clearly inside his head, Chimaca couldn't force a warning yell past the hard lump lodged in his throat. Everything happened fast after that, though the old man felt like he was trying to move in deep water. At night he always tucked his rifle into his blankets to protect it from dew. He drew it out now, his finger struggling in dream-time clumsiness before it finally slipped inside the trigger guard.

Another *rurale* seemed to materialize like a wraith out of thin air. Chimaca glimpsed his empty shoulder scabbard and the moonlight glinting cruelly off the curved blade of his upraised machete. There was a swishing whisper, like the sound of a hoe digging into flinty dirt. Then a white-hot tourniquet of pain gripped his right arm.

The rifle dropped fast into his lap. A thick stream of blood surged from the place where his arm had been nearly severed. Chimaca heard the blood splashing like horse piss onto the stone floor of the cave. His arm hung slack and useless, connected to his shoulder by the last thin rope of uncut muscle. He could see that his finger was still hooked through the trigger guard, but it was dead to his will.

Now, as the pain locked horns with his nervous system, Chimaca saw the others step inside. Even as his body went into numbing shock, he recognized the hair-face Anglo from

Tucson—the Apache-killer who talked out of both sides of his mouth, always extending one hand in friendship while the other hid a knife behind his back. And the turncoat half-breed beside him, his breath reeking of pulque—Chimaca's own nephew and Jemez's cousin, Juan Aragon.

It hadn't been the campfires that gave them away.

"Yiiii-ahh-eee-YA!"

The old man's war cry ricocheted around the stone walls, jolting everyone out of sleep like a sudden boom-clap of thunder. The high, piercing wail was compounded of rage and pain and sadness and eternal defiance.

"Maldita!" the officer cursed, pointing his pistol toward the Apache.

"Everyone knows," Chimaca said to him quickly in Spanish, "that your mother fucks Apaches."

Chimaca despised the Mexican murderers who had replaced the Spaniards. Decades of breeding with them had not made the Apaches feel any more Mexican, just as the Indian penchant for using their Spanish names made his people feel no less Apache. Now the old man had the satisfaction of seeing rage smolder in this Mexican's small, piglike eyes before an orange starburst inside Chimaca's skull welcomed him to the Land Beyond the Sun.

The cry made her think her pony was dying. Eleven-year-old Socorro woke up just in time to watch a soldier plant a bullet in her uncle's brain.

Miguelito, too, had been wakened by the old man's war cry. He lay huddled against his sister under the blanket. He started to say something, but she pressed one hand over his mouth.

More guns spat fire into the night, more curses in Spanish. Socorro watched, biting down hard on her lip to keep from screaming out, as soldiers shot their pistols point-blank into the wicker cradles and huddled sleepers. In the seemingly endless flashes of light she recognized her cousin Juan—the one who always tried to slide his hand under her dress.

In the middle of the cave Placita, her mother, sat up. Her bare back was slim and muscular and long in the stark moonlight. Placita's eyes automatically went to Socorro's. She tilted her head toward the back of the cavern, and suddenly Socorro remembered what she was supposed to do.

Placita started to rise. Another percussion cap cracked, and Socorro watched her mother collapse like a rag puppet.

The girl saw it, but it wasn't real yet. Now, as the acrid smell of cordite made her brother tense for a cough—Miguelito was sick with the croup—she quickly wrapped the blanket over his head to absorb the sound. She knew that the soldiers had not spotted them yet, partially hidden under a limestone outcropping.

"Shush," she whispered in his ear. Then she tasted salt and realized she was biting deep into her lip, drawing blood. A moment later she was up, Miguelito's hand gripped hard in hers, and they were stealing toward the escape tunnel.

The cold updraft from the tunnel entrance kissed her face. Socorro ran into the natural shaft as she heard Juan call out in Spanish, "Be careful, there's a tunnel!"

Miguelito whimpered as sharp pieces of flint cut into his bare feet. But Socorro dragged the six-year-old behind her at a reckless pace, ignoring the cuts to her own feet. Then they hit a smooth patch of water-covered shale and she went down hard on the rock, cracking her elbow. It hurt bad and she knew it was serious. But her brother cried behind her, and though he pulled back in fear, her responsibility to protect him pushed her forward.

Then the black-velvet folds of the night absorbed them as they emerged into the fertile ravine where the ponies were hidden. The area was thick with white-barked sycamores and dark, gnarled ash trees; pliant willows hugged the banks of a small river. Socorro heard voices and footsteps in the tunnel behind them, saw her pony lying dead with the others, all of them throat-slashed.

Miguelito coughed hard; a wracking, loose cough that made phlegm rattle like pebbles in his chest. Socorro's elbow hurt bad—so bad she wanted to cry. But how many times had her brother Jemez told her the Apache way? *Endure pain in silence, meet death with defiance, and if you must fall, land on the bones of an enemy.*

The noises of pursuit loomed closer in the tunnel. Still gripping Miguelito's cold little paw, Socorro headed toward the cover of the trees. When he cried in protest, she slapped him hard.

"Are you a man or a baby? Apaches don't cry!"

But as they scrambled into the darkness, she again saw her mother folding to the floor of the cave, her life cancelled by a bullet. The beadwork pattern of stars, the pale three-quarter moon, the entire night sky went blurry as hot tears filled her eyes.

PART ONE

Chapter 1

"Gentlemen, put down your pens now. That's right, put them in their holders. Good. Now clean the wax out of your ears and listen carefully. I'm about to discuss a very unpleasant order that you will never—repeat, *never*, if you value your commission—put in writing."

At these words, Cadet Seth Carlson leaned forward slightly in his seat, watching the instructor closely. Major Orrin Lofley sported a drooping George Armstrong Custer mustache, currently fashionable among the field-grade instructors at West Point. He wore blue kersey trousers with bright yellow piping, high-topped cavalry boots, a .44 caliber Smith & Wesson in a stiff leather holster over his right hip. The newly installed natural gas lights of the lecture hall gleamed off the filigreed gold hilt of his saber.

"As far as the War Department and the U.S. Army are concerned, this order does not even officially exist. But command can be a very nasty business among hostiles. So you'd better hear about it now. Especially those of you who've volunteered for immediate assignment to our new Indian-fighting regiments."

Seth felt a little insect prickle move up his spine at this last remark. He and his friend Corey Bryce had volunteered for the Indian wars even before they learned how to salute.

Lofley paused for dramatic effect and then paced from the wooden podium—painted in the Academy colors of black, gold, and gray—to the lancet-arched windows overlooking the tree-lined west bank of the Hudson River. Beyond him, Seth could see the original rammed-earth fortress that dated back to the American Revolution. Newer buildings of sturdy red brick and rough-hewn fieldstone surrounded a huge parade field now bright with new spring grass.

But at the moment the eighty cadets of Platoon 234 noticed none of this. The year was 1869, and Major Lofley had recently served two years in the Apache Campaigns. To Seth and the other cadets, he conveyed the slightly ironic, superior manner of those who have crossed over into Death's kingdom and somehow returned against the odds. Now, all eyes were on the major as he gazed out over the purling river as if searching there for the very words they would remember forever.

"Gentlemen, the great war between North and South is over, but the scars remain. The carnage cost a million casualties on each side. The United States government now has a staggering war debt amounting to seventy-five dollars for every man, woman, and child in America—thirty-eight million strong and growing fast. Quick, Cadet Bryce, you're our star arithmetician as well as our resident wit—without using your pen, how much debt is that?"

"Sir! That would be two billion, 850 million dollars, sir!" the cadet seated in front of Seth shot back promptly.

A few others whistled appreciatively, both at his quickness and at the unfathomable figure. Lofley smiled a pale little smile, nodding.

"Well done. A figure much easier to calculate than to comprehend, eh? But while white Americans were killing each other and thus placing a lien on the future generations, the red aboriginals in the Far West were having a true hey-day, count upon it."

He paused, then paced, expertly leading Seth and the rest of his young charges to the feather edge of suspense. As if timed to enhance his rhetoric, a platoon of cadets outside marched smartly past, their bold marching chant drifting into the auditorium:

"We're march-ing off for Sit-ting Bull
And *this* is the way we go:
Forty miles a day on beans and hay
In the Regular Army, *oh!*"

The vigorous cadence made Seth's skin goose-bump as he reminded himself again: Soon it would be much more than just a list of names and a ration of barroom bravado. He and Corey would have to make good on their brags and fight real by-God Indians in a land they had only heard and read about.

Lofley resumed his lecture.

"A true heyday, gentlemen. In fact, though many of the eastern greenhorns still do not realize it, the entire white citizenry of the Arizona Territory has been all but wiped out by Apaches, except for one last garrison at Tucson. It's not much safer in Texas or New Mexico, where the Comanche have earned the dubious distinction of killing more white settlers than any other tribe. The accord signed by the tribes at Laramie in 1851 isn't worth a plugged peso. Now the Indian lovers in Congress are ready to sign another useless treaty with the hostiles. But mark me, gentlemen—just be-cause a *dog* returns to its own vomit doesn't mean a nation should."

The major ran one knuckle over his mustache, smoothing it.

"Make no mistake about it, my eager young bachelors of the saddle. While the Indian lovers are persuading the hos-tiles to grow corn and raise sheep and pray to the white man's God, the U.S. Army is waging a war for its very sur-vival. Some say the ignorant aboriginals are not worth the trouble of a war, that they're just nits. But mark me, gentle-men—*nits make lice*. General Sherman is right: We feed them in the winter, then fight them in the summer. Which leads to my point: Both sides are fighting a war of extermination, and the Indian knows this as well as we blue-blouses do."

Major Lofley glanced outside again. He shook his head slowly while he spoke, as if reluctant to acknowledge certain brutal realities. The entire lecture hall was hushed with expectation.

"So now we come finally to the Unwritten Order, gentlemen. It concerns Indians, particularly the Indians of the bloody Southwest sector who zealously practice torture and other abominations against captives. Recall, this is a war of extermination, they feel they have nothing to lose. A captured child may stand a chance—if you'd call life as an Indian a chance. But when the aboriginals take a white woman captive, there is no mercy or code of honor involved.

"Gentlemen, don't be confused by the stump-screaming Indian lovers or the brotherly love claptrap the Quakers preach in their tracts. Not only will the red man torture a white woman, but as many as twenty or thirty of them in a row will also strip her naked and bull her. Then, if that doesn't kill her, they will stone her into silence about the deed. Mark me, gentlemen. I once spent an entire night trapped in an arroyo, listening to a fourteen-year-old girl's screams as a group of Kiowa Apaches taught her about the Noble Red Man. In the morning she was still alive and conscious. They slit her belly open and fed her intestines to the dogs while she watched herself being eaten alive."

Seth felt it, felt his share in it—a collective sense of outrage that charged the air in the lecture hall. It linked him and Corey to every other man in the room, bonded them in the name of duty and honor and America's ultimate destiny. Lofley slid the watch from his fob pocket, opened it to check the time, snapped the cover shut again. Again he carefully smoothed his mustache with one knuckle.

"So, in summation, I trust my point is clear. If you are escorting women and come under attack by hostiles, *under no circumstances* can you allow women to fall into enemy hands. Even if enemy success becomes imminent, a soldier is expected to die fighting. But if you know the hostiles are about to prevail, it is your responsibility to first kill the women for their own protection. Believe me, it will be the kindest cruelty of your life."

He fell silent, and too quickly Seth felt the silence grow uncomfortable. Six hours a day of close-order and horse-mounted drill, six more hours of lectures and science experiments and marksmanship training, had done nothing to prepare these neophyte warriors for such an unheroic disaster. They joked incessantly about death and losing their top-knots. But the youthful, myopic recklessness that led to either a medal or a coffin did not easily comprehend such bleak logic as the major's—men died for women, if they must, but the rules hitherto had said nothing about killing them.

The cadet named Corey Bryce leaned back a bit in his seat and said something to Seth. Both cadets stifled their laughter too late.

"What was that scuttlebutt you just passed to Mr. Carlson, Bryce?"

"Sir! Nothing, sir! Just a bit of a joke."

"Ahh, a bit of a joke? I like a good windy as well as the next soldier. Let's hear it, stout lad."

Bryce, a ruddy-complected towhead, turned a shade redder.

"Well, out with it, mister! Or is there a fishbone caught in your throat?"

"No, sir. It's just—it wasn't all that humorous, I don't suppose."

"You don't suppose? Pah! Granted, Mr. Carlson can make a mean war face. But he's a serious young lad with his nose constantly stuck into a volume of Homer. Yet *he* giggled like a schoolgirl at whatever you said."

Seth felt warm blood creeping into his face as laughter bubbled all around him. Major Lofley added, "I'm sure it's a capital hit. Now out with it, shavetail, or you'll be swamping out the stables this weekend instead of enjoying a furlough in Albany with that charming young fiancée of yours."

"Sir! It's just—well, when the major said that business about . . . about shooting women, I joked to Seth, ahh, that is, to Cadet Carlson, it was a weak joke, sir, as I said, and—"

"Damn it, cadet! You keep mealy-mouthing me and I'm marking you down for ten skins! Now *out* with it!"

Bryce nodded and swallowed audibly. "Yessir! I said to Cadet Carlson, 'Shooting the women won't bother me—I've *always* been a lady killer.'"

Laughter rippled through the auditorium, though it was brief and stopped as if on cue. Corey Bryce's brash humor and ready competence at everything he tried had quickly made him popular and a natural leader with his classmates. Now even Major Lofley allowed himself a discreet smile behind his mustache.

"Bit of gallows humor, eh?" he said, and Seth noticed a trace of cynical fondness in his tone. "Three skins for talking without permission." Then, before he dismissed the class, he added, "But I'll grant you this, Bryce—at least your men will die laughing."

From that day on, by unspoken decree, Corey Bryce was nicknamed "Lady Killer."

Chapter 2

"Sakes and saints, child, I don't credit my own eyes! Just listen to this!"

Aunt Tilly leaned forward in the high-backed rocking chair, the *Albany Journal* spread open across her lap. Bright pink spots of blood stippled her cheeks as she read out loud to her niece:

" 'The Apaches under Cochise are reported to be especially treacherous. They show a great penchant for hanging white prisoners head downward over small fires. The victims' subsequent uncontrollable jackknifing affords the savages amusement for hours while the captives' brains slowly roast until they die.' "

Aunt Tilly suddenly leaned her weight back into the rocker. Her face lost its scarlet glow as imagination transformed the words into images.

"How *can* the Army let women go out to that savage-infested desert? Worse yet, how can your own mother and father be bigger fools than God already made us mortals? Child, will you *stop* primping, the ball isn't tonight! Did you hear what I just read to you?"

"I'm not primping, I have to try on my gown. Mama sent it over to Holly Nearhood's to be altered. And yes, I heard you."

Jeanette Cunningham stood before a long cheval glass, frowning slightly as she tried to decide once and for all if her eyes were set too close together. She smoothed her soft cotton chemise, then wiggled into a corset that laced up the back and hooked in the front.

"All that's old news," she said matter-of-factly as she reached down to hook the laces. "Corey says the Kiowas like to stake prisoners out spread-eagle in the sun and slice off their eyelids. When they're bored with that, they pound pointed sticks deep under all their finger- and toenails. If you beg for mercy, they cut out your tongue. And sometimes, Corey says, they cure the tongues and hang them from their sashes instead of scalps."

She reported all this in the same tone she might use to give their maid the dairy order. Meantime, she put on a corset cover embroidered with frilly tuckwork. She was a slender, tall girl of eighteen with sea-green eyes and thick burnt-sienna hair. A slightly retroussé nose was set in a pretty, oval face that could go from silly to serious in a heartbeat.

Tilly, seated to her niece's right and behind her, looked questioningly at the girl in the mirror.

"Corey Bryce *tells* you things like that?" she demanded. "And you still want to go out there with him?"

"*You'd* have me marry a sailor like you did, and spend my hours pining away on a widow's walk! What's the point of getting married if you can never be with your husband?"

Jeanette donned a slim, tie-on petticoat and then a caged crinoline. Tilly watched her niece for a long moment, marveling at this buoyant enthusiasm still unchecked by bitter experience. Too soon old, too late smart, she thought.

"Besides, do you know what Reverend Stackpole said last Sunday?" Jeanette pulled on a pair of drawers that consisted of two cotton tubes that tied to her waist. Then she donned a second petticoat over her caged crinoline. "He said it's not the American Indian who started the barbaric customs of scalping and torturing. They learned that from the Spanish soldiers."

"Well, fine lot of good *that* little bit of history will do you, miss, under a savage's knife."

Aunt Tilly had restored her courage enough to continue reading the article.

" 'In both Mexico and the U.S. territories, newly formed cavalry units, trained for high-mountain winter hunts, have met with considerable success in searching out hostile Apaches. The new strategy of employing friendly Apaches as scouts has greatly increased Army effectiveness. A common feeling among veteran commanders is that only an Apache can catch an Apache.' "

Jeanette finally began tying on her white lace under-sleeves. When she finished, she tugged open the rosewood wardrobe beside her and removed an emerald-green satin gown from its peg. She put it on while she spoke, her eyes never leaving the mirror.

"Corey hasn't been yet, of course, But his training sergeants have. They say you never actually *see* Apaches. They blend into the landscape. For an attack, they strip almost naked. Then they wrap their head and shoulders in grass and smear the rest of their body with wet sand. Corey says they wriggle like rattlesnakes until they're close enough to kill quietly with a lance or bow."

"Almost naked . . . ? My lands." Aunt Tilly paled again as her niece eagerly reported this information.

Now Jeanette was examining her new gown in the mirror, frowning slightly.

"Child, you look beautiful. Why are you scowling?"

"It's this cadet friend Corey is bringing with him, Seth Carlson. Some backwoodsman from Michigan who supposedly knows all sorts of Latin and Greek and writes verses. I suppose he's frightfully pompous; men who like poetry usually are."

"Jeanette, you're shameless! *You* like poetry!"

"Of course, Aunt Tilly, but I'm a girl."

Tilly glanced toward the wardrobe, overflowing with fashions no longer featured in *Godey's Ladies Book*. Nearby, a gown from last season lay draped over a Chippendale settee. The only piece of furniture in the dressing room not currently draped with some article of clothing was a cherry spinet in the far corner.

"Yes," Aunt Tilly replied, "you're a girl, indeed, and not soon likely to be mistaken for anything else, dear heart."

"Well, Corey says the poor soul is practically penniless," Jeanette said to the mirror. "He only got in at West Point because his father was a hero in the battle at Shiloh or someplace. I suppose I'll have to at least dance a schottische with the poor thing—unless, of course, you had a little chat with Cousin Doris and she decided to go to the ball with him?"

Jeanette glanced slyly at her aunt. But her mischievous smile gave way to a look of wide-eyed astonishment when she saw that Tilly's eyes were suddenly bright with unshed tears.

"Aunt Tilly! What *is* it, dear?"

A froufrou of whispering skirts followed her as she crossed quickly to her aunt and hugged her.

"It's nothing, child. It was just . . . looking at you just now. Oh, Jeanette, too soon now you'll be married. Too soon after that you'll be running off to the frontier. It's all so sudden child! *Must* you go with him? I can't set the feeling to words, sweet love, but I'm frightened by . . . by something. I feel as if a clock was set ticking when you agreed to marry Corey."

Her voice climbed an octave and nearly broke as a sob rose in her throat like a tight bubble. Jeanette hugged her even tighter.

"Tilly, you dear thing, I *do* love you! Have you been having those sad dreams again?"

Her aunt nodded.

"You *must* stop taking that dreadful laudanum! Dear, I'm going to be fine. Esther Beckmann spent two years out West. The worst tragedy she can recount was the time she drank bad water and got the summer complaint."

"I suppose you're right. Still . . . ." Tilly forced out a long, nasal sigh. " 'Time driveth onward fast.' "

Jeanette drew back, her eyes moist and sparkling. " 'Love,

all alike, no season knows nor clime, nor hours, days, months, which are the rags of time.' "

Aunt Tilly looked scandalized. "Who's been giving you that reprobate Jack Donne to read? More of Reverend Stackpole's influence?"

But Jeanette ignored her, frowning again. "I suppose that if Mr. Seth Carlson likes poetry, he's a horrid dancer, too."

Chapter 3

Seth Carlson felt his scalp tighten in irritation when he recognized Sergeant Major Kinney crossing the parade field, tapping his ebony swagger stick against his right thigh. Now Seth knew it was going to be rough weather this morning. But thank God it was also going to be one of the last inspections he would stand east of the Mississippi.

It still seemed vaguely unreal to him, despite all the hard training and the final orders posted outside the duty office: He was soon bound for the frontier and the Indian wars.

But this morning he was still playing squad leader at West Point. He stood at parade rest at the head of the fourth column. Corey Bryce led the second squad, two columns over on Seth's left. When Corey spotted Kinney, he turned his head toward Seth. Making his voice deep and gravelly, he growled, "Augh! There's no glory in peace, laddiebucks!" Laughter rippled through the formation.

All eighty cadets in Platoon 234 fell silent and snapped

smartly to attention, however, when the platoon guide barked out the order. They had all turned out in full field uniform: mess kits hanging low over their right hips, sabers lined up precisely with the yellow piping of their left trouser legs, black-brimmed officer's hats, one side smartly snapped up. Each man had a blanket roll strapped to the top of his full field-marching pack. Spencer carbines rested against their right trouser seams. Those who had volunteered for the new Indian-fighting regiments wore high-topped cavalry boots polished to a high gloss like black anthracite.

"Augh! Goddamn my eyes, just look at America's future! Toting new fire sticks, and not a one of you raggedy-assed pilgrims could hit a bull in the butt with a banjo! A Sioux papoose has got a bigger set of oysters on him than any of you girls. And here the War Department is about to commission the sad, sorry lot of you as second lieutenants."

Kinney was well into his forties, long-jawed and rangy, with sallow skin. Purple veins crisscrossed his nose, the legacy of imbibing too many bottles of sour mash. He glanced out over the formation of young men. Several still hadn't mastered a straight razor, and bloody nicks pockmarked their faces.

"Hell and furies, they're all fresh from the tit," he complained to the corporal who accompanied him. "How is this man's army supposed to kill Innuns when our officers still shit yellow?" He spat a stream of tobacco juice into the grass. "Winslowe!"

"Here, Sergeant Major!"

"You're on scouting duty in hostile country. How do you move?"

"Damn slow, Sergeant Major, because it's movement, not shape, that catches the enemy's eye."

"Taylor!"

"Here, Sergeant Major!"

"It's the dead of night in mountain stillness. You're acting C.O. and your unit is approaching a camp of hostiles. Absolute silence is vital. What order do you signal to all your officers?"

"Remove sabers, Sergeant Major, so they won't clink."

"Harding!"

"Here, Sergeant Major!"

"Do you place your ear on the ground to hear sounds of nearby movement?"

"Not *on* the ground, Sergeant Major. Close to it, but not on it."

Kinney grunted after each correct response, as if mildly surprised that these toy soldiers could even speak. While he fired off questions, he prowled throughout the ranks, inspecting rifle bores for dust, tugging on pack straps, checking tunics for "Irish pennants"—tiny, loose threads. Each time he found one, the offender earned a demerit, known to the rueful recipients as skins. Seth stood by for a blast when Kinney drew nearer. The old salt had expressed definite views about cavalry officers who wrote poetry.

Kinney stopped in front of Corey. "Lady Killer!"

A quick explosion of laughter from the ranks. Kinney cut it off instantly with a low, simmering "Augh!" thrust from the back of his throat.

"Lady Killer, you're trailing hostiles. How do you know if their horses are galloping?"

"The prints will be about three and a half feet apart," Corey Bryce responded.

"What if the prints overlap?"

"That's a walk or a trot, Sergeant Major. Deeper prints mean a trot."

"Well, goddamn my ears, Lady Killer! I guess even a blind hog will root up an acorn now and then. Speaking of blind hogs—Carlson!"

"Here, Sergeant Major!"

"You're caught in blue-ass cold weather at reveille, trooper. What do you have your men do before they rig their horses?"

"Warm the bits, Sergeant Major, so the horses won't rebel."

Instead of passing on to the next man, Kinney stood rooted before Seth. Carlson was not a big lad, nor so powerfully built as his more popular friend Corey Bryce. But even early on during the training cycle, superiors noticed a quiet, determined, at times even dangerous set to his eyes when the pressure was on. It was most noticeable to Kinney during the brutal prisoner-of-war training. In the face of constant sleeplessness, hunger, verbal and physical abuse that broke bigger men, Carlson did more than endure—he silently egged his tormentors on, urged them to push him to even further limits; not from meanness, but from a tough, proud defiance that made him civil to all men, servile to none.

Nor could Kinney fault his conduct-and-proficiency reports. All his instructors concurred: He was quick-witted, well-spoken, a good listener, and a low-key but effective leader. For all these reasons, Kinney was harder on him. Corey Bryce, in contrast, was a politician's boy. Army life would coddle him despite his ample muscles. Seth Carlson was the son of an enlisted man, he'd soon find himself where the lead flew thickest. Kinney, himself the son of a coal miner, privately believed that poor officers had as much right to live as rich ones. And therefore, though he was far too irreverent to ever admit it publicly, he took with religious seriousness the prayer engraved in bronze over the entrance to the training cadre's barracks: LET NO MAN'S GHOST EVER SAY, "IF ONLY MY TRAINING HAD BEEN BETTER!"

"Carlson!"

"Sergeant Major?"

"How do you prepare your eyes for night scouting?"

"I wrap my head in a blanket for at least one hour, Sergeant Major, so my eyes will adjust completely."

"When you bed down your unit for the day, where do you graze the horses—far out, or near camp?"

This question, not covered in any class or lecture he could remember, drew Seth up short. "Sergeant Major?"

"Don't stand there with your thumb up your sitter, mister! You're burning daylight! *Where* do you graze the horses—far out, or near to camp?"

"But—"

"Put your 'buts' back in your pocket. Far out or near camp?"

"Near camp, Sergeant Major!"

"Augh! In a pig's ass, tadpole! You don't know sic 'em about being a soldier, do you? First you send them farther out with a small herd guard. Then, after dark, you bring them into camp for security. That way they'll still have some grass left to graze during the night."

Kinney stepped back in front of the entire formation.

"War is our business, stout lads, and business is still good, thanks to the goddamn red Arabs out West! There's no glory in peace, laddiebucks! When's the last time you saw a pretty face sighing after a Quaker? When it comes time for a huggin' match with redskins, Soldier Blue is the boy you send for! But ignorant soldiers like Carlson here soon get separated from their topknots."

Horse drill for the cavalry volunteers followed general inspection. Seth, Corey, and twenty others fell out and were quick-marched over to the stables. Continuing his pressure on Seth, Kinney ordered him to lead the field maneuvers.

These new units, smaller and equipped for lighter travel, were a result of the abysmal combat failures of the Third, Fourth, and Seventh Cavalry regiments. Though the newly formed Seventh, under Custer, had recently recorded some notable victories, these larger units were too burdened down to pursue the Indians across open plains on their more fleet-footed ponies. Twenty-five miles a day was all the regular units, hampered by support wagons and wheeled gun carriages, could manage. The new stripped-down mountain regiments packed everything on horseback and were expected to cover up to eighty.

Under Kinney's unrelenting scrutiny, Seth directed the preparations for a combat expedition. He visually verified that each man was equipped with the requisite hobbles, haversacks, picket pins, canteens, panniers, saddle, bridle, carbine, pistol, lariat, and shelter tents.

Seth formed the men up in the standard column of fours, then sent each trooper to the head of his mount. On his command, they stepped up into leather as one. Riding a big sorrel with a white blaze on its forehead, Seth led them smoothly through their paces around the huge expanse of forest trails and meadows reserved for horse drill.

At a full charge across a vast field, the pounding hoofs flung up divots of grass and dirt and yellow crocuses. Never breaking stride, Seth expertly formed the men into a pincers, a squad vee, a skirmish line, then performed a wheel by pivoting the entire formation from one end to change flanks.

Under Kinney's vigilant eye, he smartly formed a column of twos from a column of fours, the first and fourth squads caracoling a half turn to the right and left to mesh flawlessly with the second and third squads. Finally, with impressive coordination, the cadets reformed into a staggered echelon and then simulated a coup de main, a sudden attack in force.

"It would appear, young buck, that you're beginning to learn shit from apple butter," Kinney said begrudgingly to Seth as he dismissed the cadets for their afternoon classes. "That was some fine horsemanship, lads, all of you. Not near so fine, though, as a Comanche will show you, so don't get salty on me."

Dismissed back at the stables, Seth slipped the bit and loosed the cinch under the sorrel's belly. She nuzzled the hollow of his shoulder. He scratched her behind one ear, wondering—would he be lucky enough to draw a horse this fine at his first duty station? He rubbed his mount down good, then stalled her. He filled a nose bag with oats and strapped it on the hungry animal.

That night, during study period in the flickering gaslights of their barracks, Corey Bryce suddenly threw down a copy of *The Iliad* and loosed a high-pitched cavalry battle cry. Several cadets took up the cry until the duty NCO managed to restore order. Corey sat up in his cot and looked across the narrow aisle at his friend.

"Tarnal blazes, Seth boy! I can do arithmetic as easy as rolling off a log. But these confounded Latin poets, I've got ablatives and genitives out my eyes!"

Pure malice blazing in his look, Corey stared toward the head of the barracks. A stern-eyed bust of Colonel Sylvanus Thayer, superintendent at West Point from 1817 to 1833, stared back. Corey considered him no better than the enemy —a rigorous academician, it was Thayer who started the unpopular rule that every cadet must pass every class or make up his failure.

"*Mens sana in corpore sano,*" Seth replied, closing a copy of Dr. Johnson's essays.

"Huh. My mind was sound enough before Homer and that crowd got hold of it, damn their dead bones."

"Stand and hold, Lady Killer," Seth told him, imitating

Kinney's growl. "Won't be long before you marry the prettiest girl in New York, remember?"

"Ain't she, though? And then it's on to a brevet or a coffin out West for *these* two pony soldiers. There's no glory in peace, laddiebuck!"

Corey was in high spirits. Earlier that day he had received a telegram from Jeanette in Albany, informing him that her cousin Doris would be charmed to accompany Mr. Seth Carlson to the Albany Ladies Auxiliary Spring Beaux Arts Ball.

"This Doris, I hear she's a beauty. *All* the women in Jeanette's family are. Just think: tomorrow morning, Seth boy, we'll be riding royal as the Queen of England in one of George Pullman's new luxury coaches. Leather seats so deep you get lost in them. Augh!"

Corey lay back down, lacing his fingers behind his head and gazing at the ceiling. "You've only seen a picture of Jenny—wait till you actually meet her. By God, but she's pretty as four aces! She'll knock the wind out of you."

Seth listened, a smile tugging at his lips as his friend once again delivered an enthusiastic treatise on the subject of Jeanette Cunningham. But his happiness for Corey was not without its sting of envy. What did it matter if this girl Doris *was* pretty? Even worse luck if she liked him—marriage was out of the question for him. His father had been a good soldier, but he was not one for putting by against the future. Now he, Seth, had two younger sisters and his mother to support—an officer's pay was not much, but he could live practically free and send all of it home to them.

Besides, though he'd never say so to Corey, he was dead set against the War Department's policy of permitting women to accompany their husbands into hostile territory. With more soldiers and civilians dying out there every day, was the frontier any place for a lady?

"Taps in ten minutes!" the fire watch shouted, banging open the door at the head of the squad bay. "Lights out in ten minutes!"

That night, for some reason Seth couldn't pin down, the lone, wavering bugle notes of taps raised the fine hairs on the back of his neck as they had never done before. He felt the clear sense that it was a dirge for all he had ever been, that a door was closing on his old life and that his new life lay waiting out West. As he slowly tumbled down the long tunnel toward sleep, Corey's words formed a guilty, ghostly refrain inside his head: *Wait till you actually meet her.*

Chapter 4

The old shaman, Cries Yia, said, "Remember, Jemez, they are fortunate. When your soul leaves your body, it soars like an eagle, and finally Great Ussen allows us to see everything as we never could from the ground."

The Coyotero Apache named Jemez Grayeyes stared at the tacky blood spattering one of the wicker cradles. "Old man, you haven't got enough strong medicine to make one worm. And here you are, sending souls off into the clouds. *This* is all I know. They lived a hard life and they died a hard death. Now they're smoke behind us."

Cries Yia took no offense at the young warrior's bitter remark. As the twig is bent, he reminded himself, so the tree shall grow—and he knew Jemez Grayeyes had grown to be covered with hard bark. Over the decades, Cries Yia had watched the Apache people split into smaller and smaller bands and groups. They were forced to such fragmentation for their very survival, under constant attack in a harsh land of barren mesas, sterile mountains, and burning plains. Centuries earlier they had migrated as one people down from the eastern slopes of the Canadian Rockies. Inevitably, as Spaniards, Mexicans, and now white hair-faces in their canvas-covered bone shakers chipped away at their homeland, the rock of Apache faith also fragmented.

And truly, this thing in the cave was a hard thing for a man without religion to accept. A very hard thing. Cries Yia had no room in his heart to resent Jemez.

"They were buried soon enough," Cries Yia assured him, though Jemez hadn't asked. "Their ghosts won't come back."

The soldiers had ransacked the cavern. Tanned buffalo robes, dog skins, antelope and elk hides, pans and kettles, axes, beadwork, pipes, old moccasins, war clubs, stone hammers, grubbing hoes of bone, all lay strewn as if by a malevolent whirling dervish. Fortunately, neighboring caves had been spared. The old man Otero and his wife had taken care of Socorro and Miguelito until Jemez returned.

Jemez looked at the wicker cradle again, at the sticky patchwork of dark brown blood, and for a moment heat rose into his face. Abruptly, he stepped outside and walked back down the narrow trail to the place where he had hobbled his pony.

For a moment the sloping ground seemed to slide out from under him, and he felt like he was trying to stand up in a dugout canoe on a raging river. He saw his mother's strong white teeth flashing in laughter, remembered how Chimaca had sat up during the cold winter nights, singing the old cure songs over him after the red-speckled cough wiped out half the People. He closed his eyes hard until the dizziness passed. Then he pulled a sack of Bull Durham and some rolling papers out of the dusty aparejo dangling over his saddle.

His fingers trembled only slightly as he built himself a cigarette and lit it with a sulfur match. Like many of the males born to the seven bands of the Apache, he had grown into a big man—well over six feet, thick in the chest and stoutly muscled in his legs. His hair hung down to the middle of his back, thick, shiny black as a crow's wings, with a red flannel headband to keep his vision clear. He wore captured U.S. Army trousers and a hand-tooled leather holster with a Remington .50 caliber pistol turned butt forward to accommodate his left-handed cross draw. He had a strong aquiline nose and the distinctive nimbus-gray eyes that had earned his clan its name—cold, quick-darting eyes that missed little and revealed even less.

They revealed nothing now as he stood beside his buckskin pony and idly scratched her withers while he stared down into the craggy maw of the Cañon del Cobre. Beyond it stretched a vast expanse of Arizona desert, bright now with white-plumed Spanish bayonet, flowering mescal, prickly pear, and mesquite. Farther back from the river canyon, a broad belt of dull chaparral took over. Closer to the horizon, heat shimmered over the barren alkali flat of Sonora in Old Mexico.

Jemez had gone north to steal ponies from the Cheyenne, accompanied by a few braves from the Crooked Lance Clan of the Jicarilla. Horses were not as important to the Apaches as they were to most other plains tribes. After all, they cared nothing for counting coup or taking scalps, preferring surprise attacks on foot and practical loot, not foolish riding tricks and symbolic trophies. But good ponies were useful when fleeing from Mexicans and blue-bloused Americans. Besides, they tasted better than mule meat or beef. And the Cheyenne were renowned for their good ponies. Not so good as the Kiowa and Comanche herds, but Jemez no longer raided on them since these Southwest neighbors had sought a truce with the Apaches.

The raid had begun well, then turned disastrous. Under cover of night they had cut a good string of ponies from a Cheyenne herd grazing near the South Platte River. But they had forgotten about the Cheyenne habit of keeping so many dogs near camp—before they could escape with the horses, the wind shifted and the dogs went into a barking frenzy, alerting the camp. They had been fortunate to escape with their hair still in place and a scant handful of ponies on their lead lines.

And now he came back to this. His mother and his favorite uncle and several cousins murdered in their sleep. Once before, the Mexican *soldados* had done this to their clan, attacking the Apache stronghold at the head of Disappointment Creek in the Mescal Mountains. That was two years ago. They had killed his father that time. Knowing how Apaches feared hanging, they took him down onto the treeless plains and drag-hanged him slow, pulling him behind a horse by a rope noosed around his neck. But the officer in charge of that raid had made the mistake of getting drunk and bragging about it to the wrong people. And when Jemez tracked him down and killed him, he made sure the rest of the *soldados* knew who had done it.

But this time was different. It was not just the soldiers. He thought of his cousin, Juan Aragon, who now played the dog for the Mexicans and Americans. Jemez knew where he would have to go eventually, after he took care of Socorro and Miguelito. He would have to sneak down into Tucson. Though it was infested with blue-bloused soldiers, there was also a squalid expanse of sod shanties known as Riverbend, reserved for turncoat Indians and half-breeds who worked for the fort. Juan Aragon would eventually show up there.

Nor would the arrogant white man named Robert Trilby walk away from this. After all, Juan was only playing the fawning dog for him anyway. The hair-face whites knew little enough about Apaches. But eventually they were going to learn the same thing the Mexicans had come to learn about Jemez Grayeyes: He nursed a grudge until it called him Mother. This Trilby, Jemez knew he was the dirt-work specialist for the thieves and murderers who called themselves the Tucson Committee. He was the point man in the committee's relentless drive to profit handsomely from war contracts generated by the "Apache menace."

Up above, Miguelito suddenly coughed. The noise cut into Jemez's gloomy rumination and reminded him that his little brother and sister had been fortunate to escape. They would not have been shot—young women, and children weaned from the tit, were not so lucky. They would have been traded to the Comancheros in Santa Fe, who profited handsomely in the illegal but flourishing slave trade.

He finished his cigarette and flicked the butt away. On his way back up to the cave he stopped for a moment at the place where rocks had been heaped on the new graves to keep animals away. His eyes burned with tears for a moment, and it felt like burrs were caught in his throat. Then he swallowed hard, ashamed of his weakness, and returned to the cave.

The others were still waiting for him to make a decision: Cries Yia, Socorro, Miguelito, Otero, and the others from the nearby caves who had escaped attack. A Grayeyes man had always been their leader.

"These were Mexicans," he told Cries Yia. "So you know they were looking for me."

Cries Yia nodded. "They came to kill you. They are afraid of you. When you killed that officer, you made them put you on their special list."

"They'll look everywhere."

Again Cries Yia nodded. "Even the Tonto Basin will not be safe. Nor will they respect the border the hair-faces have declared between their two countries. You know a place?"

"I know a place. A spot way up in the mountains of Sonora."

"This place here, no one wanted it," Cries Yia said. "I watched the one who was your father sign their talking papers which gave us this land. Then the hair-faces found minerals. Now they clamor for a safe passage to the place beyond the sun, which they call California. Long ago I hated the Mexicans who replaced the Spaniards. At first I welcomed the whites. I thought they would fight beside us against the brown ones. But now we are surrounded by enemies who hate each other *and* us."

"This place I know," Jemez said, glancing at Socorro and Miguelito, "is too steep for women or children to climb to. It will be very cold there, and no fires will be permitted. There will be no milk or fresh meat."

Miguelito, sick and scared and confused about where his mother had gone, was too young to understand what was being said. But Socorro understood her older brother's meaning. A quicksilver panic glinted in her eyes.

Cries Yia understood, too. "For now the children will be better off at Mater Dolorosa. Miguelito needs medicine.

This new agent, Hays Munro, has tried harder than the others to speak one way to us."

Jemez believed this was true. Those bands of the eastern Apaches that had willingly reported to the Mater Dolorosa Reservation said things were better lately. Though it was often late, they usually received most of their ration of meat, flour, coffee, and sugar. Munro had even risked the wrath of the blue soldiers by supplying some of the hunters with old trade rifles so they could supplement the low-grade pork with fresh buffalo—though, of course, some of the rifles were eventually also turned against white settlers, causing a storm of outraged protest from the Tucson Committee.

Jemez had sworn by the sun and the earth he lived on that he would fall on his own knife before he would ever spend another day on a white man's reservation. He had been among the first Apache children educated by whites at the original San Carlos Indian Reservation. True, they had taught him the hair-face language and customs, knowledge of which had proven useful on occasion. But they could keep their stiff leather shoes and daily roll calls and parched cornfields and holy virgins who had babies without rutting.

"Tomorrow," Jemez told Socorro, "I'll take you down to Mater Dolorosa."

"No."

The sound came out more like a hiccup than a word, and surprised the others. Socorro hadn't spoken since the night of the attack. Now they all looked at her.

"No," she said again. She held her injured arm out stiffly from her side. Cries Yia had rubbed the elbow good with boiled sassafras and then splinted it with rawhide whangs and two sticks of green cottonwood.

Jemez felt anger at himself, not his sister. Of course she didn't want to go. Had he himself not warned her, over and over, that the white men meant death to all Indians? That their hospitals were places where you went to die? That their reservations were places where Indians were sent to lose their freedom and answer roll calls? Had he not encouraged her to resist the whites with her very life?

"Only for a while," Jemez promised her. "Then I'll come for both of you."

"No," she said. Crystal drops quivered on her lashes, then dripped down her cheeks. Miguelito coughed again, a whooping, wracking spasm that made Jemez wince.

That cough decided it. The boy was going to die if he took them to Sonora, and eventually so would Socorro.

Seeing a dangerous light of rebellion in Socorro's eyes, Jemez suddenly shook her hard.

"You are going, and you will *not* run away. You will wait until I come for you. Do you understand your older brother, who is now the war leader of your clan?"

Tears streamed down her face now. But Socorro nodded.

"Good," Jemez said. "Good, little sister. You may lie to hair-faces and Mexicans, but never to me. Wait for me there."

In the morning, before they rode down out of the mountains, Jemez drove a pole firmly into the ground beside the new graves. He fastened a strip of red flannel atop it; below this he attached a medal he had taken off the mutilated body of the Mexican officer in charge of drag-hanging his father.

The Mexicans would be back, and they would see the pole. And by now they knew full well what it meant when Jemez Grayeyes set up a vengeance pole.

Chapter 5

"Driver," Corey Bryce called up to the liveried cabman, "the ladies insist we must take a turn past Quackenbush Square."

It was a fine Sunday morning. The steep and narrow streets of Albany, winding uphill from the west bank of the Hudson, were alive with japanned carriages, folding-top victorias, two-wheeled hansoms, and pedestrians in their sabbath finery. The city was located just south of the busy confluence of the Mohawk River and the Erie Canal, and now tattooed bargemen strolled the waterfront on holiday. The capital's Dutch ancestry was apparent everywhere in the mullioned dormers, blunt gables, and fieldstone walls with divided doors.

Corey and Jeanette sat in the rear-facing seat of a four-passenger cab; Seth and Jeanette's cousin Doris faced them from the opposite seat. Again Jeanette closed her eyes, and Seth couldn't help admiring the way her long lashes curved perfectly against her cheeks.

Corey caught him staring and sent him a hail-fellow wink. "What did I tell you, Seth boy? *Ain't* she easy to look at?"

Jeanette met Seth's stare and held it boldly until he felt a blush creeping up from under the high collar of his tunic. He broke eye contact first and glanced out the window toward the river. He feigned sudden interest in a string of barges loaded with coal destined for Cleveland.

"Oh, Mr. Seth Carlson doesn't find *me* pretty," Jeanette said, making a little moue. "You practically had to break his arm before he would dance with me last night."

Corey winked at Seth again. "He's keen to kill Indians, all right, but he's no, uh, lady killer."

Seth felt his blush deepen. Jeanette had taken her high-hat, teasing tone with him almost from the moment when the two men arrived Saturday afternoon. The four of them had played cribbage, under the watchful eye of Aunt Tilly, until it was time for the ball. Though Seth had not cut the dashing figure Corey had, he had danced a schottische with Jeanette creditably well—yet she had embarrassed him by feigning surprise at his ability, as if a cow had cleverly walked on its hind legs.

Jeanette's cousin Doris said little. She stared out the opposite window with a bored glaze over her eyes, hands folded primly in her lap. Her matrimonial hopes for Corey's friend had suffered a visible miscarriage at the moment when she asked Seth which senator or representative had nominated him for West Point. When she found out he was a charity case selected by a lowly Army board, the son of a brave but penniless war hero, the note of false gaiety had left her voice along with every other attempt at coquetry.

For his part, Seth had fulfilled the niceties of social punctilio toward her. But he made no effort to thaw her rude coldness. Corey was right—she had a pretty enough face. But it was a brittle kind of beauty; her features could go suddenly hard and hateful in a heartbeat.

"There's the new capitol building," Jeanette said as they rolled past a partially constructed building in the French Renaissance style. Enthusiasm livened her voice, and she leaned from window to window as if she dare not let one detail escape notice.

"There, look, Mr. Seth Carlson—that's the steeple of St. Peter's Episcopal Church. That's where Corey and I will be getting married."

"Do you know," Doris said, smiling at Corey, "they have a silver communion service donated by Queen Anne herself?"

"There, Mr. Seth Carlson! That's Cherry Hill, home of the Van Rensselaer family. It's the oldest house in Albany, though I'm sure *I* wouldn't boast about that. I like modern things."

Doris laughed, as if a child had piped up with enthusiasm, if not brains. "Their money is modern enough, and Papa says they're swimming in it."

Jeanette's attention was now focused on the other side of the street. She replied absently, "That's obvious from the way Marjorie Buchanan and some of the other girls from church make shameless fools of themselves in front of young Jon Van Rensselaer. They act like a bunch of flies around a molasses barrel."

Doris put more enamel into the smile she aimed at Corey. The broad-shouldered towhead's knees nearly pressed into hers. "Well, *I'd* rather marry a handsome, dashing soldier than some puffed-up little papa's boy. But of course, Corey is a soldier *and* rich. That's even better. Mama says it's just as easy to fall in love with a rich man as it is a poor one."

"Where me and Seth are going," Corey said, "it doesn't matter a jackstraw how rich or poor you are, does it, laddiebuck?"

"It certainly matters when you come back," Doris said demurely, and Seth scooched even farther away from her.

Again, when he risked a glance at Jeanette, she was watching him with open curiosity, the chrysalis of a smile on her lips. Her scrutiny made him self-conscious about how he must look next to Corey: His brown hair had far too much wild curl to it, and his face was one the opposite sex described as "interesting" more often than handsome—though some of them seemed no less favorably impressed for the distinction.

"I hear you've a fondness for poetry, Mr. Seth Carlson?"

"Fondness?" Corey said. "He reels the stuff off by heart just like you."

"Why would anyone bother to learn it by heart?" Doris said. "It's all so dreadfully boring."

"You don't actually 'learn' it, silly," Jeanette told her impatiently. "It's not like memorizing times tables. The words stay with you because you *feel* them."

Seth watched color rise high in Jeanette's cheeks, offsetting the burnt-sienna hair, as she gazed out over a little flower park between the street and the river. Now the water was a brilliant, quivering gold as late morning sun scintillated its surface. Then she looked at Seth again. A slight edge of challenge crept into her tone when she recited:

"Calm is the morn without a sound,
    Calm as to suit a calmer grief,
    And only through the faded leaf
The chestnut pattering to the ground."

"Tennyson," Seth responded instantly, adding:

"Calm and deep peace on this high wold,
    And on these dews that drench the furze,
    And all the silvery gossamers
That twinkle into green and gold."

He fell silent, and Jeanette's sea-green eyes seemed to sparkle.

"That's all jim-dandy," Corey said, "but what in tarnal blazes is a 'silvery gossamer'?"

Doris glanced outside and said, "It all looks like boring old Albany to me."

"They're both a fine pair of dreamers," Corey said fondly. "Though I know for a fact Seth is a tough drill master. *He's* the boy to make you snap your heels together!"

"Augh! Eighty boots!" Seth growled in Kinney's gravelly voice.

"Augh! All hittin' the ground like one!" Corey shot back.

"Forty inches, back to chest!"

"You lean back, you strut!"

"You strut, you strut, you *strut!*"

"Are you two *really* going to kill Indians?" Jeanette suddenly demanded.

They both looked at her at the same moment, mildly disconcerted by her unexpected question and serious face.

"*I* am," Corey replied. "Seth boy here plans to knock 'em off their horses with bad verse."

"Reverend Stackpole talked one Sunday all about the massacre of Chief Black Kettle's Cheyennes at some place called Sand Creek. I think it was just wrong to kill unarmed women and children, especially when they had gathered under an American flag for safety."

"It's no use to lick old wounds," Corey said. "War is a nasty business. You don't kill enemy women and children because you enjoy it. A professional soldier doesn't take pleasure in killing. But he knows that nits make lice, so sometimes you have to kill the nits."

Jeanette turned to stare at him for a moment, her nostrils flaring. It was hard to tell if he was reciting training slogans or speaking his own mind.

"Nits? Is that what you consider Indians to be?"

Corey shrugged. "Well, any way you slice it, the white man's cork floats one way and the red man's another. They can't live together. One or the other has to go."

"The newspapers say," Doris said, "that the savages' days are numbered now anyway because the buffalo are dying off."

"Buff hides fetch three dollars each," Corey said. "At that rate, *I'll* tell the world they're dying off. It's a shame, I s'pose, but a man would be foolish not to profit while there's an opportunity. Besides, they knock over telegraph poles and block trains and generally make a confounded nuisance of themselves."

"How about you, Mr. Seth Carlson?" Jeanette said. "Would *you* shoot Indian women and children?"

Seth paused. "According to current regulations, any hostile Indians who surrender are to be taken prisoner and sent to the reservations."

"Are you soft between your head handles?" Corey demanded. "Indians never surrender. They go to the rez in the winter so the Quaker agents can fatten 'em up, then with the spring melt they sneak off to kill blue-blouses again."

"Well, I'm marrying a soldier," Jeanette said. "I know it's

not just pretty uniforms and stirring marches, just as I know that some of the Indians are a bad lot. But if you ever kill an Indian woman or child, Corey Andrew Bryce, don't ever brag about it around me."

She was frowning slightly in her seriousness, deepening the soft furrow between her eyebrows. Seth looked at her and suddenly felt a pang in his heart—a pang of grief, tragedy, and loss that surprised and disturbed him. For the space of a few heartbeats he felt an ineffable sense that it was dead wrong for Corey to take this fair and delicate flower and transplant her to the barren, inhospitable land out West.

She saw him watching her. The frown disappeared in a blink, replaced by her teasing smile.

"O what can ail thee, knight at arms,
    Alone and palely loitering?
The sedge has withered from the Lake
    And no birds sing!"

"Keats," he said, and he parried:

"I saw pale kings, and princes too,
    Pale warriors, death-pale were they all;
They cried, 'La belle dame sans merci
    Thee hath in thrall!' "

Corey, clearly more amused than jealous, approved this exchange with noisy applause. Doris looked embarrassed, as if one of the men had broken wind. Later, as they were waiting on the pebbled cul-de-sac before the Cunningham residence to hand the ladies down from the cab, Corey spoke low in Seth's ear.

"That Doris is a dull stick, ain't she? But you and Jenny struck it off just fine, Seth boy. Don't let her teasing fool you, she likes you. I'm glad we'll all be going to the same post. I try to be patient with her, but outside of Milton and a bit of Browning, I'm not the boy for poetry. You two can entertain each other for hours."

Again, for a moment, Seth felt a sharp tug in his heart. But before he could find words for the feeling, there was a swish of skirts as Corey swung Jeanette down to the ground.

She threw her head back, laughed. Then she abruptly looked at Seth.

"Tell me, Mr. Seth Carlson," she said with mock seriousness, "do *you* think my eyes are too close together?"

Chapter 6

More than he feared anything else, Jemez Grayeyes feared the prospect of death by hanging.

In this he was like most Indians, who preferred to cross over almost any other way. He had learned to like many of the hair-face customs: He had given up his clay pipe in favor of cigarettes, and he even preferred warm beer over pulque. But for Jemez, this fear of hanging was still the only fear that could jolt him awake at night, drenched in cold sweat. It had happened to his father, the best Coyotero warrior in Apacheria. Now that Jemez was wanted for murder in the U.S. and Mexico, the nightmare also plagued him any time he came down out of hiding in the mountains.

For several days he led Socorro, Miguelito, and four other Apache children north toward the Always Star and the reservation at Mater Dolorosa, a godforsaken, tarantula-infested wasteland a half day's easy ride east of Tucson. Several other adults had reluctantly agreed with him and old Cries Yia—

now that the Mexican and American armies were employing Apache turncoats to hunt down their own people, the constant running and hiding was too hard on the children. No one trusted the politicians and soldiers, of course. But respected Apaches had sworn that Hays Munro and Kathleen Barton, the new Indian agent and the woman he brought to teach at the Indian school, respected Indians and spoke the straight word to them.

The journey was a hard one. All the ponies had been throat-slashed on the night of the raid. Jemez had returned from the aborted trip to the north with only two—the buckskin he had ridden, and a spirited but well-broken blood bay. Now he was using both of them as packhorses for the children's possessions. Miguelito was too ill to walk, so he rode on the buckskin. Since yesterday, the youngest children had taken turns riding the bay. The rest walked.

Several of them were limping by the time they reached the dull brown expanse of the saguaro plains. Jemez halted the group and set them to work gathering wads of dry grass. He showed them how to stuff their moccasins with it for extra padding. For food they gnawed on the hard, large wafers of unleavened bread the hair-faces called hardtack. It had been raided months earlier from a supply train bound for Fort Concho. Each night at sundown the temperature plummeted and the wind whipped up to a howl like coyotes mating, pelting them with stinging sand. Jemez showed his little band how to make windbreaks out of stones placed just right. Instead of a big central fire—as the white men foolishly preferred—Jemez had them build safer and more economical personal fires over which one person leaned for warmth. When it was time to sleep, the children huddled close to each other in groups of two or three.

By day, heat shimmers floated over the plains. Water was scarce and often alkali-tainted. When the canteens were low, Jemez showed his young charges how to suck the water from rock hollows.

Jemez always felt vulnerable down here in the low country where there were few good places to hide. There were increasing signs of bluecoat troop movements, and Jemez constantly scanned the horizon for plumes of dust that might indicate riders. When they crossed a road or trail frequented by Army scouts, he made the children walk on their heels to avoid leaving footprints.

He also left a false camp behind them each night—a few burning fires and hastily built windbreaks about a mile from their real camp. Behind the windbreaks they left dirt mounds to resemble sleepers in the dark. If bluecoats or illegally patrolling Mexicans picked up their trail, the noise from the attack on a decoy camp would warn them.

Jemez was not a loner by nature, and he enjoyed human company. But he had learned, in the last few years, that talking distracted a man and got him in trouble. So he automatically hushed the children each time they started a conversation. And the enforced silence was occasionally useful; rattlesnakes idled in rock piles, and only their angry buzzing warned them in time to make a wide berth. Sometimes a careless step sent a centipede or scorpion or hairy tarantula scuttling. Frequent sandstorms cut visibility to ten yards. But finally they reached the last sandy ridge overlooking the Santa Cruz River valley and the white man's oasis of Tucson.

Jemez halted the children and made them hide with the ponies behind a thick stand of white-plumed Spanish bayonet. He lifted Miguelito down and pulled his sack of Bull Durham out of the aparejo dangling over the buckskin's saddle. He built a cigarette and smoked it, his nimbus-gray eyes gazing out across the green swath of barley land surrounding the mostly adobe town.

The sleepy, peaceful illusion from this distance was wasted on Jemez, who knew the town for what it was up close—a collection of drunken, tangle-brained fools who swaggered and boasted and shot their guns in the air while puking on their own feet. Stagnant water was purchased from an old Mexican with a cart, and garbage remained where it was dumped—in the streets. And that was the part dominated by the whites. The section reserved for Indians and breeds, a squalid appendage on the south bank of the Santa Cruz referred to as Riverbend, made the rest of Tucson seem virtuous in contrast.

Tucson was also the home of the Indian-extermination faction that masqueraded as the civic-minded Tucson Committee. Unlike many Apaches and half-castes, Jemez's knowledge of English made his eyes and ears keen to the strange ways of the white intruders. Back in the region they called the South, northern fortune hunters were causing great scandal and debt amid the ravages of war. Now new troublemakers were pouring into the Southwest, war contractors eager to profit from outfitting the U.S. Army. Some of these made up the committee. They made and enforced their own laws, claiming in their newspapers that the government lacked the backbone to handle the Indian problem the way most good Americans wanted it handled.

He finished his cigarette and flipped the butt away in a wide arc. Then he turned the children due east and led them across the last expanse of sand hills toward the reservation at Mater Dolorosa.

When their shadows were lengthening behind them, they finally came in sight of the place. Gazing out over the stark setting, Jemez felt a cold lump form in his stomach. Even San Carlos had not been this desolate. A wide gravel flat was dotted here and there with mesquite-branch jacals and dark brown adobe buildings. Scrawny cottonwoods almost devoid of leaves bordered a dried-up stream. A steady, unbroken wind prevailed over this throat-parching and unprotected land, hurling dust and gravel across the plain and leaving their eyes red and swollen.

Jemez felt the cold lump give way to hot fury. *This* was the place the freedom-loving Apaches were supposed to accept in exchange for their mountains and mesas. Land the hairfaces could not even give away free to their own people, it was so worthless.

He glanced down and saw Socorro watching him intently. Her eyes ran from his. She was the oldest of the children, and now she was responsible for them, so she refused to cry. But he saw the urge to do so in the hard, determined set of her dirt-streaked face. He looked at her splinted arm. She held it out from her body as if it didn't belong to her, and he realized it must have been hurting her all this time.

He squatted and gently held his sister's bony shoulders. "Look here. Do you see that stone?"

He let go of one shoulder and pointed.

She nodded.

"When that stone melts, little sister," he told her, "a Grayeyes will tell a lie to his own. Do you understand?"

She hesitated, then nodded again.

"Good. Remember, I'll be coming back for you and Miguelito. Meanwhile, never forget the ones who were your mother and father. As they did, keep a close eye on the younger ones. Make sure they do not speak each other's names in front of the whites."

Jemez did not really believe the old wives' tale that an Indian's name lost its power if spoken by another Indian in front of white ears. From all he had seen, Indians had damn little power to lose. But it was a good way of putting Socorro on her guard against Anglo treachery.

He had already sent a word-bringer ahead to tell the white teacher, Kathleen Barton, that he was bringing the children. Jemez refused to meet with any other officials or to cooperate with the paperwork necessary to process the new arrivals. He had simply sent word that she should meet him at the western approach at sunset on this day. Now, as they all hunkered down in a shallow arroyo, Jemez tried to place the familiar fear outside of himself: the fear of white man's cunning, of the white man's noose with thirteen coils in it.

He lost the thought—in the grainy twilight he could see a woman coming up the rise toward them. She wore a plain white shirtwaist with a blue homespun skirt. When she drew closer, he made out a pretty but prematurely careworn face dominated by big, deep-set eyes of bottomless blue. Her thick and wheat-colored hair was modestly gathered into a long braid.

He led the children up to meet her. She stopped a few paces away from the group. Her eyes flicked from Socorro's injured arm to the pistol on his right hip, turned butt forward to accommodate his cross draw.

"You know who I am?" he said in English.

She nodded, still staring at the pistol.

"You are afraid of me?"

"I am afraid of all men."

Jemez watched her face, then nodded. It was a good answer. Perhaps what he had heard his people say about the sun-haired woman was true: Like the Indians, she kept her feelings out of her face and hidden in her heart. And like the Indians, she despised a liar above all else.

"That's a wise way to feel. It makes you careful." He thought about the heaps of stone outside the cave entrance and added, "But sometimes even being afraid won't save you."

She said nothing. She was too nervous, too distracted by the fearful and dirty children, to understand his meaning at that moment. Miguelito coughed his wracking, rasping cough, and she winced.

"This Hays Munro," Jemez said. "I hear he is a good man?"

She nodded.

"Are you a Quaker, too?"

She shook her head. "Neither is he."

"You dress like one." He had never seen a white woman wearing so few layers of clothing or a full skirt without hoops.

There was a long silence.

"Well," Jemez said. "I'll be back for them."

She nodded and stepped closer, folding an arm around Socorro. To his astonishment, his sister did not draw away. Only then did he understand how badly she needed to be held and comforted.

Jemez started to leave, then turned back.

"Any news lately from Riverbend?" he asked. "Any news about Robert Trilby or Juan Aragon?"

Kathleen Barton remained silent for a long time. Jemez sensed that she wanted to trust him, wanted to tell him something.

Finally he said, "You know a Mescalero boy with a blood spot in his eye?"

She nodded. His name was Victorio, but she knew the custom and avoided saying it to an Apache she did not know well. "He lives here now."

"Yes. But he is a roamer, that one, like all in his clan. Sometimes he likes to sneak off and visit me with the news."

She understood but said nothing, waiting for more.

"Tell him, Jemez has gone to Los Clavos. If you should

decide that you have something to tell me about Riverbend, he is the one to tell. Does he like you?"

"I think so."

It was his turn to nod. He watched his normally shy sister press even closer to the white teacher. "I thought he might. Then you can trust that one with your life."

She studied his face closely before he turned away. She knew the Apaches were inherently secretive—she saw that again now in the absolute inscrutability of his young, yet somehow ageless face. His look was neither civil or hostile, a look that mixed defeat with a strong measure of defiance.

Again Miguelito coughed. The harsh bray shook his entire body. The woman crossed to him and placed the back of her hand against his face to check for fever. She pulled it back quickly, alarm tightening her face.

"Why, he's burning up!" She turned to confront Jemez. But already he was disappearing into the gathering darkness, and the sound of the ponies' hoofs was lost in the hollow shrieking of the wind.

Chapter 7

"Tarnal blazes, Seth boy! I'll warn you right now, if Jenny ever finds out you bunk with hardcases like *this*, you've had your last meal with us."

Corey Bryce gingerly picked up one of the fruit jars lined neatly along the sill of the room's only window. A hairy tarantula clung to the glass inside. Other jars held centipedes and scorpions and even one rattlesnake.

Seth hung his saber and forage cap on wooden pegs beside the window. "Every one of them, 'cept the snake, I shook out of my boots."

"Where'd you find the snake?"

Seth nodded toward the back corner and a narrow bunk with a shuck mattress. The legs of the bunk had been set in bowls of kerosene to keep bedbugs off. "I guess rattlers don't mind the kerosene."

"Speaking of rattlesnakes, did you hear the word about

Sergeant Major Kinney being posted out here from the Point? He reports in a few weeks."

Seth nodded. He put plenty of grit in his voice: "*Augh!* Goddamn my eyes, better snap those heels together!"

Corey's solid white teeth flashed when he laughed. "Hell, you do it better than me."

He glanced around the dingy bachelor officer's quarters with the superior pity of a married soldier who has not been completely deprived of the feminine and domestic comforts. Seth's quarters, located in a large adobe building beside the parade field, was a room nine feet wide and fourteen feet long, with a scant eight feet between ceiling and floor. Besides the bunk, there was a single split-bottom chair, a wooden trunk, and a washstand with a metal bowl. Corner shelves of crossed sticks held a few leather-bound books. A gaudy 1869 calendar nailed beside the door advertised the O.F. Winchester Armaments Factory. The window was clouded with fly specks.

"This place is pretty raggedy-assed, all right," Corey said. "But least there's a roof over your head at night. *This* lad has spent plenty of nights under the stars lately without once cracking a cap in combat. I feel like I'm riding herd guard over the damned Innuns."

Several months had passed since the two friends had been posted to Fort Bates in the New Mexico Territory. Both officers had been assigned to cavalry platoons, part of the newly formed Indian-hunting regiments. But as yet they had seen no major action against the Kiowa and Comanche tribes active in this region. Congress—and thus, the War Department—was currently deadlocked on the Indian question: One faction, led by the expansionist lobby, favored outright extermination of the aboriginals; another, led by Missouri senator John B. Henderson, argued for more treaties and peaceful relocation of the Indians to areas where they would be taught to farm and raise cattle.

So the Army in New Mexico, in the meantime, had cautiously hung fire. Troops from Fort Bates were mostly limited to scouting and patrolling, or to protecting supply trains from raids.

"It's not this way out in Arizona." Seth dipped his hands

into the bowl and patted the top layer of pale alkali dust from his face. Both men were tanned a deep nut-brown. "The Apaches under Geronimo are raising six sorts of hell lately, and the Army has orders to track them down."

"Sure, Geronimo is a sly devil and he's put ice in some boots. But the Indian lovers are howling like kicked dogs about the Army policy. You can put it down in your book, Seth boy—everytime Soldier Blue wins a battle, some paper-collar journalist will call it the death of the Noble Savage."

Beyond the small, fly-specked window the setting sun was a blood-orange ball balanced on the horizon. No walls enclosed the fort, which was surrounded by dull chaparral, thick stands of ocotillo, and stunted cottonwoods twisted into grotesque shapes by the desert winds. Fort Bates was a sprawling complex of dark brown adobe buildings erected around a huge quadrangle of baked earth which passed for a parade ground. From the window the two officers could see a huge pole corral and a cluster of tents where the laundry women and their children lived.

"You're burning daylight, Seth," Corey said impatiently. "Hurry up! Colonel Denton's scouts killed a few buffalo yesterday, and the old man gave Jenny some fine-looking hump steaks. Tonight, mister, we eat like by-God white men!"

Corey's quarters were located on the opposite side of the parade ground, where married officers and their families resided. The two men stepped outside of Seth's room and immediately squinted in the blowing sand and gravel. Usually the flag hung listlessly all day long and flies buzzed everywhere in the dead, hot air. But each evening, toward dark, vicious sandstorms lashed at the fort with vindictive fury.

Heads tucked away from the wind, they walked quickly past the adjutant's office, the post bakery, the guardhouse, storehouses, enlisted men's quarters, and the sutler's store. Just behind the storehouses were the cavalry stables and a blacksmith's forge.

Seth ignored all of it with the contempt bred of familiarity. He was sick of the dull routine of garrison life. For the cavalrymen, each day began at the stables. Good graze was scarce around the fort—all mounts not assigned to drill or maneuvers were sent outside the fort under guard to forage the scant grasses. Light drill and post maintenance occupied the morning; more work in the stables followed noon rations. Each afternoon was capped by a dress or undress parade. The men were demoralized and bored, and the wily fort sutler always had "oil of gladness" and cards to hand, ensuring that the boredom was occasionally punctuated by violence.

"All I've done since we got here," Seth complained, raising his voice above the shrieking wind, "is drill recruits, mount guard, lead log-cutting details and track down snowbirds for court-martial. *You're* the one who's married. Why are you always on scouting patrol?"

"Mister, where have you been grazing? I'm on scouting patrol because the old man is keen for my wife," Corey replied with a grin. "He likes to get shed of me. Jenny's got him feeding from her hand."

"So everyone has noticed. Good. Then maybe she can talk him into letting *me* lead that unit down to Albuquerque tomorrow instead of you."

The wagon-road way station near Albuquerque had recently been plagued by Comanche raids. Corey had been ordered to take his platoon south provisioned for a fifteen-day scout, both to determine the location of the Comanche camp and to establish a military presence discouraging further raids.

Corey shook his head. "Sorry, soldier. They'll serve lemonade in hell before Denton changes an order. Better polish your boots and find clean gloves."

"As usual. You'll be earning your breakfast as a soldier while I get all perfumed up for the Sunday Stroll."

Every month a detail of soldiers escorted officers' wives to the opera in nearby Santa Fe, though there had been no dangerous Indian activity near the area since the fort had been established. By now the armed escort was more a matter of military courtesy than necessity, a welcome excursion to the bored soldiers—hence the whimsical nickname "Sunday Stroll." Except this time recent reports from the Indian scouts employed by Fort Bates had been cankering at Seth.

"Jenny sure looks forward to the opera," Corey said. "Colonel Denton's wife gave her a gown a while back, and she's been frilling it up for weeks now."

But Seth knew Corey well enough by now to recognize when he was taking the long way around the barn about something. This harmless comment didn't match his worried countenance.

"I got a hunch you've heard the report. You're worried about what Goes Ahead told Denton."

Corey nodded. Colonel Denton's Papago Indian scouts had returned with more than succulent buffalo steaks. The leader of the scouts also reported a large trail, first spotted in the foothills of the Sangre de Cristo Mountains, made by unshod ponies.

"Goes Ahead couldn't identify the tribe," Corey said. "Nor determine if it's a peaceful movement. Least, that's what he says. Scouts are useful, but I don't trust the red ones. It's true that Indians all fight amongst themselves like a bunch of jealous stags. But the plain truth is, they all fly the same colors when it comes to hating the white man."

"Maybe that's so. But right now no tribe is on the warpath against the Army, not in this area," Seth reminded him.

"No, but civilians are fair game—especially to Kiowas and Comanches. And that trail Denton was told about was found close to the Old Pueblo Road."

Seth said nothing, knowing his friend was right. The Old Pueblo Road was the main link between Fort Bates and Santa Fe—the same road the opera excursion would follow. Both the Kiowas and the Comanches zealously enjoyed torturing captives. Even the most battle-hardened soldiers at the fort, those who had stood and held at Shiloh and Antietam and Bull Run, lived in fear of capture by either tribe.

"Anyhow," Corey said, "at least it's *you* who'll be heading up the Sunday Stroll detail. That makes me breathe a mite easier than if Waites or Baumgarter was in charge. If I have to be gone so much, I'm glad you're around to keep an eye on Jenny and give her some company now and then. She gets along jim-dandy with the other wives. But most of them are older than her, and none of 'em likes to read and write poetry like she does. She's a real trooper, and she won't complain no matter how dull it gets out here. But I can tell she misses Albany and her friends something fierce. If she didn't have you to talk books and such with, she'd be doing the hurt dance."

Seth said nothing, feeling a sharp guilt gnawing at him. Here Corey was, he realized, thanking him for finding time to be with Jeanette. And yet, the moments he spent with her had become the most important part of his life. Over the past months, when they had spent so much time reading to each other and playing cribbage and strolling about the remote post, a bond had developed between them, an understanding divorced from language: This wasn't just convenient companionship. Seth was convinced, in his secret heart of hearts, that they *both* spent too much time thinking about the other. Yet by not admitting anything, they could pretend nothing was happening.

"Home sweet home, laddiebuck. *Smell* that hump steak cooking!" Corey said.

The quarters he shared with Jeanette centered around a small, two-room house with walls of close-set wooden stakes chinked with mud. Several huge, comfortable tents—donated by Colonel Denton, the post C.O.—had been erected together to form a series of interconnected rooms around the hub of the building.

Jeanette's domesticating touch was apparent immediately upon entering the central house. Fresh white columbine, procured by the fort sutler just for her, spilled out of a pottery vase. White lace curtains with neatly scalloped hems covered both the tiny windows. Braided rugs covered the puncheon floor, and thick bearskin rugs softened the bare, rammed-earth floor under the tents. Cool water filled the brightly painted clay ollas suspended from the rafters.

Cooking smells and noises from the kitchen tent behind the central rooms told them where Jeanette was. When Corey called her name, she stepped past the elkskin flap to greet them.

"Mr. Seth Carlson! So Corey was right—you *would* rather eat my cooking than the Army's."

" 'Take all you want,' " Corey said, quoting the mess sergeant, " 'but eat all you take.' Makes a man partial to small portions, eh, Seth?"

Seth watched Jeanette wipe her hands on her apron while

she crossed to a chintz-covered chest. A strand of burnt-sienna hair had worked loose from her chignon and curled forward toward her chin. Again he admired the slender, tall beauty whose face was saved from a grave severity by a slightly upturned nose. Of course, with her quicksilver smile and ready flirtatiousness, she had instantly become the post sweetheart. Every soldier, from the privates swamping out the stables to the post commander, sought the opportunity to bask in her charm.

"Look, Mr. Seth Carlson," she said, pulling a folded sheet of stationery from the chest and handing it to Seth. "It's a letter from Aunt Tilly. You needn't trouble reading it, it's just boring woman talk. But look at it."

Seth unfolded it. His eyebrows rose in curiosity. "Why, she took it to a printer?"

"No, silly! It's a new machine called a typewriter."

"It's tarnal foolishness," Corey remarked as he polished an apple on his sleeve. "Why does a letter need to look like a book?"

"What would you know, Napoleon?" Jeanette protested. "All you do is chase Indians. You've never tried to write a poem in this weather. The ink turns into gum the moment it's dipped out of the pen."

"I've tried to keep a carbine oiled in this weather," Corey said. "And I've tried to keep blowing sand from wearing out the axles of our supply wagons. But even if you keep the axles in shape, the dry air shrinks the lumber and the wagon splits apart."

"Complain all you like," Jeanette said. "At least you haven't been shot at yet. And I, for one, am glad."

"There's no glory in peace, sweet love. Me and Seth both'll get shot at soon enough if old man Denton has his way. That man's hell-bent on peddling lead to some Indians."

"He's certainly tame enough around me," Jeanette said.

"*You* could charm the claws off a grizzly, Jenny. He ain't so partial to his junior-grade officers."

"He must take a fancy to Mr. Seth Carlson," Jeanette teased, smiling at their guest. "Twice in a row now he's been picked to take us ladies to the opera."

"That shines right," Corey said. "Seth is the only officer at Fort Bates who understands all that foreign caterwauling."

"Caterwauling! I'll have you know, you handsome Philistine, they're doing *Tristan and Isolt*—*only* the world's greatest love story! Oh, I know it's silly, but I cry every time Isolt's maid tells them, 'You have drunk not love alone, but love and death together,' and Tristan sings in that brave tenor, 'Well, then, come Death.'"

"Hell, the gent never bought *me* a beer." Corey winked at Seth.

But Seth neglected to grin back. For at that moment, watching Jeanette's eager face as she mentioned the opera, a cold prickling settled deep into his bone marrow. It lasted only a moment, perhaps the duration of a few heartbeats: a sharp, bittersweet pang of tragedy and loss, a pain so acute that he actually winced from the physical hurt of it.

Jeanette saw this and her pale brow runneled in a frown. "Seth? Are you all right?"

Now Corey, too, watched her closely. In her sudden concern, she had slipped into a tone Corey had never before heard her use with Seth. The furrow between his eyes deepened, more in thoughtful curiosity than jealous anger.

Seth watched Corey meet Jeanette's eyes, watched her glance guiltily away.

And in that moment, he knew.

He finally admitted it to himself for the first time: He was in love with his best friend's wife. And odds were good that she was in love with him right back.

He swallowed the hard stone in his throat, then nodded. He forced his lips into a grin. "There's nothing wrong with me, pretty lady, that a hot steak won't fix."

Later, while a pale white moon climbed toward its zenith, Corey walked Seth back to his quarters.

"Still waters *do* run deep," Corey said, meeting his friend's eyes squarely in the moonlight. The wind had raged itself out, and the usual knife edge of nighttime chill sharpened the desert air.

"What's that s'posed to mean?"

"It means, among other things, that you're stealing my girl, shavetail."

The unexpected words slapped at Seth with the force of a physical blow. But instead of formulating a response, he recalled Jeanette's sea-green eyes and the way, when she closed them, that her long lashes curved against her cheeks.

But in the same moment, Seth realized: Deep down in his secret heart of hearts, Corey was incapable of feeling any real jealousy. His money, his looks, his confidence and sense of cool command—all this ensured that he never had to doubt his security with the opposite sex.

"I think I know how you feel about her, Seth boy. Hell, only a fool *wouldn't* be in love with her."

Seth still said nothing, warm blood rising into his face. Abruptly, beyond the shadowy mass of the unwalled fort, a coyote howled—a long, ululating howl that ended in a series of yipping barks. But for a moment, again recalling the report from Goes Ahead, both men wondered: *Was* it a coyote?

Corey's next question drew Seth up short.

"Seth, did I miscalculate when I brought Jenny out here?"

Seth considered several responses. All he managed was, "It's not my place to say."

"Well anyhow, I love her, Seth. I love her more than life itself. If anything ever happened to her, I wouldn't want to live. And I just want to say it out loud one time: If anything ever happens to me, I hope she can be with you. You're bedrock, solid as they come."

Realizing this conversation had gone about as far as it could, Corey suddenly unleashed the shrill kill cry of the mountain regiment—an adaptation of the fearsome Rebel yell that had terrorized northern troops during the great war. "There's no glory in peace, laddiebuck!" he added by way of farewell, disappearing into the dark night.

His words about Jeanette—as close to deep feeling as Corey could let himself get, Seth realized—left Seth feeling dirty and mean with guilt. After tonight, after that moment of realization, he knew he couldn't pretend that nothing was happening. Neither could Jeanette. If there was no glory in peace, there was certainly little peace in love—at least, Seth figured, the only kind of love he knew about.

For a moment, just before he drifted into sleep, Seth's relaxing body suddenly gave a mighty twitch, startling him awake again.

He sat up, face stiff with fear, and spoke the word out loud into the still night.

"Jenny!"

But he had no idea what had frightened him. He lay down again, and a minute later his momentary scare was shooed away by sleep.

Chapter 8

The Papago Indian scout named Goes Ahead squatted for a long time in the lush grass bordering the Pecos River.

He had discovered more tracks made by unshod ponies. He picked up the trail a half day's ride southeast of Fort Bates. It led through a series of red-rock canyons and then veered northwest toward Santa Fe. The number of ponies—perhaps as many as forty—convinced him that these were the same riders he had already reported to Colonel Denton.

For a long time he studied the bend of the grass, determining how old the tracks were. Some of the grass was still matted, and the rest had begun to spring back up—suggesting that the prints had been made within the last day.

Goes Ahead finally rose, stiff kneecaps popping, and stared out across the long, grassy slope rising up from the river. He was short and round and wore his hair wrapped tight around his head in a braid under a floppy-brimmed plainsman's hat. He was dressed in Army trousers and a coarse gray cotton shirt with buttons. But he retained the quilled moccasins and bear-claw necklace from the days before he started praying to the white man's God.

Whoever these Indian horsemen were, he told himself, it was not the peace road they were taking. If this were a peaceful movement, involving a tribe or band, there would be lodge-pole trails in the grass. He had spotted none so far. These riders were traveling light and fast, perhaps as much as seventy miles a day—quite possibly a war party, though one hadn't ventured this close to the fort or Santa Fe in many moons.

Goes Ahead liked working for the blue-bloused soldiers. True, they were a strange and ungrateful lot. Always shouting at each other even though they stood nose to nose when talking. And the way they made greeting by grabbing each other's hands and pumping up and down—it was comical, and he still laughed every time he saw the foolish hair-faces do it. Nor could Goes Ahead truly respect a race that shoved iron bits into a horse's mouth and cruelly dug sharp-roweled spurs into their flanks.

Still, these pale-skinned intruders were rich in the things that made a hard life more pleasant: coffee, sugar, alcohol, good brown tobacco, machine-made clothing and tools. And they could be generous with these things when an Indian scout did his job well. For truly, these brave but clumsy warriors needed help from Indian scouts. Encumbered by wagons and other heavy equipment, they were no match against Indians mounted on swift ponies—Indians who, in winter, took to hiding in the high country. In spring and summer Indian scouts alone knew where the hidden water holes and graze could be found.

The Army's new strategy of employing friendly Indians to seek out the hostiles had pitted brother against brother, clan against clan. Goes Ahead had attended a mission school, and thus he knew—as most Indians still did not understand—that the red man's fate was sealed by the sheer numbers of these whites. More arrived every day from lands beyond the sun, hordes of them. Goes Ahead was no coward, nor did he consider himself a turncoat. But his tribe had tempered its personality in the blazing Southwest heat, and they had little enthusiasm for war.

He mounted and nudged his horse slowly forward, letting the mare set her own pace. He rode a tall cavalry sorrel, but used his own flat rawhide Indian saddle. The scout kept his eye on the trail, looking for more signs.

An hour later he found one.

He had reached the lee of a tall mesa. There was no evidence of any fires, but the human and animal droppings clearly indicated that a cold camp had been made. The scout was poking through some hawthorn bushes when he discovered the tiny doeskin pouch.

He recognized it immediately: It had been left behind as a gift to the place—a Kiowa custom upon leaving a camp.

Kiowas. Goes Ahead felt cold sweat break out in his armpits. Kiowas were not native to this region. So this band would surely be that of Eagle on His Journey. Normally they roamed near Medicine Lodge Creek in Oklahoma. The only reason they ever rode this far to the southwest was to join their longtime battle allies, the Comanches, under Hairy Wolf of the Antelope Eaters band.

Goes Ahead feared both tribes as he feared the yellow vomit. What they did to Christianized Indians like the Papagos was surpassed, in sheer barbarity and unspeakable cruelty, only by their treatment of white captives—especially women. Luckily, the Comanches these days seldom left their favorite hunting grounds far out on the flat Llano Estacado, or Staked Plain, a vast region covering most of the Texas Panhandle and much of eastern New Mexico.

But clearly they *had* left it: If Kiowas were in this area, they were surely riding with their battle companions. And neither tribe was one to fool with.

The Papago calculated rapidly: It was about a twenty-four-hour ride to Fort Bates. But earlier that day Corey Bryce had left with his troop of cavalry, heading south toward Albuquerque. Goes Ahead could intercept his unit in eight hours, maybe even less.

Once again he mounted and glanced carefully all around him, searching for the slightest movement. Then, pointing the sorrel's bridle north, he lashed her to a gallop with his light sisal whip.

Colonel Woodrow Denton said, "I'll give you the same warning I give all my junior grade officers, mister: Lieutenants come and go, but the Army doesn't change."

"Yes, sir," Seth replied, wondering to himself how a man could be so stupid and still pin silver eagles on his epaulets. That was why the Army forced men to respect the rank, not the man.

"There's a powerful beast lurking out there, Lieutenant, and I'm not talking about Indians. I'm talking about the chain of command."

"Yes, sir." *Just set it to music, you tiresome old blowhard.*

The commanding officer of Fort Bates pushed away from his desk and limped across the room to a Mercator map of the United States on the side wall. His left leg had been partially paralyzed by a Civil War wound, leaving him with a serious limp and a slow gait. But the great war had depleted America's manpower—if a man could walk and still had one functioning trigger finger, he was fit to soldier.

Denton absently studied the map as he spoke to his subordinate.

"The *Operations Manual* prescribes the number of guards for an escort detail—six, not counting the duty officer. You say you want to override the manual and increase it for tomorrow. In other words, you want to buck the chain of command. Why?"

"Because of the initial report from the scouts, sir. There's quite possibly a large group of unidentified Indians in the vicinity. In my judgment, this poses a threat to the women, sir."

Though it was widely recognized that Denton had enough guts to fill a smokehouse, brains were not his strong suit. His inept battlefield tactics were the butt of jokes in military circles. In one campaign up north against the Blackfeet, a regiment directly under his command expended fifteen thousand rounds of ammunition in killing six Indians, all women and children. A newspaper reporter got wind of it and dubbed the colonel "Dead-Eye Denton." His nickname caught on with the public and further tarnished the Army's image as an efficient Indian-fighting machine—thus ensuring that Colonel Denton's name would never appear on a generals' list.

"A threat? Stretching the blanket a mite, aren't you, Lieutenant? But just to be safe, I sent Goes Ahead back out to dig up some more sign, if there is any. For all we know right now, it's just a group of blanket Indians who jumped the reservation at Turkey Mountain."

"With all due respect," Seth objected, "the colonel is probably right. But when it comes to protecting the women of Fort Bates, I'd rather be safe than sorry."

Denton glanced at Seth. "Especially when one of the women is Jeanette Bryce, eh?"

"Sir?"

Denton looked at the map again. "I've seen you two together quite a bit. You appear to have some very stimulating conversations. With Bryce gone so much, it must be a solace to her to have you around."

Seth felt heat rising into his face. He forced himself to wait before he answered. His reply was civil enough, but the tone was cold and remote.

"You'd have to ask her that yourself, Colonel."

For a moment Denton frowned, his brows knitting to form a single line. He was not one to brook even mild defiance from subordinates. But this young Carlson, something in his quiet, competent manner marked him as a good man to have on one's side. The colonel suddenly relented.

"Ahh, hell, you're just a colt. Naturally you want to do a good job. Don't forget, *my* wife will be among those women, too. Stand easy, Lieutenant. Permission granted to increase the guard by two men."

"Right, sir." Seth wanted at least four more, but with Denton, even splitting the difference was a victory.

"If our scouts are telling us the straight, there's no actual, confirmed sign of hostiles or hostile activity in the area. But the scouts are Indians, and Indians like to serve up as much barroom josh as the white man. Besides increasing the guard, what plans do you have for the Stroll tomorrow?"

"The extra men will ride positions to the north and south,

the most likely directions of any attack. Also, I'm picking men from the dragoons for this detail, only the best marksmen. The usual detail will flank the passengers; and the driver, too, will be a sharpshooter from the dragoons."

Denton nodded his approval. "Don't forget they'll have my personal ambulance. That's a sturdy vehicle."

"Yes, sir."

"Most hostiles in this area are hurting for good rifles. They won't have the oysters to go up against that many carbines."

The C.O. glowered at the wall map as if he resented the way it stared accusingly back at him.

"The Army is caught between the sap and the bark on this Indian question. If the damned Indian lovers back East hadn't tied my hands, I would put paid to it *now*, mister, and make this region safe for the white man."

Denton rapped the map with his knuckles, indicating the vast Llano Estacado.

"My new mountain regiment is at full strength. Yet, it's still not authorized for combat. Even now, Bryce is limited to scouting. Never mind that the manual says twenty-five miles a day is the maximum for the regular cavalry. *Look* at this region, Carlson. We're talking about a thousand miles of desert and mountains, and canyons so deep you can't see the bottom on a clear day. And we're talking about Indians who ride with as many as five remounts on their string, remounts as well-trained as show ponies. They carry nothing but their weapons, they live on cactus, they can go two days in a hundred-twenty-degree heat without water.

"The U.S. soldier, in contrast, rides a big, strong, slow horse that can't handle the high-country trails. It is a massive undertaking to pack along the necessary rations and forage. The white-livered cowards who print the newspapers don't bother reporting *that* side of it because they'd rather write penny dreadfuls, not the facts!"

Seth only nodded politely, his eyes glazing over. Most of it was true enough. But Denton had an ax to grind, and repeated this catechism so often he sounded like a bitter Bible thumper.

Seth, however, could hear only the fearful litany of Corey's words from the other night: *Did I miscalculate when I brought Jenny out here?*

Between Santa Fe and the Rio Grande, which wound by just to the west of the City of the Holy Faith, stretched twenty miles of scrub-pine forest. On the night before the Sunday Stroll, a combined band of Kiowa and Comanche warriors made a cold camp in the pine trees just north of the Old Pueblo Road.

The Kiowa leader, Eagle on His Journey, was a member of the elite Kaitsenko, the ten greatest warriors of the Kiowa nation. He had led twenty warriors down from their hunting grounds in Oklahoma after a Comanche word-bringer arrived with a loaded clay pipe—the custom when seeking braves for a raid.

The word-bringer had been sent by his war leader, Hairy Wolf of the Antelope Eaters Clan. Hairy Wolf's Comanches claimed the vast Blanco Canyon, far out on the Staked Plain, as their home. The two bands would return to the Blanco after this raid tomorrow, secure in the knowledge that no blue-bloused soldiers had yet dared to enter their fortress.

After a hushed meal of cold ant-paste soup and wild onions, the two leaders ordered that a packhorse loaded with bladder bags be led to the center of camp. There, in moonlight as pale as bleached bones, they distributed the bags of corn beer to the clan leaders.

The drinking would not begin tonight, of course. They would never be able to control the men by morning. The bags would be broken open tomorrow before they rode out. Now, as the rest of the braves spread their sleeping robes and attended to weapons in the moonlight, the two leaders walked off some distance to counsel alone.

They made an odd pair, each typical of their vastly different peoples. The Kiowa, Eagle on His Journey, was tall, handsome, graceful on foot, broad-shouldered and thick-chested, with long, black hair flowing past the middle of his back. His Comanche ally, Hairy Wolf, was short, ugly, bandy-legged and awkward, wearing his hair just long enough to part in the center and tuck behind both ears.

Every red or white man on the plains, however, knew well

that Comanches ceased to be awkward once mounted on a horse—became, in fact, the most dreaded raiders on the plains. The best Comanche warrior could string and shoot twenty or more arrows and ride three hundred yards—all while a bluecoat was still reloading his carbine.

"Have ears for my words, Hairy Wolf," Eagle on His Journey said. "We are too close to the soldier town and too short on rifles. Only fools would linger near the Old Pueblo Road long without fire sticks. I say, never mind choosing a target. We must attack the first possible target, and then ride hard for the Blanco."

Hairy Wolf thought about this and then nodded. "Agreed. With luck it will be a supply wagon. Or perhaps a stagecoach with passengers we can ransom or sell to the Comancheros."

Each man spoke in the tongue of his own tribe. Both groups were fluent in Kiowa, Comanche, and Spanish.

"Tell your men to drink much water before they sleep," Eagle on His Journey said.

Hairy Wolf nodded. Red men were notorious late sleepers. More than one important battle had been missed—or even lost—because a tribe failed to wake up early enough. But a full bladder would ensure early risers.

"Now the talking is done," Hairy Wolf said. "Tomorrow we let our battle lances speak for us."

Just past the unwalled eastern boundary of Fort Bates grew a small copse of cottonwood trees. Some nights at sunset, when Corey was in the field, Jeanette liked to wander out to the copse and listen to the angry scolding of the jays that nested there.

She did so on the day he left for the two-week scout near Albuquerque. It was the night before the excursion to the opera in Santa Fe, and anticipation made her blood hum.

In the fading light she watched as a doe with a fawn broke from the far end of the copse and raced away. It had been a hard winter in the high country, and deer had come down into the lower, more arid regions to escape the snow.

Something in the animals' furtive movement saddened her, quickened some sense of melancholy that had plagued her throughout the day. Aunt Tilly's latest letter certainly hadn't helped her odd mood, either. The poor dear was troubled by tragic dreams lately and fairly begged Jeanette to return to Albany at once.

It was just sentimental superstition, of course. Foolish old Tilly. Even so, it seemed to Jeanette as if all day long she had looked at everything with a strange, lingering regret.

She shook off her pensive mood as the westering sun gave out its last feeble rays. The training day was over, and now Jeanette watched a detail ride out to bring the grazing herds in for the night. She resolved to return to her quarters now while there was still enough light so she could see to get a lamp going.

Watching the detail reminded her that Corey was out there somewhere in the vast, dangerous territory beyond the safety of the fort. It also reminded her, with a twinge compounded of guilt and regret, that she wouldn't see Seth this evening. By a tacit understanding between them, he never visited the Bryce quarters at night unless Corey was home.

She didn't like it when she thought of both men at once like this. Not now, not since that ineffable moment when Seth ceased to be an amusing diversion and became instead something more: a permanent reference point in the definition of her being, a needful thing answering her own need, the constant, aching *I want* of her womanhood. The two men were point and counterpoint in the tumultuous harmony of her soul, and she needed both to keep the melody of her existence alive.

She turned and headed back to the fort. She was just in time to watch a quick-darting prairie falcon swoop down on an unsuspecting squirrel that had wandered from the shelter of the trees. She shivered when the squirrel chittered in fright that quickly turned to pain.

I've got to write poor Tilly, she thought suddenly. After the opera tomorrow. And then, as suddenly, something made her change her mind—she'd write that letter tonight.

Chapter 9

The bugler sounded Sunday morning reveille at four o'clock. The sudden, harsh notes destroyed the deep stillness and quiet of the night's best sleeping hours. Corey Bryce's troops rolled out of their blankets cursing the Army, Indians, the bugler, and the crisp morning chill.

Their breath formed long feathers of smoke in the waning moonlight. The general mood improved a little after each squad built its own fire. Since filling their bullseye canteens with fresh water would be the last detail when breaking camp, the men separated the metal halves and used them to fry bacon. Corey, already up and dressed before the bugle, was working on his second cup of hot black coffee by the time a private rode out to call in the men from the picket outposts.

The platoon had departed from Fort Bates the previous day, traveling slow to the south. They stuck to the unfamiliar trails used by local Indians, staying close to the winding Rio

Grande Valley, always following the patiently searching scouts. They rode in two long columns of thirty men each, dust spiraling up all around them. Their primary mission was to show the flag in an attempt to discourage Indian attacks along the overland stage and freight routes around Albuquerque.

Exactly *who* he was supposed to show the flag to, Corey wasn't sure, but he figured he'd give it his best and trust that someone further up the chain of command knew a war whoop when he heard one. He finished his coffee and walked down to the sandy bank of the Rio Grande, squatting to rinse his cup in the sluggish current. The hollow heartbeat of approaching hooves made him stand again and glance curiously toward the north. A lone rider drew near at a run, but it was still too dark to see him well. Corey heard a sentry raise a challenge, and the rider replied with something he couldn't quite make out at this distance.

A few minutes later a shadowy form glided toward him. When the rider was almost on him, Corey recognized the floppy-brimmed hat and sorrel mare belonging to the Papago scout Goes Ahead.

"Kiowas," Goes Ahead greeted him. "Found sign. That means Comanches must be with them."

"Where did you find sign?"

"Northeast of here near the Pecos, heading toward Santa Fe."

"Santa Fe?" Corey's voice tightened an octave. "You're sure?"

Goes Ahead nodded.

"How many?"

"Maybe thirty. Maybe forty."

"A war party, you think."

"With these tribes? What else? Kiowas never come this far south for anything but raids."

Corey nodded. "The fort hasn't been warned?"

"No. You were closer. With hard riding, you might catch them before they reach Santa Fe. Also, scouts near the fort may spot them, too."

"Eat quickly, then fork a fresh horse," Corey ordered him.

"I'm forming a squad. I want you to lead us back to that trail."

His pulse thudding in his palms, Corey searched out the platoon sergeant and directed him to pick the best twenty troopers. They were to be up and on the line immediately after breakfast, full bandoliers, light-marching pack, ready to ride hard.

Then, his hands trembling only slightly, Corey picked up his blanket, saddle, and bridle and crossed rapidly to the natural shelter of thickets where the horses had been picketed in a patch of good graze. He whistled and a dark bay stallion trotted obediently toward him until it reached the end of its line.

He had already warmed the bit, and his horse took it easily. Corey saddled the bay and cinched the girth tight under its belly. He strapped his blanket roll to the back of the saddle.

Then, momentarily caught without a task to occupy him, the single word finally escaped his lips in a whisper that was almost a plea:

"Jenny!"

Corey ordered his platoon sergeant to take charge of the remaining troopers and head them toward Albuquerque, as originally planned. Then, as soon as Corey could see his hand in front of his face, he ordered Goes Ahead out on point. Rapidly, he led his squad north.

Sunday dawned clear and bright under a seamless blue sky. Seth ate a breakfast of side meat and coffee and sourdough biscuits in the officers' mess, then visited the cavalry stables. Using saddle soap, he cleaned and softened all his leather riding gear. Then he backed his horse—Comet, a chestnut mare with a white mane—out of her stall.

She nuzzled his shoulder, glad to see him. Seth had selected her from the herds soon after he reported to Fort Bates. She held the promise of being a good Indian-fighting horse—she was small but well-muscled, and sure-footed on the steep mountain trails where usually only a mule could be trusted. She had been trained to stop when her reins touched the ground, so there was no need to hobble her.

He brushed and curried the horse, then strapped a nose bag of oats on and stalled her again. Next, he visited the enlisted barracks and spoke briefly with a young corporal named Boone Maddox, a Kentucky-bred sharpshooter with a reputation for remaining cool and shooting plumb. Seth had placed him in charge of the privates who would be riding guard today.

Reassured that Maddox understood his duties, Seth returned to the cramped quarters he shared with various New Mexican fauna. He cleaned his service revolver and polished his saber. Then he shaved and donned his only clean dress uniform.

All this busywork occupied his hands, but not his thoughts. Over and over the image of Jeanette's face filled his mind's eye. And Corey's words echoed in memory like a tune he couldn't stop whistling: *I love her, Seth. I love her more than life itself. If anything ever happened to her, I wouldn't want to live.*

"Well, Mr. Seth Carlson?" Jeanette demanded. "Am I pretty or not? All this time, you've never once said it. You're hard on a girl's confidence."

"Huh! If *you* were any more confident, you could cheat the sutler."

In fact, Seth had never seen Jeanette look more beautiful than she did now in her peony-print gown. He had stopped by the Bryce quarters to inform her that the colonel's ambulance would be departing from in front of the headquarters building in thirty minutes.

The midday sun slanted into Jeanette's face when she opened the door, igniting gold flecks in her sea-green eyes. The thick hair was swept up under her gold and amethyst comb.

"You don't know much about women. How do you think we become confident? Only if you men constantly remind us how consummately beautiful we are."

She spun around for him, the satin gown whispering as it tried to keep up.

"Well? You're not going to say it, are you? Am I pretty?"

"I s'pose you're not too hard to look at," he replied evasively.

"Oh, bosh! That's what Corey always says, and you know it." She wrinkled her nose in a little moue. "Some gallants! And you two've been to West Point? I thought you had classes in proper conduct toward young ladies."

However, her eyes—wide with frank admiration for the fine figure he cut in his dress uniform—belied her bantering tone.

"Seth?"

"Mmm?"

"Speaking of West Point . . . how did Corey get his nickname?"

The question, as unexpected as a punch to the jaw, left him gaping stupidly. "What nickname?" he finally managed, knowing it sounded silly.

"Oh, don't worry, he knows I know. I heard everyone call him 'Lady Killer' when I came down for graduation, remember?"

"Well, there you are. Ask Corey."

"I did. He said to ask you sometime. I'm asking."

"Me? He said to ask *me*?"

She nodded emphatically, still waiting.

"I don't remember," he said finally.

"The only thing you do worse than dancing is lying."

"Lie or no, I'm sticking to it."

"I can see that. So I'm not going to press the point."

She affected annoyance with him for a few minutes. But the brilliant day beyond the open doorway proved too much of a diversion.

"It's a perfectly wonderful day for the opera," she declared, gazing over Seth's shoulder into the bottomless blue of the afternoon sky.

In that moment, Seth was abruptly aware of her physical nearness—aware in a pulse-tightening, throat-pinching way he'd never let himself feel around her.

Her eyes only reluctantly left the depths of sky and focused on him again.

Their eyes spoke without words, and again Seth felt it like the stirring of belly flies: that intense premonitory chill of some terrible loss. She saw in his eyes what he felt in his heart, and for a moment Seth watched the vitality inside her quicken, felt her feminine life force in all its power and vulnerability.

She spoke almost as if the words came from outside her, reciting in a clear, sad, strong cadence that made the fine hairs on his neck stiffen:

"When I have fears that I may cease to be
　Before my pen has gleaned my teeming brain,
Before high-piled books in charact'ry,
　Hold like rich garners the full-ripened grain;
When I behold upon the night's starred face,
　Huge cloudy symbols of a high romance
And think that I may never live to trace
　Their shadows with the magic hand of chance—"

Jeanette suddenly stopped reciting. Or more accurately, thought a bewildered Seth, her voice seemed to lose its will.

"I've . . . oh, dear, Mr. Seth Carlson, I've forgotten. Finish it for me?"

Seth knew she was lying. In the months they had spent reciting poetry to each other, she had never lost a single line. But the unearthly light in her eyes at that moment, the almost angelic beauty and purity—they held him in perfect thrall. And he knew, he knew they *both* knew, this was a moment marked out by an awful destiny.

"*Say* it, Seth," she pleaded when he hesitated. "Finish it? I want to hear Keats."

"And when I feel, fair creature of an hour,
　That I shall never look upon thee more,
Never have relish in the faery power
　Of unreflecting love!—then on the shore
Of the wide world I stand alone, and think
Till Love and Fame to nothingness do sink."

He finished, and in the ensuing silence time ticked out a safe and private little heaven all around them. Then Seth's voice broke the spell.

"Jeanette?"

"Yes?"

For a moment his lips almost formed the words: *Don't go today*. But that moment passed, swept away by the force of old habit, old assumptions, and the old childhood lie that everything would turn out all right—that men really *could* take care of the defenseless and keep fear at bay.

So instead Seth merely said, "I have to go tell the others we're ready. See you in a bit."

Chapter 10

A Sunday afternoon observer watching Corey Bryce's cavalry troop thunder through the Rio Grande Valley on its way north might have thought it an odd and motley sight.

The tall young towhead leading them wore a standard-issue uniform. But Army dress regulations were not yet as rigid as they soon would be. Some of the men riding with him were experienced campaigners who knew that old clothing should be worn in the field. Not one of them wore Uncle Sam's blue on this warm September day. A few wore coarse pullover shirts, others the loose four-button sack coats of Civil War vintage. Several wore straw hats, popular in the unrelenting sun.

Corey had pushed his men and horses hard, ignoring too many water holes, and by now the horses were slick with lather. Anxiously, he kept his eye on the sun and charted its progress, trying to guess where Jeanette would be at any given moment. Following right behind Goes Ahead, they had circled Fort Bates an hour earlier, dogging the Kiowa-Comanche trail as it aimed obliquely for the Old Pueblo Road.

Three miles south of the road, they found a body.

Goes Ahead sat his saddle atop a long creosote bluff, waiting for them. At first Corey thought the glistening thing lying in the grass beside the scout was an animal carcass. Then, as he rode nearer, shock and revulsion dried his mouth: the victim had definitely once been human. Among other atrocities he had suffered, a bone-handled knife had been driven to the hilt into his right eye socket.

The body had been stripped naked, crudely scalped, the genitals cut off and stuffed into the mouth.

"Comanche work," Goes Ahead said. "See? Scalp cut all ragged. Those ones always use a dull knife, do it while the person still alive."

"Holy Hannah, that's Tosh Gillycuddy!" a soldier exclaimed. "I recognize that big hairy wen upside his nose! He's a sharpshooter with the dragoons. That's Tosh, sure as hell's a-burnin'!"

"By God, you're right, Muggins!" another said. "Poor devil. You know them red niggers put him through misery liftin' *his* hair—he wore it too short to grab ahold of."

Corey ceased listening as soon as he heard the name, and realized that sharpshooter Tosh Gillycuddy was no doubt part of the Sunday Stroll detail, one of the flankers Seth had planned to send out if he got his extra men. Flankers left before the main party and rode well wide of the planned route, the first line of defense.

Every one of Corey's troopers knew their young leader had not yet been tested in combat. But Corey was one of the best-liked officers at Fort Bates, and had proven to be a fast learner in the field. His wife knew each of his men by name and always had a kind word for any she met. The general opinion among them was that she was quality goods, and any man foolish enough to imply otherwise would have paid for it dearly after taps. They knew she was along on the Sunday Stroll. Now they all looked at Corey, feeling the young officer's pain as keenly as if it were their own.

"I say it's a medal or a coffin for *this* pony soldier, sir!" the trooper named Muggins said. "It's come down to the nut-cuttin', the heathen sons o' bitches! I say we put at 'em."

Two soldiers had broken out their entrenching tools to bury Gillycuddy when Corey spoke up. "Never mind that, we'll bury him later." He mounted and gave spur to his tired bay. "Move out!" he shouted, already leaping ahead of the rest before the command was out of his mouth.

"But why on earth *aren't* you married?" Louise Denton said. "You're certainly a fine catch for some fortunate young lady."

"Oh, but Louise, Mr. Seth Carlson can't afford a wife. He sends all of *his* money home to his mama and sisters," Jeanette said. "Don't you, Mr. Seth Carlson?" she added, leaning out the window of the reinforced coach designed for use as a field ambulance.

"Well, my lands, Jenny!" put in Dorothy Gordon, wife of the quartermaster. "If that's so, you needn't torment him about it. God bless the boy for loving his family so much."

She, too, poked her head outside to smile approvingly up at Seth. Several gold teeth flashed in the sun.

"Oh, but I only tease Mr. Seth Carlson because I know that soon he'll be promoted," Jeanette said. "Then he can afford to marry a pretty girl who loves him in spite of his dancing."

Seth, trotting on Comet beside the open window of the ambulance, cheerfully touched the brim of his hat to acknowledge his lack of grace on the ballroom floor.

"Shame on you, Jenny, always picking at the lad so," another woman insisted. Her name was Helen Bursons, wife of the major who commanded the dragoons. "Although I'm the first to admit no one cuts a more dashing figure on the dance floor than your Corey."

Seth divided his attention between the six women in the clumsy but comfortable ambulance and the country surrounding them. The ambulance rode smoother than most conveyances of the day, its frame cushioned by leather braces and extra iron springs. But the additional weight also made it slower, as did the four sturdy dray horses in the traces, trained for endurance, not speed.

Boone Maddox rode about fifty yards forward, carbine resting across his saddletree. Another dragoon followed at an equal distance behind them. Two more guards rode out of sight on either flank.

The guards were in a festive spirit. For them, this was a chance to leave the mind-numbing boredom of the fort behind and spend a lively holiday in Santa Fe. Unfortunately, only the lieutenant would get close enough to smell the women's perfume.

"Tell us, Mr. Seth Carlson," Jeanette teased, leaning her head out into the sunlight again and flashing her small, even white teeth at him in a playful smile. "What kind of woman will Mrs. Seth Carlson be?"

He opened his mouth to answer, but the next moment he saw Boone Maddox abruptly slump in his saddle. At first Seth thought the trooper's horse had stumbled into a prairie dog hole. Then he spotted the fletched shaft of an arrow skewering the soldier's neck. Maddox slid to the ground like a sack of heavy grain, and immediately the next flurry of arrows rained down on the driver. He cried out sharply, then rolled forward off the box and fell, his body hung up in the traces.

Moments later a skirmish line of Indian braves attacked from out of the sun behind a long ridge on their left and rushed the little party below in the road. At the same time—in a brilliant emulation of the Army's beloved pincers movement—another line of braves closed in from the willow thickets on the right.

The sheer, hammering racket of the attackers at first unstrung the men's nerves along with the horses'. The Indians blew hard on shrill bone whistles; they shouted a yipping battle cry that pierced the ears; they fired pistols into the air; they had even captured a bluecoat bugle somewhere, and now one of them sounded a good imitation of "Boots and Saddles." The combined din was harrowing—even the well-trained team tried to rear in their traces.

Momentarily stunned by the racket and the suddenness of it, Seth watched Peterson and DeQuincey attempt to defend themselves on the west flank. But with nightmare speed and agility, several fast Comanche riders bore down on them, their stone skull crackers swinging.

An eye blink later and Seth watched the two soldiers fall to the ground in a confusion of flailing arms and legs. Their screams rose for a moment above the din of the attack. Peterson fought his way back onto his feet, staggering as if drunk, his left cheekbone smashed like an eggshell. Another swipe of the heavy club split his skull open. The body took two jerky steps while its nervous system tried to deny the fact of death, then dropped hard.

Peterson's death finally jolted Seth into action.

The chestnut was useless to him now. He swung down, even as the first screams came from inside the ambulance, and spun around to check the east flank. The two guards on that side, Robinson and Neusbaum, had gained a few precious seconds of response time thanks to the slightly later charge of the second Indian band. Their horses had been shot out from under them. Using the downed mounts as breastworks, the expert marksmen were doing a good job of keeping the Indians at bay on that side.

But with Peterson and DeQuincey dead, it was the west flank that was dangerously exposed. And the ambulance sat there like a big, clumsy boat marooned ashore.

The dragoon posted to the rear, 'Braska Sloan, raced forward to join Seth.

"Get inside with the women, 'Braska!" Seth commanded. "Direct your fire from the window. And make sure the women stay covered down!"

"Yessir!"

Sloan left his horse to its fate and scrambled inside the ambulance as ordered. Even before he could take up a position, the first fire arrows thwapped into the side of the ambulance.

Seth had not yet been able to return a shot. As Sloan's deadly carbine began to speak its piece and send the attackers scrambling back up the ridge out of range, Seth raced around to the exposed side and pulled the flaming shafts free.

Seth dove back behind cover as another flurry of bullets and iron-tipped arrows nipped at his heels. Behind him the battle suddenly heated up, as the Indians on the right flank rushed Robinson and Neusbaum. Inside the ambulance the hysterical screams of the women blended with the shrieks of dying horses and blood-lusting Indians.

The deadly accurate carbine shots held most of the attackers at bay and kept the Indians well beyond the hundred-yard range of their pistols. But a few of the best riders defiantly boasted their extraordinary skill. Despite the cold fist of fear that gripped his heart, Seth could not help admiring the way the bold warriors darted close to taunt the defenders. They held on to their mounts with neither hands nor feet and simply bounced along unconcerned. They strung their bows and launched their arrows with a rapidity that defied the eye and the imagination. Now all four horses in the traces were dead or dying, arrows protruding from them like quills.

Yipping, a Comanche with his face painted in vertical stripes of green and black leaped from his pony and lunged for the door of the ambulance. Sloan's carbine spat fire and literally wiped the war face off the brave. Seth, crouching behind a front corner of the ambulance, brought down a second brave as he attempted to reach the ambulance.

A triumphant surge of noise behind him made Seth turn around. Robinson, desperately reloading, crammed rounds through the trap in the butt plate of his carbine. A Comanche leaned incredibly wide and low from horseback and swung his stone-headed club hard enough to break Robinson's spine. Even before the man's heels quit scratching the dirt, one of the daredevil Comanche riders veered close and launched an arrow that found the meaty portion of Seth's exposed left thigh.

Sloan shot the attacker off his horse and put a second bullet into him to kill him. Seth, hardly aware of the hot sting in his leg, knew they were carrion if the east flank gave out—and right now only Neusbaum's cool aim held it.

One bullet, one enemy. Seth rallied himself as he laid the bead sight of his carbine dead center on a Kiowa and eased the trigger back.

"Get down, damnit!" Sloan's desperate voice shouted from inside the ambulance, even as another raider dashed close. A moment later the screams inside the ambulance took on a new pitch that turned Seth's blood to ice water. He looked back just in time to glimpse Louise Denton sprawled across Jeanette's lap with a double-bladed throwing ax buried in her breast.

Still hidden by one last, long ridge between them and the Old Pueblo Road, Corey's troop heard the first sounds of firing: the insignificant pops of pistols, a few sharp cracks from Indian trade guns, the more solid report of Spencer military carbines.

They drove their tired mounts forward, some of them occasionally faltering. Soon they began to discern the hideous shrieking of the Indians, the taunting notes of the captured bugle.

Corey cursed himself for leaving their own bugler behind. Weak-kneed with desperation, numb with fear for Jeanette, he knew only that they must try to announce their presence as soon as possible.

He drew his pistol and fired several shots rapidly into the air. His men followed suit. But Corey knew their efforts at noise were lost in the ferocious din of the attack.

His horse stumbled and almost fell. Savagely, Corey gouged the stallion's sides with his rowels, driving him forward.

Stand and hold, Seth boy, he said to himself over and over. *Stand and hold! Oh, God, Seth, save my Jenny!*

It was all happening fast, much too fast, as death and blood and hell-born havoc choked the air all around him.

Seth wasn't aware exactly when Neusbaum was killed. One of the Indians had shot him with Robinson's carbine. The same Indian put a slug in Seth's left forearm before the wild-eyed, cursing soldier shot him off his paint.

Blood oozed from his thigh, jetted steadily from his forearm wound. His position dangerously exposed, Seth emptied the last rounds of his seven-shot carbine to buy a little time. This sent the attackers on the east flank scrambling back toward the thickets.

Then things went rapidly to hell on the west flank.

One moment 'Braska Sloan was drawing a bead; the next,

he twitched like a gut-hooked fish and slumped forward through the window opening, blood fountaining from a bullet hole in his forehead. Emboldened now, the Indians on both flanks joined in their victory formation: the ever-tightening circle pattern.

While Seth desperately reloaded, a Comanche darted close, seized Sloan's rifle, and pumped several slugs into the ambulance. Jeanette, oh Jesus, Jeanette, he thought, but another Indian leaped to the door, jerked it open, and pulled the wounded Dorothy Gordon out. Seth snapped off a round and dropped the Comanche with the rifle. But the other managed to drive his lance through the woman's stomach before he fled.

Iron-tipped arrows pelted the ambulance. Seth suffered his third wound when another arrow struck him high in the chest, embedding just under his collarbone. Blood loss made him dizzy, as did the rapidly circling Kiowas and Comanches. Expertly, they urged their ponies in closer and closer without breaking stride. He was out of ammunition for his Spencer. Down to his last few pistol rounds, he aimed only at horses, and dropped one now and then to slow the tightening of the noose. But was Jeanette alive? Ominously, all screaming from inside the ambulance had ceased.

The Indians chose that moment to break their circle and rush the vehicle.

Seth moved with amazing speed in spite of his multiple wounds and jerked open the door on his side. He reached inside, grabbed handfuls of cloth and pulled, not even sure who he had a grip on. Louise Denton rolled out and sprawled at his feet, lips bared in a smiling death rictus above the protruding ax. Seth reached in again, grabbed more cloth, pulled. Jeanette emerged this time, barely getting her feet under her before she hit the ground.

Louise Denton's blood soaked her dress, and her eyes looked like glazed marbles. Otherwise, she was unharmed.

Helen Bursons wasn't so lucky. Three huge Kiowas grabbed her and pulled her—screaming and kicking—out the other side. Seth, down to three precious bullets now, used one to fire through the ambulance and kill one of the Kiowas. This sent the attackers back out of range again.

But the remaining Kiowas held on to Helen Bursons as they retreated. The Indians were clearly diverted for the moment by the capture of a woman—and obviously they had given up on any plans for taking live hostages. Huddled together behind the ambulance, Seth and Jeanette watched in wordless shock as several braves stripped Louise naked and raped her. Then they tied her around the ankles and towed her back and forth behind a horse through a patch of prickly pear cactus. Once, twice, again; her screams defying belief as she was literally skinned alive.

Two other women lay dead inside the ambulance. No longer capable of speech, Jeanette only stared at the horrible sight with the fascination of one whose mind has shut down completely. Her breathing was rapid and shallow, and she kept starting movements that she forgot to finish.

Seth felt himself floating toward unconsciousness as his blood continued to stain the earth. But words drifted back to him, the ancient call of duty, reminding him why he had saved these last two bullets: *Under no circumstances can you allow women to fall into the hands of Kiowas or Comanches.*

Now the combined band of raiders were tired of their sport with Helen Bursons. They massed for a final assault on the last two holdouts.

Do it, Seth ordered himself. *Now, before you die!*

As if the urgency of his last thought had penetrated her own mind, Jeanette turned and looked at him.

Wild strokes of blood smeared her face in a parody of their tormentors' garish war paint. Her eyes held his, and behind the outer glaze of shock and fear and denial, Seth read something else. He read her love for him, revealed frankly for the first time. It was clear. But what wasn't clear—what squeezed his heart into a tight fist of agony—was whether those eyes told him to kill her or begged him to save her.

She turned back around, and he slid his finger inside the trigger guard. Then he moved back a pace behind Jeanette. He raised his cavalry .44 until the muzzle kissed the depths of her burnt-sienna hair.

Corey broke over the last ridge well ahead of the rest of his men. He was just in time to watch his best friend, bloodied beyond belief and staggering, turn the .44 on Jeanette. And seeing it, his own blood seemed to stop and flow backward in Corey's veins.

"No, Seth!" he begged. "No, Seth, no God, *no*, don't do it!"

Viciously he gave spur to his mount, racing down the ridge and screaming the single word, *"No!"*

Seth hardened himself for this final duty, but still his body rebelled against his will and he could not squeeze the trigger. Yet even now the enemy pounded toward them in their final assault. In fierce desperation, his chest swelled with air and then he loosed the ferocious kill cry of the mountain regiments.

Simultaneously, the pistol leaped in his fist, a warm soup of blood and brain matter splattered his face, and Jeanette fell forward and folded to the ground.

Seth had not saved the final bullet to protect himself from Indian torture. He simply understood that if he killed Jeanette, he could not allow himself even a moment of life to think about what he had done. Now, as she fell, he pointed the .44 at himself and turned his head to fire at the base of his skull.

The hammer clicked uselessly when his weapon hung fire. A heartbeat later, in a moment that would burn itself into his memory forever, he spotted Corey racing down the ridge, his men just now appearing behind him.

Even as the Indians began to show the white feather and flee, Seth's eyes found Corey's across the narrowing distance. Never had Seth watched a man die inside as Corey did just then, watching blood blossom from his wife's thick hair. Yet what he saw in his friend only mirrored the empty desolation he himself felt where once there had been a will to live.

"Kill me!" Seth begged only a second before the ground rushed up to meet him and he blacked out. He took one last thought with him: Had he fought on for one more moment, Jeanette would have been saved.

PART TWO

Chapter 11

"Shine, senor?"

Robert Trilby paused on the swayback boardwalk of Silver Street and glanced down at a cheerfully aggressive Mexican boy about twelve years old. The kid cocked his thumbs and pointed both index fingers like twin pistols toward Trilby's oxblood leather boots.

"They look real fine now, uh? Still new. Mother of God, such fine boots! But I make them shine so good you can count your teeth in them, you betcha *que sí!*"

Trilby nodded and took a wobbly seat on the boy's up-ended packing crate. The man was big and hard-knit, with a long teamster's mustache and a bluff, weather-seamed face. He wore a new white linen suit with a silver concho belt. For reasons of professional image, he carried no weapon openly. But a two-shot ladies' muff gun was tucked into his right boot. The kid saw it there but paid it scant attention, working with a single-minded absorption that fascinated Trilby.

"Mother of God, such boots," the boy said again. As he snapped his cloth, his eyes rolled upward to admire the fine white suit, and the belt, which gave off brilliant light signals in the sunshine. The clothes were very impressive and fit the man well. But they seemed somehow wrong on this stone-eyed one, too civilized, the way a gold watch looks wrong on a gut-eating *indio*.

The cards in Trilby's wallet, printed back in St. Louis on expensive pebbled stock, modestly identified him as a "businessman's agent." In direct conversation, he more candidly called himself a profiteer and adventurer. Here in the thriving mining center of Tucson, few considered the difference a discrepancy.

The youth finished with a dramatic flourish of his cloth, and the man paid him with a generous handful of new bronze two-cent pieces.

The stunned kid was still counting the money when Trilby knelt in front of him. The words were spoken just above a whisper—compelling, confidential, intimate. "You're searching for your own grave, *muchacho*."

The boy glanced up, eyebrows forming a tent of curiosity. "Senor?"

Trilby nodded once at the coins. "Never count your money in public. Why should any man know how much you have to lose?"

The kid nodded and hastily pocketed the coins while they were still his. Some said this Anglo was loco, but nobody ever said he was stupid.

"What's your name?"

"Rafael, senor."

"You want to make more money, Rafael? A shitload more than I just gave you?"

The kid flashed a gap-toothed grin. "You betcha *que sí*."

"All right, but you got a set on you? I need a man, Rafael, not a baby."

The kid huffed up his scrawny chest. He pumped bravado into his tone and twisted down the corners of his mouth.

"*Vaya, hombre!* You kidding, man? I got a set on me like a goddamn stallion."

"We'll see. When I'm done talking, cross the street. Meet

me at Riverbend, but pretend you don't know me. You know
where the pit is . . . ? Good. Buy a ticket and wait for me.
But keep your mouth shut—*punto en boca*."

"*Claro, senor.*"

The kid took off, dirty soles flashing in the afternoon sun
under frayed cotton hems. Trilby resumed his stroll. A tolerant smile spread under his mustache as he gazed all about
him. Although the Apaches were raising hell nearby, and
the newspapers back East still called Tucson a garrison, the
quirky capital of the Arizona Territory hardly seemed the
product of a siege mentality. Even Sodom had posted
soldiers at the gate, whereas Tucson didn't even bother with
a gate.

Very few of the town's adobe-and-wood buildings were
loopholed or ported for combat. Three thousand more or less
permanent residents moved freely—if cautiously—through
the streets and numerous, unnamed alleys without benefit of
even one gun turret or revetment. The numbers of the permanent citizenry were constantly swollen by visitors and
transients as diverse and confusing as the denizens of any
exotic seaport. Spanish, English, German, French, Chinese,
and a polyglot of various Indian dialects rang out in the
streets and mingled with the dull clopping of hoofs, the in-
dustrious jingling of tug chains, the weary creaking of water
carts. The whites-only section of town was chockablock with
saloons, gaming parlors, and brothels specializing in every
color of flesh, most open day and night. But oddly, as of late
summer 1869 not a single hotel or boardinghouse had yet
taken root in this fertile soil.

It was almost as if the place was warning visitors to plunk
down their money and get the hell out, Trilby thought idly,
that the very atmosphere hereabouts was unfit for prolonged
breathing, damaging to the domestic virtues.

He turned around to watch the stagecoach from Fort
Grant, swaying recklessly on its thoroughbraces, round the
corner near the newspaper office. The driver raised a dust
cloud when he reined in his team and threw the brake forward. The coach shuddered to a stop in front of Longstreet's
Mercantile Store, the lone two-story building on the street—
and the only one in Tucson boasting the luxury of a green

canvas awning and sturdy duckboards out front when it rained.

The only passengers to disembark were an enlisted soldier clutching an orders envelope and a young woman in a cut-velvet traveling suit, both ghostly pale with a coating of alkali dust. Trilby lost interest in the coach and continued his walk.

Raw garbage and night soil choked the street, rank under a living carpet of flies and ants. Beaded lizards scurried through the dusty streets where mixed-blood children sold fruit from trundle carts as the piano notes of "La Paloma" escaped like bubbles past the bat-wings of the Three Sisters Saloon. Trilby watched a thin reef of clouds blow in from the canyon country north of town. The rest of the sky was as pure and perfect and flawless as blue china.

But Trilby had a contrary nature, and rather than triggering a good mood, all that bottomless blue sky somehow jarred an unwelcome memory chord. He glanced well beyond the fertile green and brown quiltwork of the Santa Cruz River valley, beyond the flowering yuccas and sandstone shoulders and red-rock canyons of the surrounding desert. His eyes slitted as he focused way out on the southern horizon and the high rimland where Jemez Grayeyes was probably hiding right now, plotting his death.

It was irritation, not fear, that suddenly made Trilby's face damp with cool sweat. These chilipep half-breeds on his payroll were game for just about anything. But they had no respect for workmanship. How many times had he repeated it to Aragon and the rest, reminding them until he was blue in the face: *Never step in anything you can't wipe off.* He never should have listened when—

"*Jefe!*"

The voice abruptly derailed his train of thought. Trilby glanced toward the street. The mixed-blood who had called out to him slumped forward against the bare tree of a Texas stock saddle, atop a big claybank horse. He wore a machete in a ratty straw shoulder scabbard. The objects strung on a leather thong around his neck, which many strangers mistook for dried toadstools, were shriveled human ears.

Juan Aragon nodded toward the jerry-built vehicle lumbering beside him, a mule-drawn flatbed wagon to which an iron cage had been bolted. Iron bands reinforced the axles, and the rear axle was double-wheeled. A huge brown bear—just a tad shy of a thousand pounds, Trilby estimated—had wrapped itself into a dusty ball inside. Several sharp, curved claws were cracked or broken, and one eye was swollen shut.

"I say we should just use black bears and mean dogs like we done the first few times. The honey smell lured this fellow into the cage real easy, just like you said. But he's so heavy we busted our humps, *Jefe*, gettin' that big bastard down from the mountains. You know how horses hate bears. Sonny's mare spooked bad and tossed him, broke his arm all to shit. The bear, he's played out now. But he goddamn near tipped the wagon over near Eight Mile Mesa."

"Played out? I don't want a rug. He got any fight left in him?"

Aragon shrugged one shoulder. He slipped a can of lye from a saddlebag. "He'll rise up on his hind legs when I throw some of *this* in his good eye."

"Don't let the crowd see you. The buff already in the pit?"

Aragon nodded. A sly smile creased his face. *"That* son a bitch got some fight in him, *por Dios!"*

"Who's collecting the gate?"

"Esteban."

Trilby frowned. "Will he steal?"

Aragon's smile widened from sly to foolish. He had taken the mercury cure for venereal disease so often that the doctors feared his brain had gone permanently soft.

"Will he steal? Truly, *Jefe*, would a cow lick Lot's wife? *Como no*, of course Esteban will steal. Do you trust any man who does not? But he is a civilized thief, like me, and he will steal only a little."

Trilby had to have a grudging respect for Aragon. Despite the man's at times deliberate stupidity, despite such serious miscalculation as the mistake about the whereabouts of Jemez Grayeyes during the last raid, he was fond of this Mexican-Apache hardcase. Trilby had once been a student of phrenology with ambitions to become a renowned alienist, a courtroom expert on criminal and insane behavior. Aragon's uniquely planed and sloped skull fascinated him—no doubt it was the key to the man's unfathomable behavior. It was

rumored that Aragon raped buffalo cows when drunk, and
Trilby knew for a fact he would gun down a nun for her gold
tooth. And yet he also knew for a fact that Aragon had lied
just now about stealing money. In the two years Aragon had
worked for Trilby, he had not stolen one dime from him or
Trilby's employers, despite plenty of opportunity and Aragon's tolerance for the usual petty thievery in the men beneath him. Such contradictions appealed to an observer of
human nature like Trilby; they hinted at convoluted depths
and secret personalities, and a capacity for treachery too
great to be told.

"When you were up in the high country," Trilby said, "did
you hear anything? See anything?"

He didn't need to mention any names.

Aragon finally lost his smile. "We'll see *him* when he wants
us to. Anything we hear will be a lie to keep us confused."

"Longstreet has agreed to put up a bounty on his head.
But it *must* be his head so we can see it. Spread the word to
the Mex soldiers. Two thousand in American double-eagle
gold pieces."

"It might seem a good sum," Aragon said, "to a man who
doesn't know him."

"All right," Trilby said, sliding the problem of Jemez
Grayeyes to the back of his mind. He was all business now.
"The show has been slow lately. When you get to the pit,
watch for a skinny kid with a shoeshine kit. Name's Rafael.
Tell him you work for the gringo with the fine boots. Tell him
what to do. Take care of it if he gets icy feet."

Aragon nodded and chucked up his horse to catch up with
the odd-looking wagon.

Trilby continued his leisurely pace, following the meandering street as it wound down toward the spot known as Riverbend, on the southeastern outskirts of Tucson. Here the
Santa Cruz River made a sharp dogleg turn, defining the
point of land that had become a ruffians' bazaar of the frontier town.

This collection of adobe-and-sod hovels was Tucson's
answer to the complicated problem of providing profit-
generating entertainment for nonwhites. To most Anglos,

the dark-skinned locals were simply Mexicans or Indians. But Trilby had turned a keener eye to the rigorous social structure inherited from Old Mexico. At the top were the white Creoles, Mexican-born, pureblood Spaniards; some had intermarried with Indians to produce the mestizos. Far more common, however, were the mixed-bloods like Aragon, some unknown combination of Indian and Mexican blood. Augmenting this dark-skinned horde were the Indian scouts and interpreters for the Army, as well as the reservation Indians who reported to Tucson to receive their ration allotments and sometimes ended up waiting for days. At Riverbend there was plenty of pulque and cheap wagon-yard whiskey, plenty of whores captured from various Indian tribes, plenty of clapboard shops where Indians could trade their government-issue pork, sugar, and coffee for old surplus war medals and cheap mirrors and twine-handle knives.

But the latest attraction, so popular it defied even the color barrier, was the huge pit recently dug out of the clay and sandy soil near the river.

Trilby spotted it now as Silver Street reached a dead end at the smith's shop and boarding stables which marked the outskirts of the whites-only section of town. A hard-packed path continued where the street ended, winding through a grove of scattered cottonwood trees. Deep ruts marked where the wagon had just passed. Empty liquor bottles littered the path, reflecting in the bright sun like hints of placer gold.

Before he ordered the pit dug, Trilby had often been the only Anglo on the path. But now he nodded time after time, calling out yet another hail fellow to white men on their way to "the show," as it had come to be called. Many of them smiled a bit sheepishly, and Trilby knew they were hoping their wives and mothers didn't find out they had sneaked down to the river. His contempt for these squaw-men who let women run their lives made it a special pleasure to take their money.

Trilby saw that a good crowd had gathered around the pit. It was dug deep into claybank river soil, the sides kept constantly slick and wet by a crude plank aqueduct stretching from the nearby river. The pit formed a ring, perhaps a hundred feet long and half again that wide. A stake-and-rope fence, sagging in several spots, was meant to keep the spectators from tumbling down. Crude whitewashed letters on raw planks over the entrance proclaimed:

LAST STAND OF THE NOBLE BUFFALO!!!
SEE THE MIGHTY HERO OF THE EASTERN NEWSPAPERS!!!
PRICE OF ADMISSION: FIVE CENTS
WIMMIN AND INDIAN AGENTS FREE!!!

Trilby spotted the man called Esteban standing near the sign. He stuffed coins into a fibre *morral* tied to his sash, exchanging them for admission chits. Men and boys milled everywhere: Anglos, mixed-blood Mexicans, pureblood Indians, each ignoring the other groups and sticking to his own area. Tucson's lawmen were white. Trilby recognized the deputy named Fargo Danford. He patrolled the perimeter of the pit on horseback, chasing off any spectators who didn't have chits. Trilby had recently taken care of a gambling debt for Danford, but the arrangement was risky—Charles Longstreet had claimed first dibs on the law in Tucson, and he didn't like it when his employees drank from more than one trough.

Trilby stepped through the entrance arch, nodding at Esteban. The man was already stinking drunk, but went about his duties with a methodical competence. He gave only the slightest of nods to Trilby and held out his dirt-caked palm, making the proprietor pay like everyone else. Another of Aragon's men sold whiskey and pulque from a canvas and plank stall, metal drinking cups chained to the deal counter.

The buffalo bull was already in the pit, and spectators crowded the wobbly fence.

"Lookit there!" said a young Anglo boy, voice cracking with excitement. "See the chin whiskers? The bulls all got whiskers."

"To hell with the whiskers," the man with him said. "It's the hump that makes for good fixin's. That sumbitch so juicy you doan even have to chew 'er, just falls apart in your mouth."

"Careful there, son," Trilby called out cheerfully. "That clay is slippery. You can slide right under the fence."

The buffalo, as Aragon had promised, was indeed full of fight. The last spike in the transcontinental railroad link had been pounded in just this past May, and there were still plenty of herds on the plains. But up north the white man's trains and telegraph poles and forts had driven them as far south as the Mexican border. Unaccustomed to these new routes, desperate for good graze, the animals were disoriented and nerve-frazzled.

The bull trapped below was further agitated by the powerful concatenation of unfamiliar smells, mostly unpleasant. It raced from end to end of the pit, so nearsighted that it sometimes collided with the wet clay walls. Trilby watched it repeatedly lower its massive, shaggy head and gore the claybank sides, digging out huge chunks that clung to its horns. The crowd hooted derisively each time it collided with the walls and went down.

A quick glance around and Trilby had located the boy, Rafael. Judging from the grim, determined slit formed by his lips, Aragon must have explained his part to him. Trilby grinned and wondered if the boy felt more like a gelding now than the well-hung stallion of his boast.

He saw Fargo Danford reach up to touch the floppy brim of his plainsman's hat. Only one man in Tucson could elicit such an act of courtesy from Danford, and Trilby spotted him now buying a handful of chits from Esteban.

Charles Longstreet. And the man with him, wearing a stiff felt derby and a gray duster to protect his suit, was the visiting journalist named Nat Bischoff. The usual gaggle of toadies and paper-collar types crowded around them.

Longstreet saw Trilby looking. He slid the cigar from his mouth and lifted it toward Trilby, dotting an invisible *i*. Trilby nodded back. Interesting, he thought, filing the fact away for later examination. Seeing Longstreet at Riverbend was a bit like spotting the Queen of England in Pissing Alley.

A shout went up, followed by a cheer, as Aragon and his men slowly backed the caged wagon toward the pit. The bear, reacting to the tension in the air, had come back to life. It loosed an angry, woofing bellow. The mules were unfazed, but Danford's sorrel mare sidestepped nervously and almost knocked several people into the pit.

The bear, like the buffalo, had poor vision but a keen sense of smell. At the overwhelming stink of men and horses, and now the buffalo below, the bad-tempered animal flew into a rage. It lashed from wall to wall of its cramped cage, rocking the wagon dangerously on its reinforced axles. The crowd cheered even louder, one or two firing pistols into the air.

Long handles had been attached to the flatbed of the wagon. Moving gingerly, Aragon tugged the wooden pin out of the hasp on the cage door, and it flew open. The men, three on each handle, gave the wagon bed a sudden jerk, and a moment later the bear tumbled down the steep side of the pit, scrabbling uselessly for a hold.

A roar went up from the crowd. The bull, now thoroughly agitated, picked up the motion and immediately charged, head down, hooves loosing huge divots of clay. The bear managed to hop out of the way at the last moment, moving with amazing speed. A fast swipe of its claws raked bloody furrows in the buffalo's flank.

The bull's bellow of angry pain sounded remarkably like the bear's own roar. It turned, lumbered closer in another clumsy charge, and received a new set of bloody furrows on the opposite flank.

Again the bull roared in pain, the noise amplified by the approving crowd. The bear rose on its hind legs, foreclaws dripping gobbets of flesh and gore, and beat on its massive chest. But now the buffalo had lost its fighting fettle; the crowd groaned when it slouched off toward the opposite end of the pit, tufted tail switching.

The observers rained the bear with sticks and stones, hoping to drive it in pursuit of the bull. But the big animal seemed content to merely protect its territory from invasion.

Trilby had dreaded this. The last bear, a black half blinded by lye, had put up so little fight—against just three flea-bitten hounds—that the crowd demanded refunds. He was determined to keep things from getting ugly again today. He caught Rafael's eyes and nodded at him.

The boy nodded back and moved in closer to the fence. He glanced around nervously to make sure Aragon and the others were close, as they had promised. Still, he hesitated, unable to make the final move. He glanced down into the pit. Trilby saw him swallow so hard that his Adam's apple visibly shunted up and down.

The kid met his eyes again. Again Trilby nodded. The kid looked down, then looked at Trilby and shook his head no. He stepped back from the pit.

Trilby cursed under his breath. His eyes met Aragon's. This time he didn't need to nod.

Aragon's hand moved behind the kid with almost imperceptible swiftness, pushing him forward at the small of the back. Rafael's feet slid under the bottom rope of the fence, hit the wet clay, and he was gone as quick as a blink.

The side was steep, but sloped enough to break the fall. His bare feet thwapped into the ground not thirty feet from the bear, his momentum throwing him onto his face in the mess.

"Twin balls of Christ, a Mexer kid fell in!"

"Git a rope to 'm!"

"There goes the bear!"

The huge bear lunged at Rafael as the frightened kid struggled to his feet. The crowd went wild, even the urbane Nat Bischoff throwing his hat on the ground in his excitement.

Aragon flung his long, braided reata over the side of the pit. Rafael, already in motion, grabbed for it and missed. The bear chased him partway around the pit, rapidly gaining on the boy.

The crowd cheered. Rafael's eyes were huge with panic. The buffalo, confused by all this motion, once again lowered its head and charged. Another of Aragon's men got his reata down the side of the pit, and this time Rafael gained a purchase on it. The boy was tugged to safety only moments before the bear's claws would have opened him up like the soft underbelly of a mushroom.

Thus distracted, the bear didn't move in time. The bull's horns caught him flush in the guts and lifted him off the ground.

A huge roar of approval from the spectators almost drowned out the bear's surprised bellow of pain. Trapped between the horns and the wall of the pit, the bear brought his foreclaws down over and over, ripping huge chunks out of the back and flanks of the bull, soon exposing the rib bones and gleaming vitals. Finally the buffalo collapsed in death paroxysms, the mortally injured bear still trapped on its horns.

Once the fight was clearly finished, the crowd took over.

Every man with a firearm sent at least one slug into the dying beasts, some emptying their pieces. Trilby watched as even Bischoff slid a Remington pistol from its stiff new holster and took careful aim, pretending the shot had to count.

The crowd was elated. The fight had been short, but all-out, and the added excitement of the boy falling in had sent their adrenaline pumping. Liquor sales were booming. Trilby smiled to himself. The next show would be packed. He wasn't surprised when one of Longstreet's toadies searched him out with the message that his boss wanted to see him soon.

But his contrary nature always plagued him most at moments of triumph, reminding him of dangerous things left undone. Everytime he spotted a red flannel headband in the crowd, Trilby glanced out toward the surrounding rimrock and wondered about Jemez Grayeyes.

Chapter 12

Hays Munro was gifted with a sonorous baritone, one of the chief reasons he compelled attention whenever he spoke—that, and an intense belief in the importance of his own opinions, a belief that defied listeners to ignore him. Kathleen Barton listened, completely absorbed, a pottery mug of coffee untouched on the table before her as Munro read from a copy of the *Tucson Register*.

" 'To describe what Lieutenant Carlson survived—if indeed he does survive—as just another baptism under fire would be tantamount to calling Beowulf's epic struggle against Grendel a mere fistfight. Those unpatriotic, antiexpansionist forces back East who deplore the vulgar, mean, and bloody aspect of our American frontier need only polish the rock a bit until they spot the gem shining underneath. Lieutenant Carlson's heroic struggle against an overwhelming force of hostile savages is our new American epic, our own native *Beowulf*. The entire history of manly courage and human grief was recounted in that fifteen-minute, hell-spawned skirmish in the creosote wastes of New Mexico.' "

Munro glanced up, his smooth-shaven face wrinkling in wry distaste. "It's small wonder that Nat Bischoff is the most popular writer on the frontier. He gives avarice and greed poetic underpinnings. This cavalry officer, the women who were killed, they're all small potatoes to Bischoff."

Kathleen nodded, sympathetic to Munro's angry frustration but also, by now, wary of his barbed insights. The two sat in the common room of the low adobe building that doubled as chapel and vocational school on the Mater Dolorosa Apache Reservation. Niches in the back wall displayed clay figures of the saints. But a polished clay floor and plain whitewashed walls lent the big room a hard-edged impersonality which always made Kathleen glad to get out of there.

" 'As for those nearsighted sentimentalists who argue for the rights of the red aboriginals to constitute a nation within a nation,' " Munro continued, " 'this correspondent has noticed a curious fact. The further these generous philosophers live from the sting of the warrior's arrow, the nobler the savage they praise. This correspondent, too, found the romance of the Far West all too alluring when he viewed it from afar in Boston and New York. Since actually arriving in Zebulon Pike's Great American Desert, however, he has discovered the bloody discrepancy between idea and reality.' "

Munro laid the paper down on the cloth-covered puncheon table and removed the monocle from his right eye. He helped himself to a piece of sweet mescal bread.

"Well, Bischoff's chief skill is the ability to turn dung into strawberries. But I'll give the devil his due on that last point. As I, too, have discovered, you do indeed have to go outside to find out what the weather is like."

Kathleen supposed that she herself had been exposed to plenty of weather in the year since she had been hired to teach at Mater Dolorosa. From where she sat, she could see through the common room's big arched windows, could look out onto the central courtyard of the original mission. Morning instruction was over, and the reservation Apaches were congregating for roll call and the long noon break. Despite the summer heat, the women still insisted on their many layers of clothing. Some of the younger ones carried babies in backboards. A group of adolescent boys played a hoop-and-pole game, scattering the scrawny chickens in the adjacent yard. Older Apaches squatted beneath the protruding *vigas* of the adobe buildings, rolling inferior Mexican tobacco in corn husks.

Munro finished chewing and picked up the newspaper again. He was tall, thin, and slope-shouldered, with the brusque, impatient manner of one whose kind heart was perpetually at war with his short temper.

"A-*hah*, here we are! Stand by for the blast, my dear. Now Mr. Bischoff's rapier intellect is about to skewer *us*. 'Let those in Congress pay especial attention to the thoroughly American tragedy of Lieutenant Carlson, Corey Bryce, and his wife Jeanette. For it is Congress—over the strong objection of many who have carefully studied this problem—which recently launched the so-called Quaker Policy. According to this misguided piece of legislation, experienced frontiersmen will no longer serve as Indian agents on the reservations. Instead, only nominees from approved church lists will be appointed. Corruption rules the Indian Bureau, claim the critics, and this new policy is meant to end it.' "

Munro's voice tightened in disgust as he read these last sentences. Now his cheeks went ruddy with angry blood. He pointed toward the huge windows.

" 'Claim the critics'! Bosh! Just *look* out there at those windowless shanties the contractors call 'houses.' So damned hot and stuffy even the chickens won't roost in them."

"Yes, I've noticed them," Kathleen said, an ironic smile briefly touching her lips.

"My God, these people are issued salt pork condemned for troop use, the blankets they're sent are so full of shoddy and glue they fall apart in the rain. If we leave the Indian alone, he's cursed as a godless savage. If we teach him how to plow the land and worship the white man's God, he's ridiculed as a dirt-scatterer and a praying Indian. It's greed and avarice, pure and simple, and these men of Nat Bischoff's ilk are put on the payroll to cover up the cowardly stink with brave rhetoric."

"No philosophy but in the doing," Kathleen said quietly. "What's that?"

"The afternoon session starts soon," she reminded him, rising from the table. "Juana is sick, I have to fill in for her before my classes start. Did you send that request for a clerk to the bureau? It's taking me two hours every night to keep their files up. And when do we get more medical supplies?"

Her voice, almost lost in the big, empty room, nonetheless served to jolt Munro back to more immediate matters. He dropped the paper to the table and closed both eyes for a moment, massaging the eyelids with his fingertips. Then he opened his eyes and looked up at her in silence.

He watched as she reached back to tuck her long braid behind the collar of her shirtwaist. Her homespun skirt was not quite so blue as her deep-set eyes. Frankly, with the platonic ease that had grown between them over the past months, he studied her pretty face. Youth was still quite evident in the slight puffiness of her lips, the taut and smooth flesh of the neck, the baby down on her cheeks. But there were faint lines forming at the corners of her eyes, etched by constant sun and wind and the weight of too much responsibility in a hopeless situation. During the war he had seen officers half his age with those same worry creases.

"Why push when something won't move, eh?" he said kindly. "Well, no, I didn't send in that request, but I promise to do it tomorrow. And I'll pressure Fort Grant again for medical supplies. I should just set my bellyaching to music. God knows you've heard it plenty enough by now."

Her smile was a flash of strong, even white teeth in the airy gloom. "*No hay nada nuevo bajo el sol, verdad?*" There's nothing new under the sun.

She had spoken in Spanish, and it took him a moment to translate. Then he returned her smile. "Life has taught you that much in twenty years, eh?"

"No," she said, "it hasn't. And you don't believe it after fifty. That's why I like you."

Kathleen donned her jipijapa hat and went outside into the glaring, unshaded heat of the sun. Off to one side of this central building was a slope-off kitchen house, dirty wash pots stacked out back. Nearby, a bored-looking Apache followed a mule and harrow up and down, tilling ground for another irrigated kitchen garden. Out front a few dozen Indians stood listlessly in line, government-issue mess kits in hand. This was the line for those who had used up or traded off their rations. An Indian worker ladled out portions of a foul concoction brewed from flour, water, a few beans, chopped beef, entrails, and brains, served from a large open vat. Kathleen caught a whiff of the stuff. Her face wrinkled as if she were sniffing raw sewage. The Apaches who found this too vile to eat settled for parched corn and mescal bread.

Kathleen spotted the new girl, Socorro Grayeyes, hanging back by herself in the shade of the bell tower. Kathleen waved, but the girl only looked away. Her brother Miguelito was still assigned to bed rest in the dispensary until his cough was better. Neither child had spoken more than a few words since Jemez Grayeyes had left them here. Miguelito, Kathleen cautiously predicted, was going to be all right. He was young enough to adjust. But the girl—she already had her older brother's defiant eyes. Clearly she hated this gravel-swept graveyard with an intensity like hell-thirst. She would be trouble. And Jemez . . . he would be the biggest trouble of all. Trouble for many. Kathleen had seen it in the grim set of his lips, the menace that marked his movements. She knew what they had done to his clan. And she sensed that he was the kind of man whose destiny was meant to touch others. A bloody fight was shaping up, and the dying would be hard, but also important—this Jemez was no man for trifling violence.

A well covered with a dry hide occupied the center of the courtyard. Kathleen lifted the stiff hide back and lowered a rawhide bucket tied to a sisal rope. She raised the bucket, dipped a gourd into it and drank, savoring the cool water on her tongue. Her thirst surprised her. She drank the big gourd dry and filled it again, never wanting the drink to stop or her thirst to end.

Then she hefted the bucket and angled off toward an adobe outbuilding isolated from the others. It currently served as a diphtheria pesthouse, and a half-dozen patients were quarantined inside—a result of the latest contact with white-eyes, in this case an infected clerk at one of the grog shops on the edge of the reservation. As she trudged across the arid expanse, gravelly sand hot under the thin soles of her shoes, she wondered about this tragedy in New Mexico that Hays had just read about. Against her will it made her recall the young Army officer who had proposed to her back in Springfield.

Miles had been handsome enough, and country-lad charming when sober. Her mother pronounced him a fine young man, and when the youth received orders to join the newly formed Fourth Cavalry in the Department of Dakota, her father had decanted his best port—a sure sign of paternal approval. But how vividly Kathleen still recalled Miles's first furlough after a year's duty on the frontier, fighting Sioux.

He had escorted her home from a church social, where his polished saber and bright medals had impressed everyone. Then he unbuttoned his tunic and joined her younger brother Sid and a few neighbor boys out in the orchard for whiskey and man talk. Her bedroom window opened out over the orchard. Late into the night, as liquor oiled his tongue, Miles's voice got louder, his war stories uglier.

"Indian women rut so damn much they get loose," he had declaimed to Sid and the rest of those spellbound youths. "My hand to God, chappies—I once carved out a Sioux squaw's cunny with my bayonet and stretched it over my saddle horn."

The next day, his eyes puffy from his revels, he gallantly plucked an orchid and presented it to her as he requested her hand in marriage. Calmly, looking him square in the eye and never flinching at a single word, she repeated what he'd said the night before. Then she asked him on his honor whether or not the story was true. He had flushed red clear to his earlobes and dropped the orchid. No, he'd assured her, it was a common soldier's lie, a drunken war brag. She believed him. But somehow, the fact that he could even tell such a lie, especially to seventeen-year-old boys, was almost as bad as the doing of it. She never had to officially turn him down because he at least had the decency to leave town without repeating his proposal. A month later she read an eloquent article in the *Christian Advocate*, the official newspaper of the Methodist Church, quoting several Indians who claimed their tribes longed to be Christianized and civilized. She wrote to an address in the church bulletin, and soon afterward she became a teacher for the Indian Bureau. Now she knew that article had been based on a missionary's fantasy. But she reminded herself that the fat was in the fire. One moment—one ugly war brag she never should have heard—had redefined everything she'd ever done, would shape everything she would ever do. Now she was stuck at the edge of the world in a place the zealous missionary had neglected to describe.

She had almost reached the open door of the pesthouse when a shadow slid up behind her. Kathleen whirled to confront the Mescalero boy named Victorio. He glanced up at her, his eyes slanting shyly away. Years before, a piece of buckshot had injured the sclera of his right eye, leaving a permanent blood spot against the white.

"Hello," she told him, speaking Spanish. *"Donde has sido?"* Where have you been?

He shrugged as he always did when she asked him that. They both knew she was supposed to punish him for leaving the reservation, which Victorio did frequently.

"Tio Hays is angry and disappointed. You've missed three days worth of your classes."

Victorio shrugged again. He was truly sorry to disappoint Tanta Kathleen. But he was unable to feel the larger weight of his sin. So far Victorio had learned how to scatter barren Arizona dust with a plow, how to tend a coal furnace imported from St. Louis, how to repair the tongue of a clumsy wagon he had no desire to drive. These know-it-all hair-faces who made much of pounding nails and digging post holes—few among them could even skin a buffalo properly.

"I saw Jemez," he said. "He wants to know if you have any news for him?"

She fought down a sudden wave of weary irritation. Jemez was always asking that, as if they were somehow linked in a conspiracy. Didn't she already have enough to fret about? What right did this Jemez Grayeyes have, expecting her—a paid employee of the Indian Bureau—to join his illegal schemes? It was her sworn duty to help civilize the Indians, not to assist them in acts of revenge that would only bring more grief down on the red man.

"You listen to me," she said sharply. "Jemez Grayeyes is a fugitive from the law. *Un criminal, entiendes?* If you are caught with him, you will be punished, too."

Victorio kept his feelings out of his face, as Apache men did. But the bitter hatred was clear in his voice.

"So? It is not *my* law. It is white-eye law."

"It is your law now, too."

Defiantly, he shook his head. "Jemez told me about this thing, and a Grayeyes never lies to an Apache. In the year the white man's winter count calls 1851, red men and white men signed an important talking paper in the soldier town at Laramie. This talking paper promised that white men would punish only their own criminals, red men would punish theirs. But once again the hair-faces spoke from both sides of their mouths. It is *their* law that rules us now."

We send them to school, Kathleen thought angrily, we tell them to learn. And they learn their own history well enough to hate us. Technically, Victorio was right. But white men had also forbidden the brewing of *tiswin*, Apache beer, and now there were fewer murders. And white law forbade the barbaric custom of nose-bobbing as a punishment for adultery. Let Jemez defend such Apache laws all he wished— history was turning the page, and he had no right inciting young boys to useless rebellion.

Jemez Grayeyes . . . for a moment she recalled the pistol on his right hip, turned butt forward to accommodate his left-handed crossdraw.

You are afraid of me?

I am afraid of all men.

That's a wise way to feel. It makes you careful.

Now she looked at Victorio. "Never mind, now. Go eat, and be sure to attend classes this afternoon. I will speak to Tio Hays on your behalf. As for Jemez, I have no news for him. No message at all."

Chapter 13

"See that?" Enis Hagan said. "Cut from white man's sheet iron. I'd rather get hit by a flint arrowhead any day over one of these. See there how it bent and clinched when it hit bone? Made it a sonofapup to extract. I had to hook it with a looped wire and pray the shaft didn't come loose."

Well into his forties and built stocky, Hagan had heavy burnsides and a mustache, his chin smooth-shaven. He held a palm-size iron triangle out in the fading light so that Corporal Walt Mackenzie could study it better.

"That's the one I pulled out of his chest. It grazed off the collarbone, then turned south and nicked the top of his lung. The other one in his thigh and the .44 caliber slug in his left forearm were a cinch to dig out. With all those holes in him, and moving around as much as he must have, he lost blood hard and fast before the attack was over. But all in all he was damn lucky."

Though Seth Carlson still lay near death, pale as moonstone, Mackenzie took Hagan's meaning about luck clear enough; one of these *could* have been a belly wound. On the frontier, an abdominal wound was almost always fatal. Most Indians knew this, and carefully aimed for a soldier's navel. Hagan was a contract surgeon for the Third Cavalry Regiment, and twice now he had been rebuked by Colonel Denton, post commander at Fort Bates, for suggesting that soldiers fighting Indians be issued thick leather cummerbunds.

The two men stood near the unconscious lieutenant's bed. The hospital ward was nearly empty except for a few men left hors de combat by Montezuma's Revenge—the favorite post nickname for diarrhea, which so far had proven a far worse enemy than Indians. The last of the day's sunlight tinged the windows copper. Outside, a troop of cavalry rode in from maneuvers, so dusty they sweated mud. Behind the two men, a private entered the ward with a burning taper. He moved quietly around the big room, lighting wall lamps in brass reflectors. Gradually, narrow fingers of light nudged the shadows back into the corners.

"He hasn't come to even once?" Hagan asked.

Mackenzie shook his head. He had missed the initial surgery. But the orderly had put in double shifts since Lieutenant Carlson was brought in by Corey Bryce's troops.

"Nothing you'd call bein' awake. But good God a-gorry, some of the things comin' out of his mouth fair give me the fidgets."

"Mm, I can imagine. Poor devil. He's lost more blood than a man has any business losing. His swallowing reflex still strong?"

Mackenzie nodded. The officer's wounds had been sewn with thread soaked in gentian, then wrapped in bands of bleached gauze. Every hour, following Hagan's orders, Mackenzie fed the patient four tablespoons of a warm concoction made up of milk, molasses, egg yolk, yeast, and ground calf's liver.

"It seems pretty piddlin', Doc. I wish I could do more for him."

"It *is* piddlin'. The newspapers can make him out a hero all they want, it's still the best we can do for him at this pukehole. With Mad Dog Denton in command, it's quinine and whiskey and little else but pain—there's no shortfall of *that* around here."

"No shortfall of people, neither," Mackenzie said. "Been plenty comin' by here just wantin' a look at him."

Hagan nodded. "Mm. It's the newspapers. This story was telegraphed back East before I had the first arrowhead dug out of him."

"Those women . . ."

Mackenzie trailed off and looked at the floor. "Them newspaper stories you read to me colored it up a mite, I s'pose. Still, he must've been through enough to turn ten men gray."

"Oh, the butcher's bill was steep," Hagan said. "You know I despise Denton, but it was a rough piece of work showing him his wife's body. The relatives expected us to pack them in lime and ship the bodies back for burial. Why, a couple of them, it was out of the question to do any such thing."

"If it was hard to look at the bodies," Mackenzie said, "what was it like watchin' it all happen? Not just for him, but Lieutenant Bryce, too?"

"Bryce? Christ almighty! I saw him at the inquiry, right before they sent him back East. He put me in mind of what we used to call the 'walking wounded.' "

"They say he ain't nursin' no grudge. Is it true, what they say he told the board?"

Hagan nodded. A board of inquiry had been formed immediately after that Sunday morning tragedy. Corey Bryce was asked if, in his best judgment as an officer, Seth Carlson had held on as long as could reasonably be expected. Bryce had replied tersely, "And then some, sir." But Hagan didn't trust a thing like this—severe grief could work on a man like a cactus spike. It lodged in the sole of his boot and then gradually worked its way through, so gradually he was limping long before he even realized it.

Hagan looked down toward Seth again.

"Anyway, if this one survives, the first thing he'll feel— once he can feel anything—is regret that those red Arabs didn't blow *his* lamp out, too. But he's not the man for self-slaughter. The vital instinct is too damn strong in him. So the next thing he'll want is to cut his picket pin and run. Only, there's no place to run from it. The past gets stuck on the back of a man's eyelids."

Hagan sighed and shook his head as if the whole damn world was worth less than a dance-hall token. He pulled a watch out of his fob pocket, opened the cover. "Well, I got to get. Keep feeding him. And keep his wounds clean and change the dressing. This is no time to make his body fight an infection."

Mackenzie nodded. After Hagan left, the orderly picked up the banjo he had laid across a ladder-back chair near Carlson's bed. He took his seat again and began plucking out the notes of "Wood Ticks in My Johnny."

Outside, the sun sank lower and the shadows purpled and flattened out. A platoon of dragoons marched in from the field, their unit guidon snapping in the breeze. Mackenzie picked out "The Homespun Dress" and "Little Annie Roonie" and "The Girl I Left Behind Me," his eyes occasionally slanting toward the bed and the unconscious officer.

Finally, exhausting his meager repertoire, Mackenzie stopped playing and laid his banjo on the floor. He stood, stretched until his stiff spine made a knuckle-cracking sound. Outside, the evening wind suddenly started kicking up a fuss. It sent sand stinging against the windows and made a low, moaning sound in the stovepipe—a lonely groan that filled Mackenzie with sudden dread, the kind of hollow, stomach-tickling dread a man feels when he suddenly wakes up in the middle of the night, naked and defenseless and so damn scared he can't even spit.

Feeling this, he expected what happened next. But the suddenness of it still made his bowels feel loose and heavy.

"Shoot me, Corey," the officer in the bed begged in a rusty voice like an old nail being pulled loose. "Oh, God, Corey, *shoot* me!"

Mackenzie felt his flesh crawl against his shirt. Sweat broke out on his back and his temples throbbed. Carlson didn't wake up, didn't even move. Only a few heartbeats after hearing the words, Mackenzie wasn't even sure the officer had spoken them.

But then why wouldn't his heart stop thumping against his ribs? Mackenzie crossed the bare, split-slab floor to a door that opened out onto the central parade field. The sun had finally disappeared beneath the horizon. There was no main gate or outer wall at Fort Bates, and Mackenzie could see the sand beyond the boundary of the post, an eerie blue in the new moonlight. The first desert bats were flitting about. Past the dark haze of the distant chaparral slopes, a coyote began its persistent howl.

He looked back over his shoulder toward Carlson. Hagan's recent words came back to him: *The past gets stuck on the back of a man's eyelids.* All of Seth Carlson's rantings had taught Mackenzie things he wasn't supposed to know. Such as the fact that the wounded officer had been in love with the woman he killed.

What Mackenzie felt now—this compression in his chest, exhilarating and frightening and nerve-frazzling all at once— he knew meant his life was going to change somehow, change big. He had never felt it before, not this strong. Desperately, Mackenzie looked back outside and searched for something to distract him from it.

There was an overflow of troops at the fort, mostly recruits to fill the expanding ranks of the Third and Seventh Cavalry regiments as the Indian wars heated up. Permanent barracks were still being built. Meantime, tents had been set up in pyramidal rows on the far side of the parade field. Mackenzie watched the squad fires sawing in the wind. But this time they failed to lull him as they often did. The tight fist was still lodged there inside his chest.

He turned and walked back inside the ward. Ten feet away from Seth Carlson's bed, he stopped and stared. He reached up for a lantern hanging from the crosstrees of the ceiling. His fingers trembling as if from cold, Mackenzie turned up the wick, then pulled a sulfur match from his pocket and struck it with his thumb. He opened the lantern and lit the wick. He bent toward Seth Carlson and saw that this time the man's eyes were wide open, watching him.

"Shoot me," the lieutenant whispered.

Mackenzie felt a weak, helpless shudder in his limbs. He

understood now what that strange feeling in his chest was all about. He had never learned to read, but listening to this man recite poetry from the brink of the grave—lines so beautiful they made Mackenzie's throat close—he somehow understood that those lines had meaning for his own life, that this unfortunate young officer was meant to touch the lives of others, to shape and point them.

He bent closer. There wasn't much in the world that Mackenzie knew for sure. But he was sure this gallant young officer would ride again, and Corporal Walt Mackenzie knew he was going to ride with him, and die if he must. He knew it sure in his skin, the way a Baptist knows Jesus.

"Sir," he said, out loud but quiet, so as not to disturb the other men dozing, "do you understand me?"

Carlson only continued to stare, saying nothing. But Mackenzie went on as if he had nodded.

"Right now none of what I'm talkin' will make any damn sense to you. But please listen to me. I've washed your wounds, fed you, took out your slops. I've listened to you rant crazy and wild talk and spout poetry that come damn near to makin' me bawl like a titty baby. Now you please listen, sir. I got a request. I know you got the devil hisownself to face first. But you're a soldier, and you'll whip Old Scratch and come through this like a soldier. And when you do, I want to be one of your troopers."

Mackenzie bent even closer and whispered the rest of it.

"Sir, I ain't no killer, but I ain't no coward, neither. I got what the trappers use to call buck ager. That's how come the Army put me in this job. I can whup on a man good with my fists, but I get the shakes bad whenever I point a gun at a person and try to squeeze the trigger. But it don't mean nothing on account of I can make myself more useful than ten sharpshooters. I ain't no coward. You take me with you."

He stopped and studied the lieutenant's face. "You understand any of that, sir?"

"Shoot me."

Mackenzie shook his head. "I guess you didn't hear me. Shoot you? No, sir, that I won't. Wouldn't even if I could. And I'll stomp a picket pin through the balls of the first sonofabitch who tries. But sir, please tell me—did you understand *any*thing I just told you?"

Seth Carlson nodded once. Mackenzie grinned briefly.

"Good. Welcome back to the world of the living. Now go to sleep. Sir."

Chapter 14

"All this Noble Red Man claptrap for a pack of heathen gut-eaters too stupid to harness the wheel," Charles Longstreet said. "Now this stump-screaming senator from Missouri, this —this—"

"Henderson," Nat Bischoff said. "John Henderson."

"This Henderson. I see now he's talking up another peace initiative with all the tribes west of the Mississippi. But he's an Indian-loving fool. Give the red aboriginals Phil Sheridan, not phil-anthropy, eh, Bischoff?"

Nat Bischoff occupied one of two leather wing chairs located at opposite corners of Longstreet's huge scrollwork desk. Robert Trilby sprawled comfortably in the other, his legs crossed at the ankles.

"Sheridan?" Bischoff said. "Now *there's* a mad dog off his leash. I hear he wants to turn Old Iron Butt Custer loose up in Dakota. That's because Custer showed his Indian-fighting philosophy at the Washita. The man knows only one strategy: charge. But he does it quite effectively."

"Well, then!" Longstreet said. "Effective leadership is precisely what we need. When it comes to redskins, I say send for a man who's willing to exterminate the lot of them."

Trilby ignored Longstreet's familiar tirade and watched Bischoff with curiosity. Although his shoes barely touched the floor, this journalist of such small physical stature had nonetheless become a consequential figure on the American frontier. He had gained instant notoriety, and set the irreverent tone for a new breed of pro-expansionist editorialists when he employed the phrase "Slightly Recumbent Gentleman Cow" as a sardonic moniker for Sitting Bull.

"And how about you, Mr. Trilby?" Bischoff said. "Do you subscribe to Longstreet's extermination theory?"

A smile flickered for a moment in Trilby's big, bluff face. "I think a man should be careful what he says he wants. Charlie has some fine contracts with the sutler's store at Fort Grant. He also supplies the reservation at Dolorosa. If he settles the Indians' hash, there too go most of his profits."

Longstreet forgot to puff on his cigar, staring with cold reproof at his subordinate. "Most of *our* profits you might have said. You're the one sells scalps."

"Ahh, but I'm branching out, Charlie, like any wise man of capital. You've seen my little amusement down at Riverbend."

"It's not so little. And some of the others on the committee aren't too damned 'amused.' Frankly, neither am I."

"I thought it was a capital hit," Bischoff threw in. "That was a brilliant touch, nudging the Mexican boy down into the pit."

Trilby threw his head back and laughed. "Oh, Charlie here enjoys it as much as the next fellow. It's just that, with me in the game, it's too many pigs for the tits, eh, Charlie? You big nabobs're just begrudging of the profits I'm making. It chaps your asses that you didn't move in while the gate was still open. But Riverbend is Mexers and 'breeds, so you all left it alone. And you miscalculated bad. Now it's my territory to graze."

"That's up to the committee," Longstreet said.

Trilby smiled pleasantly. "Is it?" he said softly, and Longstreet looked away.

Trilby didn't consider Longstreet a coward. He had led a rifle company in the war, and Trilby suspected the man had buried an enemy or two in his rise to prominence on the frontier. But he was like the rest of the "respectable" hypocrites who called the shots in Tucson: They packed weapons and made the he-bear talk, but when you got down to essentials, they hired out the rough work and let their lives be run by women. Wives, mothers, daughters, sisters—in these tidy little houses it was the cows who bellowed to the bulls. And because these men were run by women, hardscrabble trash like Trilby could not be publicly acknowledged—although it was fine to employ him secretly as a dirt worker, the man who strikes in the night to grease the wheels of progress. But Trilby knew that all of them were destined to be mere cinders on the roadbed of his own success, one way or the other: He was a man for keeping careful records.

Trilby lifted his chin toward a shelf on the wall behind Longstreet. "You talk about me selling scalps. Has your wife seen the little trophies you paid me to procure for this office?"

Upon the shelf sat the white, sun-bleached, eerily grinning skulls of two long-gone Apache warriors. Someone had painted satirical messages on them. SAFE ON THE RESERVATION AT LAST proclaimed one; NOBLE, SAVAGE, AND DEAD boasted the other.

Longstreet opened his mouth to retort. But Bischoff had been waiting for an opportunity to test Trilby's intellectual fettle a bit further.

"Surely," he persisted, still looking at Trilby, "you are not so cynical as to see an entire page of national and international history as merely a sheet from an accounts ledger?"

"History? Personally, I feel no need to invoke Manifest Destiny and the supposed superiority of civilized whites. The sun travels west, Mr. Bischoff, and so does opportunity. *Any* man who survives out here is a savage. History? Add 'history' to a spent cartridge, mister, and you're out of ammo."

"Money talks and horseshit walks, eh?" Bischoff was not at all offended. Trilby had said all this in a civil enough tone, and Bischoff dearly loved a capable debater. "But you're so busy selling off the trees, you can't see the forest. This territory represents far more than a war contractor's dream come true. America is poised on the brink of becoming the greatest nation in the history of the world."

"Do tell?" Trilby said.

"Yes, indeed, your bemused smile notwithstanding. It's been just two years since Juarez's guerrilla army captured Mexico City and executed Maximilian. Now we see that proud old Benito is sincere about the Reform. But his country is in a shambles as the result of nearly a century of revolution and banditry and sheer chaos. As we speak, there's not one bank or functioning railroad in Mexico. The people are far too poor to mount a force against the Indians terrorizing their northern states. By current treaty agreement, it's up to the U.S. to stop Indian raids into Mexican territory. We do that, and you're going to witness a sea change in the Mexican attitude toward their gringo neighbors. Do you realize the wealth of natural resources in Mexico, the opportunities for trade? This isn't just monetary profit for a few, Mr. Trilby. It could be a golden age for the common man in America, the beginning of a new empire, a new world order."

"Balls," Trilby said. "But I see now why the *New York Herald* pays you so well."

"Gentlemen," Longstreet interrupted impatiently, "my schedule is full and we have various business matters to discuss. Perhaps you two could chew it fine on another occasion."

Bischoff made an expansive gesture with both hands, giving the floor to Longstreet. The town's leading businessman, Longstreet also headed the Tucson Committee's effort to end the Indian problem by whatever means necessary. The committee was particularly active now that the Indian Bureau's new Quaker Policy had, in their collective view, hobbled the Army. In truth, Trilby knew, the committee was delighted with Indian treachery so long as it didn't include attacks on their interests—a mistake the disrespectful Jemez Grayeyes had made once too often.

Longstreet said, "I'm getting up a new business venture, and I need help from both of you. As you know, the campaign to wipe out the buffalo is going great guns. The government resisted until the frontier lobby finally convinced them that the quicker we get rid of the buff, the quicker we throw a harness on the Indians."

Longstreet paused to fidget with the diamond-headed pin in his cravat. Then he looked at Bischoff.

"I mean to profit before this opportunity is lost. I've placed advertisements in the *London Times* and elsewhere. Advertisements for a unique international sporting venture on the far frontier of America. I'm going to make it easy for greenhorns—rich greenhorns, of course—to go home with a buffalo robe as a trophy. I'm going to provide comfortable wagons to shoot from, liquor and whatnot, crews to steer the herds their way and do the skinning. I'd appreciate it if you, Nat, would go along on the first expedition, maybe write it up for your column if you wanted to, tell everyone how exciting the experience is."

Bischoff nodded. "Deal me in. Sounds interesting. I plan on staying in Arizona until my editor cuts off my remittance."

"And you, Bob," Longstreet said. "I'd like you to round up some reliable men for the hunt crews. I'll pay them good money. I'd prefer white men over pepper guts."

"I can't get you many white men unless I ride way the hell to Prescott. Mostly you'll have to settle for Mexers. I'll talk to Aragon."

Longstreet frowned, pulling the cigar out of his mouth. "You sure you can trust him? That man looks over his shoulder plenty."

"I trust him as much as I need to. He'll do."

"What about the stories I hear? The stories about him topping buffalo cows?"

"Buffalo cows?" Bischoff looked asquint at Trilby. "Have we found yet another use for this versatile beast?"

"When he's drunk, he's a mite skewed in the head," Trilby admitted, grinning. "But he's smarter than he looks. I trust him."

"I hope so."

Something in Longstreet's tone alerted Trilby. He uncrossed his ankles and sat up a little straighter, his interest piqued. It was a tone that usually meant profits were in the wind.

Longstreet leaned back and tugged at the bottom of his calfskin vest. He slid tapered glasses and a wicker-covered clay jar of wine across the desk, but the other two men ignored it.

"Gentlemen, I recently spoke with one of my associates at Fort Grant. It was discouraging. Both of you know damn good and well that the Apaches have this entire territory in a constant uproar. Reservations have been set aside for them, but only a few of the western tribes have settled on them. The eastern bands, particularly the Chiricahuas, are recruiting small groups of criminals and malcontents. Under the likes of Victorio, Nana, Geronimo, and that thieving crowd, they travel light and fast, seldom in bands of more than a hundred. Their battle strategy is brilliant: They strike hard and fast in one area, then ride like the devil and strike the next day at a place a hundred miles away. They've hit military work details, stagecoaches and stations, mail riders. They've also been raiding cattle, trading them down in Old Mexico for tobacco and coffee and liquor. They are masters of the ambush, and will turn on the most capable trackers in a heartbeat. Thirty warriors on the move like this can keep five thousand troops in the field."

Trilby nodded. The Apaches were the only people in this vast region to successfully resist the Spaniards for over three centuries. But Longstreet's spiel just now was old news—clearly he was leading up to something besides a lesson in military tactics.

"Unfortunately, the interests of several of us on the committee are seriously jeopardized by a certain . . . unpredictability in the present situation. Most of the raiding lately has taken place far to the north and east of us, around the Glen Canyon freight terminal and the Butterfield Overland routes. For this reason, according to my associate at Fort Grant, the garrison there might be moved to a new command sector. That would of course include redeployment of the troops kept here in Tucson."

Now Trilby understood the real purpose of this meeting. Located fifty-five miles northeast of Tucson, Fort Grant was a major remount post. A troop of cavalry from that fort was kept on extended bivouac at Tucson. Longstreet and his colleagues on the committee held numerous contracts to supply meat, horses, blankets, and other goods to the fort, as well as to the reservation at Mater Dolorosa. Another "Indian attack" in this region would help justify keeping the fort where it was. And why was Longstreet boldly leading up to such a plan in front of Bischoff? At first Trilby had been surprised that Longstreet would reveal his hand so frankly to an outsider—a journalist, at that. Now he understood: Every literate person in America might know Bischoff's name, but that name was just one more for Longstreet to add to his payroll. Besides, Bischoff was in the newspaper business. And it was important to keep the newspapers interesting.

"According to my associate," Longstreet continued, "the Mater Dolorosa Reservation has become a hotbed of Apache intrigue. The agent there, Hays Munro, is an Indian-loving malcontent. He has filed formal complaints against several of us on the committee who supply goods to the reservation, claiming we are engaged in fraud against the Apaches and the U.S. government. Worse, the renegade Apaches are using Mater Dolorosa as a sort of staging area, working in cahoots with the praying Indians."

Trilby had to stifle a laugh at this last claim. Pure malarkey! The Mater Dolorosa Apaches were a sorry lot of flea-bitten blanket asses. But Longstreet looked squarely at Trilby now. It was not Longstreet's way to issue a direct order for a raid. Nor was it Trilby's way to require one.

"If there were trouble at the rez," Longstreet said, "it might prove mighty providential. The military would take a serious look at their plans to move Fort Grant to another department. And perhaps enough pressure will bring about the . . . removal of Hays Munro and his staff, replace them with an agent more amenable to the businessman."

Trilby kept his gaze lidded, his face inscrutable. Bischoff poured himself a glass of wine. Then he stood, wandered to the shelf behind the desk and picked up one of the skulls. He examined it with minute attention, discreetly ignoring the other two.

"What kind of trouble?" Trilby said.

"The worst kind. The kind the Indian Bureau hates most. Indians attacking fellow Indians. Proof that an agent has no control over his wards, that his policies invite nothing but chaos and anarchy."

Trilby nodded. "That *would* be trouble, wouldn't it?"

"Of course," Longstreet added, "it would *not* be a good thing if Munro got in front of a bullet. His family are well-placed back East. It might precipitate too . . . *thorough* an investigation by the government. Still, perhaps a death or two would lend a certain urgency to the public outcry."

Trilby looked past Longstreet to Bischoff. "Might be an exciting story, too. Part of the new world order, eh?"

Bischoff put the skull back on the shelf. Then he smiled an enigmatic little smile and raised his glass. "Gentlemen, a toast: to history—and the men who make it."

Chapter 15

Seth Carlson seldom suffered from nightmares. For him, the hard times came in the empty, breathing stillness of early morning, lying there wide-awake with dawn still hours away and no help to be had.

Dreams at least dulled the rough edges, symbolized the pain; memories were literal brutes, at times even hostile, and these were the hours when they caught him defenseless. It was always the same. Again he would see Jeanette in the final moments of that fatal Sunday, turning to look at him for the last time. Her face blood-smeared, her eyes glazed marbles, and that urgent plea in her look that would haunt him unto death: Was she telling him to kill her? Or begging him to save her?

His ferocious kill cry, the pistol leaping in his fist, that loathsome spray of blood and brain matter, Jeanette folding to the ground, and then the useless click of the hammer when he turned the .44 on himself. After that, oh merciful God, after that, Corey's eyes . . .

Each time, a knife twisted deep into Seth's guts. Now his body twitched and a moan escaped his lips, sounding oddly disembodied amidst the rhythmic snoring of the other patients. And then the hurt was on Seth, so hard his face crumpled, and the loss was in him, so deep and desperate and irretrievable that his mind shut down the images completely to protect his body from the shock.

He slumped back heavily into the pillows, a patina of sweat glistening on his forehead in the raw white moonlight.

Walt Mackenzie watched Carlson's jaw clench so tight the muscles formed huge knots. The lieutenant's eyes went wide, his face pale, and Mackenzie thought, for one scary moment, that his patient was having some type of seizure.

"Good God a-gorry! Sir? You all right? *Sir?*"

But though his eyes stared at something, Carlson was still seeing deep inside, not without. Walt wanted to shake him, wanted to bad, but in truth he was afraid for both of them. It just might be dangerous. A man's face, it can't get that way, Walt thought—not unless a man was hurting so deep it took over all of him, and that could get dangerous in a hurry.

Mackenzie, too, looked physically pained when Seth's right index finger crooked, as if curling around an imaginary trigger, repeatedly squeezing it.

"Sir?" Mackenzie said again. "You all right? You need something?"

This time the orderly's voice jolted him back to the present. Seth shook his head.

He looked at Mackenzie, his eyes lucid now.

"All I need," he said with a calm conviction that surprised Walt after what he had just witnessed, "is to get the hell out of the Army."

"Every week," said Brigadier General Ferris Ablehard, "we set up another cracker-and-molasses chief on the reservations. Or we capture another renegade leader and ship his raggedy ass out to the Dry Tortugas. In either case, more rations for the American people to buy. The Mexicans have the right idea. They call it 'Ley Fuga.' Shoot the devils in the back while taking them to jail, then claim they tried to run. Saves a lot of money and trouble, and—say, shavetail, is there wax in your ears?"

The distracted glaze over Corey Bryce's eyes melted away only slowly. "Sir? Oh . . . no, of course not, I'm listening. I'm sorry, General. My mind just wandered for a moment."

Ablehard reached across the table toward a glass carboy filled with bourbon whiskey. He had suddenly recalled, with a twinge of guilt rare for him, the lad's recent tragedy and the damn good reason for his distraction.

"Of course it did, son." His voice softened with paternal solicitude. "Have a spot of the giant killer."

The two men shared a table at the Saber House, a civilian-owned establishment on Washington's fashionable Independence Avenue which catered to military officers. The walls were upholstered in maroon velvet; on all four sides, mounted in giltwood frames, early Wild West scenes painted by Rindisbacher and M'Laughlin alternated with regimental flags and portraits of great Civil War leaders for the Union. No women were permitted in this wing, and spittoons were scattered about among the tables and leather club chairs. Most of the officers were still in uniform, tunics unbuttoned for evening. Some stood engaged in animated conversations or arguments at the bar, one foot propped on the brass rail; others sat in small, quieter groups at the tables, playing monte and faro amidst blue clouds of tobacco smoke.

"How long has it been now since . . . ?" Ablehard's voice trailed off delicately.

"A month tomorrow, sir."

"Ahh, a month. Well, life goes on, m'boy. I spoke with your father at Jeanette's—at the funeral. He's the one suggested to General Drummond that you be assigned as my aide-de-camp."

Corey nodded. "He mentioned that to me, sir. I was surprised, though, when the orders came through."

"It's hard to ignore the suggestion of a congressman. Anyway, your father and I go back a few years. I owe him a favor or two, and I told him I'd keep an eye on you."

The U.S. Army, in 1869, still issued no regulations for

officers' hats. The broad-brimmed gray hat on the table near Ablehard emulated the style made popular by Old Iron Butt Custer: the brim turned up on the right side and held to the crown by a small hook-and-eye, so a rifle could be aimed from horseback even at a gallop.

"Your father mentioned that you had considered resigning your commission. I'm happy to see you gave it further thought."

Corey nodded. He tried not to be aware of all the officers glancing over at him. It's the damned newspapers, he thought, with a warm flush of irritation. A month, and they still wouldn't let it alone. And it was the paper-collar newspaper boys who predicted he would no longer have the stomach for Army life.

"Yes, sir. But when I made the decision to stay in the Army, I didn't have Washington in mind. Another of my father's suggestions?"

Ablehard shrugged one shoulder. "Perhaps. Who knows? As I said, it's hard to ignore the suggestion of a congressman. At any rate, you've only got to put in a short stint here. You're a cavalryman. They can't keep you east of the Mississippi forever. I take it you're keen to kill some savages?"

"There's no glory in peace, sir."

"*There's* your fettle! Hell, you're just a colt. What happened out West . . . why, it was enough to unstring any man. You'll soon come sassy again."

Ablehard had developed an affinity for Army life during the Civil War. The only way to perpetuate this lifestyle was to volunteer for Indian fighting. He had chased a few Sioux out of the Black Hills, clearing the way for the white miners the Army was supposed to keep at bay by order of the treaties signed with the Sioux Nations. He talked up a stout campaign, but he had no zeal for actual warfare and was an indifferent field commander, though brilliant at tapping the talents of others and taking credit for it without offending them. The general currently served as Special Liaison between President Grant and the field commanders out West. But in truth the well-intentioned president was distracted by the great regional battles over future railroad routes. He had little time for the Indian Question. So Ablehard spent most of his time drunk and otherwise amusing himself.

Ablehard drained his glass, filled it again, picked it up with a little flourish. "To the cavalry," he said. "May your testicles survive the pounding."

Corey forgot to laugh along with his superior, still uncomfortable at the unwanted attention from all sides. It had all started with that stirring piece of idiocy penned by Nat Bischoff. Corey, crazy numb with grief, had not wanted to read any of it. But ignoring it was like trying not to peek at a dead body. And then reading it had been so much worse: Bischoff had cast Seth as heroic, Corey as pitiable, and those basic characterizations had shaped the subsequent articles. These men looking at him now with secret, slanted glances—Jeanette's death had been a nasty piece of business, all right, and they were genuinely sympathetic. But it was sympathy tainted, Corey felt, by a measure of scorn for this supposed leader of warriors—this leader who could only sit his saddle, foolishly screaming "No!" while his wife was killed before his very eyes.

Ablehard quaffed another glass of bourbon. Twin points of color had risen high in his bony cheeks, and his enunciation grew a shade less precise.

"Listen up, mister. What say the two of us pay a little visit to a hog ranch tonight? I know a superb place over on Mount Vernon Square. Not a lass over twenty, and they've all been to finishing school. Not a coarse or vulgar one in the lot—though, of course, some men *like* cheap whiskey."

Corey shook his head. "No, thank you, sir. I've got no heart for it."

"That's the beauty of it, lad. In a brothel you leave your heart at the door!"

Corey shook his head again, and Ablehard reached across to pat his shoulder.

"I understand, shavetail. I met Jeanette at the wedding, remember? She was pretty and charming, and of course you loved—love—her. But when it comes to women, I've got a bit more time in grade on you. I'll tell you this much, and you can write it on your pillowcase: Marriage isn't all it's cracked up to be, and a bachelor's life has more to recommend it than the poets and old maids will allow."

This was wasted on Corey. But by now Ablehard was too inebriated to notice the fact.

"Marriage? I've worn *that* old moccasin, lad, and it's not always a good fit. Single men think it's idyllic to have a regular night woman. Well, good luck! Rare is the married man who gets a fair ration of his bedroom pleasures. Women are as temperamental as close-bred horses, and they get all those damnable female complaints, so that much of the time a man's got to shoot at targets of opportunity, if you take my meaning? I—"

"They're treating *him* like a damned hero!" Corey blurted out, oblivious to Ablehard's lecture. "And him still alive while she's dead!"

Corey, not a veteran campaigner when it came to drinking, had all at once felt the heady effects of the bourbon he drank far too quickly on an empty stomach. He was hardly aware that he had spoken his thoughts—until he saw the general gaping at him in stupefied amazement.

"What's that?"

Corey shook his head, gathered himself up. "Nothing, sir. Sorry. Just thinking out loud."

By now Ablehard was vaguely impatient with Corey, but he said nothing. Secretly, he considered it unmanly to wallow in grief. If a man got tossed hard, he simply had to shake it off and climb right back on the same damned horse. Of *course* the girl was pretty, but they all looked alike in the dark.

"Well," Ablehard said, "this old war-horse is about blown in." He winked at Corey. "Though I believe there's still enough wind left in me for a bit of sport before I'm stalled for the night. Sure you won't join me, meet some of the ladies?"

"No. No, sir. Thank you."

"Suit yourself. Least I could offer for a fellow pony soldier. Cheer up, lad, soon enough you'll feel fit as a ruttin' buck."

Corey had enough presence of mind to stand up when his superior rose and left the table. But instead of returning to his own quarters, he sat down again and filled his glass one more time from the carboy.

Ablehard was wrong: Liquor didn't kill the giants. But Corey had lately discovered that if he drank enough of it, the giants didn't matter so much.

Chapter 16

*T*he rope felt like scabby fingers scratching at his neck.

He wanted to reach up and pull it away, but his wrists were bound tight at the small of his back. The rope-fingers tightened, pressed into his windpipe when his executioner snubbed the coils close against the nape of his neck. He could smell the clean, heavy tang of creosote soaking the new rope. Beneath him, the horse whickered and tried to crow hop, but someone gentled it.

Panic welled inside him, threatening to explode his chest like potsherds. It wasn't the dying, that part was just the familiar fear. But this rope, like some sere, scaly snake coiled around his neck: It meant more than just death. It meant bad death, the worst kind, the unclean death of the white-eyes. How a man dies is how he spends eternity.

His eyes were open, but they must have placed a blindfold over them—he could see nothing, though he felt the sun hot on *his skin, felt a pinyon-scented breeze tickling his face like exploring fingers.*

But the panic—cold, brittle, expanding inside him.

A voice dry as sotol stalks whispered close in his ear:

"Hey, 'Pache? You know how's come they call a man 'well hung'? When that noose goes snug, all the blood gets cut off from your brain and shoots down into your peeder. If we do it right, you'll die with a big ol' red boner."

A rattling, phlegm-clogged laugh, the stink of bad forty-rod whiskey. The sun hot, the breeze cool, and then a sudden whip crack, the horse surging out from under him, his voice welling up in a scream as the fingers around his neck turned into fangs—

Jemez Grayeyes started awake, a scream trapped in his throat.

Sweat chilled him to shivers, and he could taste the fear on his tongue, thick as alkali dust. The pale density of the sky, the dawn star glimmering low in the east, told him it was just sunup. For a long moment he couldn't understand why he had slept here at the cave entrance. Then the last cobwebs of sleep cleared from his mind, and he remembered the soldiers below.

Had he caught his scream in time?

He sat up and peered down the steep talus slope that led up to the cave. It must have been their noise that woke him —the squad of Mexican soldiers was just now breaking camp below. He spotted the officer in his green uniform and high black boots, the enlisted men with their crossed bandoliers and tall shako hats with metal facings.

Jemez had spotted them yesterday, riding up toward his position in a narrow enfilade formation from the broad soda plain below. They were led by a Pima scout who stopped often to bend low from the saddle and scour the ground. None of them had yet spotted his cave entrance, but he knew why they were lingering in this area: He had watched the Pima break apart droppings left by his horses, determining whether they were made by the horses of Indians or of soldiers.

Jemez cursed himself for not disposing of the droppings earlier as he had meant to. At least his ponies should be safe for now. They were well grazed and watered, hidden in a distant barranca. It worried him, though, that the Mexicans —notoriously lazy soldiers, in his experience, though ruthless —had endured the considerable hardships of traveling this far up into the remote sierras of northern Sonora. This spot could be reached by only one trail, one so steep Jemez had once seen a pack mule lose its footing and tumble to a hard death on the basalt turrets below. It was made treacherous by steep shale slopes, surrounded by unscalable traprock shelves.

Only a strong sense of purpose—and perhaps a good bounty—would send Mexican soldiers this high into the arid wastelands near the Mexican-American border. Nor could the bloody goal of their mission be doubted; the shotguns some of the soldiers carried balanced over their pommels meant they had come with close-range killing on their minds. So far, though, this remote detour had given them nothing more than an opportunity to boil their clothing to kill the lice and vermin. Jemez had watched them yesterday, sitting naked in the sun with their clothes drying on rocks all around them.

He had replaced his U.S. Army trousers with long-fringed buckskins—he knew from too much experience as a fugitive that the fringes would come in handy for repairing his gear and providing thongs. He also wore a fur-lined leather shirt against the chill of high-sierra nights. He slid a strip of flannel from his sash and tied his long black hair back away from his face.

The night before, he had laid his weapons carefully to hand at the entrance, wrapping the firearms in coyote fur to protect them from the damp: the Remington .50 pistol in its hand-tooled leather holster; a big Sharps .45-120 rifle, its cracked wooden stock reinforced with a buckskin patch; a double-bladed throwing ax, its wooden helve carved with the totems of the Grayeyes clan; a Spanish bayonet with blood gutters carved into the long blade to facilitate rapid bleeding.

Again his swift eyes returned to the soldiers. In the early morning stillness he could hear their horses snuffling, the clinking of harness and gear. While the men strapped their bedrolls to their cantles, and the Pima looked about half-heartedly for sign, the officer slid a pair of brass binoculars from a saddle pannier. Jemez pressed even tighter against the walls of stone at the entrance, making sure to stay out of the slanting sunlight.

Clearly this was a final look around before they pushed on. While the officer patiently traversed the surrounding crags and pinnacles with his binoculars, Jemez let his own gaze drift out toward the distant sierras to the south, where the great cordillera formed Mexico's spine. Bald peaks of granite marked the highest mountains. Rough-hewn lava rocks made great, jumbled piles of scree at their base. All of it abruptly gave way to the flatlands on either side, mostly sparse desert grass dotted with palmilla.

Jemez, like most Apaches, hated forced solitude. For any Indian, true death was to be alone. But he loved this vast, lonely, uncompromising country that had taught his people the hard lessons of survival. Thinking these things, he suddenly saw an image of his little sister, Socorro. He remembered, so vividly it still ached inside him, saying good-bye to her and Miguelito at Mater Dolorosa. She had the defiant Grayeyes blood in her, that one did.

Again, against his will, his mind's eye saw the wicker cradles, tacky with blood after the assault on his clan's cavern stronghold. Those cradles were indelible pictures etched in his memory not as mere traces, but deep scars. They were the proof that nothing was left for the Dineh, the People: no heritage, no destiny, the last survivors of the race either answering roll calls on white man's reservations or living like hunted animals in the barren hinterlands.

No, he told himself, nothing was left except *this*—the white-hot hatred, the blood lust for revenge. Meanness had nothing to do with it. Without revenge, there was no point left to existence, no reason to keep on working so hard just for bare survival. Nothing else was permitted by white-eye law but this implacable thirst for vengeance. Die if you must, but fall on the bones of an enemy.

Thinking abruptly gave way to a cool prickle of apprehension—the officer below was staring directly at his cave entrance, adjusting the focus on his binoculars for a closer look.

Jemez pressed farther back into the shadows. He was fairly certain the entrance could not be spotted at this distance, even through field glasses. But he hoped that he had not inadvertently allowed the copper and silver brassards encircling his arms to glint in the sunlight.

Behind him, in the cramped interior of the cave, he had dug a pit for cooking mescal after dark, when the smoke couldn't be seen. Nearby, a bladder bag full of water hung from a braided-horsehair rope. His saddle and bridle, and a pile of gnawed bones, completed the meager contents of his rude bastion.

Again Jemez looked downslope, and now the cool prickle of apprehension became a cold, numbing fear. The officer, surrounded by several men, was pointing in his direction and issuing orders. A moment later a half-dozen men fanned out in a wedge, heading up toward his cave through the jumble of boulders.

Jemez held the all-important high ground, but his ammunition was scarce. Knowing he could never sustain a gun battle against several adversaries, he had prepared a more natural and perhaps devastating defense. Now, as the soldiers neared his position, he half crawled, half rolled to a slight depression just to the right of the cave's small, recessed entrance.

Here, held in place by several strategically placed rocks, a huge boulder the size of a fat pony waged a tug of war with gravity. Painstakingly, over the course of several backbreaking days, Jemez had pried out most of the smaller rocks that kept the boulder from tumbling down the steep slope. The slope, covered with loose rocks and stones, would instantly turn into a heaving chaos once that boulder sprang into motion, a juggernaut of death.

The first of the soldiers were close enough now for him to make out their faces. Those not armed with shotguns carried new Springfield breechloaders. Sweat beaded on his upper lip, but now, so close to action, Jemez felt his fear replaced by a cool sense of purpose. Carefully, he slid one of the restraining rocks out from under the boulder. A little trickle of gravel slid down as the boulder edged forward slightly.

The soldiers picked their way closer, crouching behind

rocks. I'll never kill all of them, Jemez thought. But a rock slide might be enough to scatter the survivors. Unfortunately, this was only a squad. Surely the rest of their unit was in the area. If he did manage to rabbit, he could never return to this cave.

The lead soldier suddenly dropped into a crouch and snapped his Springfield to his shoulder. He's spotted me, Jemez thought, loosing another rock. Now he felt the boulder shift slightly, on the feather edge of hurtling downward.

The soldier's rifle cracked, and the bullet whanged from boulder to boulder, ricocheting in a long echo. A moment later Jemez glimpsed a streak of tawny fur as a mountain lion leaped from hiding and scrambled down the slope. Now the other soldiers opened fire, raising excited shouts as their bullets splatted against rocks and the quick animal darted to safety. The officer good-naturedly cursed their bad marksmanship. Five minutes later the troops were disappearing down the trail.

Jemez allowed himself to exhale, and wedged the restraining rocks back into place under the boulder. When he was sure the Mexicans were gone, he returned to the cave and pulled the sack of Bull Durham and the packet of rolling papers from his shirt pocket. He built himself a smoke while he turned his thoughts to Juan Aragon and Robert Trilby.

The Sioux had the right idea, Jemez thought. The best way to negotiate with whites was to avoid them. This advice was even wiser for dealing with Mexicans, and his mixed-blood cousin, Juan Aragon, was far more Mexican than Apache in temperament. Nonetheless, Jemez planned to learn as much as he could about the activities of both men— and whoever else drank from their trough.

There were other Apaches like him, holed up between northern Mexico and the uppermost reaches of the Arizona Territory. Information was passed through a system of smoke signals, mirror flashes, and runners—dubbed the Moccasin Telegraph by the blue-dressed soldiers. And thanks to a visit from Victorio, the Mescalero boy from Mater Dolorosa, he had already heard about the new "sporting" pit at Riverbend. According to Victorio, the pit drew quite a motley crowd. Good. Jemez was thinking about visiting the place himself.

He stood in the cave entrance and looked out over the land, over the desolate spine of talus, scree, crags, pinnacles, and distant, snow-streaked sierras. For one unsettling moment he recalled his life's worst nightmare and the rope fingers closing around his neck. But he put the fear outside of himself and spoke two brief sentences out loud in that vast stillness:

"This place hears me. My enemies have no place to hide."

Chapter 17

"Shine, senor?"

The youth named Rafael fell into quickstep beside Robert Trilby, dragging his battered packing crate behind him.

"I make those fine boots shine so good you can shave in them, you betcha *que sí.*"

"I'm in a hurry, *chico.* Here. You can owe me a shine."

Trilby fished into a pocket and removed a few silver and copper coins, handing them to the youth.

The kid flashed his gap-toothed grin and shoved the coins into his pocket without even looking at them.

"*Dios le bendiga, senor!* See? Just as you told me, I did not count them. Why should any man know how much money I have, *verdad?*"

"That's the gait, kid. Hold your cards close to your vest."

Rafael was running behind him again. "Senor? You need somebody to fall into the pit again? I was just *acting* scared last time, I got a set on me."

Trilby waved him off and stuck to the Sunday morning shadows of Silver Street. His boot heels thumped on the boardwalk. A water cart creaked by, and a few soiled doves in ruffled satin dresses crossed the street to an eating house that stayed open night and day. Now and then Trilby nodded to an acquaintance. But when the day's first stagecoach rounded the corner near the newspaper office, trace chains jangling, he turned his gaze upon it until it had passed.

Trilby always carefully monitored new arrivals to Tucson. Years earlier he had made his way west by posing as an independent conductor organizing a train of wagons. After collecting the fee for passage and supplies in advance, he'd left a hundred families stranded in the St. Louis settlements. Several people had died in the subsequent riot, and at least one politician won reelection by swearing to bring him to justice. He regretted nothing he had done, and he was the last man to fear threats from a cheese-gut politician. Yet he also knew from experience that a man seldom hears the shot that kills him.

The huge frame building that housed the boarding stable stood where Silver Street gave way to the path to Riverbend. The hostler, an acerbic old Irishman named Cedric O'Flaherty, sat on a rain barrel just outside the big front doors, swatting at flies with a quirt.

"Heigh-up, old-timer! You didn't send my horse out to graze, did you?"

"The hell, you always talk at me like I'm a damn soft brain. You told me yesterday to leave her stalled, dint you? So that's what I done."

"No need to get on the peck. I was just asking you."

"Ahuh. And looks like I'm just tellin' you."

Trilby moved back through the dark, manure-fragrant interior of the building. He stopped at the last stall on the right. His horse, a dark cream with a black mane and tail, nickered in greeting and nuzzled his shoulder. She was sleek from regular graining, and Trilby kept her muscle definition strong by paying the stable *mozo* extra to exercise her daily.

He scratched the mare's withers and spoke to her fondly. Then he crossed to the tack room in a slope-off partition. From nails on the wall he took down his bridle and bit, then threw his saddle, pad, and blanket over his shoulder. He returned to the mare and unstalled her. She took the bit easily, eager to run, then snorted impatiently while he saddled her, cinched the girth, double-checked the latigos.

"*Jefe*."

Trilby turned around and immediately smelled the powerful stench of pulque on Aragon's breath.

"I asked you to hold off on the drinking until we're finished today," he said irritably.

Aragon smiled his sly smile and raised both hands like a priest blessing his flock.

"*Jefe*, you are right. You *asked*. That is why I am drunk. Had you ordered me not to drink, things might be different. However, drunk or sober I would follow you into the jaws of hell. But truly, you can be an unreasonable man! You know I cannot sit my saddle when I am sober."

"You can't sit your saddle, period. I never even saw a tenderfoot ride as sloppy as you do, and you were born out here. Are the men ready?"

"Does corn beer make your piss yellow? *Como no* they are ready. They will meet us at Cañon de Oro."

Trilby led the mare outside. Aragon's big claybank stood in the shade, stamping its foreleg in irritation at the pesky flies. Trilby watched his companion mount from the right side of the horse—the Indian side. Again Trilby took that as a reminder and a warning. The phrenologist in him could marvel at the mixed-blood's uniquely angular skull structure, so similar to that of the great European military geniuses. But the frontier survivor must never forget Aragon was also half Apache.

From habit, Aragon slumped lazily against the bare tree of his Texas stock saddle. The movement swung his machete forward in its tatty straw scabbard.

"You bring the carbine?" Trilby said.

Aragon slid a seven-shot Spencer from his left saddle scabbard and handed it across. Trilby carried no weapons except the muff gun in his boot, but he liked the small cavalry-issue carbine when he was riding out on a job such as this one. It was accurate, the .56 slug deadly, and the piece easy to handle and load from the saddle since all you had to do was shove rounds through a trap in the butt plate. He tucked it into his own scabbard, which was tied high on his saddle so the weapon could be lifted and fired without removing it from the scabbard.

"Any more news about Grayeyes?" Trilby asked.

For a moment Aragon pictured that vengeance pole high up in the mountains, and he felt a queasy churning in his stomach.

"Nothing, *Jefe*. As I said, we will hear from him when he chooses."

"So you say. But I'm notional, and I've decided it's not his game to call."

Aragon glanced at his boss, his curiosity piqued. Amusement twitched his lips. "No?"

"You said his younger brother and sister are at Mater Dolorosa now?"

Aragon nodded.

"Would you recognize them?"

"*Cómo no?* They are my cousins."

"If we grab them, will Grayeyes come for us?"

"Is a whore's bath quick?"

"Good," Trilby said. He swung up into leather. "I'm tired of waiting for him to make his play. Let's stir up the shit a little."

"Sin," said Father Montoya, "is Satan's yoke on mortals. Through sin does the Most Low work his malevolent scheme of destruction and chaos. Through sin does he attack God's perfect plan for man. Through sin does he attempt to drag all mankind back to the graceless condition from which we were all saved by the great and gracious sacrifice of Jesus Christ."

Kathleen watched Father Montoya pause and pat his sweat-mottled forehead with a handkerchief. Sunlight slanted through the big arched windows, forcing some in the congregation to squint. The original Mater Dolorosa Mission had been sacked in the Yaqui uprisings, and the chapel badly damaged. Now a portable altar and long, backless benches had been dragged in, converting the schoolroom into a chapel. Attendance at religious services was mandatory, but far from popular with the Apaches at Mater Dolorosa. So now that roll call was over, Hays Munro stood at one door, Kathleen at the other, guarding against the inevitable escape attempts.

Kathleen curled her toes in frustration. An opportunity was being squandered here, and it was a crying shame. For sadly, Father Montoya's piety far outstripped his rhetorical prowess. He was a short, plump, balding man whose heart was in the right place, and Kathleen liked him immensely. When an Indian was sick or dying, he was tireless in his efforts to help and comfort. Unlike many others in the religious community, he did not consider Indians beasts without souls. He was utterly sincere in his efforts to guide these rude pagans through the gates of paradise alongside their white brethren.

But unfortunately, she thought as she glanced around this place where joy couldn't seem to take root any better than crops, he had no concept of the red man's notions. He valued the aboriginal soul but despised aboriginal ways. The Apaches, though not so religious as some tribes she had met, nonetheless set great store by medicine men. But they expected a show, an entertainment. This medicine man named Father Montoya—his monotonous, droning voice, stiff movements, and strange concepts such as sin, salvation, and immaculate conception—bored and confused them.

"Sin weakens creation just as sickness weakens a body, devouring the healthy and good parts and leaving behind a putrid mass of corruption. . . ."

Kathleen had left her hair unbraided today, tying it in a wheat-colored knot on the back of her neck. She glanced around again and felt a flush of irritation when she realized what was niggling at her: the rebellious youth named Victorio was gone again. He must have slipped off right after roll call. Unless he showed up for the evening roll, Hays would find out about the absence. This time the boy would surely be punished.

From where she stood, she could glance out the windows at the desolate wasteland of the reservation. She saw the flat, gravel-laden, wind-scoured expanse that would neither hold nor nurture seeds; the creosote bushes and paddle cactus and prickly pear which did not supply enough shade to succor a jackrabbit. *All silent, and all damned.*

Many in the congregation, too, gazed out the windows. But their eyes seemed to focus much farther beyond, perhaps as far as the Superstition, Dragoon, and Mescal mountains. There, life had been hard but free; cold water crashed down from roaring cataracts; cool, thin air invigorated the flesh and made the blood sing in tribute to Great Ussen and the High Holy Ones who first made the days and then gave them to men.

"Sin," Father Montoya droned on, "is an invisible worm eating its way to the core of this precious but fragile fruit called life. . . ."

Outside, the wind gusted up, and Kathleen could almost feel the stinging grit on her skin. By now everyone in the congregation had a frozen glaze over their eyes. Children fussed and fidgeted, adults shuffled their feet and coughed. One exception, she noted with a wry smile, was Miguelito Grayeyes. The boy's cough was much better and he was out of the dispensary. Now he sat down in the front row beside his sister, rapt with attention as he studied the priest's embroidered silk stole. Not so his defiant sister. Her eyes darted constantly about the big room, as if she were watching for a war party to spring her from this white-eye prison house.

Kathleen looked at Hays Munro and saw him turn to stare out the door behind him. The movement was casual enough. Yet a moment later Socorro Grayeyes also turned around and —rare for her—met Kathleen's eyes. Some knowledge down deep in Kathleen brought a cool tingling to the back of her neck.

"Even now," Father Montoya said, "sin mounts its everlasting assault on the soul of man. Even now the legions of hell are bearing down upon the citadel, and all too soon the blood of the lambs will feed the barbarous horde. . . ."

There were six of them and they rode wide abreast in a skirmish line: a white man, a mixed-blood, and four full-blooded Apaches. Yellow dust plumes spiraled up behind them and vanished like wraiths in the wind.

They rode through thick stands of ocotillo, across sandy washes, past spines of wind-sculpted rock. They crossed a dry pan, then miles of rolling scrubland, escarpments visible in the distance. Wild lavender bloomed up in the mountains and purple sage tinged the horizon in a wavering haze. Closer at hand, an occasional dwarf oak popped up amidst the cactus, twisted into bizarre shapes by the vindictive, unrelenting wind.

With Jemez Grayeyes so much on his mind lately, Trilby appreciated this open country. Good ground cover was scarce, and the mountains were too far distant to darken the approach of an enemy.

All four Apaches were turncoats sought out by Aragon, required to keep a low profile this close to Tucson. The four had waited for them at Cañon de Oro. They had no saddle scabbards, riding with their rifles resting across their saddle bows or pointing straight up, butt plates pressed into their thighs. Two of them were Chiricahuas dressed in the distinctive manner of their clan: knee-length moccasins, elkskin clouts, copper brassards, flexible hide helmets sporting plumes. The other two Trilby recognized as a pair of Aragon's favorite dirt workers, Mimbrenos named Janos and Loco, who always rode together. They were clad in more motley garb: Janos wore cowhide boots broken down at the heels, a flannel shirt and Mexican army trousers made of kersey; Loco was clad in captured American cavalry trousers and a bone breastplate stolen from a drunk Kiowa. All four Indians used hide headstalls without bits on their horses, and wore cartridge belts crossing their backs. All four also felt a common contempt for Dust Scatterers—the reservation Indians trying to raise crops instead of living as hunters, warriors, and marauders.

Trilby knew from experience that Apaches were bad shots, as a rule. But he wouldn't be needing accurate marksmen for this raid. He had spent two years as a scout and pathfinder for the Kansas–Santa Fe freight line. He had kept his eyes open and his mouth shut, and had learned some fundamental things about Apaches. That learning was important—whereas whites had managed to learn the ways of many Indians, Apaches were inherently secretive.

An hour west of Mater Dolorosa they crossed a high saddle and then descended into the mostly deserted pueblo of Poco Agua, a handful of mud hovels crumbling into dust. Frequent Indian raids had sent most of the population to Tucson or San Manuel. But in the middle of the pueblo, Trilby spotted a handful of raggedy-looking Mexicans. They were roasting a mule over a big fire made from the *vigas* of ruined buildings. A woman with waist-length hair stood over a big, flat rock. Trilby saw that she was crushing coffee beans with the butt of an old dragoon pistol. He counted four men. The pistol had no hammer, and he dismissed it.

The Mexicans wore raw wool serapes and rope sandals. They glanced up when the riders approached, accompanied by the light clinking of bit rings, their hoof clops echoing off the crumbling mud walls.

For a long time none of them moved. Then one of the Mexicans rocked back on his heels slightly and said something to the others. Trilby watched one hand go out of sight behind his serape. The rest now ignored the roasting mule, watching the new arrivals with caged eyes. It cost Trilby an effort not to grin when he saw how they watched the Apaches most of all. If there was one race Apaches hated more than whites, it was Mexicans. At least Apaches would shoot a white man. But unless forced to it, they refused to waste a bullet on a Mexican. They killed them as they might a snake, with rocks.

As if by silent accord, the riders stopped when only a few yards away from the little group.

The man who had spoken to his friends now stared at the wrinkled human ears on the leather thong around Aragon's neck. Then he looked at Trilby.

"*Buenos dias,*" he said.

Trilby nodded. Thunderheads boiled in the distance. It was so still the air seemed to ring.

"*Me gusta su caballo,*" the man said, nodding at Trilby's cream-colored mare.

Trilby understood the compliment but said nothing.

The man gestured toward the mule. "*Hay bastante. Tienen ustedes hambre?*"

Trilby shook his head. "We're in a hurry."

"*Jefe*," Aragon said in a quiet, pleasant voice, "these are not people bound for heaven. They plan to kill us for our stock after we pass by. The speaker and the skinny one over there have guns."

Again Trilby nodded. "As I said, best to take the bull by the horns."

He tipped his hat to the group on the ground, touched his horse as if to leave. But as he rode past the man who had spoken, his right hand lifted the carbine—still in its scabbard—and he snapped off a round.

The bullet struck the man in his lower jaw and knocked him sprawling into the dirt. Aragon's pin-fire pistol cracked, there were several more solid reports from the Apaches' British trade rifles, one of the horses nickered and reared. Moments later the men were all dead or dying, and the woman threw down the dragoon pistol. She bolted down the street, long hair streaming out behind her.

Aragon unsheathed his machete at the same moment the Mimbreno named Loco brandished an oak war club bristling with spikes. The Apache reached her first, swung his arm back in a wide arc, and caved in her skull. Immediately nerve-dead, she shambled forward a few more paces from sheer momentum and then collapsed.

Trilby sat his saddle, indifferent to the others, as Aragon and the Apaches dismounted. Loco squatted near the woman, grabbed her blood-and-brain-mottled hair and twisted it tight around his wrist. He made a swift outline cut around her scalp with the tip of his twine-handle knife. Then, standing with one foot on her neck for leverage, he jerked the scalp loose in one powerful snap. Aragon and the other Apaches scalped the rest.

Trilby thought of Nat Bischoff and the little ironies of history as he watched Loco return to his horse and add the woman's hair to a string of several such scalps dangling from a leather whang hidden under his blanket. Apaches normally disdained taking scalps. But profit was the great flywheel of mankind, and now they, too, were selling scalps for bounty. Technically, the bounty on Indian scalps was illegal. But the governor of Chihuahua still paid a hundred pesos for the scalp of Apache men, fifty pesos for those of women and children. When some enterprising Apache turncoats couldn't find enough fellow Indians to scalp, they would occasionally slip into Sonora and lift the hair of a few pepper guts—there was no shortage of coarse black hair in this territory. One naive Mexican *gobernador* had even been known to pay top price for several cleverly clipped horse tails.

Trilby patted his mustache with three fingertips.

"You, John," he said to one of the Chiricahuas, using the name commonly employed by frontier whites in direct address to an Indian. "When we ride out of this place, wait up there at the head of that bluff. Wait as long as it takes the sun to travel the width of two lodge poles. *Entiendes?* Then catch up to us."

The Apache avoided eye contact with him but nodded. He hated whites like he hated catching the drizzling shits. But truly there were times when this Robert Trilby thought like one of the Dineh. Trilby had fought southwest guerrilla warfare long enough that he had learned to take a leaf from his enemy's own book—best to watch your back trail after a skirmish, when the elation of victory could make men cocky and careless.

Aragon broke out a flask of pulque and passed it around.

"All right," Trilby said when it was empty. He pointed his bridle east toward Mater Dolorosa. "We're burning daylight. Let's get 'er done."

Well-hidden behind a spine of rocks in the high rimland, the Apache youth named Victorio hobbled his mustang foreleg to rear with a strip of rawhide. Then he watched the six riders below.

They loped across a dry alkali pan, white dust plumes rising behind them. He couldn't make out much at this distance, though clearly at least two were Chiricahuas—he recognized the plumed helmets of their warlike tribe. But whoever they were, they were obviously racing toward Mater Dolorosa. Nothing else lay in that direction except desert and rolling scrubland.

Victorio, unable to bear the alien monotony at the reservation, had slipped away again to ride south and visit his friend Jemez in Sonora. But now, something in the riders' urgent pace, the grim determination suggested by their tight formation, made Victorio's armpits and groin go cool with sweat.

He knew a shortcut down out of the high country. If he pushed his sure-footed mountain pony hard, he might be able to reach Mater Dolorosa first.

Socorro had tried, at first, to focus on the hair-face shaman's sermon. Not because she would ever want to believe their foolish lies, but only because it kept her mind from looking elsewhere.

But it was no good. No matter how hard she tried not to, again she was forced to hear that last defiant death cry of her uncle Chimaca—a cry so like the death whinny of a pony. She missed her pony, and she missed her mother. But it hurt too much inside, felt like sharp prickers caught in her throat, to think about her mother.

Beside her, Miguelito squeezed her hand. The white shaman droned on. But over his meaningless words she again heard the solemn promise of her brother Jemez: *When that stone melts, little sister, a Grayeyes will tell a lie to his own. I'll be coming back for you and Miguelito.*

Mercifully, the priest seemed to be concluding. Socorro glanced over her shoulder and saw Tio Hays staring out the open door. That was all, yet something about the way he held his face made her heart turn over.

Kathleen wasn't sure she really heard anything—just a faint, hollow drumming that might have been a slow muttering of thunder. But she stepped quickly out into the glaring sunlight and stared toward the vast sweeps to the north. She spotted him almost instantly, recognized his buckskin mustang: Victorio. He was racing toward her across the flat, hugging his pony's neck and lashing it with his light sisal whip.

She took a few more steps and stopped in confusion.

She heard a light, insignificant popping sound. Again, and a geyser of dirt shot up near Victorio's horse. A third pop, and a heartbeat later Victorio's mustang went down hard and the youth was tumbling headlong over the ground. When he didn't get up, Kathleen felt a flash of cold and then started running toward him.

A moment later the old Spanish church bell rang once—a sharp, clear, sudden ringing—and Kathleen stopped. A bullet had just struck the bell.

She stared west, squinted into the sun and saw them. Riders approaching at a gallop. Hays stepped out the other door. Her eyes met his.

"Get back inside," he ordered her, "and tell the rest to stay inside and take cover."

"But what about Victorio?"

"If he's alive and half smart, he'll stay right where he is. Now do as I told you!"

Trilby and his raiders struck in classic Apache fashion, swooping in fast from the direction of the sun.

Some mules and other stock were kept in a pole corral near the kitchen gardens. One of the Chiricahuas veered off in that direction, halted his mount and slipped inside the corral. He made short work of throat-slashing the docile stock. An eerie trumpeting noise broke out as air rushed through the animals' severed windpipes.

The other riders made straight for the low central building. They swept around Hays Munro and hardly broke stride. Trilby and Aragon had pulled bandannas up around their faces, tilted their hats low. Now, with a triumphant shout, Trilby spurred his mare over the broad, low sill of one of the windows and landed on the polished clay inside with a wild skittering and clattering of shod hooves. Aragon and the rest followed suit.

All had received careful instructions from Trilby. Kill all the animals they could, destroy or steal any property they wanted, nab the Grayeyes children and any other youngsters who might be salable to the Comanchero slave traders. But kill no one. That option would be left to Trilby alone.

Terrified screams broke out as the intruders entered. Weapons were illegal on reservations. The unarmed Apaches were all huddled tight behind the makeshift altar. Trilby saw a white woman and a Mexican priest standing before them, eyes huge with fright. Guns blasted with a deafening, ear-ringing roar in the big room, horses whinnied, the screams now unrelenting.

Trilby's blood was up, his face flushed with excitement. At moments of violence like this, his mind relaxed and saw everything with crystalline clarity. He fired and a clay saint exploded into shards. In the corner of one eye he saw Aragon drag a girl—kicking and screaming—up onto his saddle. The man who had been standing out front now ran in behind them. One of the Apaches whirled and smashed him in the face with a rifle butt. The Anglo woman tried to claw the Apache girl down from Aragon's horse. The mixed-blood kicked the woman hard in the chest and she went down.

One killing, Trilby thought. One killing to keep the Apache menace alive. He levered his carbine and pointed it at the woman on the floor, fighting his mare to hold her still.

"No!" the priest shouted. "For the love of God, no!"

Only Trilby's eyes showed above his bandanna, aglitter with sudden inspiration. It had just occurred to him how priest slaughter would foment anti-Indian unrest in the border newspapers. Besides, the woman had some good flesh on her. She shaped up mighty fine. Their trails just might cross again when he had more time.

" 'Sta bien, Padre," he said cordially. "For the love of God."

He swung his muzzle dead center on the priest and planted a slug in his chest.

Chapter 18

"So the little ripple of fame has become a ground swell," Enis Hagan remarked.

Mackenzie dropped a canvas mailbag beside Seth's bed. The young officer sat propped up against a bank of pillows. He was still confined to bed most of the time, though he was now permitted to walk around the hospital ward with the aid of a cane.

"There's plenty of packages, too," Mackenzie said. "I brought the ones from your mother. The mail clerk is holding the rest for you, sir, but it's certain-sure he's fair out of room to store 'em."

Seth nodded slightly to acknowledge that he'd heard. He was finally wearing issue trousers again, with a loose gray cotton shirt to accommodate his bandages.

Hagan sat on the edge of the bed, listening to Seth's heartbeat through a tubular stethoscope.

"Well," the contract surgeon finally said, "your pump

sounds good. You've got no fever, you're holding down solid food, and the wounds are finally starting to knit. I was a mite worried about infections, you were so weak there for a while. But I'd say you're finally and definitely out of the woods, soldier."

Seth said nothing, his eyes unfocused but leveled at an oblique angle toward the windows. It was late afternoon, the day still and warm. Across the parade field the sides of the squad tents were rolled up. The training day was over for most, and now the men had gathered in little groups, playing checkers and whist and betting on foot races. A larger group formed a huddled ring just past the pyramidal rows of tents. Excited shouts went up as they incited a battle between colonies of red and black ants.

Mackenzie and Hagan exchanged quick glances when the officer refused to respond.

"Sounds like good news to me," Mackenzie finally said.

"Better than a poke in the eye with a sharp stick, I reckon," Hagan said, snapping his leather medical kit shut.

Seth stared toward the window, his gaze still unfocused. A soft whimper from beside the bed made him glance down. Mackenzie had caught a coyote pup and given it a home in an ammo box to amuse the bedridden lieutenant. At first Seth had been indifferent to its presence, letting Mackenzie and the other patients play with it. Now he reached down and absently scratched it behind the ears.

"You wantin' to read any of your mail, sir?" Mackenzie said.

"Not particularly. Send it to Nat Bischoff. He's the one they're writing to, not me."

Seth's voice resisted any tone. Again Hagan and Mackenzie exchanged a quick look. Both men were now too close to the young officer's life not to appreciate his remark. Nat Bischoff was practically making it his career to turn Seth into a national institution. As a result, mail and gifts were pouring in. Yet no one seemed the least bit daunted by the cruel irony of it all: Absolutely nothing, in strategic terms, had been "won." But Seth's very survival had become charged with symbolism. An editorialist in Chicago had referred to him as "invincible." Another, in Jeanette Bryce's hometown of Albany, even insisted that Seth was God's appointed agent, sent to fulfill the Great White Destiny.

Bischoff's latest column had reported on a renegade Indian raid at the Mater Dolorosa Apache Reservation in the Arizona Territory. A priest had been killed, several children kidnapped. And though Seth had been flat on his back during the strike, Bischoff managed to work his name in no fewer than six times. It was yet one more story that had gotten the American public on the scrap against Indians, and now there was even a popular slogan anytime the Red Peril was mentioned: "Send Seth!"

Nat Bischoff was one of the few subjects that could bring a spark of animation to Seth's torpid eyes. At first the man's incessant campaign to lionize him had only mildly irritated Seth. But when it dragged on, that mild irritation had quickly given way to strong resentment and dislike. He had never met Bischoff, yet the journalist claimed omniscient privy to his innermost thoughts and feelings. The lifeblood of Jeanette and five other women—not to mention eight good soldiers—had stained red the ground, and now this clever scrivener from Boston was using their deaths as a sort of hawker's bark to sell the Expansionist philosophy. Seth was mainly indifferent to whatever battles were raging in the barrooms back East—but it cankered at him, this being used to shore up a political agenda.

Even the soldiers at Fort Bates were not immune to the journalistic hyperbole. Mackenzie had caught several of them trying to snip buttons off Carlson's clothing; others had visited the stables to cut hair from his horse's mane and tail.

The young corporal wasn't sure just how much Seth recalled of that night when he had first regained consciousness, the night when the orderly had opened up his heart to him and requested assignment under him. But the officer must have remembered that request and mentioned it to someone who mattered—Mackenzie had been immediately reclassified from Third Regiment orderly to service as Carlson's personal orderly, effective as soon as a replacement could be trained. Since junior-grade officers did not normally rate such privileges at Army expense, the speedy reassignment told Mackenzie that Lieutenant Carlson had new friends in very high places. It also hinted that Carlson had a hefty promotion in the works.

Enis Hagan, an ironist at heart, read the disgust in Seth's face and clucked sympathetically.

"Thoreau was right, may he rest in peace. 'The newspaper is the lowest common denominator of the masses.'" He slipped his watch out of his fob pocket and thumbed back the cover. "Well, got to get. You're officially on the convalescent list now, fella."

Mackenzie followed Hagan outside, heading to early mess before he fed the patients. Moments later a familiar voice bellowed from the bay of the ward:

"Don't expect *me* to call you sir, shavetail," Sergeant Major Jay Kinney said. "I *trained* you. Hell, I was busting caps against Yellow Bear's Northern Cheyenne while you were still on Ma's milk."

Kinney swaggered toward the bed and seemed unperturbed by the shocking change in Seth Carlson. The visitor's blustering bravado implied that he was completely unimpressed by living legends.

"Hell you gawping at? You *did* know I drew orders to this shithole, didn't you?"

Seth nodded. "I heard. Corey . . . Corey mentioned it."

"Better get those heels together, mister. I'm your new top sergeant for the Third Regiment. Back in the harness after kickin' all you turds around at the Point. Well, don't get salty on me, Soldier Blue. I'm still meaner'n a badger in a barrel. I may be twice your age, but by-God I can knock your dick into the dirt."

It was only a glimmer of a grin. But seeing it on the younger man's face made Kinney toss back his head and laugh. It echoed through the ward.

"Pipe down!" a disgruntled patient in the far corner complained. "This is a hospital, rank don't matter here."

"Augh! In a pig's ass, you malingering civilians!" Kinney roared. "This here is a foofaraw house, and I come to plant my carrot. Drop your trapdoors, we'll start with the volunteers."

A long moment's shocked silence, and then the few men scattered around the ward burst out laughing as one.

"You Company Q slackers won't be haw-hawing when it finally dawns on you I am a truly crazy-by-thunder sonofabitch who is going to unscrew your head and shit in it. Cowards to the rear, laddiebucks! There's no glory in peace! Augh!"

More laughter. But abruptly the grin deserted Kinney's face. He surprised Seth by stepping close to the bed and sitting on the edge. His voice quieted, lost its jocular edge, took on the old authority of West Point.

"You lissenup, sprout. I'm here to tell you the truth about Ruth. The pus-guts and paper collars who run this man's Army from their desks in Washington have got plans for you. Big plans. Pretty damn quick, things're gunna be a-hummin ten ways a second."

Seth turned to look at the older man. "What's that supposed to mean?"

"It means what it means, boyo. The Army has got plenty of enemies besides the Injin lovers. There's them in Congress thinks there shouldn't even *be* a standing Army, though I say, what else is America going to do with her common criminals? Anyway, now here *you* are. All of a sudden you're a damn symbol—a symbol the War Department plans on milking for all it's worth."

"Top, you sure are one for taking the long way over the hill."

"That right? Who *wouldn't* be a soldier? Just chew on this for now: You're in a queer position. Never mind that you're still frying size, you're all at once a damn popular hero. Truth is, you've been under hellacious fire and acquitted yourself well. But you're also still a greenhorn, there's a thousand little tricks you'll be needing to know."

"Needing to know for what?"

"You got wax in your ears? I told you, you'll twig the game soon enough. And when you do, make sure you tell them you want an old Indian campaigner assigned to your unit, somebody who ain't fresh from the tit."

"Them? Spell it out. And *what* damn unit?"

But Kinney stood up, shook his head. "You'll see."

"No I won't."

"Why the hell not?"

"Because I'm resigning my commission."

Kinney watched him for perhaps ten heartbeats, scrutinizing him with the same eagle eyes that used to search his person for loose threads and unbuttoned pockets.

"Pah! No you aren't."

"The hell I'm not. I already made up my mind to do it."

"No you aren't," Kinney repeated with conviction. "I know you, tadpole, I've seen you when the pressure's on. And I've got a gut hunch. Your kind is cut out to do the thing that matters. And the thing that matters here is staying and doing. You'll stay, and by the bleeding Christ, you'll do."

"I'm quitting."

"Horseshit. 'Sides, what's the point? Whatever you plan on rabbiting from, it won't go away when you quit the Army. Believe this old war-horse, it just goes with you."

Kinney bent down, gripped Seth's arm. When he spoke, his voice was barely above a whisper.

"*You* didn't kill her, Seth, the goddamn Innuns did. You and Corey Bryce are the most squared-away officers I ever trained. And I'm going to help you give a few red Arabs a comeuppance they ain't never going to forget."

Chapter 19

"Here's the part tickles me most," Charles Longstreet said. "Listen: 'Those who spin the familiar tale of the Noble Savage cite, as proof these rustic gut-eaters possess souls, the care most tribes vest in preparing their dead for the afterlife. Yet, more german—'"

"Germane," Bischoff corrected him.

"'—more germane to note what any red tribe will casually do to the remains of other tribes. A Mandan, for example, will tear down the funeral scaffold of a Cheyenne as casually as a bear will rip open a rotted log in search of insects. For in truth, an aboriginal is capable only of superstition, not enlightened faith, and superstition can bring down a civilization as surely as the plague. No people capable of enlightened faith could slaughter a priest so calmly as the renegade criminals who attacked Mater Dolorosa.'"

Longstreet lowered his copy of the *Tucson Register* and looked across his desk at Trilby and Bischoff.

"That's a lode! The mealy-mouth reformers are forever harping on how God has a place in heaven for the nigger and the Indian. Next thing you know, they'll be baptizing horses."

Longstreet realized his cigar had gone out and laid it aside. He raised the paper again, shook it, let his eye fall farther down the narrow columns.

" 'History is cruel to those who scorn her. Let they who decry spending money on the Army reflect instead on the price of their craven thrift. Better an ounce of prevention now than a pound of cure later. The thoughtful citizen cannot but doubt the patriotism of those who blindly champion Chingachgook and Uncas while it is the daily heroes like Lieutenant Seth Carlson who must bear the brunt of this seditious sentimentalism.' "

Robert Trilby's eyes showed a glint of amused admiration as they cut to Bischoff. " 'Seditious sentimentalism'? I'd say *that's* firing live ammo."

" 'What oft was thought, but ne'er so well expressed,' eh?" Longstreet threw in.

Nat Bischoff acknowledged the compliments with a gracious nod.

"I spoke with the other members of the committee," Longstreet said. "Needless to say, they are all quite pleased. Both of you gentlemen did a crackerjack job. Letters are pouring in to the newspaper office. Even better, there's already serious talk about leaving the garrison at Fort Grant right where it is."

Longstreet's Mercantile was the only two-story building on Silver Street. From the upstairs office the entire street was visible, also part of the unsavory section known as Riverbend, where the Santa Cruz River skirted town to the west. The roar of a crowd went up from that direction, and Trilby crossed to the window. He glanced to the left and saw a huge throng gathered around the bull-baiting pit.

"Sounds like the groundlings are well-amused," Bischoff said.

Trilby nodded. "That's the sound of money."

"Speaking of money," Longstreet said, "have you . . . made arrangements for the children yet?"

Trilby's bluff, weather-seamed face turned from the window to stare at his employer. "The children? But Charlie, you know selling Indians into slavery is illegal."

Longstreet, busy relighting his cigar, only snorted. "I never knew that to slow down your man Aragon. I'm told he's thick as thieves with the Comancheros."

Trilby maintained a poker face, volunteering nothing. After all, it was none of Longstreet's mix. The Comancheros made good profits by acquiring captives from the plains Indians, trading whiskey and weapons for them, then selling them into prostitution and other forced servitude in Old and New Mexico. Aragon had indeed already entered into negotiations with them concerning the Apache children.

Bischoff had mentioned the four missing children in his article. But no one had told him that two of them were Jemez Grayeyes's siblings. Trilby was convinced, however, that Jemez himself already knew about it, or soon would. He was also convinced the crime would not stand, that trouble was surely coming. Well, let it come. That was the point of taking them in the first place. Jemez would respond, and soon; the question was, how?

"The amorous Mr. Aragon," Bischoff said, a humorous inflection in his tone. "He who tiptoes up behind the buffalo." Bischoff's eyes met Trilby's. "I'm just curious. Do you suppose the cows ever even notice he's back there?"

"'A man's reach should exceed his grasp,'" Trilby rejoined, "'or what's a heaven for?'"

All three men enjoyed a good laugh, Longstreet so carried away that his cigar dropped from his mouth and he was forced to hawk up phlegm into his handkerchief.

Outside, another crowd roar from Riverbend. It seemed to sober Longstreet and remind him he was acting like a silly schoolboy, not a civic leader and head of the Tucson Committee.

He looked squarely at Trilby. "The committee was pleased with Sunday's events," he repeated. "Still, one question troubles several of us. Will Hays Munro see which way the wind sets and clear out, leaving the job to someone less hostile to the businessman?"

Trilby said, "It's still too early to call that one. He's surely smart enough to know he *could* have been killed. A word to the wise."

"Well," Longstreet said, "let's hope that, even if the Indian Bureau doesn't remove him for this, he'll be sensible enough to pull up stakes on his own. If not?" He shrugged. "If not, it would be a damn pitiable tragedy if something happened to that teacher."

"I interviewed her for my story," Bischoff said. "She's quite a looker. Is it true that she's more than just Munro's employee? I know they share a house together."

"She's damned easy to look at," Trilby agreed. "I couldn't tell you, though, if the old boy is poking her. She could certainly do better, although white men are scarce out her way."

"The American people," Longstreet said, "were mad enough to grease hell with war paint when that girl was killed in the New Mexico Territory, that—that—"

"Jeanette Bryce," Bischoff said.

"Her. If this Kathleen Barton ended up the same way, the public outcry would be tremendous. Hays Munro would be left riding the grub line."

Trilby nodded. "Better just wait and see for now. A 'public outcry' might end up destroying the grass just to get at the weeds. I got a feeling Hays Munro *and* the lovely Miss Barton are taking a hard look at their lives."

The official residence provided for the Indian agent at Mater Dolorosa was simple but quite comfortable by frontier standards. A single-story house of cottonwood logs chinked with adobe had been built in a slight hollow to blunt the fierce windstorms. The ramada shading the front of the house was no mere decoration—not one tree broke the sandy expanse that passed for a yard, though an irrigated and carefully tended kitchen garden grew in the shade of the west wall. Two small rooms under a slope-off partition behind the house were provided to house the reservation teacher. However, these rarely received any breeze, and for most of the year were unbearably hot until late at night, after the desert had cooled.

A small but sturdy pole corral behind the house held a team of blood bays provided for the agent's personal use. A mesquite-branch shelter near the corral housed a buckboard, harnesses, and trace chains, as well as one old saddle and bridle and an iron drum filled with grain.

Kathleen Barton had learned the grim truth long ago: Thanks to the stifling heat, which lingered until late fall, the only hours she could reasonably hope for sleep were between midnight and sunup. She and Hays had gradually settled into the after-dinner habits of old acquaintances, sharing the front parlor for several hours each evening. Two windows opened toward the east and often caught a cool breeze, and the room was pleasant enough with its rose-pattern carpet, walnut sideboard, and comfortable crewel-work armchairs.

Some nights Hays would hitch the buckboard and they would ride out to visit some of the Apache families. And usually they would pass at least one hour taking turns reading to each other. Recently they had begun reading Thackeray's *Vanity Fair*, and both found it engrossing enough that they seldom missed a night's reading. Tonight, however, Hays was far too angry and preoccupied to enjoy literature. For the latest *Tucson Register* had printed Nat Bischoff's story on the Mater Dolorosa raid. Now Munro turned up the wick of a coal-oil lamp and read out loud the parts that disgusted him most, his compelling voice pitched an octave higher than usual from anger.

" 'There is no question that the marauders were Apaches. But in the confusion of the attack, it is impossible to say which Indian fired the fatal bullet that killed Father Montoya. One fact, however, only a fool would deny: This attack was symbolic, a direct assault on the U.S. government's sovereign authority. And since it appears to have been planned and mounted from the reservation itself, it casts serious doubt on the appeasement policies of the Indian Bureau and church-appointed agents like Hays Munro. It matters little how honorable one's intentions may be if those intentions issue from a false and sentimental view of the red man's inherent nature.' Bosh!"

Munro removed his reading monocle and looked at Kathleen, who was seated at a little escritoire composing a letter to her parents. The right side of his face was still puffy and grape-colored from the blow that had knocked him out.

"This Nat Bischoff is a Janus-faced liar working for that damned Tucson ring! That deceitful scoundrel! My dear, *you* were present when he interviewed me. Indeed, I recall that your hair was unbraided and he couldn't keep his eyes off you. You know that I insisted at least one of the attackers was Mexican, another an American or European. And I didn't see the shooting, but you did. You *told* Bischoff you thought the murderer wasn't an Indian, I heard you. Both of us told him this was the work of outsiders, and he pretended to believe us."

Kathleen nodded. They had both been impressed, too, when he asked her to translate while he questioned several of the Apaches who had been present during the raid. Not one had been quoted in the article.

"I know," she said. "But I can't swear it wasn't an Indian who did the shooting. A lot of guns were going off, it was all so confusing, I—"

"Of course it was. We were both scared witless. But don't you see? This entire story is a deliberate and malicious whitewash! We are not just talking about the usual journalistic garbling and misquoting. This story is a deliberate fabrication, and there are vested interests behind it."

Kathleen didn't know what to say. Hays was enraged by the sinister underlying plot—she, in contrast, was still numb from the direct consequences of the attack. The property damage had been bad enough: stock killed, the common room shot up, the cook house partially burned, gardens trampled. But far more important, at least to her, the marauding force had made off with four children. Besides the Grayeyes children, they had grabbed another boy and girl around Miguelito's age, maybe five or six years old: Kato and Rosario of the Dragoon Mountain Apaches, some of the most recent to trickle in to the reservation.

As required, Hays had filed a complete and detailed report with the Army and the U.S. Marshal in San Manuel. Kathleen knew that was the end of it. No white man was going to waste time or energy tracking down missing Indian children, not even children who were wards of the federal government. The soldiers had, however, staked out the passes and water holes along the common escape routes at the borders of the reservation. This move was designed to reassure the white settlers that the rez was under control.

"If Bischoff thinks he'll get away with this," Munro said, "he's even more stupid than he appears. It's one thing to create 'heroes' out of hapless soldiers, as he's doing with this lad Seth Carlson; another thing altogether to represent criminal interests under the guise of reporting frontier news. I've already drafted a formal letter of protest. Copies will be sent to Congress, the Indian Bureau, the War Department, and major newspapers throughout the country."

His words sent a little prickle of alarm down Kathleen's spine. "Hays? Are you sure that's wise?"

He glanced at her sharply, his thin, slope-shouldered body leaning forward in the chair. "What do you mean?"

"You know how you sometimes regret those huffy letters, once you calm down. Besides, as you yourself said, why push when something won't move?"

"Fair enough, my dear. But you can't *know* if the thing will move until you at least give it an exploratory nudge."

She nodded, knowing he was right, yet fearing the result of that nudge.

"I'm going to walk outside for a bit," she told him, "take some fresh air."

The night was cool against her skin. A three-quarter moon shone from a clear, star-shot sky, bathing the sand in an eerie blue glow that made everything seem painted. She drifted across the barren yard, the ground still warm through the soles of her shoes.

Again Kathleen thought about the missing children. She had heard of the Comanchero slave traders, knew something —from talking with the reservation Apaches—of the degradations those children faced.

Socorro Grayeyes . . . the girl's quiet defiance had worked at Kathleen, the rebellion at times an almost welcome sign of human spirit in this place where no joy lived, nor hope that it ever would. And Miguelito—again Kathleen saw him in church, his legs swinging on the bench, his eyes fascinated by the embroidered silk of Father Montoya's stole. For a moment Kathleen also recalled her fears as Jemez Grayeyes led those children up out of the hidden arroyo to meet her secretly at the edge of the reservation.

I'll be coming back for them.

She thought of his pistol, turned butt forward on his right hip. The cold, nimbus-gray eyes that gave his clan its name.

You are afraid of me?

I am afraid of all men.

Sometimes, even being afraid won't save you.

What had he meant by that? It made her think of the fear she had tasted just now when Hays told her about the letters he was writing. Jemez scared her, and Hays scared her when he talked about fighting back.

One of the bays abruptly nickered, and a voice whispered distinctly in Spanish, *"Callete, caballo!* Hush!"

She drew up short, her breath snagging in her throat. Her first impulse was to turn and run back toward the house. But by now her eyes had adjusted to the moonlit night, and she thought she recognized the figure ahead of her, standing near the mesquite-branch shelter.

"Victorio? *Qué haces aqui?"*

The Mescalero youth started, almost dropping the saddle he had been about to fling over one of the bays.

"Tanta Kathleen!"

In the luminous moonlight she could see the new scabs forming on his skinny chest—legacies of his hard tumble to the ground when the raiders had shot his pony out from under him.

"What are you doing here?" she demanded again, though indeed she could see easily enough.

He finished adjusting the pad, threw the saddle on and cinched the girth.

"I am taking this horse," he said defiantly. "They killed my pony. They have stolen four of our people. I am riding to tell Jemez what I know."

"You'll do no such thing. Jemez can hear things without your help." After a brief pause: "What do you know?"

"I know what the white-eyes said in the newspaper. White men piss down your back and tell you it's raining. I know what kind of horse the turncoat Juan Aragon rides. And I know the hair-face Robert Trilby's horse, too."

"Victorio! You know I can't let you steal a horse! And don't you know there are soldiers surrounding the reservation?"

"Soldiers! An Apache can steal a soldier's groundsheet from under him without waking him. I know how to get around the blue-blouses."

"Tio Hays is very angry right now. This is no time to push him, he will punish you severely."

Victorio shrugged and gave one last tug to the latigos. "So? White-eyes always punish us. Punishment is all they know."

"Victorio! Unsaddle that horse!"

"No." He looked at her with that trademark Apache defiance in his eyes, but otherwise held his face impassive, as the warriors did. Only women and squaw-men like the Poncas showed their feelings in their faces like white men.

"What if I try to stop you by force? Will you hurt me?"

He was silent for perhaps ten heartbeats.

"No," he said finally, his voice softening. "I like you, Tanta Kathleen. But if you stop me now, I will go tomorrow or the next day. I will go if I have to take a mule from the common corral. Or I will leave on foot and steal the first horse that is for the taking. I *will* go to Jemez."

"So there will be more trouble," she said bitterly. "More fighting and killing."

"Yes. Of course. We did not send out the first soldier. The white-eyes did. We only sent out the second."

The wind gusted hard, whipping up a spray of gravel to pelt their skin. She looked at the boy's scrawny chest and determined face. She looked at the desolate land around them, looked beyond to the dark silhouette of the sierras. Again she saw Socorro's face, frightened but defiant. And she saw Father Montoya, sprawled dead in the tacky pool made by his own blood.

"Then go," she finally told him. "I will talk to Tio Hays and do what I can for you. But *ten cuidado!*"

"I will be careful," he promised, mounting from the Indian side.

She watched him for a long time in the silver-white moonlight, bearing southwest at an easy lope. Then he disappeared suddenly as he entered a draw, and she was alone with her fear and the wolf-howl of the wind.

Chapter 20

Soon enough Seth found out why Jay Kinney had dropped so many hints about "big plans."

The odd little delegation appeared in the bay of the hospital ward an hour after breakfast: Colonel Woodrow Denton, commanding officer of Fort Bates; Kinney himself, the new regimental sergeant major; George Henning, a senior civilian administrator for the U.S. War Department; and Second Lieutenant Abe Worley, Henning's military aide. They were accompanied by an enlisted Army artist named Ladislaw from the Archives Department, who specialized in quick sketches of important occasions. The Army had its own photographers now, but Henning wished to accommodate the civilian magazines back East which were clamoring for sketches of Seth Carlson.

Seth was composing a short letter of resignation to the Department of the Army when a familiar voice abruptly claimed his attention:

"Top of the morning, *sir!*" Kinney sang out from the wide door at the head of the ward.

The sergeant major turned so the others couldn't see him and scowled a war face at the supine officer, letting him know it was hard duty to "sir" his young ass.

"Hell, it's ol' Dead-Eye," Walt Mackenzie whispered to Seth, frowning when he spotted the C.O. "I ain't in no mood for that yack. Anybody asks, I suddenly got me a bad case of the droppins. I'll be out back at the latrine."

Mackenzie put his banjo on an empty bed and scuttled out the side door. Seth swung his legs off the bed and absently straightened his shirt, watching the others cross to his bed. He showed far less interest than did the other patients, who gaped in outright amazement at sight of the administrator. The civilian was astonishingly tall and rotund, dressed in an immaculate white linen suit, fancy brown kid boots, and a white pith helmet. Lieutenant Worley trailed behind him carrying a folding canvas camp stool.

"So here's the man of the hour at last," the giant boomed in a hearty basso profundo voice that made the coyote pup beside the bed whimper in fright.

The artist, too, carried a canvas stool. Without a word, he opened it up and sat down in the middle of the aisle, unfolding a sketchpad across his knees. The speaker gripped Seth's right hand in a hamlike fist clammy with sweat.

"Lieutenant Carlson," Denton said, "Mr. George Henning of the War Department. He just made a long journey from Washington to visit with you."

Worley unfolded Henning's camp stool, then hovered in the background, constantly on the verge of getting in the way as he strained to be useful. Seth nodded at Henning. Kinney caught his eye and winked. Henning eased down onto the stool with a dramatic sigh, buttocks oozing over the edges.

"It's both a great pleasure and a great honor, Lieutenant Carlson," Henning assured him. "America is extremely grateful to you."

Ladislaw caught his lower lip between his teeth, studying Seth's face intently as he sketched. Seth watched Denton self-consciously turn until his left profile was presented squarely to the artist. At first, after Denton's wife, Louise, had been killed with the other women during the Sunday Stroll, there had been widespread sympathy for Denton, even among those who most disliked him. But as Seth's national prominence grew, Denton's quiet grief gave way to showy, blustery talk about revenge—usually when newspapermen were around, and lately they often were.

As a commander, Seth considered Denton a little tin-god martinet incapable of distinguishing sadism from good discipline. On the hottest days he ordered his troops to form up in ranks with their blouses buttoned. Even when there was no enemy within a hundred miles, troopers in the field were forced to march or ride in full battle rigs with full belts of ammo. He was constantly having men lashed, their heads shaved, the letter of their petty offenses branded into their skin. As a result of such brutality and suffering, one-third of the recruits at Fort Bates took what was known as French leave—they deserted.

"In fact," Henning added, opening a large tow wallet in his lap and removing a sheaf of papers, "many Americans are so grateful to you they're actually petitioning the Army to reward you. So many, soldier, that the Army has gladly obliged them."

He handed the papers to Seth. The young officer assumed, at first, he was receiving yet another award citation. The Army had already cited him for extreme heroism in the face of overwhelming enemy fire. But Seth had quietly refused the medals—he had been so spirit-broken, so full of self-loathing, he couldn't bear the sight of them. Despite the genuine respect of those around him, the act of killing the post sweetheart while he somehow survived had left him feeling like a freak intruder among real soldiers. But refusing those medals only seemed to ennoble him further in the eyes of soldiers and civilians alike. The medals were tactfully withdrawn, but his right to wear them was entered in his permanent service record.

Henning was not, however, handing him more award citations. This was a letter of promotion: a brevet appointment to the rank of lieutenant colonel, certified by the congressional seal. Seth would assume this temporary rank and authority while holding his permanent commission as a lieutenant, accruing time in grade toward permanent promotion.

"You and Iron Butt Custer." Henning beamed. "The Boy Wonders of Michigan!"

Kinney didn't like what he read in Seth's eyes. Before the young officer could speak up, he said hastily, "This promotion is more than just a personal honor, *Colonel* Carlson. It's also a practical move by the War Department."

"Just so, just so," Henning agreed. "The rank of lieutenant colonel, as you of course know, is a major-command rank. Suitable for the commander of a battalion or even a small regiment. And that's precisely what the Army has in mind: a new unit to serve as the spearhead of our Indian-fighting regiments. An elite fighting organization to be known as the First Mountain Company. And we'd like you to command it."

Henning paused and watched Seth as if the lieutenant were supposed to care. Seth said nothing. Henning read his quiet indifference as attentive curiosity.

"In the beginning the First Mountain Company will actually be only a platoon. Forty sharpshooters, a few guides and scouts and interpreters. An experiment, really, in taking the fight directly to the Indians in their farthermost hiding places."

Denton, through all this, had been paying close attention to the artist. He shifted around in case the man might want to include the leg that had been partially paralyzed from a Civil War wound. Now he spoke up.

"The point is to break up the bands against themselves. Injuns are so damned hard to chase because they keep dividing and subdividing, setting up new trails to follow. Eventually, they take to the high country in small bands and the cavalry is forced to give up pursuit. Then the bands reunite after the spring melt."

"That's where the First Mountain Company comes in," Henning said. "Instead of giving up the chase, the platoon will trail the groups to their very mountain strongholds. The First Mountain Company won't ride the bigger American cavalry horses, but tough little Indian pintos. American horses are spoiled by grain, but Indian ponies can survive a hard winter by nibbling on bark."

In spite of himself, Seth was paying more and more attention. The nubbin of an idea was forming. Kinney seemed to notice the new glint of interest in the younger man's eyes.

"This new platoon will carry no Gatlings," the sergeant major said. "The carriages are too damned clumsy for high country. Each gun requires four horses. Half the time you end up unhitching them and dragging them over something by hand. Same thing with the twenty-four-pound Napoleon cannons. You—that is, those in the unit—would carry only powder, pig lead, molds for casting bullets. That's lighter than lugging full ammo belts all the time, and you won't have to worry about the sand and the cold weather ruining the bullets. The men would be armed with carbines, pistols, sabers, knives only."

"Cross out the sabers," Seth said automatically. "Useless weight and they're a noise risk."

Kinney grinned. "No cheese knives. Right, *sir!*"

Henning flashed an ear-to-ear smile. "That's the spirit, stout lad. Personally, I'm an admirer of General Sherman's philosophy: Do a thing by halves and it ends up half-assed done. After what the heathens put you through, soldier, I can understand why you'd be breathing fire to put at them."

"*If* I was to command such a unit," Seth said, "I would not let a personal vendetta against Indians drive me or my men. Nor would I be interested in hunting down any and every group of redskins that rustled a few head of cattle. I'd want the hard cases only, the bands following the worst renegades. I'd want the criminals, the killers."

"Hell!" Denton said. "They're *all* hostiles to a soldier."

Seth leveled a cool glance at his superior. "If you really believe that, Colonel, you should've remembered it when I came to you requesting more guards for the Sunday Stroll."

Denton's face flushed. Henning, ever the capable diplomat, smoothly interceded. Clearly, he had deliberately been holding this next enticement in reserve.

"The criminal faction is precisely what the War Department has in mind. Eventually you would move your men farther west into Apacheria, route out the bands under Geronimo and that crowd. For now, though, you would remain here at Fort Bates while forming up the unit. And then you would use this post as a staging area to launch an inaugural campaign against Comanches and the Kaitsenko war leader, Eagle on His Journey."

Seth nodded, allowing nothing to show in his face. The Kaitsenko was a Kiowa warrior society made up of the tribe's most elite fighters. In concert with the Comanche band under Hairy Wolf, they had terrorized Texas and the New Mexico Territory, eluding even the highly respected Texas Rangers. And as half the people in America knew by now, Eagle on His Journey's band had been along for the Sunday Stroll massacre.

"What do you say, saddle soldier?" Henning said. "Hairy Wolf was killed by Mexicans just south of Juarez, and his band has scattered. But the Kaitsenko are on a rampage. Are you ready to give those young testicles a real pounding? The entire nation is praying you'll raise a war whoop. When you survived that skirmish, it left a feeling in the air, a certain sense of expectation. The average citizen wants to see justice done and figures you're the man for the job."

Seth debated, feeling Kinney's anxious eyes on him. The situation was clear enough. As Kinney had once said, the Army had plenty of enemies in Congress and elsewhere. No veteran campaigner would be fool enough to think Seth and forty sharpshooters could make much of a dent in the Indian problem. But the potential gain to the Army's image was enormous. "Send Seth!" the country was crying, clamoring for a real-life hero to tackle the Red Peril. And what more dramatically satisfying enemy than the Indian who led the Sunday Stroll massacre?

In one sense, Seth knew that his recent decision to leave the Army was the easy thing to do. But again, Kinney was right: It would leave him with the rest of his life to relive that horrible Sunday. On the other hand, immersion in this hard campaign would leave him with no luxury for rumination. This was a chance to occupy his mind and body doing what he'd been trained to do. It would be a hard fight just to survive—and if he did lose the fight, what of that? No more wide-awake hours just before dawn, feeling his insides torn apart as he saw again Jeanette's eyes, begging him, begging him . . .

He met Kinney's eyes. "There's no glory in peace," the sergeant major reminded him.

"If I were to accept this command," Seth said, "could I pick my own men?"

"Of course," Henning said. "I assume you'd want volunteers?"

Seth nodded, watching Denton now. "Among others I'd want Walt Mackenzie. And the sergeant major here."

"Walt Mackenzie?" Denton looked puzzled. "The hell for? The man has to squat to piss, he's worthless with a weapon."

"You don't know your men, Colonel, so you end up wasting their talents. Mackenzie is a first-rate soldier. I want him along, he'll ride as our combat orderly."

"Then you'll have him," Henning assured him, shooting a warning at Denton when he was about to object to this insubordination. The C.O. shrugged off his resentment. Clearly he, too, had his orders from high places: make sure Seth Carlson accepts this new assignment.

"So . . . do we have a commander for the First?" Henning pressed, his tone cajoling.

Seth let his attention focus out the windows. "You say the unit would eventually be posted to the Arizona Territory?"

"That's an affirmative. The Apaches have that sector paralyzed. This priest-killing at Mater Dolorosa has the public outraged."

"Not the ones that don't like Mexicans," Kinney said, but the rest ignored him.

Good, Seth thought. The Department of Arizona was the end of the earth, so far as the Army was concerned. The farther away from here, the better.

"I'll do it," he said.

Henning stood up in an impressive burst of energy.

"Outstanding! I hear you've a fondness for poetry. Do you know this American fellow, Whitman?"

Seth said nothing, but Henning needed no encouragement.

"There's a nice bit appropriate to this occasion:

"Beat! beat! drums!—blow! bugles! blow!
Make no parley—stop for no expostulation,
Mind not the timid—mind not the weeper or prayer
Mind not—mind not . . ."

Henning faltered, looked sheepish. "Thought I had it by
the tail, but it got away."

" 'Mind not the old man beseeching the young man,' "
Seth finished for him, his voice deadpan.

Henning cocked his head, genuine admiration sparking in
his eyes. "Just so, just so. You know Whitman?"

"He never bought me a beer."

"Fuck him, then," Kinney said, and Denton was the only
one present who didn't laugh.

Trooper Mackenzie peeked through the side door, and
Seth gave him the high sign.

"Gentlemen," he called out, "with all due respect, Lieutenant Carlson is still under Dr. Hagan's orders. He's got to
rest up now. I'll have to ask y'all to leave."

"Of course," Henning said. "Of course. We'll stop by
again before we return, talk over a few more details . . .
Only, that's *Colonel* Carlson now, Corporal."

When they were gone, Mackenzie looked at Seth and said,
"Jesus! Colonel Carlson. We got some hard riding ahead, I
take it?"

Seth met his eyes. "You asked for it, trooper. Just remember that. You're free to cut your picket pin at any time, and
that'll go for every man in the unit."

"I *will* remember it," Mackenzie said, picking up his banjo
and settling it under his arm. "Man likes to have a choice."

"Not always," Seth replied in a voice just above a whisper.
"Not always."

Chapter 21

"Gentlemen, I believe in mixing scientific fact with plain speaking. And in that spirit, I submit that the American people are being seriously flummoxed on this Indian question. The Quakers and other sentimentalists would change their tune in a hurry if they ever had to pull an arrow out of their sitter."

Laughter bubbled all around Corey Bryce. On the third Tuesday of each month, a fraternal association calling themselves Americans United for Survival met in a red-granite building at the end of Washington's Virginia Avenue, where Georgetown Channel curved past deserted lots once chockablock with Union Army tents. Shortly after reporting to the capital from New Mexico Territory, Corey had received a cordial invitation to attend the group's meetings. Only after repeated prodding by General Ferris Ablehard, however, did he muster up enough interest to visit. Now he sat on a crowded bench, pinched between Ablehard and a civilian friend of the general's, a hearty, hail-fellow type named Eric Hupenbecker.

Ansel Drouillard, the guest speaker, acknowledged the laughter with a saturnine smile.

"But gentlemen, proponents of the Noble Savage theory sedulously avoid any facts. Too much 'milk of human kindness' can choke a man *or* a country. Yes, to give the devil his due: There *is* a certain 'nobility' to the red aboriginals, just as there is to any animal in nature. The Creator made no mistakes when fashioning His creatures. However, the point the Noble Savage zealots fail to grasp was best immortalized by Dr. Johnson in a remark to Boswell: 'I believe in subordination, sir, as the proper condition of mankind.' The jackleg philosophers who abound today deny God's Great Chain of Being in a headlong rush to mongrelize heaven."

Corey watched Drouillard, a professor of Natural History at nearby Georgetown College, turn to a chart on an easel beside his lectern. It showed two skulls in cross section, one labeled CAUCASOID, the other ALGONQUIN.

"Gentlemen, never before in human history has man been so close to solving the essential mysteries of his own existence. Through enlightened science we have finally 'dragged Diana from her car,' as Poe phrased it. Right now the new and revolutionary ideas of Charles Darwin are being rigorously tested in the experimental laboratories of Germany and England, where overzealous Christian piety has not stifled the quest for knowledge as it has, unfortunately, in our own great nation. And what, if I may be allowed to paint for a moment with wide strokes of the brush, is one important upshot of this new experimentation?"

Drouillard paused dramatically, gazing out over the hundred or so men—many in uniform—obscured by a blue pall of tobacco smoke.

"I could merely repeat the physiological facts I've already reported about the diminished capacity of the aboriginal brain. Instead, let me close by quoting a popular journalist of our day, Mr. Nat Bischoff."

Hearing the name, Corey felt warm blood creep up the back of his neck. His lips tightened in a grim, determined slit. Whether it was true or not, he suddenly felt as if every man in the room was staring at him.

"Gentlemen, Bischoff is no scientist. Yet he turned up a choice nugget of knowledge when he wrote this: 'In truth, an aboriginal is capable only of superstition, not enlightened faith, and superstition can bring down a civilization as surely as the plague.' Preaching gospel to savages is worse than casting pearls to swine—swine won't scalp you in your sleep!

"The Indian lovers cry out that the red man can be Christianized, taught to make higher moral choices, to value thrift, hard work, and the concepts of private property and severalty of the land. I wouldn't stake one copper cent on such flummery! Science has proved beyond question that the aboriginal brain—like that of all races, white or colored—has been purposely fashioned by a knowing God to suit His sometimes obscure purposes. As soldiers who lead, as responsible citizens, you gentlemen need to remember that the decisions our government reaches today about the red man will affect generations to come. Will they admire us for having the courage to ensure the survival of the great white promise, or will they revile us as cowards who were afraid to act while action was still possible—and thus, squandered the potential glory of empire?"

With that, Ansel Drouillard abruptly ended his talk. Enthusiastic applause and calls of "Hear, hear!" filled the meeting room. Now the men slowly adjourned to the foyer and formed up in small groups to discuss the lecture.

"Glad you could make it this evening, m'boy," Ablehard told Corey. "Many of our members have been inquiring after you."

"Quite so," the civilian named Hupenbecker said. Like Corey, he was well-knit, with an athlete's ruddy complexion. "Matter of fact, your being here is a bit like having a second guest of honor."

Corey, not sure what to make of that, decided to let it pass with a polite nod.

Ablehard held his broad-brimmed campaign hat, toying with the hook-and-eye that kept the brim bent back. "Say, shavetail, what'd you think of the talk?"

"It was interesting, the business with skull size. This Drouillard seems to know his facts."

"*I'll* tell the world! It was a jim-dandy lecture," Hupenbecker said with enthusiasm. He was an investor in a newly formed western-based land company that had recently taken the federal government to court in efforts to open up the huge tracts of Indian grant land to white settlement.

"Here's one for you," Hupenbecker said. "Upon signing a new treaty, a Quaker Indian agent and a Sioux chief are celebrating by traveling across the country in a Pullman car. They're accompanied by the agent's mother, wife, and daughter. After two days on the train, the shocked matron takes her boy aside. 'Son,' she tells him, 'do you realize that savage has been enjoying carnal knowledge with your wife and daughter?' 'Oh, don't worry, Mother,' the Quaker answers proudly, 'it's a tough treaty—he can't touch *you*.' "

It didn't strike Corey as particularly funny, but the other men laughed with gusto, Ablehard even declaring it a "lulu." Rather than come off as a curmudgeon, Corey laughed, too. Hupenbecker slapped him between the shoulder blades.

"Good to see you joshing, soldier. You've looked too serious all evening."

"Now listen up, mister," Ablehard said, "because my friend Eric speaks straight-arrow. That's why I've been after you to stop by one of our meetings. We're not just a political organization with a serious agenda, we're also a club."

"Friends, having a good time among other friends who share similar ideas," Hupenbecker said.

Suddenly, Corey realized these two were selling him a bill of goods. But the pitch had been on before he even recognized it as such.

"As you can see," the general told his young aide, "many of us are military officers or civilian workers for the government, as Hupenbecker here used to do before he struck out on his own. So in a certain sense we have one common interest: We are working from the 'inside' to influence government and military policy."

"The main goal of our efforts," Hupenbecker said, "is a rapid, effective solution to the Indian question. We want our government committed to an all-out postbellum Indian campaign. No Indian reservations, no Dry Tortugas, no 'nation within a nation.' We want the heathen aboriginals exterminated—nothing less—once and for all for the good of America's future."

Ablehard said, "How do you feel about our mission, Corey?"

He shrugged. "I'm not much for politics, sir," he said evasively. "That's my father's bailiwick."

"We ask," Hupenbecker said, "because quite frankly you'd be a prominent addition to our group. You're pleasing to look at, well-spoken, and most importantly, you'd be crackerjack as a fund-raiser. Your name is prominent and would generate immense sympathy because of your personal suffering at the hands of savages."

"Wha'd'you say, lad? Will you nail your colors to our mast?"

Corey looked at his superior, then at Hupenbecker. "I'll give it some thought," he promised.

"Good man!" Ablehard winked. "Eric and I plan on doing a little hog ranching this evening. Have you changed your mind yet?"

Corey shook his head. "Not yet."

"Suit yourself. But do think about the invitation to join our little association."

"And remember," Hupenbecker added, "no man alive has a better right than you to see the Indian wiped off the face of the earth."

Corey declined Ablehard's offer of a ride in his coach. He decided to walk until an available cab passed him. He followed Virginia Avenue southeast toward the lights at the heart of the city, his mind a riot of confused thoughts.

The damp November wind was raw with the promise of a hard winter just around the corner. Corey welcomed the slap to his senses, this clean air bracing him after the lethargic smoke and body warmth of the meeting hall. Slim silver flasks were fashionable with many of the single officers, and now Corey slid one out of the inside pocket of his tunic. The bourbon burned in a straight line to his belly, reminding him he hadn't eaten all day.

The street intersected with New Hampshire Avenue, and here began an even row of natural-gas street lamps. Corey stepped into a tobacconist's shop to purchase a few cigars. He had paid and was about to step outside again when he spotted the magazines, stacked up on a deal counter beside copies of the *Washington Post*.

On top was the latest issue of a popular new magazine called *Frontier America*. A highly romanticized sketch of Seth Carlson gazed off the front cover, under the huge scrollwork banner SEND SETH! But Corey had already seen the magazine —a copy showed up in his letter box earlier that morning, without benefit of postage or an address. So clearly, it had been hand-delivered, but by whom and why?

The article was about Seth's new promotion and the creation of the First Mountain Company. Corey's momentary resurgence of curiosity and suspicion again gave way to another onslaught of humiliation and rage. Without willing them to, his fingers opened the top magazine. He'd read them earlier, and now his eyes fell to the offending words as if they'd been printed in red to mock him forever.

For Corey Bryce, perhaps Fate's true victim in this oh-too-American tragedy, comes the emasculating sorrow of a man who can only sit and watch, helpless to influence the outcome, as cruel destiny destroys the woman he loves. Seth Carlson at least acted. Tragically, to be sure. But like a man he made his destiny, he did not merely observe it happening.

Blood throbbed hard in his palms as he threw the magazine back down and stepped outside to hail a hansom cab just then turning the corner. He gave the driver his address near West Potomac Park. Then, grateful for the solitude of darkness, he settled back into the tucked-and-pleated upholstery of the seat.

He slid his flask out and emptied it, lulled by the rhythmic *clop-clop* of shod hooves on cobblestones. But inevitably, the sound put him in mind of another cab ride, and memory's eyes recalled the steep and narrow streets of Albany. He saw Jeanette and Seth, eyes radiant as they recited poetry to each other. And with that memory came the realization, sharp and shockingly new to him: Seth and Jeanette had shared so much that he was never part of. All that time at Fort Bates, when he had been out in the field . . . after dark a man could easily sneak undetected from the bachelor officers' quarters to the Bryce quarters. . . .

Corey banished that thought before it got a good hold on him. But for the first time since the long numbness caused by Jeanette's death, he let himself admit it: He despised Seth Carlson. If not for killing Jeanette, then certainly for erecting a tasteless and cruel monument to his own glory on her bones. "Send Seth!" What the hell for? Better to send for the damn grave diggers—that glory-seeking sonofabitch *killed* Jeanette!

Corey seldom dreamed about what had happened. Not directly, but as if his mind were making only a sidelong glance to protect him. Then one night recently his mind failed to protect him, and a dream came dangerously close to the truth. He was riding by himself across a flat, baking alkali plain. He spotted a buzzard flying overhead, a bright blue swatch of cloth caught in its claw—the same color as Jeanette's best gown.

Is it? he asked himself in the dream. *Is it?* He rode hard, topped a long rise, then felt his stomach turn over: Below stood Seth Carlson straddling a grisly heap of unrecognizable remains, fanning the hammer of his service revolver as he emptied it into the slick, bloody mess. And as Corey bore closer, screaming the single word "No!" over and over, Carlson turned, met his eyes, smiled mockingly, and then unleashed the cavalry kill cry.

The cab hit a pothole and the driver swore at his horse, jolting Corey back to the present. The grief, like broken glass grinding in his gut, was replaced by a dull, pulsing anger. Hupenbecker's words from earlier returned to him, meaning far more now because they helped him focus this rage: *We want the heathen aboriginals eliminated—nothing less—once and for all for the good of America's future.*

Chapter 22

"Some say he is the white man's answer to Geronimo," Victorio said. "Indian bullets and arrows cannot find him."

"Geronimo fights like five men, little brother. But he cannot turn bullets into sand. Neither can this white-skin."

"It is what the people say, Jemez."

"People say many things, do they not? Each time a comet flashes overhead, someone plays the big Indian and claims credit for it. Geronimo will die, and this blue soldier, too, will die."

Jemez had already heard these stories from Jicarilla Apaches in northern Sonora who were part of the moccasin telegraph: the growing legend of the white-skin pony soldier with the powerful battle medicine. He was not impressed. Besides, he had vengeance on his mind, not white legends, as he and Victorio rode down out of the sierra, late in the Fall Moon, and headed for the Arizona Territory.

Jemez had loaned Victorio his buckskin, leaving the sorry

reservation nag to graze in the lush grass of a remote barranca south of the cave. At first, familiar landmarks were scarce in the open desert. They traveled by night, orienting themselves by the Always Star to the north. They crossed cracked alkali flats and broad soda plains, raised plumes of gray lava dust skirting the volcanoes east of Cibuta in Old Mexico. The route took them past basalt formations, then mile after mile of prickly pear and the spiked cactus called Spanish bayonet. The land changed gradually as they rode farther north. Rolling scrubland alternated with saltbush and soapweed and creosote and endless expanses of purple sage and dull chaparral.

In the Sonoran Desert of the southwestern Arizona Territory, Jemez stopped Victorio atop a long rise.

"Look over there," he said, pointing toward a long slope between two red-rock bluffs. "Never cross the sand there between those two bluffs."

"Why, Jemez?"

"Just stay away. The Pimas call that place the Devil's Floor, and I have seen why. When you are a little older, I'll show you more about it."

Coyotes and wolves trailed them at a distance, often in plain view and always more curious than menacing. Water holes were scarce, so they carried a full gut bag tied to the buckskin. Victorio told him about the bluecoat pony soldiers patrolling the reservation far to the northeast. Jemez knew that also meant they'd be watching the usual Indian trails up from Sonora, too. So after they passed Nogales, still riding only at night, they boldly followed the wagon trail of the Santa Cruz Stage and Freighting Line. Often Jemez dismounted and placed several fingertips lightly to the ground, feeling for the rhythmic cadence of cavalry horses.

The short white days were coming to the mountains, and even down here in the low country the air was cold at night now. Each morning at dawn, their fingers and toes numb as dead sticks, they made a rock windbreak. Behind it they each built the tiny personal fires preferred by Apaches—just enough flame to warm one person if he huddled close.

While they rode, Jemez thought constantly of the things Victorio had told him about the raid at Mater Dolorosa.

"You are certain about the horses?" he asked. "The ones you say you recognized?"

"I swear it. They belonged to Juan Aragon and Robert Trilby."

"And the four Apaches? You are certain two of them were Mimbrenos?"

"Yes, and others said so, too."

"While the other two wore plumed helmets?"

"Yes, they were Chiricahuas. Only they wear such hats."

Jemez nodded. "I know nothing of those two. The Mimbrenos, however, I am sure I know: Loco and Janos."

Two of Aragon's favorite dirt workers. When they had money, they could often be found in Tucson, well after dark, swilling wagon-yard whiskey in the Indian bars at Riverbend.

Victorio watched him for a few moments. "What about Aragon and Trilby? Are we going to kill them, too?"

Jemez turned a sharp look on him. "*We* are not going to kill anyone, little brother. As for Aragon and Trilby, they are safe until I know for sure where Socorro and Miguelito are."

But the Mimbrenos, Jemez told himself, were worthless. They would know nothing. And they were going to die because it was important to send a signal to Aragon and Trilby, to let them know they were not forgotten—to let them know how vulnerable *they* were, too, should anything happen to Socorro or Miguelito.

Socorro and Miguelito . . . during the third night of their journey, Jemez and Victorio stopped in the lee of a mesa to shelter from the wind while Jemez built a cigarette. He thought for a long time about his dead parents and his little brother and sister.

"Why do you smile?" Victorio said.

"Have the white-skins passed a law against smiling, too?"

"None I have heard of. Why do you smile?"

"Because I'm thinking how different Socorro is from Miguelito. If I did not know better, I would swear they sprang from separate loins."

Victorio, too, grinned. "Straight words, Uncle. Miguelito does not lack spirit or courage. He does not hang back when the boys catch a snake or play at war. Still . . ."

"Still, you mean to say, he will be an indifferent warrior, and you are right. But Socorro, she is more like you."

"Me?" Being compared to a girl made sudden anger darken Victorio's face.

"Yes, like you. Quick to get blood in her eyes, and defiant in her very bones."

Different from each other they might be, but his younger brother and sister were both Grayeyes—the last surviving members of his family and the future of the Grayeyes clan, if indeed it were to *have* a future. In them, too, lived the memories that were Jemez's past.

He thought about all of that, then remembered the desperate hope in Socorro's eyes when he said good-bye to her at Mater Dolorosa. Never mind clans, and never mind family names—nothing lasted, not even the mountains. He was a man, and he could accept that hard truth; he needed nothing of immortality. But those two children were his blood, and they were alive now and they were alone in this world without him. Besides all that, he loved them, and this place knew he meant to get them back.

Jemez flipped the butt away in a glowing arc. They caught up their ponies and pointed bridles north toward Tucson.

On the northern outskirts of Madera Canyon, Jemez realized his pony was limping slightly, favoring her left foreleg.

The night was clear and moonlit. He dismounted and spoke to the blood, calming her. He lifted her foot and spotted a slight bruise to the pastern.

"Not too bad," he told Victorio. "A sharp rock flew up, maybe. She'll hold up if I don't push her." Jemez knew he was fortunate. In this country, a rider without a remount was carrion fodder if his horse foundered.

Later that same night they came across many tracks, all fresh.

"Soldiers moving at night," Jemez said. He pointed. "See all the rocks turned over? Daylight riders would have missed them. That means the white-skins may have scouts or flank riders around here. Be careful going over ridges."

They crossed a broad wash where the sand was so deep Jemez feared injuring his pony's bruised leg. He dismounted and led the mare, the exertion quickly warming him despite the white plumes of his breath. On the horizon a silent electrical storm sent blue fireballs flashing from peak to distant peak.

By day, they holed up in places long known only to the Apaches who had traveled this route for centuries: small red-rock canyons, limestone caves, sometimes merely a deep arroyo or a jumble of boulders. Fresh meat had been scarce in Sonora, and Jemez knew he would need strength for what was coming. One morning, just after sunup, he shot an antelope and butchered it, then used its ribs as a cooking rack. They cooked a hindquarter and made a nourishing soup of the brains, blood, and tender morsels of marrow and fat meat. After eating, they scoured their few utensils in the sand and moved on to a new campsite, leaving most of the antelope for the wolves. Jemez never slept near a meat camp —even if the fire was hidden, cooking smells couldn't be.

Victorio noticed that before Jemez spread out his ground-sheet and buffalo robe, he always carefully wiped and lubricated the bore of his rifle.

"Uncle, I have never seen any Indian fuss so much over his weapon," the youth said.

"Nor will you ever meet many Southwest Indians, besides me and the Navajo, Armijo, who shoot straight with long irons. Do you know that your own people are among some of the poorest shots in all the red nation?"

"I have heard this said of the Crow tribe, truly."

"They are bad, but Apaches are worse. No need to frown, buck, it is only the straight word. Too many of our men are bad rifle shots because of the same foolishness that grants 'magic powers' to this white battle chief. To red men a rifle is medicine, a magic fire stick that kills on its own. Watch them. They can kill at close range with a pistol, because they need only point and shoot. But this is foolish when shooting long distance with a rifle."

He opened the action, worked the mechanism while he inspected it.

"Nor do Apaches like to clean their weapons. This is why they have so many misfires and stoppages. Copy the whites in little else, Victorio, but learn to shoot like they do. Aim steady, keep your weapon clean, hoard your bullets. One bullet for one enemy."

On the last night before they reached the saguaro hills south of Tucson, they stopped at the hot springs in the Coyote Mountains. They stripped and immersed themselves for a long time in a steaming pool under a traprock shelf. Jemez felt the big muscles of his back, chest, and thighs go slack and heavy, felt pores opening to expel the grit of the hard journey.

And while he sat, letting his mind go as slack as his muscles, he again thought about this white-eyed legend in New Mexico, this soldier Victorio insisted was immune to Indian bullets.

His fear was back, itching like a new scab.

Jemez had ordered Victorio to wait outside of town. Now he crouched behind a deep-ridged cottonwood, knowing he shouldn't be this close in broad daylight. Only the placid Santa Cruz River separated him from the boisterous throng circling Trilby's bear-baiting pit. And if he were caught here now, his only fear would be realized: not fear of dying, but of dying unclean at the end of a white man's rope.

But even with a bounty on his head, he couldn't resist this opportunity to spy on his enemies. And here two of them were, like flies buzzing around a molasses barrel, accumulating the gold they valued more than their manhood.

Jemez couldn't see into the pit itself. But he could hear the black bear roaring, hear the snarling and barking of the dogs as they goaded it to a murderous fury. There sat his arrogant mixed-blood cousin, Juan Aragon, perched on a wagon seat with one foot up on the brake. Even from here, Jemez could make out his necklace of human ears. And there, playing with the hair on his face while talking to the deputy named Fargo Danford, was Robert Trilby.

He saw Indian women with bear grease in their hair, an old man selling pinole and *menudo* from the back of a donkey-drawn *carreta*. Like it was a goddamn holiday, Jemez thought, with a hot flaring of anger at these stupid people. These greedy white-eye and Mexican murderers would rut on their own mothers if an audience would pay a handful of beans to see it.

Even from here he could smell the stinking bat-board jakes. Just as, even from here, he could see the little group of mud hovels where he planned to kill the Mimbrenos.

Riverbend was genuinely democratic in its degradation of the human spirit. Frontier capitalism provided vice for all who had the means, which included even Indians or those who lived in the section near where the river flooded every spring. Most of these were reservation Indians or scouts and interpreters employed by freight companies and the U.S. Army. But all Indians looked alike to non-Indians, and questions were seldom asked in Riverbend, especially after dark. It was not unusual for an Indian scout in Army uniform to share a bottle of whiskey or an Arapaho whore with a renegade officially classified by the U.S. government as a hostile.

Jemez paid special attention to the largest hovel of all, constructed of sturdy adobe with a rawhide door hanging askew and a corral out back made of branches. There was no stock in the corral, only several U.S. Army tents. All were in ragged shape, with crude patches made of wagon canvas or burlap. The place was a whorehouse and cantina run by one of Trilby's mixed-blood minions. Trilby supplied the liquor, Aragon the Indian whores through deals with the Comanchero slave traders.

Jemez knew the members of the Tucson Committee would shit bullets if they had any inkling that hostile Apaches and other Indians visited the place. But what transpired in Riverbend was beneath their notice. It was supposedly the job of the white-skin deputy Fargo Danford to maintain law and order in Riverbend. But though Danford was Longstreet's man, he was also drinking out of Trilby's trough. So the law steered clear of Riverbend, and the number of shallow, unmarked graves on the western flank of this pariahs' colony grew steadily larger, without benefit of funerals or inquests. Someone had started covering the newer graves with rocks after predators dug up several bodies and left them partially devoured.

Again, as he eased back through the cottonwoods toward his hobbled mount, Jemez thought about Loco and Janos.

They would probably have money these days, judging from things Victorio had told him. If so, they would be showing up after dark to spend some of it. He planned to be there when they arrived.

Another roar from the crowd, a piercing howl of pain from one of the dogs in the pit. Jemez slipped the hobble from his pony's leg while he tried to ignore that whispering voice—the same voice of the white-skin hangman in his dreams.

Apaches didn't like to fight at night, and Jemez had never considered himself an exception. But things were the way they were, and therefore he had learned to make a virtue of necessity.

Despite the night chill, he had stripped almost naked for combat, wearing only a doeskin clout. He smeared his entire body with red clay from the banks of the Santa Cruz, and soaked his flannel headband in mud before tying it back on. He had already unbuckled his Remington in its hand-tooled holster, leaving it with Victorio. He also left the big Sharps in its saddle scabbard. He would take only his Spanish bayonet, carrying it always in his right hand, close to his leg and low.

His plan was to infiltrate Riverbend from the west, fording the river where it narrowed at the bend. A gravel bar extended across at that point and kept the water shallow at this time of year for easy crossing. Then he would hobble his pony where she would be quick to hand in case everything went to hell fast and Victorio had to bring his mount on the run.

The fording went easy, their feet never once getting wet. Before they led their ponies out of the cottonwood grove, Jemez handed Victorio some squares of buckskin. "Wrap your ponies' hooves with these," he told the boy. The ponies were not shod, but bare hooves were hard enough to make plenty of noise on stones and packed earth. He wanted no one to spot him—he was well-known in this area, and bounty hunters would be unleashed on him like a pack of hounds on a blood scent.

Riverbend was without illumination except for an occasional shaft of lantern light slanting through a window or open doorway. Jemez dismounted and, Victorio still following, led his pony toward the big hovel with the corral out back, staying close to the river and skirting the other hovels. Dim lights glowed inside the tents and cast dream-distorted shadows as the occupants moved around inside them. Occasionally he heard muffled laughter, a voice raised in argument, snatches of Apache and Spanish and other languages he didn't know. Shadowy figures glided here and there through the streets, as sinister and obscure as the place itself.

They were slipping between two buildings when Jemez spotted them, sharing a bottle of whiskey at the end of the short alley he was about to enter—Loco and Janos.

Fear jolted him like a mule kick. Both Mimbrenos wore sidearms, and this was close range. The buckskin pony started at the sudden halt and the abrupt presence of the two men. Moving quickly before she could whinny, Jemez employed the same trick that had saved his hair up in Cheyenne country: He reached back and pinched his pony's nostrils shut.

Sweat broke out in Jemez's armpits and groin as he eased himself and the pony back out of sight. One of the Mimbrenos glanced in their direction but failed to spot him and Victorio in the grainy darkness. It must be Loco, Jemez thought, seeing stray light reflect off the bone breastplate he never removed. He spoke quietly to the buckskin, gentling her as he pushed deeper into the shadows. Then he whispered to Victorio, telling him to wait there with the horses.

She was a Northern Cheyenne, and Loco could see in the dim light of a tallow candle that she still wore her knotted-rope chastity belt.

He grinned at his good fortune. He had heard rumors about a new shipment of girls, but this would be fine sport indeed! Cheyenne girls were not only pretty, but famous for their chastity—unmarried girls wore these knotted-rope belts over their crotch, and any Cheyenne brave fool enough to touch it without first undergoing the squaw-taking ceremony would end up hanging from a penance pole.

"Shit, that rope don't fool me," Loco told the frightened but submissive girl, kicking off his cowhide boots and shucking the Mexican army trousers. "I can splash mud on a pinto and call it a claybank, too."

He stood there, naked except for his breastplate. He never took it off because he believed it improved his fighting skills *and* his sexual prowess. He had stolen it from a Kiowa—a tribe noted for lusty warriors who left their women limping in the morning.

A sudden, high-pitched masculine shriek from the tent beside this one made Loco laugh out loud. That Janos was a bull in the hot moons when it came to the glory of the rut.

"Turn around," he told the Cheyenne girl. "I do it like the dogs."

When she didn't respond, he reached down toward the heap of skins she lay on and flipped her easily around. Even in the dim light he could see the tight dimples at the base of her spine. He pulled the twine-handle knife from his trousers and cut through her rope, casting it aside.

Another high-pitched shriek from the adjacent tent, this one particularly loud. Loco laughed again. He gripped the Cheyenne girl tight by the hips, and he could feel her trembling.

"I'll make you howl and see the Wendigo, you little she-bitch," he promised, pushing hard and deep into the steamy wet of her. No virgin, he thought, but her belly-mouth was still tight as a new moccasin. . . .

His breathing went raspy. The girl's knees left the ground as he pulled her up by the hips to thrust deeper, deeper.

A cool lick of breeze on his bare buttocks, then Loco felt something light hit the middle of his back, heard it fall to the robes beneath him. Dimly, through a welling of hot pleasure, he thought of the beaded lizards that were so common around here. But what if it had been a tarantula or a scorpion instead? The goddamn thing was still crawling around somewhere.

Reluctantly he withdrew from the girl and picked up the little metal dish that held the stub of candle. He bent down carefully, saw something, moved the circle of light closer.

Then he realized what it was, and fear lanced through him.

The panic was on him, cutting through the dense fog of

his drunken lust. Loco didn't bother to grab for his clothes or weapons. He burst through the fly of the tent just in time to watch the girl Janos was with racing across the corral toward the cantina.

Those shrieks . . . Loco threw the fly of the next tent wide, looked inside. Janos had died with fear starched deep into his features. Loco's glance dropped to the bloody place where his friend's sex was missing. And now he knew who the killer was—Apaches customarily mutilated dead enemies, believing they must thus spend eternity maimed.

When he turned, Jemez Grayeyes stood before him.

"No," Loco said, piss suddenly spurting down his thigh as his bladder emptied in reflexive fear. "No."

Jemez was satisfied. He had terrorized his enemies before killing them, not showing himself until the moment of death, so that the face of their executioner was their last image on earth. Now his bayonet came up from his side, and he neatly slid the blade between two bones in the breastplate and straight into Loco's heart. Before Jemez melted into the surrounding shadows to meet Victorio, he served more direct notice to Trilby and Aragon by leaving an eagle-tail feather stuck in the blood on each body—the traditional battle totem of the Grayeyes clan Jemez now led, even in exile.

Soon, with Nat Bischoff's help, would begin another legend to match that of the invincible blue soldier in Arizona: that of Jemez Grayeyes, the implacable Apache renegade bent on blood justice.

PART THREE

Chapter 23

Holding double columns at parade interval, the newly formed First Mountain Company rode out from Fort Bates, Department of New Mexico, early in the winter of 1870 under the command of Lieutenant Colonel Seth Carlson.

They bore due east toward the vast Llano Estacado, or Staked Plain, the unsettled wasteland covering much of the eastern New Mexico Territory and the Texas Panhandle. This remote, arid, almost treeless region was seldom visited by whites. It was home to buffalo, antelope, wolves, coyotes, jackrabbits, prairie dogs, rattlesnakes—and Comanches, arguably the most fearsome pony soldiers in the New World and known by friend and foe alike as the Red Raiders of the Plains.

The unit's mission, as every newspaper in the country constantly reminded nervous Americans, was twofold: First, they were to cut sign on Comanche marauders under the renegade brave Iron Eyes, tracking down and destroying as many as possible and forcing the rest to flee from areas of white settlement and back out onto the Llano, where they could do little harm to settlers. Then the First Mountain Company was to recruit briefly back at Fort Bates before heading south to concentrate its attention on close Comanche allies—a band of Kiowa warriors that included the battle chief Eagle on His Journey and several other Kaitsenko warriors, the best fighters among this tribe known for its love of warfare.

The newspapers constantly reminded readers that Eagle on His Journey might well have personally killed some of the women under Seth's protection on that bloody Sunday. But Seth still felt no burning thirst for revenge. Somehow, to him it seemed as if a need for revenge would only be a way of denying his own guilt. Indians killed and pillaged, that was their nature and everyone knew it; it was his job to stop them, and he had failed.

The Army's elite Indian-fighting unit was just over forty strong, each man a volunteer picked by Seth and Sergeant Major Kinney without regard to rank: forty Army sharpshooters, the Papago Indian scout named Goes Ahead, and Walt Mackenzie to handle the remuda and serve as medical orderly. Several of the volunteers had served under Corey Bryce and were with him on that fatal Sunday outside of Santa Fe. More guides and interpreters were not necessary because many of the men were selected on the basis of previous civilian experience and were veteran frontiersmen. A few knew this territory well.

The War Department insisted the First Mountain Company must ride out in full uniform, post band blasting out "The Grenadier's March" while a dozen journalists raced alongside, trying to elicit quotes from the stone-faced men. But once in the field, they stripped off their uniforms and buried them, changing into civilian clothes. One reason was purely practical: Relations with Mexico were shaky, and the company had secret U.S. clearance for hot pursuit of hostiles who fled south of the border. Mexican officials could wink at occasional forays across their border by civilian militiamen armed with letters of marque from their government—after all, what did it matter *who* killed the Apaches, so long as the red vermin were killed? But an incursion by American government soldiers—this would be seen as yet another gringo assault on Mexico's sovereignty, invoking bitter images of General Winfield Scott and bloody Chapultepec.

Seth's unit crossed the Sangre de Cristo and Turkey mountains in good time, encountering light snow, although the valleys were not yet locked with ice. In one day's hard ride they raced across the eighty-mile expanse of grassland east of the giant hump called Wagon Mound—a three-day journey for regular cavalry troops. They skirted the Staked Plain itself, following reports that Iron Eyes and his Comanche band were farther south, harassing miners near the Red River. The First Mountain Company surprised the enemy in a pincers movement near Logan, then engaged him in a fierce running battle as the Comanches fled north toward their stronghold in Blanco Canyon, the only break dividing the Staked Plain.

No soldiers had ever persisted very far in a chase across this vast desert of bone-dry arroyos and chalky alkali dust. The First Mountain Company, however, seemed undaunted by this sterile land of tarantulas, centipedes, and scorpions, of tainted water and fierce sandstorms that cut visibility to less than ten yards. It was a brutal expedition. The enemy could travel all day on a handful of parched corn and rode horses trained as well as circus ponies. So Carlson drove his troops to exhaustion and then demanded more: reveille at two A.M., moving out before three o'clock, not stopping again, even to eat, until late afternoon.

But the grueling pace paid off. The sharpshooters often edged into effective range, and soon a trail of Comanche bodies littered the Llano; for the first time Iron Eyes realized there was no safe haven from some hair-face devils. The braves eventually reached the safety of the Blanco, and the soldiers were forced to return to Fort Bates before heading south after Kiowas.

Part One of their mission, however, was a clear strategic victory for the Army. When the unit had first ridden out, the combined national mood of relief mixed with expectation was perhaps best summed up by an exuberant headline in the *Philadelphia Inquirer*: SETH SENT!!! But privately, no one in the upper echelons of the War Department expected one gutsy company to accomplish what entire regiments could not. Now, with this sweet taste of partial victory, the symbolism was potent, and the national conviction strong that finally the Army was, by-God, doing something about these damned redskins—thanks to their Indian fighter extraordinaire, Seth Carlson.

As for the newspapers, with this successful campaign against the Comanches, Seth went from being lionized to being canonized. His indifference to his own danger—bordering at times on recklessness—only enhanced his romantic image as a tragic but indestructible warrior. Indeed, Seth thought the newspapers just might be right—except that it was the devil who had made him indestructible, and only so that he could torment him forever with the memory of killing Jeanette.

"I could shorely wrap my teeth around some Cincinnati chicken right about now," Walt Mackenzie said, two days after a pack mule plunged to its death and took all their bacon with it. "The Innuns don't kill you, beans and hardtack will."

"*Augh!* Long as you're ordering lemonade in hell, turd, might as well order a heap of flapjacks with molasses, too. And why not a foofaraw house full of whores so we can all drain our snakes?" Kinney added.

The First Mountain Company had stopped to make a nooning deep in the Sierra Perdida of northern Chihuahua State. Normally the Kiowas could be found far to the north, ranging around their Medicine Lodge Creek homeland in Kansas. But this band of a hundred braves, led by Eagle on His Journey, had become highly nomadic as their campaign of terror forced them to elude more and more pursuers.

Seth Carlson rode back from the point position, joining his men in a grassy hollow beside the narrow and tortuous mountain trail. He dismounted from his powerful little calico mustang and stamped his picket pin into the cold but still unfrozen ground with his heel. He knotted the end of the reins, buried it deeper with the pin and stomped the earth around it.

"Any sign?" Kinney said.

Seth shook his head, squatting to pour a cup of coffee. The heat from the fire felt good on his face. "Nothing straight ahead."

"No, but they're out there, all right," said a mustang lieutenant named Charlie Plummer. He was the only other officer in the unit, a dragoon who had made it to captain twice and been busted both times for drunkenness and insubordination. Almost thirty, his career in the Army was highly doubtful due to abysmal conduct-and-proficiency reports. But he was a dead shot, an experienced mountain fighter, and spoke some Spanish, as did many Kiowas and Comanches.

"Hell yes they're out there," Kinney said. "Eagle on His Journey has been giving the slip to shavetails since most of you tadpoles was in three-cornered britches. He's watching us right now and laughing his red ass off."

Seth nodded. The sergeant major's gut hunches were the product of long experience and had proven valuable during their pursuit of the Comanches. "They could hit us anytime. Pass the word: Every man is to make sure he has thirty rounds crimped and ready. But no more. We may have to make tracks fast."

A sentry up in the rimrock called out that Goes Ahead was riding in from a scout along the west flank. Seth watched the Papago ride carefully down a loose shale slope above them. His favorite cavalry sorrel had been replaced, as were all the men's mounts, by a sure-footed mustang broken in by Indians employed at Fort Bates. The men used flat, buffalo-hide saddles, and no bits were shoved into the pony's mouths— they were controlled with headstalls only. Goes Ahead had selected a stocking-footed chestnut. From force of habit he sat hunched low in the saddle, as if looking for sign.

"What's on the spit?" Seth greeted him.

Goes Ahead dismounted and squatted to hobble his pony. "Last night they camped on the next ridge over. Made two campfires, one built in a hole for cooking."

Goes Ahead stood back up. His long hair was braided tight under his floppy-brim hat. His feet looked oddly misshapen because he had fashioned his own silent footgear out of sponge and leather. The strange shoes barely left a track or made a sound.

"The other fire was because they gave a victory dance," he added. "The grass is trampled flat in a big circle. They left gifts to the place."

" 'Victory.' In a pig's ass," Kinney said. He spat into the fire. "You know damn good and well it was that bull train they wiped out south of Artesia."

Again Seth nodded. Since cutting sign on the Kiowas north of the wagon-road way station at Roswell, the First Mountain Company had borne grim witness to the aftermath of their foe's brutality. At Roswell the Kiowas had killed four employees of the Overland Freight Company and burned the station to the ground, cutting the telegraph wire as they left. In this they were different from most tribes, who steadfastly refused to touch the white man's singing wires—such powerful medicine was best left alone.

Then, thirty miles south of Artesia, they attacked a pack train bound for Carlsbad. The bull whackers had all been slaughtered, most of their shipment of dry goods looted and burned. But not one man had been scalped. Like most Southwest tribes, the Kiowas were bored by such northern plains customs as taking scalps and counting coups. To them, the point of battle was to seize goods and take captives—torture being a favorite source of entertainment for the entire tribe.

Now Seth felt a thin geyser of bile erupt in his throat as he recalled the bull whacker they had found near the Rio Penasco, clearly a Kiowa captive. The renegades had sliced his eyelids off, then completely flayed his soles. Deep into the raw, exposed meat of his feet they jabbed hard kernels of corn, then left him in the desert to walk, wrists bound tight behind his neck. When Seth's unit found the body, the pain and suffering etched deep into the dead man's face defied belief. At Seth's command every man in the First Mountain Company had filed past the grisly sight, staring into that grim death mask—a reminder of why they were here and what they could expect if they got careless.

Seth spilled the dregs of his coffee out and scoured his cup with a handful of grass. He glanced around the clearing, looking at the men huddled over small fires. Then his gaze focused past them, farther down the rock-strewn slope toward the vast and desolate terrain of Old Mexico.

Kinney moved up beside him. The sergeant major was the oldest man in the unit, and the rigors of this mission showed in the slack weariness of his face, the soft and sallow pockets under his eyes.

"It's godforsook country, all right," he said, looking out where Seth was gazing.

"It's an enemy," Seth agreed. "It has to be whipped along with the Indians."

He wasn't waxing philosophical. Thus far the company had lost almost as many men to terrain and weather as it had to Indians. They had slogged deep into sierras covered with icy slopes; across dry plains where they had to water their horses from their hats; through dunes and spoil banks and deep sand washes that could break a horse's leg; up treacherous mountain slopes covered with gravel. They had to contend with loose shale, miles and miles of slagland, steep and twisting trails, open alkali flats and broad soda plains and endless gypsum lakes. Lightning had knocked one man off his pony and killed him, another drowned when a sudden downpour created an instant torrent in the gorge they were crossing.

Walt Mackenzie sauntered over to join Seth and Kinney. Like most of the men, the lanky corporal had stopped shaving at the beginning of this campaign. His beard was blond and fine, red-streaked in the sunlight.

"How's Helzer doing?" Seth asked him.

So far Mackenzie had lived up to Seth's expectation that he would prove valuable to this mission. He knew how to make pastes of yarrow root to soothe saddle sores and blisters, how to treat cuts and wounds by packing them with balsam and gunpowder. He could also remove superficially embedded bullets and arrowheads efficiently. But Jimmy Helzer, the victim of Kiowa snipers, was wounded too seriously to recover with Walt's help alone.

"That bullet is damn close to his spine," Mackenzie said.

"I got the bleeding stopped. But it fair gives me the fidgets ever' time that mule stumbles."

For a moment, frustration showed clearly in Seth's unshaven face. They were forced to carry their wounded in cacolets, crude mule litters. Every movement in this terrain could become an agony of pain to an injured man. As for their dead, ceremonies were brief and brutally spartan: They were sewn up tight in their blankets and ponchos, then buried in shallow graves under rocks. Their names were written on slips of paper, then inserted into an empty cartridge and hammered into the top of a wooden stake. The gesture was useless out here where no one would ever read it, mere sand thrown against the wind. But Seth refused to leave any man in an unmarked grave—almost as if, by leaving his name somewhere, the man's dying took on a particular significance, if not for history, at least in the memories of his comrades.

All three men dropped back down the trail to visit with Helzer for a moment. The ashen-faced soldier was wrapped in several blankets and an oilskin, his canvas litter now lying on the ground. Seth winced, trading an uneasy glance with Kinney. Helzer looked bad. His eyes had an ominous glaze to them and were slow to record the presence of his comrades.

"Hey, Jimmy," Seth greeted him, working to keep his tone casual. "When you gonna quit malingering in Company Q and give me a break on point?"

Mucus smeared one side of Helzer's face. Walt Mackenzie reached down and wiped it off with his coat sleeve.

"I don't know, sir," Helzer replied, too miserable and scared to muster much bravado. "That bullet's dealing me misery."

Seth knelt close and gripped one of the youth's shoulders. "You lissenup, trooper. You hang on, do you hear me? I'll make you a deal. You hang on just until we get down onto the flat again. Then we'll send a man to splice into the telegraph line at Malaga, and wire for an ambulance out of the garrison at Carlsbad. You hear me?"

Helzer nodded, hope sparking in his eyes for just a moment. "Yessir. That sounds like a deal, all right. I'll take it."

Again Seth felt the sudden anger of frustration. Helzer tended to complain a lot and was a bit of a shirker when hard work was doled out. But he was disciplined under fire, and Seth had watched him pull a wounded comrade to safety through a flurry of Comanche arrows and bullets.

Kinney and Walt exchanged a long glance. Each of the two men, in his own way, had noticed it: Seth was driven by an almost obsessive need to protect his men while still getting the job done. So far he had repeatedly risked his own life rather than give an order that would endanger another man. In the First, no man punished another, and rank was enforced only to maintain order, not social status. All men ate the same food and split such unpleasant tasks as riding point and manning picket outposts. Seth adamantly refused to give any order he himself wouldn't be willing to carry out. As a result, his unit—to the last man—were fanatically loyal and would follow Colonel Carlson into hell carrying empty carbines.

All the men sensed it: Despite their cynicism over the paper-collar journalists and their high-blown pronouncements, there was indeed something different about Seth Carlson. He *was* marked out by destiny, as Nat Bischoff had written, and all the men felt it—that, and their own part in it. Every man there somehow sensed that all their present suffering would give meaning to the rest of their lives and mark an indelible page of history, a feeling they had never known under Denton back at Fort Bates.

Now Seth squeezed Helzer's shoulder again, then stood back up. He glanced over toward the neighboring ridge, where Goes Ahead had found the Kiowa camp. The hard battle was looming. Their enemy was retreating farther and farther into the high country—soon they would have to dig in and fight these determined soldiers. And every man in the First knew what set the Kaitsenko warriors apart: They had taken an oath never to surrender. When it came to a final stand, they were all bound by honor to either win or fight to the death.

"All right!" Seth called back toward the men in the clearing. "Cinch up!"

When the tired men were slow to move, Kinney took over.

"*Augh!* You ladies got a cob up your sitters? If I have to come over there, I'll open up your trapdoors and bugger every one of you! You heard the man, pony soldiers. Hop your hosses and let's pound those testicles some more!"

Chapter 24

"I took your advice, Bob," Charles Longstreet said. "You told me I should just lay low and see if that raid on the reservation would straighten Hays Munro out. Well, *here's* how he's come around."

Longstreet slapped at the open pages of a recent *Rocky Mountain News*, which had just arrived by post.

"You've both read the same letter in other newspapers," he said to Trilby and Nat Bischoff. "It names me and Nat openly and accuses both of us of lying and conspiring to hornswaggle the government and the Indians. You read that passage about how this pepper-gut priest, this—this—"

"Montoya," Bischoff threw in.

"—this Father Montoya's blood is on our hands. This is the fourth newspaper I know of that's printed it. Has he mailed one to the goddamn Queen of England, too?"

It was early afternoon, a cool but sunny January day, and the three men were drinking whiskey at a deal table, one of about two dozen scattered about the spacious Three Sisters Saloon on Silver Street. It was a favorite with Tucson miners, a big, raw-plank building with a board canopy and a long hitching post out front. A huge, sawdust-covered dance floor filled more than half the structure. The player piano was silent now, but soon men would be drifting in for the evening to buy dances from the girls who only gave a man a dance for his money, and thus lorded it over the soiled doves who tendered their bodies.

Trilby, mellowed by the good rye, had no share in his employer's anger. It was no skin off his ass if Longstreet and Bischoff were worried about the attention. Longstreet was hogging too much for himself, anyway, and Trilby figured a man had a right to work ahead of the roundup to get his own fair share.

"I miscalculated Munro," Trilby admitted. "I figured him to fold up the tent and go home."

"It's no say-so of his how I make my living, that goddamn pus-gut Indian-loving sonofabitch. If he thinks he can go toe to toe with the Tucson Committee, he ain't even *pretending* he's got more brains than a rabbit."

"He certainly writes well," Bischoff put in. "Could be he's one of these Byronic intellectuals willing to die for his beliefs."

"Balls," Trilby said. "He's talking tough now. But that's because he got off too light. He'll show the white feather."

Longstreet pulled his cheroot from his mouth and pointed at Trilby with it as he spoke. "Maybe. But we've got to be careful with this reservation situation, or we'll end up trapped between the sap and the bark. We want to quiet Munro and get him the hell out of there. But go too far, and we'll get a damned government investigation started."

"Perhaps," Bischoff said, looking at Longstreet, "you were on to something when you mentioned the girl, Kathleen Barton. Munro is too well-connected to touch, but I know from interviewing her that her father is a harness maker in Illinois with no friends in high places. Still, it would certainly go badly for Munro if it was perceived that his policies and behavior jeopardized a woman's safety."

Trilby was only half listening, still trying to bite back a

scornful smile as he studied the other two men. Longstreet wore his usual respectable businessman's garb, a vest and string tie. But Bischoff looked like he had just stepped off the cover of a dime novel, in his brand-new straw Sonora hat and leather *chivarra* pants with a beaded silk shirt.

"Still, the raid was a good idea, eh?" Longstreet said. "The Army has decided, after all, to stay at Fort Grant. In part we can thank Nat for that much. That piece he did on Jemez Grayeyes has terrified the white settlers. The C.O. at Fort Grant told me letters and telegrams have been flooding Washington nineteen to the dozen, demanding the Army stay put. Have some more coffin varnish," he added, sliding the whiskey bottle across to Trilby. Then he went on:

"This two-bit Apache criminal, this Jemez Grayeyes. He's got to go, and you can chisel that in granite. It was a brilliant move, Nat, when you hinted that *he* killed that priest. The committee is matching the bounty I've already put up. It's up to four thousand dollars now."

The Apache had not contented himself with a revenge strike in Riverbend against the Mimbrenos. Since then he had been steadily harassing Longstreet's various business concerns. Freighters hauling goods for his mercantile and mining-supply business had been shot at, cattle on his range south of town throat-slashed.

"Grayeyes has got me worried," Longstreet admitted. "I already told you boys about this international buff-hunting expedition I want to get up. I won't be able to do it unless I can free up enough manpower. Thanks to this goddamn red nigger, I've had to double the number of line riders on my spread, and more men have been assigned to other security jobs."

Trilby was about to say something. Then he heard the familiar crunch of iron rims. He excused himself, crossed to the bat-wings and glanced out over them. It was nippy outside, but pleasantly sunny and clear, the shadows crisply etched in the winter air. He watched the stage from Fort Grant lurch to a stop in front of Longstreet's Mercantile. The driver swung down from the box and stretched. Trilby could see there were no passengers this trip.

Nat Bischoff had watched Trilby scrape back his chair and

cross toward the doorway to glance outside. When Trilby returned and took his seat again, Bischoff said:

"Not only do you always keep a wall behind you, but I've noticed you never let a stage roll into town unobserved."

Trilby patted his long teamster's mustache with three fingertips. His weather-seamed face revealed nothing.

"There's careful," Bischoff said, "and then there's *careful*. If I didn't know better, Bob, I'd say you were a man with a past. In fact, I'd wager that Robert Trilby is what you frontiersmen call a summer name."

Trilby flashed his tolerant smile. He had been expecting this moment to finally arrive. Bischoff was intelligent enough, but he was a self-inflated fool who believed his power over a gaggle of enthralled, newspaper-reading squawmen back East somehow conferred a set of oysters on him out here among men. So once again Trilby decided it was time to take the bull by the horns.

"And *I've* noticed something, too, Nat. I've noticed that once you set that golden quill of yours in motion, a man can suddenly get a whole damn lot of attention. Maybe attention he doesn't want."

Bischoff smiled a brief Gioconda smile and made an expansive gesture with both hands, conceding the point.

Trilby deliberately maintained a longer than usual silence, until the other two men were watching him curiously.

"So, Nat. I hear you're a family man like Charlie here?"

His tone was amiable. But the long pause before his comment, the careful emphasis of his words, the fact that Trilby never discussed domestic matters—all this made his ominous hint clear enough and took both men completely by surprise. Bischoff paled a bit, then nodded.

"Yes. Yes, I am. A lovely wife and two little girls five and seven."

"Ahh, little girls. Do tell? I love children."

Longstreet pulled a handkerchief out and wiped his brow, not liking the turn this trail was taking. He looked at Bischoff with a warning clear in his eyes.

"One thing makes us different out here, Nat," Longstreet said, "is we don't pry into a man's past. So long as he pulls his own freight, we don't much give a damn if he goes by a summer name or not. We judge the man, not the name."

"After all, Nat," Trilby added, "you're a man of the world. You know full well *any* man is guilty if you ask him the right question."

"Touché. Discretion is the better part of valor, eh?"

Trilby shrugged. "We must take the world as we find it."

"Speaking of taking things as we find them," Longstreet said, nodding toward the bat-wings.

Juan Aragon stood in the doorway, his gaze slitted against the sun. His eyes prowled the room until he spotted Trilby.

Bischoff wrinkled his nose, making a show of delicately sampling the air. "Is it just my imagination, gentlemen," he said in a low voice, "or do you smell the distinct fetor of . . . buffalo?"

All three men shared a laugh. Trilby scraped back his chair again. Mixed-bloods were not permitted inside the Three Sisters. As he stood up, Bischoff said, "I hear that not all those ears on that necklace of his came from Indians."

"None of them did," Trilby said. "A trophy has to have value or it's not a trophy. If you gentlemen will excuse me . . ."

He joined his lackey out on the boardwalk.

"*Jefe,*" Aragon greeted him, his tone more urgent than usual, "Jemez has been spotted."

Trilby hung fire for a long moment. His face showed nothing as he gazed out over the rutted, garbage-strewn expanse of Silver Street. "Where?" he finally said.

"South of here near Madera Canyon. He was heading northeast. Maybe toward Dolorosa."

"Who saw him?"

"Pass the Pipe, a Pima who scouts for the cavalry. He saw him through those whatchacallems. . . ."

"Field glasses?"

"Those. Swears it was him."

"You worried about it?"

Aragon looked at him as if wondering what world Trilby inhabited. Aragon was completely sober, a fact that surprised and worried Trilby.

"Does a big-titted woman sleep on her back? *Como no* I

am worried. You did not see how those Mimbrenos died, *Jefe*. I did."

"A fish always looks bigger underwater, '*mano*. He killed two drunk Indians in Riverbend and hacked off their pizzles. So? It doesn't put snow in *my* boots." Trilby paused, added: "Do you think he knows about the children?"

The four abducted Apache children had been sold to Enrique Padilla, a wealthy *hacendado* in Chihuahua, former administrative capital of Old Mexico. The haciendas of Sonora and Chihuahua were excellent markets for kidnapped *indio* children—slave labor was technically illegal in Mexico, but Mexicans despised Indians even more than the gringos did, and questions were never asked.

"No," Aragon said. "If he knew, *por Dios*! We would both be sleeping with the worms, and he would not be around here."

"Horseshit. Worry about the man, not the scuttlebutt you hear. He's a blood Indian, he thinks more like an animal. The thing of it is, we have to make sure that when the showdown comes, it's on our terms. *We* have to control the fight, not him."

Aragon flashed his deceptively foolish grin. "Will you tell the wind which way to blow, too? Might be easier."

"He's only a man," Trilby repeated. Despite his bravado, he knew damn good and well Grayeyes was indeed a serious threat. But his contrary nature was at work: Bischoff's remark earlier had him thinking about Kathleen Barton, not Grayeyes.

Aragon's grin melted away like a snowflake on the surface of a river.

"No he's not," he said. "*Jefe*, I like you even though you sit swilling liquor with your gringo friends and laughing at me. And I tell you now, hombre, when he gets blood in his eyes, this Jemez Grayeyes is a devil from hell."

"Well, that's it," Hays Munro said in a tone laced with disgusted defeat.

He threw down the letter he had just read and took the monocle out of his eye.

"The commander at Fort Grant maintains his position

that he has no authority to investigate the raid. All he can do, he insists, is to continue patrolling the periphery of the reservation. As for the bureau, they thanked me for my detailed report and promptly filed it away into oblivion. The War Department and the U.S. Marshal in San Manuel haven't even acknowledged receiving it."

Kathleen sat reading at the little escritoire. She lay her book down and looked across the room at her superior. Supper was over, the night a louring gloom beyond the windows. Though it was nippy outside, a cheerful fire crackled in the fieldstone fireplace and threw dancing shadows on the chenille curtains.

"Are you really surprised?" she said.

"Of course not. But actually reading their mealy-mouth, cowardly responses is galling. It's one thing to know abstractly that men spew vomit, another to have to watch them do it."

"I wish," she said, a smile glittering in her eyes, "that you'd compose different analogies so soon after supper."

If he heard her, the fact didn't register on his careworn face.

"That damned Tucson Committee is behind this. Bischoff has been bought off. And I wouldn't be surprised if they're all tight as ticks with the commander of Fort Grant."

He went through some version of this familiar litany every day. But since the attack on Mater Dolorosa, she was no longer simply inured to his articulate complaints—a little spring of spiteful anger was coiled tight inside her, too, and she owned a growing share in his indignation. Nonetheless, Hays was brooding in a way that bothered her. He was not one to brook being ignored like this—especially not when he was adamantly convinced that he was right.

She said, "I've noticed that you've been writing more letters lately. If this Tucson Committee is as ruthless as you imply, is it wise to keep antagonizing them?"

"Bosh! Let them stew in their juices."

"Hays, you're not a lawman. It's dangerous."

"It always is when you come between dogs and their meat."

"You've been working too hard and worrying too much. No

offense, but you look just terrible. Let me read to you tonight."

Munro shook his head, smiling wanly. "No thanks, Kath, flattery will get you nowhere. I couldn't relax enough to enjoy it anyway, despite your wonderful reading voice. I'm going to finish that editorial I've been invited to write for *Harper's Weekly.*"

She gave up with a resigned sigh. "Write a good one. I'm proud of you, it'll reach a lot of readers."

She stood, taking the coal-oil lamp with her, and crossed to his chair, kissing him on the cheek. "Think I'll retire early. 'Night, Hays."

"Good night, my dear, sleep tight," he muttered, already sifting through his notes.

A short dogtrot led from the kitchen to her quarters under the slope-off roof. She lifted the latch string, opened the door, set the lamp on a highboy beside a narrow iron bedstead with a blue taffeta coverlet.

Kathleen sat on the bed and was letting her hair down when she suddenly realized she wasn't alone. She glanced to her right. Jemez Grayeyes sat in her rocking chair, watching her with unblinking eyes.

She felt nothing: no fear, no anger, not even very much surprise. In an odd way, it was as if he belonged there.

"Hello," she said.

He nodded, still watching her with nimbus-gray eyes too vague and distant to reveal motives. She took in his filthy, long-fringed buckskin trousers, spattered with dark stains she suspected were blood. He wasn't very clean, and the smell coming off him made her breathe through her mouth.

"*Cómo entraste?*" she said. How did you get in?

"The same way I'll get out," he answered in English.

"If you insist on visiting the reservation illegally, I'd appreciate it if you'd pick some other place to confront me."

"Don't want to get caught with an Apache anywhere near your bed, huh? Especially one who smells this bad."

"I'd rather not be 'caught' with *any* man near my bed. Though yes, you could certainly use a bath."

His eyes had not left her alone once, but oddly, his intense scrutiny did not bother her. He had a way of looking close but impersonally.

"Don't you know this place is surrounded by soldiers?"

"I saw them. I guess you could call them soldiers. They carry guns."

"Bullets, too. It's not safe for you around here. You've been blamed for killing Father Montoya."

He nodded, reaching up to adjust his red flannel headband. "Nat Bischoff," he said. "Know him?"

"I've met him, and I don't like him."

"He's a liar. He lies to cover for murderers and thieves. If he crosses my path, I'll kill him."

After another long pause, she said, "What do you want?"

"I want to know where Socorro and Miguelito are."

"I wish I knew, but I don't."

"You've heard nothing?"

She shook her head.

"Nobody on the rez knows anything?" he persisted. "A lot of them got clan to the south, they hear things."

"If they do, they've said nothing to me."

"Could you ask around? I can't. There's some here would sell my hide to the committee."

She hesitated. For a long time their eyes held.

"I don't understand," she finally said. "Victorio would know more than I do. Why did you risk coming here to see me?"

"I think you're a good woman," he said. "I like you. So I came to say something else, too. This Hays Munro, the Dineh say he bores them, he doesn't feel comfortable around red men, he never knows where to put his hands or how to be easy in their company. But they like him well enough. They say he speaks one way to the Indian, that he's not afraid to anger his big chiefs in Washington."

Kathleen felt the nape of her neck tingle. She knew Apaches well enough by now to know they seldom came at a thing too directly.

"I like you, too," she admitted. "I think you're a good man. But I also know that trouble comes with you, and I'm afraid."

"I am, too. Do you understand that I don't make the

trouble? I want you to understand that because I respect you."

Her throat pinched closed, and Kathleen fought back a hot welling of tears as she began to sense his urgency. "This is important, isn't it?" she said.

He nodded, the rest of him as still as stone.

"Yes," she said, "I understand. You're telling me that Hays is in trouble?"

"He's in bad trouble, and so are you."

"You're telling me that I'm going to have to be strong." The words felt like nails in her throat.

"You're strong already. I'm asking you to get even stronger and to be careful. You didn't understand the way things are before you came out here. But you're here, this place has you, and now you're part of the trouble. You could rabbit now, but I don't think you will. I *wish* you would, I like you. But you won't. Neither will Hays Munro."

"I'm afraid," she said again.

"I told you, I am, too. Will you ask around the rez about those kids?"

She nodded. Her hot tears made the room go blurry.

"Stop it," Jemez told her. "You can cry after I leave. I want you to know that I'm your friend, but you can't cry around me."

"Then get out of here, because it's *my* room and I want to cry."

He grinned, stood without moving the rocking chair a fraction of an inch. "Big baby," he said fondly, crossing toward the room's only window. "I'm going. You just be careful."

Chapter 25

Steadily, like a sinewy, many-headed death machine, the First Mountain Company wound its way farther and farther into the highest reaches of northern Chihuahua's Sierra Perdida range, fighting a running battle with the band of Kiowa renegades led by Eagle on His Journey.

Seth Carlson took the point position almost exclusively now, setting a hard pace on his tough little calico. "Carlson's Raiders," as they had lately been dubbed by the American press, rode either in columns of two abreast or in single file, depending on terrain. The unit's grim sense of purpose was reflected in the determined set of Seth's mouth, the unrelenting pursuit that allowed the Kiowas no respite—a type of pursuit they had never believed white-skin soldiers capable of.

Occasionally, one group came within rifle sights of the other. The sharp, thin crack of Indian trade rifles was answered by the heavier report of the Army carbines. The soldiers paid no attention to the occasional small bands of Yumas or Pimas who scattered in panic at their approach, homing in on the Kiowas like wolves on a blood scent. Only once did they pause to hide, after spotting a group of riders down on the flats, a red and green Mexican flag flying above their unit guidon.

At night, when it was secure, they gathered briefly around fragrant fires of pinyon wood. Seth made one exception to the strict rule about hauling nonessential gear: Walt Mackenzie's banjo. Walt wasn't particularly blessed as a musician. But on nights when battle silence wasn't enforced, the tired troopers were glad enough to sing along to "Little Brown Jug" and "Bonny Jean" and "Lightly Row" before snatching a few hours of uneasy sleep. Some nights they were caught in freezing rainstorms, and the men were forced to button their shelter halves together and borrow each other's body warmth. If the weather hadn't cleared by the two A.M. reveille, they rode out anyway, thin tendrils of icy rain lashing at their faces and pattering off their oilskin slickers.

On the sixth morning after they rode into the sierra, Seth led his men in single file up a particularly treacherous stretch of mountain trail. The night before, Goes Ahead had reported that their Kiowa enemy was about to reach the end of his tether: a little teacup-shaped hollow just beneath the peak of the tallest mountain in the range. Further flight was impossible, the Papago scout explained, because of precipitous limestone cliffs that covered the south slope.

At the moment, however, Seth was worried about negotiating the trail without serious mishap. It rose at a steep angle, talus-strewn, with sheer cliffs dropping off on either side. Each time he turned in the saddle to glance back, the deep, recently knit wound under his collarbone—aggravated by the constant cold and damp—shot a twinge of pain through him.

Behind him, Walt Mackenzie led their small remuda, which included the mule rigged with Jimmy Helzer's litter. Seth had already made up his mind not to wait until they returned to the flats before evacuating Helzer. Goes Ahead reported a passable side trail just ahead. As much as he hated to lose the firepower, Seth planned to send a small detachment down with the wounded man.

All was cold and silent under a sunless sky the color of dirty bathwater. Seth heard only the snuffling of the horses and an occasional curse as one of the men fought to control a nervous pony on the dangerous trail.

Abruptly, he heard the loose sliding of rocks, heard Walt Mackenzie's urgent voice slice through the silence: "Good God a-gorry!"

Seth whirled in the saddle, then felt his face drain cold. The mule hauling Helzer's litter had slipped from the trail, its hind legs flailing uselessly in thin air. One leather strap securing Helzer's litter had snapped, the litter now dangling like a sheath. Only two thin security ropes kept the injured man from tumbling out. Mackenzie, his face bloodless above his sparse beard, was hanging on for dear life to the guide rope tied to the mule's bit ring.

Seth's momentary shock passed in a heartbeat. He whirled his mount, desperately searching for the nearest man.

"Charlie!" he bellowed, spotting Plummer below. "Eyes front!"

Plummer, busy watching the narrow trail right in front of him, snapped his head up. A moment later, mindless of his own danger, he loosed a brisk "Gee up!" and savagely kicked his pony's flanks with both heels. He surged up the trail even as Seth started back down.

The mule slid another few inches, dragging Walt dangerously close to the edge. But the frightened orderly stubbornly refused to let go. His muscles strained like taut cords as he dug his heels in and leaned back on the rope.

"Goddamnit!" he shouted. "Goddamnit, somebody help!"

Seth's calico almost lost her footing, but the lithe officer instantly counterbalanced by leaning far out and down on the opposite side. He reached Walt at the same time Plummer did. Both soldiers had grabbed their ropes, clearly thinking the same thing: Get the ropes around the dangling mule and then secure them to one of numerous huge boulders nearby.

"Let go, soldier!" Seth told Mackenzie, seeing that the corporal was on the verge of plummeting off the trail.

Mackenzie, both hands bleeding as the rope cut in deeper, refused with a grim shake of his head.

"Goddamn fool," Seth muttered, flinging his rope out over the mule's back at the same time Charlie did. Seth had pulled his carbine from its scabbard when he dismounted. Now he quickly fixed his bayonet to it, giving him just enough reach, if he leaned out precariously far, to snag the dangling rope.

The next moment, the mule's clawing forelegs lost their struggle and the beast plunged out of sight, Helzer and the litter with it.

Seth reached out desperately, caught Mackenzie by the belt as he surged forward, felt himself going over with them. Then Plummer grabbed Seth's legs in a bear hug and plopped down hard on his butt. The two men fell back onto the trail, Mackenzie crashing down on top of them.

Helzer's scream melded with the mule's agonized death bray, the sound scraping along Seth's spine like a rusty knife blade. Long moments later the mule and Helzer were crushed on the lava rock nearly a thousand feet below.

The three soldiers lay there gasping from the sudden exertion and the shock of their near miss. Then Seth stood and caught up his nervously sidestepping calico before she, too, plunged off the trail. The slope was too steep and narrow for the rest of the men to join them—indeed, the men at the drag end of the formation hadn't even seen the mishap, though all heard the screaming man and beast.

Walt suddenly turned his head aside and vomited.

"Damnit," he said, wiping his mouth on his sleeve. "Aw, damnit, Jimmy."

"Snap out of your shit," Seth ordered him, a bit too sharply. "It's nobody's fault."

Seth stood, helped Charlie up, then glanced back down the trail. For a moment, despite the fact that it truly was nobody's fault, Seth lost his strong sense of command and felt the familiar doubt come over him. He hadn't come through for Jeanette when it had counted, either. Jimmy's scream was just one more thing to relive in the dark hours before dawn. Then he reminded himself: Hostile Kiowas were watching them even now, and his men were lined up like clay targets. It was his responsibility to get them to safety, to bring them back from this mission.

He spotted Jay Kinney and raised his right fist high, pumping it up and down twice: the signal to move out. His top sergeant shouted the command, and it was repeated down the winding file until the unit was in motion again.

That night, the First Mountain Company sheltered under a big limestone outcropping. Seth sent out the picket outposts, then disappeared for a long time. He returned to the fire just before the men started to spread their groundsheets. Every head turned to look at him. Walt had not touched his banjo tonight. All the men sat in a glum silence. They had expected death and suffering on this expedition. But Helzer's demise had left all of them feeling vulnerable in a way they hadn't expected—there were many ways to die a bad death, here in the mountains.

Seth spoke a few words quietly, his voice calm and devoid of emotion. "Today a man fell to his death. I'm never going to forget Jimmy Helzer, and I'm never going to forget any of you men who rode with him. You're the best soldiers I've ever known, and I'm proud to fight beside every one of you. But tonight that applies especially to Walt Mackenzie and Charlie Plummer.

"Unfortunately," he added, "the dying isn't over. Not even close to being over. As I said before, any man can cut his picket pin at any time and return to regular duty, no questions asked."

He shut up and sat down. There was a long silence while the green firewood crackled and a cold night wind howled up through the remote passes of the sierra.

"*Augh!*" Kinney suddenly roared. "Who *wouldn't* be a soldier? If we can't rut nor drink knockum stiff, let's at least have some music here! Where's my regimental band? Rock me to sleep, mother!"

Walt snatched up his banjo and launched into "Drill, Ye Tarriers," and for the first time, Seth joined the voices singing around the fire.

Chapter 26

Just after sunup the next morning, Goes Ahead reported to Seth after making a forward scout of the enemy's position.

"They have no food. They stopped to slaughter and cook a pony and have lost much time. I think we could catch them before they reach the hollow at the end of the trail. The fight will go much better for us if we catch them on the trail."

Seth nodded. Once those Kiowas, led by a fanatical Kait-senko warrior, holed up for a final stand, the fight would be bloody. Though they were not all armed with rifles, there were nearly a hundred braves compared to Seth's force of forty. During a close-in fight from a fixed position, the Indian arrows would prove as deadly as bullets. It was best to engage them in the open and rely on the superior shooting of the Army marksmen.

They rode hard for the rest of that day, then well into the night, keeping Orion at their left and pushing steadily higher. They snatched three hours sleep and then moved out again. Now the fleeing Indians were rolling huge boulders over the trail, forcing the soldiers to constantly dismount and then exert their already weary muscles to clear a path. Toward late morning Seth began to notice occasional bright flashes of light up ahead.

"Close now," Goes Ahead said. "They turn around often to look back. That light come from mirror glass they put in their shields. Blinds their enemies in a charge."

Soon the trail straightened out and widened somewhat, and Seth could spot the Kiowas up ahead. He signaled for Charlie Plummer to move his squad of ten sharpshooters forward. Firing offhand from horseback, they dropped several of the enemy's ponies before the Kiowas went into defensive positions behind several huge jumbles of scree beside the trail.

"Picket your mounts here out of range," Seth ordered the men. "We'll form in a wedge and advance on foot under cover of the rocks. If they run, let daylight into their horses."

The mountain troopers leap-frogged from boulder to boulder, easily dodging bullets at this range. As they drew closer, arrows rushed past their ears.

"If one lands close, snap the shafts so they can't be used again!" Seth yelled.

Maintaining the taut battle discipline that characterized the unit, Carlson's Raiders refused to fire unless they had a sure target in their bead sights. Each man carried only thirty rounds, and every one had to count. No battle cries resounded, no one made any heroic individual charges to count coup on the Indians. They advanced methodically, smoothly, so far without taking a casualty, though several dead Indians had tumbled down out of the scree. Soon the entire unit was massed behind a short basalt parapet just beneath the Kiowa positions.

Kinney eased up beside Seth. "What's the game, Soldier Blue?"

"We can't draw a good bead on them from here," Seth said. "But they can't hit us, either. We have rations, they don't. Plus we have a clear field of fire to the only trail. I say we wait them out for now. From here, they can't break for the trail again without us picking them off."

"Fish in a barrel," Kinney agreed.

However, the Kiowas clearly had no intention of cooperating. Nor, Seth soon discovered, was he precisely correct that hits couldn't be scored from the Kiowa position. He and the rest were taken by surprise when the enemy launched a continuous volley of arrows almost straight up into the air, dropping them down onto the unseen soldiers below.

Seth hadn't clustered his men, so only two were hit, neither fatally. Even as Walt Mackenzie scuttled through the rocks to tend to them, a group of mounted Kiowas broke from hiding and raced for the trail. A fast volley from the soldiers dropped every one of them.

"They're carrion bait now!" Kinney exulted. "That's holding and squeezing, laddiebucks!"

A long silence ensued. Occasionally, another flurry of arrows dropped in, but the men had covered down better and no one else was hit.

The day dragged on, the sun climbing higher and higher across the sky, bringing some welcome warmth. The men chewed on hardtack, smoked, made small talk in low voices to stay alert. Now and then someone told a joke, and the men around him would laugh. But their fingers were curled inside their trigger guards, ready for the expected attack. Occasionally one of them was tricked into wasting a shot at an "Indian" that turned out to be buffalo hair on a stick, raised above the rocks to lure their fire.

"How they playing it?" Seth asked Kinney.

"Waiting until dark, I'd wager, so's they can sneak off on us."

"Then they'll have to use the trail. It's too steep behind them unless they desert their ponies."

"An Apache would, but not a Comanche or a Kiowa. They'll muzzle their mounts, then lead them up the trail."

"We'll have it covered and hope for a clear sky and a good moon."

But late in the afternoon, a white flag was thrust out above the scree. A moment later a brave stood up and shouted something in Spanish.

"What'd he say, Charlie?" Seth called out.

"They want to parley. He said they'll send three men out if we send three men out. No weapons."

"Fuck the red sonsabitches," Kinney said. "It's a trick. Why three? And their leader is a Kaitsenko, they never surrender."

"Might not be a trick," Charlie said. "Kiowas worship the number three, think it's holy or some such. They always parley that way. And they didn't say nothing about surrendering. They just want to parley. I ain't saying I trust 'em, but I know the Kiowa tribe is one for making deals so's the big Indians can save face in the eyes of their warriors."

"Trick," Kinney insisted.

"Maybe," Seth said. "But we can't charge them, and if they decide to wait and get a dark night to aid them, I can't see us stopping all of them. Which means one more fight up in that hollow, where we'll have to drive them out of breastworks. You saw what happened to Helzer. Besides all the men that'll sure's hell get killed, what if we end up with a lot of wounded men to pack out?"

This time Kinney nodded. Seth was right. A serious wound, even a moderately serious wound, was fatal up in this high country. And many men would surely be wounded.

Seth told Plummer, "Have them send out their men."

Charlie called up to them in halting Spanish. A few minutes later three braves scrambled nimbly up over the top of the scree and started down. They lifted both hands out before them to show they held no weapons.

"That big, hairy buck in the middle must be Eagle on His Journey," Kinney said. "*Look* at that sneering bastard. I'd like to pop that red Arab on the snot locker."

Seth did look, though he refrained from any comment. The Kaitsenko leader wore captured bluecoat trousers, tall cavalry boots, and a fur-lined leather shirt. He was huge—well over six feet—and thickly muscled, with a Roman nose and long, flowing black hair that fell below his waist.

"I'll need you to translate, Charlie," Seth said.

"I'll go too, sir," piped up a private named Bonaventure Lagace, who had been recruited from the dragoons.

Seth nodded. "Ground your weapons."

"It's a trick, shavetail," Kinney insisted.

"I half think you're right, Top. But let's go ahead and stir up the shit a little, I'm falling asleep. Lagace, you heard the top. You might be walking into a trap. Sure you want to go?"

"I'm a crazy sonofabitch and always have been, sir, it runs in my family. I wanna see me a live Kiowa up close."

"By-God, you're all stout lads! Hell, you gotta die sometime," Kinney called behind them as Seth and the others scrambled over the protective basalt embankment to meet the Indian delegation.

The trio of Kiowas halted and waited for them.

"I don't like it," Plummer said. "I've parleyed with Kiowas. They always come out halfway. These have stopped way back."

Plummer was still speaking when Seth spotted it: another flash of light as a hidden Indian slipped out from cover up in the scree. But before he could do anything about it, several trade rifles cracked. A slug whirred past Seth's ear with the sound of an angry hornet, and another tugged at his pants leg as it passed through. Plummer cursed and clutched at blood blossoming from his right thigh, and Lagace dropped in his tracks as a bullet tore through his neck.

"Cover down!" Seth screamed to Plummer.

While the two unarmed men made themselves small, the air suddenly erupted in a loud, singsong chanting.

"We got a fight coming now!" Goes Ahead shouted out. "That's their death song, here comes the charge!"

Sure enough, a pony and rider suddenly raced from behind the left flank of the scree and plunged down toward the white-skin position. Startled by the sudden and brazen attack, and the warning of a massed charge, the men opened fire as one, wasting far too many bullets on one target. Seconds later they sheepishly realized the "rider" was in fact a buckskin suit stuffed with grass.

Only now, however, did the full extent and brilliance of the Indians' diversionary tactics reveal itself. Behind the dug-in soldiers, a shotgun roared. Moments later their panicked ponies, picket pins dragging behind them, scattered both ways along the trail. Under cover of the confusion, a Kiowa had circled around behind the hair-faces and pulled their picket pins.

Now, above them, the Kiowas broke for freedom while the cursing soldiers tried to capture their mounts. They couldn't even get in any last shots at the fleeing braves for fear of hitting their own ponies.

Seth and Charlie Plummer leaped out from their cover and joined the men who were grabbing ponies. Several of the mounts that had run forward had been killed by the Indians. Inadvertently, they thus aided the soldiers by causing a gruesome choke point of dead ponies across the narrow trail, stopping the rest so they could be caught. Other men, however, were still running back down the trail, chasing the rest.

This time the victory clearly went to the enemy. The final toll was grim enough to a proud unit unused to serious setbacks: Though Lagace was the only man killed, and Plummer's wound was minor, three frightened ponies had plunged to their death, taking much of their owners' equipment with them. A fourth pony had broken a leg and had to be shot. This left only two remounts in the already sparse saddle band.

It was almost dark by the time Lagace had been buried in a shallow grave and covered with rocks. Those men not on guard threw out their bedrolls early, uneasy from the day's odd encounter. Seth was one of the last to leave the dying fire, accompanied by Kinney and Walt Mackenzie, who plucked quietly at his banjo but didn't bother to sing.

"Do we push after them?" Kinney said. "Now, I mean?"

"What's the point now? There's only one place they can go. Goes Ahead says the hollow's already built up and reinforced, so catching them there early won't help much. The men are tired, and the horses still nerve-frazzled. We'll post guards and get a good night's rest. Goes Ahead is making one final scout, then we'll make our plan."

"That shines right. Them Injins bamboozled us good. Hell, they had us shootin' at goddamn scarecrows."

Seth nodded. "I figured the parley was just a smokescreen. But as long as they were making a play, it seemed better to do something than risk a night battle. Expert marksmen aren't much use if it's too dark to draw a bead."

"Tits on a boar hog. You played it right. I was all for waiting, but take a look at that sky. No stars, and the moon's

been covered by clouds. You called it right, shavetail, but
then, I trained you, so what the hell? Mackenzie! The hell
you so mournful for tonight, you sad sack of shit? Pluck me
out a jig, boyo!"

"Ain't got no fettle for it, Top. I'm worn down to the
nub." Mackenzie stood up and headed out to check on the
horses.

"Moody fucker," Kinney said. "The hell's his problem?"

"Get some sleep," Seth told him. "We all got the same
problem, and it's waiting for us at the end of that trail."

Eagle on His Journey posted two sentries along the steep
trail that ended at the rocky hollow where the Kiowas had
taken refuge. The first, located farthest out, was situated at
the top of a razorback with a good view down the trail for
miles. He was within sight of a second sentry closer to the
hollow.

Early on the first morning following their clever escape
from the white-skins, the first sentry spotted the enemy approaching. He raised his streamered lance high to catch the
other sentry's attention. Then he pulled one finger slowly
across his forehead, signifying the brim of a hat—sign talk
for white men.

The second sentry, well out of sight of the approaching
column, uncrimped a rifle cartridge and shook the grains of
powder out onto his palm. He licked the filed-flint point of
an arrow, pressed it into the powder, then notched the arrow
into his osage bow and drew the string taut. He dipped it
into a small fire burning at his feet, then shot the heavily
smoking arrow up in a high arc. The black-smoke parabola
lingered in the air, warning the rest back in the hollow: *Enemy right on us, soon comes the attack!*

A light rain tickled his face as Seth clawed his way over the
mica-and-quartz rimrock and cautiously peered into the hollow below him. The Kiowas had formed battle groups behind
breastworks of piled stone. As he had hoped, all were staring
intently forward, watching for the attack up the trail. He
prayed that none would think to look straight overhead in
the next few minutes.

His carbine was slung across his back. He secured a rope to a boulder, then tossed it back down the sheer cliff face behind him to the narrow shelf where Charlie Plummer—his right thigh wrapped in a bloody bandage—waited with his squad. As the troops climbed up to join him, Seth began securing more ropes to other boulders.

The bold plan had begun with Goes Ahead's discovery of a very narrow trace that bypassed the main trail and the hollow where the Kiowas were holed up. Perhaps made by the Caddoes who used to explore this region, it was barely wide enough for one pony at a time and passed close to the Kiowas, but remained out of sight under a traprock shelf. The soldiers had passed a shoeing hammer from man to man, removing their horses' iron shoes to cut noise. They had also muzzled the ponies with their belts to keep them from nickering while they sneaked around their enemy. Now the ponies were all bunched in a tiny clearing at the end of the hidden trace.

It was Larry Muggins, a private who had served under Corey Bryce, who suggested the idea of using ropes to drop down silently on the enemy, taking them by surprise. Muggins had fought under the Methodist preacher Chivington and his Pike's Peakers when the Colorodans had used the same trick to destroy the Confederate Army massed at La Glorietta Pass in New Mexico.

As more and more men crowded up beside Seth, they began knotting lengths of rope to those their leader had already secured.

"Good time to put at 'em," Kinney whispered in Seth's ear, swiping rain out of his eyes. "Wet weather loosens the animal tendons they use for bowstrings."

When all the ropes were ready, each man went through a final weapons check and fixed bayonets. Seth met Kinney's eyes, then Plummer's, nodding to each in turn.

"Here goes for a brevet or a coffin!" Kinney whispered. A moment later Seth lowered himself hand over hand down the stone face, the rest spilling out all around him.

Seth had given strict orders to hold all fire until he fired the first shot, unless they were spotted first. But the descent went perfectly: The hissing rain and the steady mutter of distant thunder covered the light scraping sounds of their cloth-muffled boots on the rocks. Seth dropped lower, ever lower, searching as he descended for the tall Kiowa leader. His pulse throbbed in his ears and sweat broke out in his armpits. He reached bottom and shrugged his carbine off his back.

Then one of the soldiers fell as he landed, carbine clattering on the rocks, and the Kiowas whirled around.

Eagle on His Journey met Seth's eyes. Seth waited long enough for recognition to dawn on the Kiowa's face. Then the soldier's first shot punched into the battle chief's chest and sent him tumbling over the breastwork. In rapid succession Seth emptied the rest of his seven-shot Spencer, killing or wounding an enemy with almost every shot. And now the air around him fairly crackled with the sound of unrelenting carbine fire and the death shrieks of the Indians.

As spent cartridges clattered to the rocks, the soldiers surged forward, mowing their enemy down before them. Seth crammed rounds through his butt plate, felt his carbine kicking into his shoulder over and over, the stock slapping his cheek with each report. A Kiowa unleashed a savage kill cry and lunged at him with his deadly skull cracker—a tapered stone war club. Seth tucked and rolled, came up in a crouch and drove his bayonet deep into the brave's vitals.

In an eye blink Charlie Plummer was in trouble beside him. Spencer carbines were sturdy and accurate, but the soft copper shells had a tendency to stick in the breech. Plummer was desperately prying a stuck cartridge loose when a Kiowa brave lifted his rifle at almost point-blank range. A moment later Walt Mackenzie, one of the last to come down the ropes, kicked away from the stone face and swung his right foot hard into the Kiowa's face. Charlie freed the stoppage and shot the brave dead as he struggled to his feet.

Very few of the surprised enemy even got a shot off. The fight was over quicker than a hungry man could gulp a biscuit. Dead and dying Kiowas lay scattered everywhere. Soldiers, their faces powder-blackened above their beards, moved quickly about the hollow, finishing off the wounded with bullets to the brain.

Seth still had half his rounds left. But those he'd fired had been in such rapid succession that a wiping patch would sizzle if he shoved it through his bore now. His ears still rang, and the acrid stink of cordite hung thick in the damp air. A quick battle muster revealed that only two men were hurt, one shot through the knee, the other the victim of a broken ankle when he landed wrong coming down the rope.

"It went slicker than cat shit on oilskin," Kinney gloated as he removed a bone choker from a dead Kiowa. Other men, too, had started to gather up trophies.

Seth spotted Walt Mackenzie. The orderly stood apart from the rest, ignoring everything and gazing out down the trail. Seth walked over beside him. "You all right?"

Mackenzie glanced at him, nodded. "I asked to go along, sir, and I'm with you from here to the harvest. I know the Innuns we done for today was some mighty hard cases, I seen the things they done. And I'm happier than a pig in shit about you killing Eagle on His Journey—the murderin' bastard. But I got to say, this today, it wasn't no battle. It don't seem right, somehow. It just wasn't no kind of battle at all."

Walt walked off. Seth stood for a minute, watching him. Then he turned toward his men.

"Lissenup!" he shouted. "We take nothing from this place, and that's an order. I'm not going to lose any sleep over the Indians I killed here today. They were murdering criminals who torture and kill noncombatants, and they fired on us after showing a white flag. But they were also a worthy enemy and ran us ragged. We got awful damn lucky just now. No trophies. I'm proud of all of you, but we got enough gear to pack out already."

"Jesus," Kinney groused. "You been drinkin' with Quakers?"

"You shut your goddamn mouth. I gave an order and I expect it to be carried out."

Kinney seemed almost pleased by the harshness of the rebuke. He threw the choker quickly down. "Yes, sir, Colonel!"

Kinney turned to face the rest. "Augh! You heard the man, ladies! Drop that goddamn contraband before I unscrew your heads and shit in them!"

Chapter 27

"Ladies and gentlemen, those I represent agree there is indeed an 'Indian problem.' That is why we so readily accepted the challenge of a public forum to debate the subject. However, we radically part ways with my colleague here, Senator Jeffries, on the precise definition of that problem. So not surprisingly, we also differ fundamentally as to the most appropriate solution for it."

Pennsylvania senator Josiah Hopewell paused, his shrewd, intelligent eyes sweeping the vast auditorium. Today's widely publicized debate was being held in a little-used theater annex of the U.S. Capitol, but it had drawn enough spectators to fill the neoclassically vaulted main chamber. One reason was the athletic and ruddy-complected soldier seated in the cordoned-off box reserved for guest speakers. Corey Bryce's clean-cut good looks and smart dress uniform drew admiring glances from every female present, and today they were nearly as numerous as the men.

"Yes, there is certainly an Indian problem," Senator Hopewell conceded again. "We simply urge our government to approach it using something other than force. Force is counterproductive in the long run. The Sand Creek massacre, for example, forced the Cheyenne to make common cause with the Sioux, and the results have been devastating for all concerned. You heard Lieutenant Bryce describe his terrible ordeal. My heart, too, went out to this fine young man. But you also heard me read the letter from Hays Munro, agent at the Mater Dolorosa Reservation in the New Mexico Territory. Nothing in Munro's background shows him to be an 'Indian lover,' yet he, too, has learned how human greed leads to unnecessary force.

"We also urge our government to honor treaties already in place. Senator Jeffries is an enthusiastic supporter of John Bozeman's road through Wyoming. Fine, but that road clearly violates earlier treaties with the Sioux. It's small wonder, to quote an Army officer fighting on the frontier, that 'the American Indian despises a liar'!"

Hopewell relinquished his spot at the podium to a smattering of polite applause, a few low hisses and jeers. He was a small, slightly stooped but energetic man in a charcoal frock coat. The speaker who took his place seemed like a deliberate contrast: Senator Boone Jeffries of Kansas was big and hale and flamboyant, drawing plenty of attention to himself in his buckskin trousers and a fringed buckskin coat.

"I say to my esteemed colleague what we always say out West to yarners who outbrag each other around the campfire: *horse apples!*"

Laughter rippled through the high-ceilinged room with its steeply banked tiers of seats. The audience included Brigadier General Ferris Ablehard and his civilian associate Eric Hupenbecker, the investor whose fledgling land company was currently suing the Indian Bureau to open grant lands up for white homesteading.

"Senator Hopewell eulogizes the aboriginals, tells us they despise a liar. Oh? And do pigs fly, too? Does this Noble Savage of Senator Hopewell's bucolic West also despise murderers, thieves, and—pardon my range manners, ladies—rapists? I submit that Senator Hopewell and his clamoring followers want the American government to stick its own head in a noose."

Jeffries wore his sandy hair long and tucked behind his ears so that it flipped over his collar. He paced before the podium, bent slightly forward at the waist as if ready to pounce.

"It is a grievous mistake, ladies and gentlemen, to coddle the savages. Witness all the dead Texans who tried to accommodate the dreaded Comanche, the Arizonans who even now are being felled daily in the Apache reign of terror. Ask any family of settlers who has filed a homestead, staked out a tomahawk claim, then worked for years to prove up their land, only to see Indian lovers in Congress take it all away from them and give it to heathens and bison."

Jeffries crossed to the box and stopped in front of Corey.

"Ask this courageous young Army officer, this leader of men who has already described for you in heartrending detail what it was like to watch, helpless, while gut-eating animals destroyed a man's very reason for living! Jeanette Bryce would tell us all about the Noble Savage, if she were alive today as she *ought* to be!"

Corey flushed as every face in the annex turned to stare at him as if he were a bit of curiosa in a freak show. The pity in those eyes made him curl his toes in silent anger and curse the entire lot of them for fools.

"Ladies and gentlemen, I'm proud as a game rooster that Lieutenant Bryce has finally chosen to break his agony of silence by testifying here today. Such courageous and heartbreaking testimony balances the rhetorical books a little by showing the price—in human suffering—of Senator Hopewell's misguided sentimentalism.

"I leave you today with some pithy advice from this city's own distinguished Professor Drouillard of Georgetown College—a man known, as we westerners like to put it, for shooting straight from the shoulder. 'Preaching gospel to savages,' the professor has opined, 'is worse than casting pearls to swine—swine won't scalp you in your sleep.' Even more to the point: 'The decisions our government reaches today about the red man will affect generations to come.' "

Jeffries fell silent, and applause erupted throughout the theater. Corey flushed again when Jeffries, on his way from the podium, followed a showman's instinct and suddenly stopped in front of him again. He tugged him up from his seat to turn and face the audience.

"Ladies and gentlemen, I give you the backbone of America—our fighting men in blue!"

The applause grew deafening, and almost every woman in the place now cried openly. Even a few men swiped at their eyes. Corey's humiliation was complete when a young girl of nineteen or so surged forward, hugged him desperately, then burst into tears. With a gallant flourish, Jeffries produced a handkerchief and escorted the distraught young thing back to her parents.

"Say, shavetail," Ablehard congratulated him when Corey joined the general and Hupenbecker in the cloakroom. "You were in good form today."

"Capital," Hupenbecker said, adding, "no pun intended. That was a nice bit with the hysterical young girl. I wonder if Boone put her up to it, the rascal? The newspapers will milk it good. A few more episodes like today, and my company will be issuing land warrants hand over fist."

Corey ignored them. "Was he there?" he asked Ablehard.

"Who? Trapp, you mean?"

Corey nodded.

"Of course, m'boy, of course, didn't I assure you he would be? He was there, all right, taking your full measure. And I could tell he liked what he saw."

Lieutenant General Nelson Trapp was currently the most powerful three-star general in the U.S. Army. Head of the War Department's Operations and Planning Section, he was direct advisor to President Grant on the matter of combat strategy for fighting the postbellum Indian campaign.

"You won't forget, sir, your promise to introduce me to him?"

Ablehard and Hupenbecker exchanged quick glances.

"Lad, *this* old war-horse doesn't forget a damn thing. I've already spoken with Nelson, told him what a bright young man my aide-de-camp is. Everything in its own time, Corey. Just be patient."

"Don't forget," Hupenbecker put in, "Trapp is a member of our organization, too, just like Senator Jeffries. Now that you've joined, you and General Trapp share an important common bond. He'll be sympathetic to your suggestions."

"The more you make appearances like this one today, acting as a spokesman for Americans United for Survival," Ablehard said, "the more aware Trapp becomes of you. I happen to know he's an admirer of your father's politics, too. It won't be long, you mark my words, and you'll join a select group of officers on his staff at Ops and Planning."

"All this brouhaha over railroad routes," Hupenbecker said, "is keeping President Grant busier than a one-legged man at an ass-kicking contest. Right now Trapp's section has damn near a free hand."

Corey nodded, helping Ablehard into his wool greatcoat. He thought again about the dime novel he'd found in his letter box last week. Rage clutched at his stomach. Like all the magazines and newspapers lately, it had arrived without benefit of an address or postage. Entitled *Frontier Destiny*, the story used thinly disguised names and was based on the Sunday Stroll tragedy—except that in this version the Corey figure died, while Seth and Jeanette survived to get married and have children.

"That's what I want," Corey said. "A free hand."

Mexico's northern state of Chihuahua is mostly an elevated plain, much of it located between the rugged peaks of two mineral-rich cordilleras, the Sierra Madre Occidental and the Sierra Madre Oriental. The western mountains, especially, are separated by fertile valleys whose lush splendor sent early Spanish explorers into descriptive rhapsodies. One of the most remote and beautiful of these valleys, Valle del Lago Azul, was home to La Esperanza, a hacienda owned by the Spanish monarchist Enrique Padilla.

La Esperanza had been considered a showcase of successful enterprise under the recently aborted reign of Austrian Prince Maximilian of Hapsburg. Now, like the rest of the dwindling *hacendados*, Padilla ruled over a medieval-style manor which comprised a self-sufficient unit and cared little about supplying the rest of the war-ravaged country. The fields and pastures of the fertile valley produced the "five C's" of hacienda commerce: corn, cotton, cattle, coffee, and cane. The higher elevations added a sixth: vast, high-grade deposits of copper. The latter was sold exclusively to the North Americans, as the Spanish called citizens of the U.S.

Indeed, Mexico was still New Spain to Padilla. He was a Spanish-born white sent from Spain as a child with his parents. That had been in 1835, well after Mexico's first bloody revolution in 1821 had led to political independence from the mother country, though the ties were still strong. Thus, he had grown to manhood in a land where power by brutal violence was the rule, not the exception.

He had seen governments change so often they were gone before the leader's name reached the peons in the countryside: fifty different administrations in just thirty-five chaotic years. And more rebellions than a man could follow even if he tried, over 250 of them. "Sides" didn't matter, and in fact had no meaning—success went to the strongest generals with the strongest armies, and they fought for whichever *patrón* fed them best. And naturally, those armies were raised, in part, by looting the haciendas of Chihuahua and Sonora, by driving their cattle across the border into Texas and Arizona, where it was sold to purchase guns and ammunition.

La Esperanza did not escape the damage, but somehow it had survived. And now it even thrived, in large part because of Los Bendigados, the Blessed, Padilla's name for the cost-efficient *indio* peons who worked his land and mines. Truly blessed, for they received good food and shelter, unlike the starving masses in this war-weary nation: Yaquis, Mayas, Aztecs, Pimas, Karankawas, Apaches, some a *mezcla* of two or more tribes. They were not officially slaves—the Constitution of 1857 had outlawed this practice. They were nonetheless forced laborers who were delivered by slave traders and broken in young. They were well-enough cared for, Padilla being a practical man who liked to husband his resources and maximize profits. But he also believed that certain realities about their wild blood must be faced. When they grew old enough, the boys especially, they were carefully monitored by Padilla's *segundo* and the *jefes*—recruited from the army or the Seguridades Publicas, the private army of the Governor of Chihuahua—in charge of the hacienda work crews. Any

child who represented even a remote threat was taken on
work details deep into the copper mines, never to be heard of
again.

But this winter day was a pleasant one, and Enrique Padilla had no room in his mind for violent thoughts as he
surveyed the grounds of La Esperanza in the company of a
former vaquero named Jesus Gallegos, now employed as his
segundo. The two men rode in a calash, a light conveyance
with its top folded down, offering a beautiful view of the
fields and orchards, the lemon and tamarind trees that bore
delicate and fragrant flowers almost year-round in this valley
of mild winters. From the lane that neatly divided the fertile
valley, they could also glance up the nearby slope and see the
head frame of the most productive copper mine.

"This last group we got from Aragon, the four Apaches.
They are young and the *norteamericanos* have not been feeding them so well. But they are healthy enough. I think they
will work out fine. The girl, the oldest one. She will perhaps
bear watching. She is defiant now, but give Gabriela some
time with her, she will come out well, *ojalá*."

Gallegos fell silent and Padilla nodded slowly, thoughtfully, offering the grave and careful attention he lavished on
every matter presented him, monumental or trivial. He was a
pale, handsome man in his forties, his hair still dark, though
thinning, his skin clear and unlined. Though he had never
served in any army, he wore a richly embroidered tunic with
a fourragère looped around the left shoulder and a silk handkerchief tucked into one sleeve.

"Were the boys sent to the mine?"

Gallegos nodded. He was perhaps fifteen years younger
than his *patrón*. Compact and powerfully built, he wore tight
black trousers and a silver-frogged jacket with a flat leather
shako hat. He was considered the best rider in the valley, and
an expert with his braided-leather reata. He had filed the
sight off the bone-handle Volcanic .38 in his holster so it
wouldn't snag coming out—and it was known to come out
very quickly indeed.

"I put one back in the stopes, another on the slusher line."

"Let's see how they're doing."

Gallegos nodded and tugged the reins.

They veered right onto a side trail just ahead, the light vehicle beginning to lug as they ascended toward the mine entrance. From here Padilla could look back down toward the white Moorish arches of the *casa grande,* could see the neat spread of the stables, the granary, the chapel, the dairy. Beyond all of it were the lines of rock-and-adobe shelters where Los Bendigados lived. A Mexican woman wearing a dark rebozo, with a lace mantilla wrapped around her head, hurried out of the *casa grande* and began to chase some chickens running free in the side garden. Padilla grinned. When Gabriela caught the one she wanted, she would wring its neck with a decisive snap that always truly impressed him. The hard-boiled old woman disgusted his wife, who had even resorted to tears in her efforts to get rid of her. But though Padilla was usually doting where his wife was concerned, he had put his foot down on the matter of Gabriela. She was a mean one, but good at handling the *indio* women, who could sometimes be very difficult.

The *indios.* Like most Catholic *hacendados,* Padilla preferred a simple and convenient morality when it came to justifying slave labor. The pureblood Spaniards, the Mexican-born Creoles like his wife, even the mixed-blood Mexicans and South Americans like Gallegos: according to the Church, all these were sentient creatures with souls that would rejoice in heaven or burn in hell. But the heathen *indios . . .* they were not blessed with the vital élan, and thus like the animals and plants, had been put on earth to serve man's pleasure and merely dissolve back into the clay from whence they came. Padilla gratefully accepted this doctrine and was generous to himself in his interpretation of the word "pleasure."

The vehicle rocked to a stop beside a huge steam boiler. It powered a cable line that extended back into the successive stopes of the mine shaft. As the stopes were blown deeper, the ore and waste were removed in big iron buckets connected to the cable. Well back from the mine entrance about a dozen *indios,* all boys between four and twelve years old, sat on tall three-legged stools while the buckets moved past them. It was their job to sort the good chunks of ore from the mucking waste, tossing them into cars on the narrow-gauge tracks behind them.

As the two men climbed out, a burly man in a jipijapa hat crossed from the group of boys. Thick lumps of scar tissue crowded his eyes. An old eighteen-inch bowie was tucked under his belt without benefit of a sheath.

"Don Enrique. Cómo se encuentra, patrón?"

"Bien, Ramon, bien, gracias."

He nodded toward the boys. "How are the new ones doing? The Apaches?"

"Good workers, Don Enrique. Quiet boys who pay attention. This one, I have checked his buckets, and he misses very little. They hold themselves back from the others, but have caused no trouble."

"Do they eat well?"

Ramon bared his broken yellow teeth. "Like two starving pups."

Padilla walked closer to the slusher crew, Gallegos dogging his heels. The *segundo* carried a rawhide quirt, now and then whacking his boot with it.

"Chico," he said to the Apache boy named Miguelito, *"cómo estás?"*

The boy met his eyes with a friendly, curious candor that momentarily disarmed the *hacendado*. But seeing Ramon nearby, the boy quickly turned back to his work. Padilla had heard good things about this one—docile but plucky, Gabriela had described him.

"Bien, senor," the boy finally answered.

Padilla placed his hands on his thighs and bent forward a bit, bringing his face on a level with the boy's. "Do you like it here, *niño?*"

Miguelito hesitated before he answered. *"Si, senor."*

Padilla lowered his voice. "Tell me the truth. Does Ramon treat you bad? Hit you, frighten you?"

The question seemed to almost panic Miguelito. His eyes slanted up briefly to meet Padilla's, then returned to the buckets.

"No, senor," he replied.

Padilla looked at his *segundo* and both men laughed. Gallegos whacked his boot so hard the boy winced.

"He learns quickly," Padilla said. "You are right, I like him."

"As I said, it is his sister who worries me."

Padilla cast another glance back down the slope toward the house and yard. For a moment he pictured defiant eyes in a high-boned face that held the promise of great beauty. It was a type of finely delineated, Romanesque beauty he usually associated with North American women, for it was one of the secret disappointments of his life that he had married a dark Spanish beauty instead of a blonde. Fortunately, a man could find little ways to compensate for the big disappointments. But now, thinking about such defiance and hatred in one so young made Padilla wonder if *indios* were indeed devoid of the spirit flame within. Then he reminded himself that animals, too, could become enraged.

"If the girl worries you, Jesus," he told his subordinate, "then by all means, let us go visit her, too."

Chapter 28

By the spring of 1870 the U.S. Army's postbellum drive against Indians had quelled or seriously weakened most of the northern plains tribes. Abetted by melodramatic journalism and a welling American fear of the Apaches that sometimes bordered on hysteria, that drive became a single-minded campaign to exterminate this tough southwestern tribe—the most enduring and humiliating reminder that primitive savages could match wits with West Point's best.

Back East, deadlines had already been set, ignored, set again—final dates by which each of the many scattered bands was to report to the reservations at San Carlos, Bosque Redondo, Mater Dolorosa, and elsewhere. Many had done so. But many others had not. Now, led by savvy battle leaders such as Geronimo, Nana, and more recently, Jemez Grayeyes, the holdouts had formed many small, highly mobile bands. Linked by the elusive moccasin telegraph, they were conducting a defiant and superbly coordinated guerrilla war against the vastly more numerous white-eye invaders. Their goal was to confuse both troops and settlers, to spread fear and make life hell for all the hair-faces who had pushed into Apacheria. Especially hard hit were the merchants of the Tucson Committee.

Amid clamors of "Send Seth again!" the First Mountain Company was deployed by special troop train from Fort Bates to Fort Grant. The elite Indian-fighting unit had returned from its successful defeat of the Kaitsenko to a newspaper fanfare unprecedented in American journalism. Carlson's Raiders rested and recruited at Fort Bates. Seth turned his tough little calico out to a long, well-earned graze and selected a blaze-faced sorrel trained to hate the odor of Indians.

Led by Nat Bischoff, writers throughout the country had offered their own stirring—and mostly fictitious—accounts of the indestructible Seth Carlson's devil-may-care heroics: how he had faced sure death over and over, reins in his teeth, sidearm blazing, knocking the Grim Reaper from his pony each time. Bullets, one writer even hinted in an especially purple passage, were destined to fly wide around Seth Carlson, destined to turn to sand because the Divine Commander had marked him down for a greater fate than death.

Newspapermen and other sensation seekers hounded the troop train at every stop and clamored like beggars, thick as flies in a Mexican marketplace. Seth's policy now was to maintain an indifferent silence around them. But Kinney's constant threats to "bugger the lot of you scribbling pansies" kept them thinned out. And thus the First Mountain Company arrived in the Arizona Territory, ready to take on the Apache menace which had already defied some of the toughest soldiers in the world for 350 years.

A commodious pavilion had been erected in the center of Governor's Park on the northern outskirts of Tucson. Under a gaily colored canvas awning, couples in Sunday finery danced to dizzying Virginia reels played by an Army band from Fort Grant. A banner, surrounded by red, white, and blue bunting and mounted between upended corral poles out front, proclaimed: WELCOME, FIRST MOUNTAIN COMPANY!!! Behind the open-sided tent, mixed-blood menials roasted a young goat on a spit.

"The thing of it is, Colonel," Charles Longstreet said, "the treaties aren't worth a busted trace chain. As I'm sure you've learned by now, eh?—notions held by the greenhorns back East don't cut much ice out here."

Seth held the place of honor at the head of a long trestle table covered with ivory-lace cloths. To his left sat Charles Longstreet, to his right Nat Bischoff. The VIPs scattered along the table's length included Matthew Lewiston, Governor of Arizona Territory.

"What's the point of making a kick to the paper-collars who sit behind desks in Washington?" Longstreet added. "A man wants a thing done right, he's got to do it himself."

Seth met Bischoff's eye as he answered Longstreet. There was no animosity in his tone, just a pointed irony. "And of course you haven't got time to fight the Apaches yourself, what with looking after all your business concerns."

"It would be a stretch," Longstreet agreed amiably, not once feeling the barb. But Bischoff smiled wanly and sipped from his wineglass. He never missed a trick, and this wasn't the first time since Carlson's arrival that the officer had shown his contempt for both men.

Other guests at this and nearby tables included several officers from Fort Grant and a slightly wall-eyed captain named Dennis Moats, the stolid and stern-jawed commander of the cavalry troop garrisoned at Tucson. All had been deferential, to the point of fawning, since the First Mountain Company had deployed from the train. Seth, in turn, was civil but distant, interested neither in impressing nor goading them. The War Department had been generous in allowing him a free hand to run his troop as he saw fit. So he had made little protest when Washington officials insisted on this formal reception; he had even borrowed a sad-iron and pressed his best tunic. Seth saw the entire affair as a good feed among pretty, perfumed women—and a passel of mostly harmless fools who were actually quite amusing once Old Tanglefoot started humming in a man's blood. However, he had never expected to end up within spitting distance of

Nat Bischoff. Nor had closer scrutiny done one damn thing to temper his loathing for the man.

Governor Lewiston tapped on his wineglass with a fork to get everyone's attention. A mine owner, he was also a Tucson resident and a member of the committee.

"Ladies and gentlemen, officers and men! I think most of you can feel it in the air as I can—a sense that we're *all* a part of history here today. The young officer at the head of this table has got the hopes of an entire nation resting on his capable shoulders. But he isn't alone in this most important of missions. He's got forty good men pushing him on to victory. And so, I propose a toast: to Carlson's Raiders of the First Mountain Company. 'These are the boys who fear no noise where the mighty cannons roar.'"

Seth lifted his glass to applause and shouts of "Hear! Hear!" His eyes briefly met those of his other comrades at the table, not holding any of them long for fear they'd all burst out laughing in scorn at this dog-and-pony show. Charlie Plummer was there, already flushed with drunkenness. Kinney sat beside Plummer, matching him shot for shot from a bottle of good grain mash. Walt Mackenzie, clean-shaven now and attending as Seth's orderly, sat just beyond Longstreet. Mackenzie wore an ill-fitting uniform, and the other officers present clearly did not think much of the corporal's easy, familiar relationship with Colonel Carlson. It reflected badly on Carlson—fraternization with enlisted men was the mark of a weak leader. It was as if Carlson felt a cool contempt for the privileges of rank.

Lewiston nattered on, but Seth missed most of it, watching as Bischoff slipped off to join a young blond woman at the next table. She wore a gown of silk twill, and her thick hair was pulled back tight and coiled in a Psyche knot on the nape of her neck, held by a tortoiseshell comb. She was pretty, her face unfashionably tanned from exposure to the sun. He wondered if the man with her was her father or a much older husband. Probably not her husband—not the way Bischoff and Captain Moats were vying for her attention.

". . . can't trust the greasers, either," Longstreet was advising Seth, "or you'll end up rotting in a *cárcel* in Mexico."

Seth listened, a glaze over his eyes, nodding now and then to humor the fool. The woman at the next table met his eyes, and he realized she was doing much the same as he was: merely humoring her interlocutors. The wall-eyed officer had scarlet pinpoints in his cheeks from imbibing too much wine. For a moment his voice rose above the hubbub, pedantic and slightly belligerent as he addressed himself to Bischoff, leaning rudely in front of the woman.

"No, sir, you're confused on your terminology. 'Skyline' means to foolishly show yourself on a ridge. 'Skylight' is when you attempt to *spot* someone who's skylined."

The woman was clearly bored. She met his eyes again, and Seth smiled. She looked quickly away without acknowledging him.

"He keeps looking over at you, my dear," Hays Munro said, "and you keep looking rudely away. Interesting. Is this a case of 'the stage lighting up,' as the playwrights put it?"

He had spoken low so Bischoff and the cavalry officer couldn't overhear him.

"If I were in the mood for intrigue," she answered, "I'd hardly select the nation's top Indian killer."

"I don't know about that. Surprisingly, I *like* him," Hays said, looking closely at this celebrated young man with the weather-rawed face. His dark hair curled down onto the collar of his tunic. "There's real character stamped into that face. And certainly," he added, casting a sidelong glance past Kathleen, "from a young lady's point of view, he surpasses the potential competition."

"Touché."

Munro leaned even closer to her. "I'd wager anything that it was Bischoff himself who had us invited. My letters to the newspapers, and my essay in *Harper's*, have got them worried. We were asked only to keep up amiable appearances. They never expected us to actually show up."

Kathleen recalled that visit from Jemez Grayeyes, his warning about the grave Hays was digging himself into. A cool shiver moved down her spine.

"Your letters have got *me* worried, too."

"To quote my favorite reservation teacher: 'No philosophy but in the doing.'"

Bischoff leaned forward and looked past the obnoxious cavalry officer to Kathleen. "No secrets from the press, you two," he called over playfully.

"Rot in hell, you corrupt bastard," Munro muttered.

Kathleen kicked his ankle under the table. "Hays, please! You promised to avoid trouble if I agreed to come. Remember?"

"Oh, damnit, I remember. It just galls me, his sitting there acting as if he didn't lie through his teeth in that piece on the raid."

Munro looked at Seth again. "By God, *look* at him—this is all a fool's game to him. It's just as I thought. That jackass Bischoff has appropriated the man's very identity for his own purposes. He knows nothing about Carlson, or if he does, he doesn't care."

"He's an Indian killer."

"Bosh! Some Indians need killing." Munro glanced meaningfully toward Bischoff and Longstreet. "So do plenty of white men. I'm going to invite him to the reservation."

"Who?"

"Seth Carlson."

Alarm tightened her voice. "Why?"

"Why not? He's officially the second-ranking military commander in the area after the C.O. at Fort Grant. I intended to invite him anyway, even if I instantly loathed the sight of him. It's my duty. If he's here to kill Indians, then in fact I'm obligated to consult with him."

Munro watched Seth meet Kathleen's eyes again, again watched her turn away. His thin lips creased in a smile.

"Interesting," he said again. "Something is definitely germinating here."

Charles Longstreet was in the midst of making a point—dotting invisible *i*'s in midair with his cigar—when he saw Seth's eyes focus somewhere behind him. Longstreet turned around and immediately fell silent.

"Why, hallo Charlie! Hallo over there, Nat! You boys seem surprised to see your old drinking companion."

"Evening, Bob," Longstreet said.

Seth took in a big, powerfully built man with bluff features and drooping mustache. He wore a leather weskit, a black wool hat, well-polished oxblood boots. He was one of the few men Seth had noticed going around Tucson unarmed.

"Hell, boys," the newcomer said, "I'm dried to jerky! How about some panther piss? I guess maybe you boys forgot to invite me."

Longstreet frowned. He avoided looking at the table where his wife and many other respectable women of Tucson were glowering at Robert Trilby.

One by one Trilby met the eyes of every man who dared look at him. And one by one they all looked away first—all except one, Trilby noticed. The young officer at the head of the table watched him with utter indifference.

"Here," Seth finally said, tossing a bottle of mash to the new arrival. "If you're dried to jerky, best have a drink."

Trilby caught the bottle neatly and grinned. "By-God! Who's your friend, Charlie?"

"Colonel Carlson, Robert Trilby."

Both men nodded, neither offering his hand.

"Seth Carlson," Trilby said. "Well, this *is* an honor. Your reputation has preceded you, sir. Ol' eloquent Nat over there has called you an American Beowulf. No offense, but that only means something to them that read. You don't stand deuce-high with the Apaches. Be careful, Colonel. By the time you see them, it's too late."

Seth felt the blond-haired woman's eyes on him. " 'Preciate the warning, Mr. Trilby. I'll keep it in mind."

Trilby nodded. He spoke clearly enough. But the puffiness around his eyes suggested that he'd already enjoyed an ample ration of whiskey.

"I wasn't invited tonight, Colonel, because I'm not a decent family man. You a family man?"

By now everyone in the tent had fallen silent, listening. Trilby's blunt question left menace hanging in the air.

Before Seth could answer, a chair scraped the planks about halfway down the table. By the time Plummer made it to his feet, there was an old dragoon pistol in his fist—the early Civil War model manufactured by the New Haven Arms

Company. It fired big, conical balls capable of shocking a man to death even when they struck an arm or leg. The business end of the muzzle was leveled at Trilby's belly. Several women gasped.

"Put your weapon away, sir," Trilby said calmly. "I'm unarmed."

"Like hob I will, you greasy shit-stain. I'm drawing down on you cuz I mean to kill you. Besides, you ain't unarmed. You ain't decent enough to wear your weapon where a man can see it. Cockroaches like you always carry a hideout gun."

Plummer looked at Seth. "Permission to kill him, sir?"

"*Augh!*" Kinney set the bottle down, his purple-tinted face going even darker with excited blood. He was enjoying this impromptu turn of events immensely.

"Why?" Seth asked. He was far more amazed than angry.

"Why? Hell, because he's garbage, Colonel, that's why. He's bad trouble. Look at him. I mean really *look*. He's going to deal us a world of hurt. I say let's kill him now while I got the fettle for it."

Trilby held his cool, mocking smile. But Seth watched a line of sweat break out just under the brim of his hat.

"Wha'd*you* say, Top?" Plummer shouted.

"He's a bent shooter, you ask me. Besides, he never bought me a beer," Kinney answered. "Air the ugly sonofabitch."

Plummer's eyes landed on Mackenzie. "Walt! Wha'd'you say?"

"It's no mix of mine, so long's I don't have to clean it up."

"See?" Plummer looked at Seth as if he had a strong and reasonable case. "The men are all for it. Give me the nod, Colonel, and I'll knock him out from under his hat."

Seth felt Trilby's eyes on him; felt, too, the weight of the blond-haired woman's stare.

"Well, Colonel Carlson," Trilby said quietly, "this is a familiar drama for you, nazpaw? Playing God with another person's life, I mean."

The remark brought a dead, almost painful silence. Seth felt dizzying heat rise up into his face, tasted bile erupting up his throat. His arms went weak and useless as the rage gripped him. All that passed quickly, and a cold calm settled into his muscles.

"Bob," Longstreet warned Trilby quietly, "that was uncalled for. You're out of line."

Seth looked at Plummer. "You're right, Lieutenant. He needs killing, and the sooner the better."

Plummer grinned like a happy baby and thumbed his hammer back to full cock. A gasp shivered through the tent. Several people took cover under tables. For the first time, Seth noticed, Trilby's insouciant smile was in trouble.

"You're right," Seth repeated, "he needs killing. But you'll go to jail, Charlie, and I won't be able to help you. And I can't afford to lose a good squad leader. So put your gun away."

Plummer looked disappointed, but offered no further argument. He returned his hammer to half-cock and slipped the leather thong back over it. He sat down, laid the pistol beside his empty plate, and poured himself a drink with a rock-steady hand.

This time, when Seth met the pretty woman's eyes, she didn't look away immediately. But he wished she would have. For the look she gave him back told him clearly: *I see how it is, and I don't like it. Men like you live in two worlds. The cool, competent killers who also dress for dinner and engage in urbane banter.*

"Mr. Trilby," Seth finally said, "nobody is playing God. There are women here, this is a friendly gathering, not a dueling field. You come here today complaining about the way you're treated. Fine, you spoke your piece. I can be sympathetic to a man's claim that he's being high-hatted. Personally, I won't drink in private with any man I'm ashamed to drink with in public."

Trilby's strong white teeth flashed under his mustache. "By-God, then! Will you have a drink with me now?"

Seth watched him for a long time. "No, Mr. Trilby," he finally answered. "I won't."

"I s'pose that means *you* are a gentleman, too?"

"I still have the option of that title, yes. You don't."

"How can you know that?"

"I feel it more than I know it. It's a matter of trusting my instincts—and Charlie Plummer's."

Trilby stared until his eyes filmed with dull smoke. Kathleen watched, her lower lip gripped between her teeth as Seth leaned slightly forward, nerved for action. He spoke so low that only those nearby heard him.

"You have two choices, Trilby. Leave quietly now, or you and I will step outside. No more tough talk in here."

Trilby's anger seemed to pass in a heartbeat. "You're all right," he said. "All grit and a yard wide. The man who kills you will earn the right to piss on your grave."

A moment later he was gone.

"Shoulda let me kill him," Plummer said again. "That one is trouble plenty."

Chapter 29

Just as dawn began to pale the eastern horizon, Jemez Grayeyes finished climbing the latticework structure of a nearly completed railroad trestle spanning a steep gorge in the Sierrita Mountains southwest of Tucson.

The climb had been long and slow, but although his muscles ached from chill and exertion, at least his eyes were well-adjusted by now to the dark. He could easily make out the big Sibley tents and serried stacks of railroad ties scattered throughout the work camp on the eastern rim of the gorge. The huge pinyon-wood fires of the night before had burned down to low heaps of glowing embers.

He watched carefully for sentries before heaving himself up onto the tracks. Jemez paused in the crepuscular stillness to pull a long pine sliver out of his palm. His hands were sticky with resin from the new, unpainted wood.

He knew he didn't have much time, but he tried to fight down the urgency that makes a man careless. His plan was to strike before the work actually began for the day, yet only after there was enough light to permit him one good shot with a bow and arrow. The bow, made of sturdy osage wood, was strung with buffalo sinew. And his foxskin quiver contained only three arrows, all specially modified by Jemez.

Despite his leggings and knee-length fur moccasins, he could feel the sweat chilling on him in this high and thin air of the spring morning. The new trestle was part of a spur track connecting with the new Southern Pacific Railroad. It would link the mountains with the Brawley Wash below, beside which ran the federal freight road which eventually linked up to the San Pedro River in San Manuel. It was a joint venture of Charles Longstreet and Matthew Lewiston, the territorial governor of the white-eyes. The two men owned productive silver mines in the Sierritas. But so far they had been forced to sink too much of their profits into slow, expensive bull trains for packing out their ore. This spur track, once completed, would enable them to haul it directly to the federal road, where loading and shipping were vastly easier and less expensive.

Jemez hunched low and crept down the track even closer to the quiet camp. He studied the area straight on for a long time. Then he turned sideways and studied the same area from the corner of his eye—an oblique look could sometimes detect motion a direct glance missed.

All still appeared quiet. Now he turned and studied the western rim of the gorge. Earlier he had tethered his horse in the hawthorn bushes there, bridle down. The spidery frame of the trestle touched the western rim, though the rails had not yet been laid all the way across. But a full moon and periodically roving sentries had forced him to come up from the bottom of the gorge instead of simply sneaking across from the western rim.

For days he had watched the white-skin work crews. First came the Pima scout serving as pathfinder, then a surveyor with a level and a long Gunter's chain had gone through accompanied by a well-armed assistant to hold the sticks for him. After the numbered markers were pounded into piles of stone, the grading and roadbed crew came through, leveling the track bed and occasionally shoring up boggy places with crushed rock. They were followed by the crews that laid down the fresh-cut ties and spiked the rails into place.

Jemez couldn't see his horse from here, but neither could he see any guards. He had noticed how they got lazy late at night, when the Irish gang boss was nowhere to be seen. Crouched over and moving quickly, he headed toward two handcars parked on the tracks near the beginning of the trestle. The nearest car was piled high with ties. The flat canvas packs stacked up on the most distant car were solid two-pound blocks of the powerful new explosive the hairfaces called nitro. Jemez had first learned about it from talking to Indian scouts employed by mining companies. Safe to handle, it was nonetheless easy to detonate. The crews had been using it from time to time to blast out stubborn bluffs and piles of talus.

Jemez reached the second car and paused again, his heart racing now that he was in his enemy's camp. Here and there men snored from their tents, horses and mules snuffled from the temporary rope corral, and there was a clattering of pans from the cook shack across the way. Soon the first mess would be called to breakfast. He had very little time now. If he miscalculated by even a few minutes, he'd be spotted. And that meant death: a bullet, if he was lucky. But these white-skin devils, they knew how much Apaches feared death by hanging. Perhaps they would even skip the tree and simply drag-hang him behind a horse as the Mexicans had killed his father. *How a man dies is how he spends eternity. . . .*

The fear sent belly flies stirring, and he carefully sequestered his mind from such thoughts. He pulled two of the canvas packs of nitro off the top of the stack and hung them over the end of the first car by their carrying straps, weighing them down with ties. He grabbed several more and stuffed them down between the ties. Now it was time to think only with his senses, time to move that first handcar out onto the trestle.

Although Jemez worked alone now, he had recently joined a band of renegade Mescaleros and a few of their Navajo cousins who had fled their reservation at Bosque Redondo. Some women and children were with this band, holed up in the catacombs of the Sierra de Las Cruces. But the warriors remained highly mobile. The strike here this morning was part of a three-pronged attack to step up the defiant pressure on the Tucson Committee. They would be reminded that blood begets blood, that this vast region known as Apacheria was not for the taking. They could boast all they wanted to about this Seth Carlson, this blue-bloused soldier with powerful battle medicine. He would learn as all the rest had: for every Apache killed, two invaders would die. Just as Robert Trilby and Juan Aragon would die once Jemez knew where to find his younger brother and sister—information he was becoming more and more desperate to learn as time diminished his chances of ever finding them.

But for now he shut his mind off from everything except the task at hand. He could not use the hand lever to propel the car—it would creak and be too loud in the dawn stillness. So he bent down and set his shoulder against the iron bed of the cart. His tired muscles leaped out in rigid definition as he pushed, biceps straining against their brassards. The car's iron wheels grated on the tracks and made him wince. But soon it was in steady motion and rolling smoothly toward the center of the trestle.

He stopped about halfway out and climbed over the car to the other side. Then he double-checked to make sure the nitro packs were still in place. Jemez knew the holes in the top of the packs were for the blasting caps stored in side pockets along with crimping tools and red coils of fuse. But he knew nothing about using them and had no intention of blowing himself to hell while trying to learn.

By now, more gray light had leaked into the sky, and fear made his mouth feel like it was stuffed with cotton. As he finally finished rigging the packs, the first startled shout went up behind him: "What in tarnal hell! Who goes out there? Give the pass!"

Jemez leaped from tie to tie, keeping the car between him and the camp as he raced toward the far end of the trestle. The last thirty feet or so lacked rails or any support base, and he was forced to scramble along the wooden braces, which edged him into view of the camp.

"There!" another voice shouted. "Out scrambling on the span, see him?"

A rifle cracked, another, and bullets chipped wood into his face and whanged past his ears. Then he heard a hollow drumming and realized the hair-faces were out on the trestle. He couldn't let them figure out why that car was pulled out this far nor let them discover those dangling packs of nitro.

Another slug rushed past, so close he heard a sound like a bumblebee. Jemez reached across his chest with his left hand and drew his Remington .50. One hand holding on to the trestle, he snapped off three quick shots and sent his pursuers onto their faces.

Jemez heard more shouts from the camp. He finally reached the west rim of the gorge and leaped off the trestle. He drew one of the arrows from his quiver and leaned his back against the trunk of a tree to steady himself while he strung it. The arrow was an invention copied from their Cheyenne enemy: the exploding arrow. Jemez had tied a primer cap to the edge of a flint arrow point with a piece of sinew thread. Then he tied a small rawhide pouch filled with black powder over the point. With luck, the primer cap would hit just right and ignite the powder. The resulting explosion could start fires, and made the arrows useful against supply wagons and guns mounted on wooden carriages.

Using the car as a shield, two of the whites had sneaked up behind it to the middle of the trestle. Now they fired at Jemez from around both sides, still unaware of the nitro packs hanging down off the front of the car.

A bullet thwacked into the tree just above his head. Holding steady, placing the fear outside himself, Jemez drew a bead on the packs and launched his first arrow. It flew high by inches, skimming over the car and landing harmlessly beyond it.

Jemez cursed and strung a second arrow even as slugs parted the air all around him. This one flew straight and struck one of the packs, but nothing happened. Fighting back his desperation, Jemez pulled the final exploding arrow from his quiver.

"That red nigger is by himself, and he's out of bullets!" one of the whites shouted. "He must be, he's down to arrows."

Jemez cursed again when one of the brazen hair-faces scrambled over the car and sheltered in the wooden braces, getting a better line of fire on him. The white leaned out, levered his rifle, shot at the same time Jemez launched his final arrow.

A white-hot wire of pain creased the Apache's left cheek as the bullet grazed him. An eye blink later he heard a loud snapping noise like a giant gas pocket igniting, and then Jemez was blown onto his back as the entire world exploded around him.

The shattered trestle in the Sierritas was still smoldering when, sixty miles north at the base of the Picacho Mountains, three of Jemez's Mescalero comrades successfully infiltrated a white-skin "buffalo fort." Stripped naked, clumps of creosote tied to their backs, they used rawhide-wrapped rocks to cave in the skulls of a half-dozen sleeping hunters, all wealthy foreigners who had invaded Apacheria in response to Charles Longstreet's advertisements for exotic sport.

Later that morning, in the Green Valley grazeland south of Tucson, the rest of Jemez's band killed a line rider and attacked a herd of cattle belonging to a Tucson Committee member. They slipped in quietly among the cows, calves, yearlings, and steers, throat-slashing nearly two hundred animals before the rest of the herd stampeded to safety. The well-coordinated strikes soon contributed to the widespread white-skin panic—the fear that there were many more Apaches than anyone knew, and that no one was safe from their murderous wrath.

"Well, we aren't at the dinner table, so I don't have to be polite. Let me just ask you point-blank, Colonel, and get it out of the way. Do you, like many of your colleagues, advocate the notion that the only good Indian is a dead Indian?"

Seth paused with a china coffee cup halfway to his lips. He returned the cup to its saucer and set both on his knee. He glanced first at Kathleen Barton, then at Hays Munro. Both of them watched him intently, waiting for him to answer Munro's question.

"I don't know what I advocate. I guess I believe in live and let live," he said finally. "And I guess I also believe in giving as good as I get."

"None of this turn the other cheek business, eh? Fine, you're not offending me, I'm no pacifist, either. But do your personal beliefs influence the way you carry out your orders?"

"I don't follow you, sir."

"I mean, belief doesn't always translate into behavior. If your superiors ordered you to exterminate the residents of an Indian camp, would you do it?"

The day was unseasonably warm, and two windows on the east side of the house were open to a pleasant breeze. Seth watched an Apache on a mule pass by on the wagon road out front.

"Frankly," he replied, "one of the few benefits of being a darling of the newspapers is that I don't have to take many direct orders. To answer your question, I take the fight to warriors, not to tribes. Anyone who surrenders, warrior or not, goes to the reservation unless there's an arrest warrant for them. On the other hand, *anyone* who takes up weapons is a combatant, including women and children."

"Fair enough." Munro noticed all the sidelong glances Kathleen and Carlson were sneaking at each other. Interesting, he told himself again.

"As I understand it, Mr. Munro, you didn't ask me out here to quiz me on my personal philosophy?"

"Actually, you're wrong there. That was indeed one of my reasons for inviting you. You see, it does matter how you feel, Colonel, because you're in charge of the Indian problem, and the dominant tribe in your sector now are Apaches. Concerning them, your comments about surrendering are irrelevant."

"I understand. You mean because Apaches are known for making the most fanatical last stands."

Munro nodded, leaning forward in his chair. "Exactly. I know you faced down the Kiowa Kaitsenko. You can expect every fight with Apaches to be more of the same."

"That's their choice. Can't say as I blame them, from what I've seen of Mater Dolorosa."

Color rose in Kathleen's cheeks. Her hair was down this evening, tumbling in a tawny confusion to the middle of her back.

"You can say that," she said, "and kill them anyway?"

"Really, my dear," Munro interceded, "Colonel Carlson isn't responsible for the deplorable state of the reservations nor the U.S. government's inflexibility. He's a soldier, not a politician. I noticed, Colonel, you've met Charles Longstreet and Nat Bischoff. Do you mind, sir, if I ask you your impression of them?"

Seth hung fire for at least ten seconds, watching Kathleen watch him. He looked at the even, finely etched features of her face and told himself: *My God, she's beautiful.* But the anger and resentment burning in her bottomless blue eyes—he resented it in turn.

"My impression? I know I've got no use for either of them."

Hays nodded, leaning even farther forward in his gathering excitement. "Good. Because they're both lying, criminal trash. In fact, it was they who were behind the attack on Mater Dolorosa, not the Apaches."

Seth was familiar with Munro's allegations that the two men, and others of Longstreet's associates on the Tucson Committee, were conspiring to defraud the government and violate the treaty rights of the Apache peoples. He had read about the corrupt Indian Ring back East and seen plenty of criminal profiteering while garrisoned in New Mexico. Finally meeting Longstreet and Bischoff had done little to weaken Munro's charges.

"Even if you're right," Seth said, "you've got to remember that there are criminals enough on both sides. Apaches *have* committed other crimes, if not the Dolorosa raid."

"True enough, and there definitely were Apaches involved in the raid, though they were surely paid to do it. But there's also such a thing as a preponderance of guilt. When whites poison a tribe's rations, or deliberately infect their blankets with smallpox, it's not even worth a column inch in the newspapers. But when the Apaches strike back, as Apaches always will, suddenly the Red Peril gets national attention."

Seth said nothing, watching Kathleen again. She surprised both men by suddenly speaking up just as Hays was set to talk again.

"Jemez Grayeyes is an example. He's not near so black as

he's painted. Yet Bischoff has maliciously maintained a campaign against him, beginning with the false implication months ago that he was present at the raid and killed Father Montoya."

"How do you know," Seth replied, "he's not so black as he's painted. You know him?"

She looked down in confusion. "Not exactly. But I've talked to him a couple times, and I certainly know what he looks like. He definitely was *not* present at the raid. Bischoff all but condemned him—and neglected the fact that horses belonging to Robert Trilby and one of Trilby's toadies, Juan Aragon, were definitely recognized."

"Trilby? He was in on it?"

She nodded. "He led them. Now Jemez is being hounded as the killer of Father Montoya. There's a bounty on his head. Not only did he have nothing to do with it, his brother and sister were among the children taken."

Seth watched her, saying nothing. Knowing about the children helped explain all the strikes lately against the committee's interests—as well as Bischoff's written campaign against Jemez. Seth looked at the Indian agent.

"Mr. Munro, without taking sides, I can understand your animosity toward Longstreet and his bunch. I think you're trying to uphold the terms of the treaties, and I admire that. But you're also making a serious mistake to push Longstreet and the committee too hard. That Trilby, he's as mean and low as they come, and it's clear Longstreet knows him better than he cares to admit in public. I advise you to go easy on the letters to newspapers."

"Bosh! Thomas Paine was right when he said it's a sin not to speak up against scoundrels. If—"

"Hays," Kathleen cut in sharply, "to hell with Thomas Paine. Colonel Carlson is serious about this. And he's right. You *must* be careful."

Again both men glanced in surprise at Kathleen. The determined set of her face, the fervid plea in her eyes, made both of them uncomfortable. For the first time her argument seemed to sink home to Munro. He paled, losing his usual self-assurance.

"Well," he said, finally breaking the awkward silence, "the lass is certainly spirited today."

Three loud knocks at the front door saved them.

Munro pulled out his watch, then stood up. "If you two will excuse me, that's Taza with a load of firewood. I forgot he was coming by."

The moment he left the room, the silence grew unbearable.

"What's your grudge against me?" Seth finally blurted.

She flushed but matched his aggressive stare. "It's presumption on your part to assume such importance in my life. Perhaps all the newspaper stories have gone to your head. I hardly know you well enough to harbor a grudge."

"Nor well enough to insult me, but you do. Something about me rankles in your craw."

"Maybe . . ."

"Maybe what?" he encouraged her when she paused.

"Well . . . maybe it was that run-in you had with Trilby at Governor's Park."

"What about it?"

"You enjoyed it."

"Now, hold on. *He* turned over my rock first."

"I know that. He's sick, and that remark he made . . . it was cruel. But I think maybe there's some truth to it."

"What remark?"

"The business about . . . about how you like to play God with other people's lives."

Kathleen had been thinking only of the Apaches when she said it. As soon as the words were out of her mouth, however, she remembered the tragedy that had landed Carlson here in the first place. The young officer went pale and set his cup down, hands visibly shaking. For a moment he saw an unwanted image of Corey Bryce's agonized face, grief etched deep into every feature, and then it was gone.

Seth stood up and clapped his hat on. "Why don't you just say it plain?" he said coldly. "Those Comanches might have let her live, right? They might not have raped her and fed her guts to their dogs. She might have had a good life with them in spite of the fact that they were a war party bent on murder, in spite of the fact that she watched them kill just about every friend she had at Fort Bates. Or *I* might have been more of a man, instead of playing at being a god, right?"

Anger pinched his throat closed, and he abruptly strode from the room.

"Wait!"

Kathleen rose and followed him. Seth brushed past Hays and the old Apache unloading split-slab stove lengths from a donkey cart.

"Good day, sir," he said curtly, heading for the small corral to retrieve his horse. "I'll stay in touch."

"Colonel Carlson," Kathleen called out again. "Please wait! I didn't *mean* that, *wait!*"

The momentary look of surprise on Munro's smooth-shaven face was replaced by his more usual ironic grin. "So," he said to no one in particular, "the plot thickens." In a louder voice he called out behind Seth: "Well, *I* like you, Colonel. Do come back, the latchstring is always out."

Chapter 30

A roar went up from the Riverbend crowd when Juan Aragon's crew tipped back the flatbed of the jerry-built wagon. The door of the iron cage banged open and a frightened black bear tumbled down the wet, slick-as-ice wall of the claybank pit.

The crowd surged against the dangerously sagging stake-and-rope fence, eager to see into the pit. The black bear—six feet long and weighing perhaps three hundred pounds—landed heavily. A pack of bull terriers on the other side of the pit had already started growling and barking when they smelled the bear up above them. Now they broke into a yapping frenzy and attacked the confused animal.

The short-haired dogs were a strong, swift breed with long and powerful jaws. The bear, weak eyes and ears failing it, lifted its long snout and sampled the air. The powerful dog scent alerted it just in time—one swipe of its right forepaw, all five toes ending in a heavy claw, and a bull terrier was instantly ripped open and tossed twenty feet away. It crawled off a few more feet, dragging its entrails through the clay, howling piteously, before it went into death convulsions. The rest of the dogs, suddenly respectful, leaped back to safety.

It was an auspicious beginning, and the crowd roared its approval. Nonetheless, Robert Trilby's contrary nature made him worry most when all seemed well. Bull terriers were known for their courage, yet he sensed in his bones that this pack would turn cowardly. And consequently, the crowd's mood was going to turn ugly in a hurry.

"I swear," Nat Bischoff said, watching Aragon's foolishly grinning face, "that man is not all there above the eyebrows."

"Of course not," Longstreet said. "Half his blood is Apache, the other half is Mex. Two doses of crazy in one man."

"Judging from that wiry hair of his, might be a little buff mixed in him, too," Trilby said.

But this time, Trilby noticed, neither of his companions laughed. The easy camaraderie between the three men had been permanently strained during their last meeting at the Three Sisters Saloon—when Trilby had felt himself being forced to a thinly disguised threat against Bischoff's family as the only way to stop the man's prying. Nor had Trilby's drunken indiscretion, at the reception for Seth Carlson, endeared him to his two companions. Longstreet, especially, was in a foul mood. Recent events had set the wheel of fortune on a long downward spin for him.

The three men stood apart from the crowd, near the little canvas-and-plank stall where whiskey and pulque were sold. The mixed-blood named Esteban still stood near the rickety entrance, a fiber *morral* on his sash bulging with coins. Fargo Danford, the white deputy, circled the pit on horseback, making sure everyone had an admission chit.

"Crowd's down," Bischoff said, glancing around. The day was sunny and bright, but cold from a stiff northern wind off the Colorado Plateau. In his dark wool overcoat the journalist looked even more diminutive than usual. The bear suddenly roared in savage wrath as a dog bit the sensitive tip off its nose. The crowd whistled and cheered, several men firing their weapons in the air.

Trilby nodded. "Way down. It's Jemez Grayeyes. He and his renegades've got Aragon's men scared spitless. They won't go out in the open country after buff, nor up in the high country to capture a brown. So I'm stuck with black bears and dogs with piss-poor breeding behind them."

"The hell *you* bellyaching about?" Longstreet demanded. "That red bastard was spotted near the trestle in the Sierritas before it was blown. And I'd wager anything that was his bunch that attacked my buff-hunting expedition. Thanks to them, I threw my money down a rat hole on that deal. Not to mention that it's permanently ruined my name overseas and destroyed a good source of profit."

Longstreet fell silent and glumly chewed on his unlit cheroot. His situation was getting desperate. As Jemez Grayeyes and his bunch continued to torment Longstreet's men, more and more were quitting. Now he was scrambling for enough help to keep his enterprise intact.

"Grayeyes's strategy is starting to work," Trilby agreed. "Make all the cracks you want to about ignorant savages, that 'Pache is savvy."

"He doesn't need to be," Longstreet riposted. "He's got you on his side."

"Balls! Spell it out."

"You call yourself a businessman's agent and ask me to spell it out? Do you realize that I was starting to soften Seth Carlson up, that I could have had him flying our colors by now? Then *you* had to show up, drunk as the lords of creation, and get into a pissing contest with him."

"You can't read men, Charlie," Trilby said, "so you end up grabbing at farts. Carlson can't be bought. He'll have to be killed."

"Bob's right," Bischoff cut in, speaking to Longstreet. "Granted, his little drunken exhibition was pointless bravado and didn't help our cause any. But Carlson can't be bribed—he's right there. You couldn't see it, Charlie, but he was sneering at you the whole time you were buttering him up."

"Well, then! Either way it doesn't matter. I'm on the brink

of going into a deep hole. From here on out it's going to be root hog or die."

Down in the pit, all had grown ominously quiet. The crowd, too, had quieted. Trilby felt sweat break out on his back. He looked at Aragon, and his lackey shrugged one shoulder in lazy helplessness.

"Don't worry about the arrogant Seth Carlson," Bischoff said. "His rising star has already begun to plummet."

"That last piece you wrote was a good one," Trilby agreed. "Hinting that he might be suffering from combat fatigue, that's good. Subtle, but it plants the seed of his destruction."

"It's the beginning of the end for that goddamn fence-post digger from nowhere. *I* made that arrogant, stuck-up sonofabitch into a national hero, and the fool hasn't enough sense to be grateful. You saw how he snubbed me—that glory-grabbing rube honestly thinks it's *he*, not I, who got him where he is."

"Don't worry about him giving us the frosty mitt," Trilby said. "Who cares about that? Worse, it looks like he might even be throwing in with Hays Munro."

All three men were silent at that, realizing the possibly serious consequences of such a liaison. Trilby didn't give a tinker's damn about the interests of Longstreet and the rest of the squaw men in the Tucson Committee. But clearly his own interests were already being harmed by Jemez Grayeyes and his defiant Apaches. Trilby didn't need an Indian lover like Hays Munro teaming up with a man as influential—and clearly as tough—as Carlson was.

"It's root hog or die," Longstreet repeated. "I see now Hays Munro is not going to fade out. Not on his own."

"No," Bischoff agreed. "He's not. It's best to pop this blister now before it swells too big. But whatever is done, it must be dòne carefully. After all, he's in tight with the Northeast intelligentsia and the Tidewater aristocrats."

"I don't trust the woman, either," Longstreet said. "This —This—"

"Kathleen Barton," Bischoff supplied.

"Her. She's an Indian lover, too. If we . . . remove Munro from the picture, she might become a martyr to his cause."

Trilby was surprised. Longstreet had shown an unusual discernment in making this point. He thought of something Aragon had recently reported.

"The Comancheros are heading down into Chihuahua soon with another bunch of Indian kids. Apparently, this wealthy *hacendado*, Padilla, has a powerful yen for Anglo women. We could not only get her out of the picture, but pick up a little scratch into the deal."

Further discussion now, however, was impossible. There was very little action down in the pit, and the crowd was taking over. Somebody fired a pistol shot, one of the dogs leaped into the air and came down dead.

"We've all been sold, by-God!" someone else shouted, and suddenly the air bristled with shots. When the mad volley finally ended, the bear and the rest of the dogs lay dead in the pit. Fargo Danford sent a helpless look across to Trilby. The big man shook his head once, warning the deputy to back off.

"Free drinks for everyone!" Trilby bellowed. "*Copas gratis para todos!* Whiskey for white men, pulque for the rest!"

A raucous cheer broke out, and the crowd surged toward the liquor stall. The three men got out of the way just in time.

Bischoff caught Trilby's eye. "Quick thinking."

Trilby nodded back, mentally calculating what this spontaneous crowd sop was going to cost him in profits.

"Maybe," he said. "But between Munro, Grayeyes, and now Carlson, we're fighting a retreating battle. We've got to take the bull by the horns, or that sonofabitch is going to gore us."

"The Southwest-sector aboriginals are keeping us busier than a moth in a mitten," Lieutenant General Nelson Trapp said. "So far they've had the upper hand, there's no gainsaying that."

Trapp, General Ferris Ablehard, and Corey Bryce shared a table at the Saber Club. It was the dinner hour and the place was crowded with officers, some unbuttoned for evening, others in mufti. The thick and shifting pall of tobacco smoke lent a lurid blue cast to the air.

"They're ruling the roost," Ablehard said, "because the Army's left hand doesn't know what its right hand is up to. That's why I mentioned Corey to you, Nelson, and wanted you to meet him. Frankly, that Ops and Planning section of yours needs an infusion of fresh young blood—somebody who not only understands what needs to be done, but is capable of leading the effort in the field."

Trapp nodded amiably, casting an approving eye over the squared-away young officer seated next to him at the table. Head of the War Department's Operations and Planning Section, Trapp was small and powerfully built. Although well into his fifties, he spent thirty minutes every day punching a full sandbag. He also, Corey had noticed, indulged a penchant for violet-scented throat pastilles. Now the cloying smell wafted into Corey's nostrils as the general appraised him.

"I was present when this courageous lad spoke at the Jeffries-Hopewell debate on the Indian question. He's straight grain clear through."

"That's an affirmative. And speaking of fresh young blood," Ablehard said, "did you read Nat Bischoff's piece in the *New York Herald* last week?"

Corey watched Trapp's amiable grin give way to a pettish frown. More violet scent blasted his face in a cloying vapor when Trapp looked at him again and leaned confidentially closer.

"I know Seth Carlson was . . . *is* your friend. But I wonder if Bischoff wasn't on to something when he hinted that a nation can ask too much of one soldier? Bischoff was cautious. One gets a distinct impression, however, as to what he is intimating—namely, that young Carlson is too soft on the aboriginals, despite some notable battle victories to date."

Corey played it careful here and only nodded. But secretly, he was elated. He, too, had read Bischoff's piece. Seth Carlson had made all Corey's hope for the future suffer an eclipse. Now, for the first time, a slight wrinkle had appeared in the hitherto unblemished veneer of Seth's renown. The Army had no shortage of glory seekers, and Seth's prolonged hogging of the limelight had engendered plenty of animosity and jealousy.

"No doubt Carlson is a good soldier," Ablehard said, topping his glass from a carboy of bourbon. "But frankly, *all* the attention has been going to him. Bluebellies are dropping like flies all over the West, but if you take it from the newspapers, there's a one-man army in America."

"That rings right," Trapp agreed. "He's apparently got the knack for killing Indians. But how would he have done at Bull Run against white generals trained in modern warfare?"

"No matter how you slice it," Ablehard said, "the job will have to go to a man who thinks like Americans United for Survival."

Trapp looked at Corey. "How would you handle this Apache uprising, Lieutenant?"

"Well, sir, deadlines for reporting to the reservations have been consistently ignored. The Mexican army, too, is eager to end this Indian problem. So I would impose one final deadline as a gesture of good faith. The savages would, of course, ignore it. After that deadline, all Indians who had not surrendered would be considered hostiles and killed in a joint sweep by the Mexican and American militaries. Once the date passes, no prisoners, no surrendering."

Trapp's eyes puckered with satisfaction. "You're not timid about it, are you, Soldier Blue?"

"Not a bit, sir. It's no job for a faint heart. Matter of fact, I'm keen to crack the first cap."

Trapp watched him for a long moment, thoughtfully sucking on a pastille. "Your father is William Bryce? The congressman from Virginia?"

Corey nodded. Like several in Congress, his father ruled over a tobacco fortune that had given him the clout to enter politics and remain influential. Urbane and honest, he was nonetheless considered a friend of the Army and pro-expansionists.

"You know," Trapp went on, "I have to make a recommendation to President Grant soon about a strategy for the Apacheria campaign. Ferris tells me you're a crackerjack pony soldier?"

"Top of my class at West Point, sir. Plus time leading a platoon in the field in the Department of New Mexico. But I'm getting holed-up fever here in Washington."

"Eager to pound those testicles again, are you?"

"War is our business, sir, and business is good."

Ablehard and Trapp exchanged smiling glances. Both old war-horses saw younger versions of themselves in this fire-breathing officer.

"Right now I can't promise you anything, shavetail," Trapp said. "But we'll see . . . we'll see."

Corey was satisfied with that. Clearly General Trapp liked him. No other military man in Washington had his clout. One way or another, Corey planned to get back out West.

For a moment he recalled it again: the odd, terse note he had found in his letter box a few days ago, signed only "A Friend." *Her name was not Jeanette,* it read, *but Hagar, and Carlson was Abraham.* Rusty on his Old Testament lore, Corey had been baffled by the note until he looked into his Bible and discovered that Hagar was Abraham's concubine.

Chapter 31

In May 1870, as the result of recent and costly Apache raids, members of the Tucson Committee filed a formal complaint with the military commander of the Department of Arizona. Their complaint was referred directly to Lieutenant Colonel Seth Carlson, commanding officer of the First Mountain Company.

The highly mobile First currently had no permanent garrison nor even a built-up camp as a staging area. Like the Indians he fought, Seth was uncomfortable forting up to fight from a fixed position, preferring instead to harass his enemy in running battles. So the First lived almost entirely in the field, authorized to recruit horses and supplies as needed from Fort Grant, Fort Bowie, Camp San Carlos, and other garrisons in the Arizona sector.

Military couriers served as the only liaison between Seth's unit and the regular cavalry troop camped at Tucson under the command of Captain Dennis Moats. Determined to con-

vince superiors that no imported glory seekers were needed
to safeguard the settlers, Moats launched his own showy and
ambitious campaign against the Apaches. Dozens of mirror
stations were established to flash signals whenever any
Apache movement was spotted. Gatlings and Parrot muzzle-
loading artillery rifles were requisitioned from Fort Huachuca
and shipped to Tucson on a spur track of the Southern Pacific Railroad. Moats spent the next few weeks trying to
guess, from scouting reports and map patterns, the next
probable targets of the renegades. Then the clumsy gun carriages were laboriously hauled into place and camouflaged—
only to be hauled out again, unfired, when the uncooperative
Apaches struck somewhere else fifty miles away.

The First Mountain Company, in stark contrast to this
scattershot approach, cut sign on one band of hostiles west
of Tucson and began dogging them mercilessly.

They first picked up the trail near the old freight line
known as Cooke's Wagon Route. They followed it northwest
toward the Gila River. It led them into high country where fir
trees pointed into the sky like spear tips and there was still
frost at night. Then it veered southwest again, and the tim-
ber changed to grassland, then to sand and cactus.

Though there was plenty of evidence of the Apaches, the
horse soldiers never actually spotted them. It was warm during the days now, but the brief desert rainy season had set in,
and the constant wind and rain kept wiping out the trail.
Sometimes the onsweep of dark clouds was sudden, and the
heavens opened up with a vengeance, rain hurtling down like
buckshot. They were forced to button their shelter halves
together and build their cooking fires under a canvas ground-
sheet.

Still, they pushed relentlessly on, never spotting the
Apaches, but sensing they were gaining on them. Grain bags
full of oats and corn strapped to their saddles, they crossed
desolate mineral wastes, traversed vast tracts of greasewood
thickets. The sun blazed torturously during the days without
rain, forcing the men to slip eyeshades on their horses and
blacken their own eyes with charcoal. Near the meandering
Gila River valley, they rode through deserted settlements
where crops had been ravaged by thick clouds of locusts.

As was his custom, Seth took the point often, scanning the horizon for dust puffs, feeling the ground with his fingertips to detect the movement of enemy horses. At night the exhausted men rubbed their mounts down with handfuls of dry grass, then ate the day's only hot meal. When meat ran low and resupply was impossible, they relied mainly on parched corn and "baled hay"—Army-issue desiccated vegetables known to the disgruntled troops as "desecrated vegetables." The Civil War vets made Burnside Stew by soaking hardtack in water, then frying it.

Two weeks into the campaign, Goes Ahead returned from a forward scout. Seth spotted the Papago's paint mustang topping a rise just ahead. The men had been riding for hours, and the horses' manes were matted with sweat. Seth signaled a halt.

"Closing in on them," Goes Ahead greeted him. "Their horses are tired and need good graze. The Apaches, they eat little but corn now."

"Spot them yet?"

"A few times, but most I see just smoke from their fires. Some sign by the river."

"What sign?"

Goes Ahead shrugged. Why were white men so interested in talking about things that only needed to be looked at? "You will see it if you just keep riding ahead."

A few rods farther they rode into a patch of reeds near a slough. Now there was ample evidence that many riders had spent some time around a lick located there—salt-impregnated earth surrounding a saline spring, a good spot to lurk for deer, elk, buffalo, and other game as they came to the salt.

"They killed an animal and dressed it out before leaving," Goes Ahead said. "See the blood trail?"

"It ain't turned very tacky yet," Charlie Plummer said, squatting to feel it. "They can't be far off. We'll soon be huggin' with 'em."

Holding double columns, riding at wide intervals, they crossed a series of narrow sand blights, then entered a string of long and narrow red-rock canyons. Seth ordered a rearguard out and sent flankers to scan the walls and rimrock surrounding them. They were halfway through the canyon when a sudden and eerie piping noise began echoing off the canyon walls, making the horses sidestep nervously.

"The hell's that?" Seth asked Goes Ahead, craning his neck to look all around them.

"Flutes they make from human bones," the scout replied. "Means they get worried, try to blow death down on us. Try to scare us and the horses."

They rode through more narrow canyons, and the Apache campaign to frazzle their enemy's nerves grew even bolder. Though they spotted no one, the soldiers clearly heard the scornful hoots and catcalls from the surrounding rock. The eerie piping continued, too, making the men glance uneasily all around them.

The sun sank lower in the sky and their shadows grew long behind them. Seth watched Goes Ahead swing off his paint and squat beside something. The soldier joined him. Plummer, Kinney, and Mackenzie edged up around them, then a few of the others.

"Holy Hannah! What is it?" the trooper named Larry Muggins asked.

Like the others, Seth stared at the rock covered with broad stripes of bright red and black paint. Then he looked at Goes Ahead.

"Deathrock," the Papago explained. "Red stands for blood, black means joy at the death of an enemy. Apaches warn us one last time. They say go back now. Go forward past this place, our bodies will feed the coyotes. Means they won't run much more. They cannot. This the boundary of Apacheria, now they have to fight. Their God, Great Ussen, expect them to protect it."

Seth turned away and watched a lone eagle soaring over a peak. His face was set hard as granite in the gray half-light. For a moment, vulnerable in his weariness and the weight of his responsibilities, he let his mind's eye conjure up the image of Kathleen Barton. Despite the anger and resentment churning inside him ever since her "playing God" remark, her face lingered in his mind like a favorite poem, beautiful and comforting and vaguely exciting. He recalled, too, what she had told him about Jemez Grayeyes's brother and sister

—information the Tucson Ring had left out of their indignantly worded complaint against him and the other Apaches. Just as Nat Bischoff had left Robert Trilby's name out of his story about the Mater Dolorosa raid.

Then, in an eye blink, he shut all that out and returned to the problem at hand. He looked at Goes Ahead.

"You're paid to scout, not fight. You don't like the look of it, you're welcome to fade."

"I might," the Papago said. "Or I might stay."

"*All* you goddamn Injins are notional," Kinney groused.

Seth decided to make camp right there. The picket outposts were set up, with orders to be especially vigilant. Throughout the night Apaches hidden in the rimrock kept up a constant shouting and hooting, as well as the steady piping of their eerie bone flutes. Although the constant harassment was beginning to take its toll on the men's nerves, Seth had to grudgingly admire the Apache's spirit of defiance. For in truth, it matched his own mood lately.

But the next morning, riding out ahead on point, Seth got a more personal dose of that defiance.

He was making a hard climb up out of a narrow defile and had given his horse a loose bridle. Abruptly, as he debouched at the top, something moved in the corner of his eye, a fast streak coming from a jumble of rocks to his right. He saw it all happen, but it was so quick he didn't register the fact until it was too late. The streak was a young Apache still in his teens. He leaped onto the sorrel's right foreleg and wrapped himself tight around it, tripping the pony and bringing it and Seth crashing down.

Somehow, neither Apache, horse, nor rider was seriously hurt. Seth scrambled to his feet, trying to get out of the sorrel's way even as he fumbled for the snap of his holster. But the youth hadn't come to fight and was even quicker. A few heartbeats later he disappeared into the surrounding boulders.

"*Jee*-zus jumping Christ," Seth said out loud, his heart slowly crawling down out of his throat.

He dropped back to warn the rest against any more ambushes. They pushed hard that morning, leaving the canyon country and entering an open stretch of white-sand desert. Goes Ahead returned at midday.

"They head for the catacombs in the Sierra de Las Cruces," he announced. "Got to be. Only shelter between here and Fort Yuma. Push hard, we maybe catch them down on the flat."

Catch the Apaches they did—several hours later, with the westering sun a dull copper orb suspended low in the sky. For the first time the soldiers actually spotted their quarry riding out ahead of them across the arid vastness: a band of perhaps fifty braves, leading a small remuda.

Charlie Plummer had been watching them through brass field glasses.

"They've halted and they're digging sand wallows," he reported. "They figger to pick some of us off. At least a few of them red niggers've got sixteen-shot Henrys, prob'ly heisted them from sage freighters. Good guns, but 'Paches are piss-poor marksmen. They're hoping to turn us back now."

Seth nodded. "Since they're going to all that trouble for us, least we can do is attack. Spread the word: We approach at a right oblique in a wedge formation. We can't risk turning our horses into targets, so we'll dismount and hobble 'em back behind those dunes off to the right up ahead there. We'll make our final movement to contact on foot. Tell the men to fix bayonets."

However, Kinney was right about Indians being notional, and the confrontation turned out to be short-lived. The First rode on until the bullets forced them to dismount and low-crawl through the sand. Clearly, the Apaches had not expected their pursuers to close the gap so determinedly. Loath to fight an entrenched battle in the open, they laid down covering fire and quickly retreated to their ponies, resuming their flight. The well-disciplined sharpshooters had not fired a return shot.

But a man had been wounded in that last, frantic volley and was patched up by Mackenzie. Since the trooper was not fit to ride, a side sling was rigged from a horse blanket. Then, because the terrain was flat and smooth, they fashioned a travois for him as soon as they reached sapling thickets growing near the Rio Llorrana. They shot an antelope and made a meat camp that night beside the river. The unit's mood was optimistic: Their bellies were full, their enemy was on the run, and so far casualties had been light.

But they underestimated Apache stealth, as well as their determination to unnerve the white-skin enemy. The next morning, when the picket guards were called in, one was missing: Larry Muggins, one of the volunteers from Corey Bryce's old unit. His horse lay dead near the outpost, its entrails pulled through a huge slit in its side.

"Shouldn't we split up and look for him, sir?" Mackenzie asked.

Seth shook his head. "That's what they want us to do. We stay together."

Kinney nodded agreement. "It ain't no sense to look for him, turd," he told Mackenzie. "He'll turn up, and you won't be so glad to see him when he does."

Just past noon they reached the last sierra between the desert scrubland behind them and Fort Yuma ahead. This was the site of the catacombs Goes Ahead spoke of. They had just entered the foothills when Plummer, riding point, dropped back to halt them.

"I found Muggins," he said, his face as pale as gypsum sand. "Or anyhow I figger it's Muggins. Get ready—it ain't very pretty."

Ahead, in a rolling sward, they came upon a huge circle of still-warm ashes. A body, naked and castrated, lay near the fire. Pointed sticks had been driven deep under the finger- and toenails, the skin pocked with scars and burns. The severed genitals had been spitted with a green stick and now protruded from the ground like a grisly totem.

They found the head in the ashes, roasted so hot the brains still simmered.

"We'll bury him here," Seth announced in a grim voice. "And then we're pushing on. By nightfall they'll be holed up in the catacombs. We're moving into place after dark, attacking at sunup."

Seth, Kinney, and Plummer conferred on strategy. Agreeing that intense, concentrated firepower would be the key to routing the Apaches from the caves and catacombs above them, Seth suspended the thirty-round limit. The men crimped plenty of extra cartridges, filling bandoliers by the light of a well-sheltered fire. Seth, like most of the men, slept very little that night. He listened to the horses snorting and stomping, the wind blasting through the canyons ahead and shrieking in the caves and crevasses. When the first light of dawn rimmed the eastern horizon, the First Mountain Company was up and on the line.

They sheltered the wounded man and the horses under guard in a protected hollow. Then the men deployed in three battle groups, led by Seth, Kinney, and Charlie Plummer.

"All right," he finally called out. "Let's earn our pay. Keep your intervals as we advance."

"You heard the man: no cluster-fucking. Stay frosty and shoot plumb," Kinney added. "And don't none of you shitbirds worry about your wife or colleen back home. You get killed, *I'll* poke her for you. What's a comrade for?"

"You'd fuck a snake, Top," a trooper yelled back, "if somebody'd hold its mouth open for you."

"*Augh!*"

Kinney grabbed his crotch and leaped about like a drunken ape while the rest laughed at his buffoonery. Then Seth, shaking his head in mock dismay at these sick, soft-brained soldiers who comprised the modern Army, moved forward. The offensive had begun.

At first, leapfrogging from boulder to boulder, they made good time and moved steadily higher. The Apaches, well hidden above them, made no attempt to pretend they weren't there. They held their fire until the invaders were close enough to insult in Spanish and English. Then they began firing in earnest.

The men covered down as ricocheting bullets whanged from rock to rock. So far the soldiers had held their fire.

"Seth!"

Seth spotted Plummer in a pile of scree to his right. The lieutenant pointed up toward a place where a pile of boulders formed a natural breastwork between two traprock shelves.

"I seen muzzle flashes up there. Ten o'clock! Some of 'em are holed up there."

Seth nodded back. "Lissenup!" he shouted to his unit. "Sustained field of fire, ten o'clock high, on my command. Group leaders, repeat the order!"

First Plummer, then Kinney, reiterated the command. When Seth was sure all the men had heard it and drawn a bead on the right target, he bellowed, "Fire!" and squeezed off the first round.

An ear-shattering din of rapid fire. The expert marksmen concentrated a withering, sustained volley on the designated target, sending a deadly hail of ricocheting bullets back into the cave. As fast as they could cram rounds into their Spencers they emptied them again, the sharp, precision cracks of the carbines sounding like a huge ice flow breaking apart.

Sporadic fire was returned from other positions. But not from the location between the traprock shelves. Seth heard cries of pain from some of the Indians hidden there. Suddenly, a woman clutching a small child tumbled down out of the rocks and landed on the bottom shelf below the protected cave entrance.

Seth didn't need to halt his men's fire. Not chivalry, but shock at the unexpected sight, brought all of them up short as if by tacit command.

Kinney first broke the ensuing silence. "Well, I'll be go to hell!"

The woman lay stone-still, the child still clutched in her arms. A faint cry told them it was still alive, though the woman had absorbed the impact and could not have survived the fall onto those harsh rocks even if a bullet didn't kill her. Faintly now, Seth could hear more children crying from the cave. He swore out loud. They weren't riding with the group during the chase, so they must have been holed up there all along.

"Charlie!" he shouted.

"Yo?"

"Tell them we want to parley."

"*Oye!*" Plummer shouted in Spanish. "*Queremos hablar con ustedes!*"

"Fuck your whore mother, pig's afterbirth!" came an answering shout from above in clear English.

"Listen!" Seth called up. "I won't ask the warriors to sur-

render because I know you won't. But send your women and
children out. We'll let them go. We have no fight with
them."

"It is common knowledge," the taunting voice replied,
"that white-skins rut on sheep and turn the offspring into
soldiers."

"Sir!" Mackenzie called out from his left. "Look!"

Seth saw that the naked child had crawled from its
mother's arms and was moving dangerously close to the edge
of the shelf.

"Come down and get that kid!" Seth called up. "We won't
shoot!"

"Hair-face, do you take us for loco peyote soldiers? Come
earn your kills, long knife, we will not make it easy for you."

"Shit," Seth muttered. Then, seeing Walt was about to
spring forward, he picked up a stone and hurled it toward
him, the sudden impact sending the orderly scrambling behind a rock.

"Stay put, trooper," he ordered, "or I'll kill you graveyard
dead myself!"

The child, a boy about two years old, was bawling now as
its mother failed to respond. He edged even closer to a steep
fall.

"Listen!" Seth called out to those above. "Hold your fire.
I'm bringing the kid up. I also want to parley. I won't have
any weapons."

Seth ignored the protests from Kinney and Plummer. This
gamble might not be as risky as it looked—Goes Ahead had
told him that, despite the Apaches' harsh code of survival,
their children were very important to them. They weren't
indifferent to this child's fate, but extremely battle savvy. Its
falling had been an accident, but it had stopped the bullets.
They would let the soldiers make the next move. Seth
grounded his carbine, unsnapped his holster belt.

Then, nervous sweat cooling him, he rose and scrambled
up toward the shelf, climbing from boulder to boulder. He
expected a shot at every moment, but none came. He
reached the shelf, hoisted himself up, picked up the skinny,
dirty, crying child. A quick glance at the woman's broken

neck and the ugly, puckered gunshot wound to her temple confirmed that she was dead. Holding the little boy awkwardly under one arm, he finished the climb to the entrance.

The Indian waiting for him just behind the protective heap of boulders looked small for an Apache adult, but the hard set of his face reminded his enemies that killing was mostly a matter of will. A flannel headband restrained his hair and made his forehead look even lower and more wrinkled. The sere face was as weather-gnarled as a peach pit. The Henry in his hands was cocked and pointed at Seth's belly. Seth set the child down. A woman ran forward and scooped him up, taking him to the rear of the cavern where more noncombatants huddled.

Seth watched the Apache's finger ease inside the trigger guard and take up the slack.

"Look at the noble white-skin soldier! Saves a child to impress his men and thinks we will admire him, too, the fool."

It dawned on Seth then that the Apache was about to kill him. For a moment his stomach tightened into a fist as his body reacted in spite of his mind's indifference. A moment later someone moved out of the shadows and caught hold of the rifle barrel, lifting it so it pointed well over the soldier's head.

Seth's eyes met the nimbus-gray stare of a big, well-muscled young Apache about his own age. Seth took in the broad, heavy nose, the sharp and straight mouth with no weakness about it. The eyes seemed to miss nothing, yet revealed little as they took careful measure of this tenacious enemy.

"Jemez Grayeyes," Seth said finally, not making it a question.

"Seth Carlson," the Apache replied. "The famous bluecoat who cannot be killed."

"He can be killed," the older Apache insisted. "Just watch."

But Jemez caught the barrel again. "Let it go," he said in Apache. "Can't you see that he is not afraid? Look at him. He did not bring little Delshay up here to impress his men.

Death holds no sting for this one. Indeed, he may even be tempting it now. Why help an enemy?"

In English he said, "Speak words we can place in our sashes."

"I'm here to enforce the treaties Cochise and your other leaders signed. I'm here to remind you you're required to report to the reservations and that bust-outs are illegal."

Jemez shook his head. "I have no ears for such foolishness. Whatever papers Cochise signed have nothing to do with us. We Apaches are not one tribe, but many separate bands under leaders who never signed anything. I lived on the reservation at San Carlos, and I tell you now: I choose life on the run."

"I'm a soldier, I had nothing to do with the treaties. I can only repeat: I *order* you to report to the reservation."

"And if we do not?"

"You'll be hunted down and killed."

Jemez laughed. "So. You save a child today so that you may kill him later. And the white-eye legend brazenly announces it to our faces? Perhaps he has read too many stories about his powerful magic that can stop the sun from rising. Perhaps he truly believes Indian bullets fall from their guns around him?"

Seth hesitated. "Will you send the women and children out?"

Jemez shook his head, still mocking the whiteskin with cold, unfathomable eyes. Behind them a child cried piteously. Seth saw a woman wiping blood from one of them.

"All right," he finally decided. "There's nothing else for it. This time I'm ordering my men to leave. But so long as you remain at large, you're officially considered hostiles. Remember—you can't hide behind noncombatants forever without putting them at risk, too. I'm backing off this time, but tomorrow is another day."

"It is," Jemez agreed, "for those who are alive to see it."

"If that's a threat," Seth replied, "you're wasting your breath. Go ahead and kill me. *I* don't care, but I'll warn you —lay a hand on me, and my men will make sure not one of you—man, woman, or child—leaves this place alive."

Jemez nodded. "That's the way it is?"

"That's the way it is."

"Your men are loyal to their battle god. Then go, battle god. I confess, I like you and can understand your men's loyalty. But things are the way they are, and liking you will not keep me from killing you."

Chapter 32

"I tell you," Morela said, "it is not so bad at La Esperanza, sad-faced one. True, Gabriela is an ugly old *bruja*. And we are harshly punished if we are caught alone with any of the boys, and the *jefes* take their pleasure with us when they will, following the example of Don Enrique. But the food is good, and if you are pretty as we are, the work is pleasant and easy. Some girls in my village, they come here on their own asking for work. You—no, *querida*, don't jerk the onions out like that, as if you are angry at them. Dig under them and lift them out gently, like this."

Socorro ignored the pretty Mayan girl. Instead she watched a horse rolling in the grass of a nearby meadow. Again she thought about her own pony, lying throat-slashed with the others in that ravine near the Rio Bravo.

Morela was right: In many important ways, life here was not that bad—better than Socorro had ever known. This lush garden, where they now gathered vegetables for the tasty

pozole stew served daily to the slave workers Padilla called the
Blessed, was ringed by flower beds and brawling fountains. It
was as pretty and perfect as everything else in Valle del Lago
Azul. As for not being allowed to be alone with boys, what
did *she* care? This was the Apache way, too, and besides, she
had only twelve winters behind her—ponies held far more
attraction for her than boys. But here at La Esperanza it
wasn't boys she feared.

As if sensing her thoughts, Morela ducked lower in her row
and whispered, "*Mira!* There goes Jesus with Doña Elena.
They make a pretty couple, *verdad?* He is good with the gun
and said to be her bodyguard when she goes to mass. And of
course, she goes every day. But some of the *criadas*, they say
things. They say that, while Don Enrique sneaks back to the
caseta with his little girls, Doña Elena is kind to Jesus, that
he does more than guard her body. They say Don Enrique
knows about it, but winks at the *segundo*. Because the whole
world knows, though *el patrón* truly loves his wife and dotes
on his daughter, Elena is now barren and cannot give her
husband the son and heir he craves."

Socorro watched the *segundo* escort a slender woman,
wearing a narrow-waisted gown and a lace mantilla, from a
light calash to the front entrance of the main house. Jesus
wore his usual tight black trousers and short frogged jacket,
but in place of his leather shako hat the former vaquero had
donned a black sombrero ringed with pieces of silver. All this
menacing black emphasized the bone handle of the pistol
riding high over his hip.

At the mention of the *caseta*, Socorro had automatically
glanced back toward the neat lanes of rock-and-adobe shelters where most of Los Bendigados lived. One hut, the very
last one, was set apart from the rest and equipped with a
hasp and lock on the door.

Morela saw her looking. "Never mind," she said. Then,
curiosity getting the better of her, she added: "He hasn't
taken *you* back there yet, has he?"

Socorro shook her head. Several times Padilla had visited
with her. So far he hadn't put his hand under her dress, like
her cousin Juan Aragon used to do. But he had smiled and
spoken gently, almost urgently, to her, saying the oddest

things, stroking her face until his breath whistled in his nostrils and his voice took on a rough husk.

Morela, who was several years older than Socorro, leaned closer again. She had pretty, even features, flawless skin the color of topaz.

"He will take you, eventually, because you are lighter-skinned than most of us, and the whole world knows he pines for fair women like the *norteamericanas*. But I tell you, it is not so bad," she repeated. "He is . . . unusual. After it is over, he sometimes cries and broods. Or he can get angry as a jungle beast when—when it—when he has difficulties with his thing. Sagrada Virgen, how angry! But his thing is little, and few girls have been hurt badly. Usually it is over quickly, and he is ashamed afterward. After a girl has had her turn, Gabriela has instructions to give her pleasant duties. Doña Elena knows about the *caseta* and hates it, just as she hates Gabriela for assisting *el patrón* in this. But she has Jesus to console her. These *ricos*, they are a queer lot."

Socorro thought of Padilla, his sickly sweet cologne, the ridiculous embroidered tunic with its fourragère draped over the left shoulder, a silk handkerchief tucked into his sleeve. The image made her flesh crawl against her dress. How could Morela say it was not so bad? And how could she simply shrug when Socorro asked why there were few boys older than fifteen or so working on the hacienda, when she asked where the rest had disappeared to?

Thinking of this, Socorro looked out beyond the cluster of low stone buildings that housed the stables and the dairy, up the scarred mountainside to the head frame of the copper mine where Miguelito worked on the slusher line. Her brother seemed content enough these days, if not exactly happy. But again Socorro pictured the big *jefe* Ramon, with the huge bowie knife in his belt. Would Miguelito be one of the few males who was allowed to grow to adulthood as one of the Blessed?

Socorro could never forget that Apaches were taught to escape from an enemy, not to submit to capture. Was it better to forget that she was an Apache, to forget the defiance against their enemies which Jemez had once encouraged in her? And must she also forget the names which, by

Apache custom, she could never again repeat, the names of her mother and father and all the rest of the dead. For the sake of food and shelter, was she supposed to forget all this and simply submit when Padilla finally lifted her dress?

"*Ojo*," Morela whispered, spotting Gabriela coming out of the *casa grande*. "Careful! Here comes the witch, look busy now."

Socorro resumed her work without looking up. But she thought again about her brother Jemez and his promise that she would see him again—his promise that a Grayeyes never lied to an Apache. It was her only hope, and she clung to it like a drowning man to a branch.

If Jemez was still alive, she told herself, he would find her.

" 'The question is not one of honor or gallantry—Seth Carlson has proven he lacks neither. Rather, it is a question of sound judgment and natural suitability. Has the right man been sent to deal with this thorny problem of the Apaches, the aboriginal tribe that has remained not only the most intractable, but the most inscrutable to the Christian race? As for the ill-advised decision to let Jemez Grayeyes roam free, perhaps King Lear spoke for Seth Carlson, too, when he lamented: "We are not the first who, with best meaning, have incurred the worst." ' "

Hays Munro lowered the *Tucson Register* and took the monocle out of his eye. He looked at Kathleen.

"Thus the eloquent Mr. Bischoff turns the screws tighter on our young officer. Little did the erstwhile scrivener realize, when he created the myth of Seth Carlson, that he would eventually have to turn this rising star into a falling meteor."

Kathleen watched Munro take a peppermint for his stomach—his dyspepsia had been troubling him more lately. Despite his little ironic grin, there was a rough grain to his voice that made her nervous. She had heard it before—the suppressed anger and indignation that almost always hinted at a confrontation of some sort. She knew he had been dashing off more of his acerbic letters lately, all directed at Nat Bischoff and the Tucson Committee. The more she implored him not to, it seemed, the more determined he became to force their hand.

"Seth Carlson makes one big mistake, my dear, at least from the point of view of his military career. You cannot be a public figure and yet be as indifferent as he obviously is to the political climate of the times. Casually admitting that he let those Apaches—including Jemez Grayeyes—in the Sierra de Las Cruces go, instead of pressing for a total defeat, has made him an Indian lover."

Kathleen sipped at a glass of plum brandy, nodding occasionally but saying nothing, only gazing with unseeing eyes toward the mud-daubed chimney and flagstone hearth. It was early in June, the day's heat finally beginning to ease as twilight darkened the windows. Jemez, she thought suddenly, had not been back to see her since the night he sneaked into her room. But their conversation burned as strong in her memory as if it had been only yesterday:

You're telling me that Hays is in trouble.

He's in bad trouble, and so are you.

A sudden voice, not from memory but from the open window behind her, startled Kathleen.

"Tanta Kathleen?"

She and Hays both looked at the same time.

"Victorio," Hays said. "*Qué quieres? Por qué no vienes al puerto cómo es costumbre?*"

The Apache youth shrugged. Tio Hays always got upset when he called from this little entrance instead of the big one. What did it matter, so long as they heard him?

"I want to speak to Tanta Kathleen about my lessons."

"Now I *do* believe in miracles. Come in, come in," Hays said impatiently, "but don't climb through the window, use the front door."

"I want to see her outside," the Mescalero insisted.

Hays was about to object, but Kathleen shushed him with a glance and went outside.

"What's wrong, Victorio?"

She couldn't see him very clearly in the dying light, but she wasn't as gullible as Hays. He wasn't here about lessons.

"Jemez sent me."

Her breath caught in her throat. "Why?"

"To tell you a thing. He has found out that Juan Aragon is soon to meet the Comancheros in Riverbend. They will have several Cheyenne girls. Aragon is buying them to work as whores at Trilby's cantina."

Kathleen stayed silent, listening to the low groaning of the wind. Out in the corral one of the bays snorted.

"Why did he send this message to me?" she finally asked.

"Because he wants you to tell Seth Carlson. He told me to tell you he trusts this soldier, that he is a decent man who speaks one way only."

Now Kathleen understood. One reason why Bischoff and the Tucson Committee were undermining Seth Carlson was his public position on the subject of Comanchero slave traders. He had already flatly stated—in an open letter to all area newspapers—his intention to fight the illegal practice of kidnapping Indian children, citing it as a major cause of Apache unrest. To her knowledge, he was the first soldier who had publicly spoken out against this barbaric practice, the first soldier to argue that it was not just an "Indian problem."

"Will you tell him, Tanta Kathleen?" Victorio said.

Again she hesitated. In truth, she now deeply regretted that her natural mistrust of all soldiers had caused her to offend this strong-willed young officer. This time Hays was right: Despite Carlson's curt cynicism and abrupt manner, he was a good man who was trying to do the right thing in a horribly complicated situation. Letting Jemez and his band go in spite of the public outcry proved that. It would be difficult to get word to him, but not impossible—he had told her and Hays that messages for him could be sent by way of the Adjutant's Office at Fort Grant.

"Will you tell him?" Victorio pressed.

Again Jemez's words drifted back to her, triggering fear and resentment and nagging doubt: *You're strong already. I'm asking you to get even stronger.*

Finally she met Victorio's eyes and nodded. "Tell Jemez no promises, but I will try."

Robert Trilby threw a blanket and pad over his mare's back, then tossed the saddle on her and cinched the girth. She took the bit easily when he slipped her bridle on her.

"You drunk?" he asked Aragon.

Since waking up that morning, Aragon had been sipping from a flask of liquor brewed from maguey cactus. Now he flashed his sly smile.

"Truly, *Jefe*, must a fat man fish for his pecker? *Cómo no* I am drunk. You know I am useless when sober. Out of great respect for you, I have gotten drunk enough to do my best work."

Trilby glanced over at Aragon, who stood just outside the cream mare's stall. The mixed-blood looked feckless and pathetic in his sleep-rumpled clothing, machete dangling in its tatty straw shoulder scabbard. But once again the phrenologist in Trilby was forced to marvel at the unique slopes and planes of the man's skull. Somewhere in his mongrelized history flowed the blood of aristocrats.

"You're sure," Trilby said, "that Padilla will buy a white slave? It's one thing with Indians, but even the Mex government might not stand for selling a white woman."

Aragon's yellow teeth flashed. "What government, *Jefe*? There *is* no Mexico, only a pack of starving curs stealing each other's meat. A *hacendado* makes his own laws, and I tell you this Padilla dreams of tasting some creamy white gringa flesh. These Spanish *perfumados* get an itch, and it must be scratched. He has asked about it before. And once he sees this *rubia* beauty Kathleen Barton, *ay mamacita!* He will pay in good coin of the realm."

Trilby bent down to check the latigos and stirrups. Again he thought about his meeting earlier with Charles Longstreet and Nat Bischoff. The word had come down from Fort Grant through Longstreet's contact there: An Indian courier had been sent from Mater Dolorosa with a message from Kathleen Barton to Seth Carlson. Longstreet's contact had been unable to learn the contents of the sealed envelope. But the specific message didn't matter: What did matter was the fact that Hays Munro and Kathleen Barton were both clearly becoming tight as ticks with Carlson, feeding him information inimical to the merchants and businessmen of Tucson—a group Trilby didn't give a hoot in hell for, except that it included him.

Cedric O'Flaherty, the crusty old hostler, limped past the stall leading a dun stallion out to graze.

"*Hola, viejo,*" Juan called out. "Gettin' any of that fresh young cunny?"

Cedric stopped and stared at Aragon as if he were something nasty he had just scraped off his boot.

"You'll shovel coal in hell, greaser half-breed. My old peeder might be turned to cheese, mebbe, but the best part o' *you* dripped down the hog's hind leg, you thievin', murderin' shitheel."

Cedric moved on while Aragon howled with laughter, spooking the mare. "*That* sonabitch don't need teeth to bite, *por Dios!*"

Trilby ignored his lackey, still thinking about Seth Carlson and how the man had stared him down with utter indifference, how—in front of all the big nabobs in Tucson—he had refused to drink with him. That arrogant bastard was still strutting around like the lord and master hereabouts, despite Bischoff's clever campaign to turn the national tide against him. It was time to give him a taste of humility while also eliminating the growing threat of Hays Munro and Kathleen Barton.

Trilby shook his right leg a bit to settle the muff gun in his boot. "Come on," he said to Aragon, leading his horse out of the stall, "let's get 'er done."

"We really do require a servant," Hays Munro said. "This is above and beyond the call of your duties—not to mention completely unchivalrous of me."

"Nonsense, I've got it," Kathleen insisted. "It's not heavy, it's just clumsy. Ready?"

Hays gripped one side, she the other, and they threw the harness on the team and hooked up the traces. When the hitching was complete, Hays threw the reins back into the buckboard and climbed up onto the board seat. He chucked up the horses and drove it out of the mesquite-branch shelter while Kathleen picked up a large wicker basket covered with a clean cloth. It was stuffed with food for a clan that lived near the eastern border of the reservation. Several members of the clan were seriously ill with diphtheria. No priest had yet been located to replace Father Montoya, so Hays and Kathleen spent more evenings lately making visits.

The western horizon was a rim of ruby-red flame, the vast dome of twilight sky aglitter with the first fiery pinpoints as the stars winked to life. Kathleen set the basket in the buckboard. Hays reached down to help her up.

From behind the mesquite-brush shelter came a pathetic whimpering.

"Why, that sounds like a puppy," Kathleen said. "What in the world? Hold on a second."

"Careful," Hays warned her, starting to wrap the reins around the brake. "A coyote bitch may have whelped back there. If so, she'll be protective of her pups. Let me go with—"

"Oh, stay there, silly," she said, already halfway to the hut. "I'll just take a quick peek."

She reached the back corner, looked around, felt her heart turn over with shock. Before she could regain her wits, two powerful hands gripped her like talons and pulled her the rest of the way behind the hut. One of the big hands, rough with calluses, slipped tight over her mouth.

The light was dim and grainy, and the man who grabbed her wore a bandanna over most of his face. But she thought she recognized Trilby from his brief but dramatic appearance at the reception for Seth Carlson. The other man, the foolishly grinning mixed-blood with the curved machete in his hand, was a stranger to her.

The one with the machete widened his grin, still watching her as he again gave a good imitation of a puppy in distress.

"Kath? What is it? Kathleen?"

She heard Hays swing down from the buckboard, grunting at the effort, heard the gravel crunching under his soles as he approached.

"Kathleen! What the devil *is* it?"

Only now did it sink in, her stomach forming a huge, solid knot: Hays was about to die! She watched the mixed-blood set his heels firmly with his back to the wall of the hut. He raised the machete in both hands above his right shoulder.

Kathleen tried to scream, to kick free, but the man holding her was big and powerful. His grip on her mouth was so tight, she tasted the salty tang of blood, and her front teeth were on the verge of cracking loose. The scream never got up past her throat.

"Kathleen, what's the—"

Hays broke into view, the mixed-blood swung hard, Munro's eyes found Kathleen's, and then there was a noise like a butcher's cleaver ripping into a shank. She was still staring into his face when it suddenly tilted sideways as the decapitated head rolled off the shoulders and thumped to the ground.

The headless body took one more shambling step, blood spuming from the severed neck, before the lifeless hull fell to the ground like a sack of grain.

Kathleen's legs went rubbery. The full enormity of what she had just seen had not yet registered—for her sanity's sake, it could not. Now her captor held her with only one hand.

"Nice work," he told his companion. "Make it look Apache."

A thin wooden stake honed to a sharp point at both ends leaned against the hut. The mixed-blood picked it up. Rolling the head into position with his boot, he crammed one end of the stake deep into the severed neck.

"Take it out front of the house," the bigger man said, "stick it into the road. Then go get our horses. We'll check the house before we leave."

A hot numbness took over, the strength left her legs completely, and Kathleen suddenly sat down.

"Hays," she said. "Oh, no, Hays."

The mixed-blood did as ordered. The remaining man fumbled at his belt. "*That's* the spirit," he told her, looking down at her as he undid his trousers. "Might as well lay all the way back and enjoy the ride."

Chapter 33

Again risking the dreaded white man's noose, Jemez Grayeyes came down from the sierra strongholds to infiltrate Tucson and the dangerous adobe-and-mud appendage called Riverbend.

Through the moccasin telegraph he had heard rumors that Juan Aragon would be meeting a band of Comanchero slavers here tonight. They had Southern Cheyenne girls to sell, nabbed when the entire tribe migrated south for their annual buffalo hunt. As badly as he thirsted for Aragon's blood, tonight Jemez had a more important purpose: He must try again to learn where his little brother and sister had been sold. So far all inquiries had proven fruitless. This trip was even more dangerous now that he was also wanted for the murder of Hays Munro and the abduction of Kathleen Barton. Nat Bischoff's account of the incident had included "witnesses" who claimed they saw Jemez Grayeyes on the reservation at the time of the crime. Never mind that he had also supposedly been sighted during a raid near Bisbee on the same day—over a hundred miles away.

Now, as evening gathered itself around him, he gazed out from the shelter of a cottonwood copse on the outskirts of Riverbend. He watched a lone rider in woolly chaps and a broad-brimmed slouch hat wrap his reins around the tie pole in front of the adobe hovel with the crude branch corral out back—the same tent-filled corral Jemez had visited when he sent the Mimbrenos under. The rider lifted the latchstring of the hovel's rawhide door and disappeared inside.

Jemez hugged the ridged bark of a cottonwood and waited patiently as the last light of day bled from the sky. He had stripped to his clout, darkened his body with mud. He planned to leave his Sharps in its scabbard, and wore no holster, but carried his Remington pistol cocked in his left hand. He also carried his long Spanish bayonet handy in a coyote-fur legging sash.

While he waited, feeling his heartbeat gradually synchronize with the slow-pulsing *chirr* of cicadas, he wondered about Kathleen Barton. Why hadn't Trilby and Aragon killed her, too? Or had they, somehow hiding the body? Jemez meant to do whatever he could to find out. She was one reason why he had decided to cooperate somewhat with Seth Carlson.

It had been a gamble, notifying Carlson of this meeting—if indeed he had been notified. If Carlson did decide to take action against the Comancheros, Jemez knew it could jeopardize his ability to learn anything useful about Socorro and Miguelito. Nor did Jemez assume Carlson would let him go if he got him in his sights again. But the Apache had taken both chances out of respect for the soldier's unpopular decision to fight these Comanchero devils. Now he suspected he had overestimated the Anglo's determination to break up the Indian-slave trade. Carlson would not interfere tonight. Perhaps he had not even received the word, perhaps Kathleen Barton had been seized before she could contact him. And perhaps, Jemez forced himself to admit, she had been seized *because* she contacted him—at Jemez's request.

He respected the white-skin battle chief. For all of his formidable combat tenacity, Seth Carlson followed a clear code: Despite the wishes of many superiors, he would not risk the lives of Apache women and children. He took his battle directly to the warriors. And he fought like a man, not by infecting blankets with disease or poisoning meat rations. Thus, despite his well-earned reputation as an effective Indian hunter, Carlson had also earned the grudging respect of Jemez Grayeyes and many other Apaches who admired a gallant warrior even among the ranks of their enemies. So far, Jemez and his new band had not been seriously pressured again by Carlson's Raiders. But as other Apaches learned they could trust this bluecoat's word, more and more bands were surrendering peaceably and reporting to the reservations.

Jemez was a freedom-loving Coyotero, an Apache band long resistant to relocation, and had no plans to ever surrender. But life was hard for other Apache bands, and though Jemez was against it, he forgave those tormented leaders who were surrendering for the sake of the starving women and children. For these bands, it was a choice between the dreaded reservations or sure extinction. Unfortunately, the trend toward peace upset Robert Trilby and the white-skin war contractors he represented. It—

His thoughts scattered when the rawhide door flapped open and Juan Aragon stepped outside of the hovel.

Jemez felt his pulse quicken. Aragon stepped behind the hut and returned with his claybank—clearly, thought Jemez, he had hidden it. He expected trouble. Jemez watched him mount—from the Indian side, he noted with wry disgust at this turncoat who played the dog for white murderers. Jemez, too, quickly returned to his horse and mounted. Then, holding back inside the trees, he watched Aragon and the Comanchero emissary ride toward the shallow bend in the Santa Cruz River, where a long gravel bar made the ford west of Tucson an easy one. Relying on a cloud-mottled sky and a weak crescent moon to obscure him, Jemez followed them.

For perhaps an hour he trailed the two riders as they headed due south of town. Finally they halted in the lee of a mesa. About a dozen horses were tethered under guard. Men waited near a big jacal a few dozen yards farther on, a branch hut roofed with straw rushes. A small fire blazed inside, where Jemez assumed the girls must be. When Aragon and the other man arrived, several of the Comancheros stepped inside the jacal with them. The rest milled around outside, smoking and drinking, rawhiding each other in Spanish and English, keeping an eye out for trouble.

Jemez hobbled his pony on the far side of the mesa. He reminded himself that an Apache had no business doing this at night. Then, relying on the patient art of movement and concealment which made his band the most highly feared guerrillas on the vast frontier, he began sneaking closer to the jacal. He slithered forward, low to the ground like a snake, waiting for gusts of wind to cover his sound.

All day long, according to Goes Ahead's report, a group of heavily armed mixed-blood riders herding six Cheyenne girls had dusted their hocks toward Tucson. Since the Papago scout had trailed them to the jacal earlier, Seth Carlson, Charlie Plummer, and Jay Kinney were well-hidden in sand wallows near the brush hut by the time Aragon arrived. The soldiers had picketed their horses out of sight, haltering them with nose bags of grain to keep them quiet.

"There's only one guard back with their horses," Charlie Plummer reported in a whisper when he returned from a brief reconnaissance. "The men outside are all armed, but they don't seem to be expecting any serious trouble. Most of 'em are liquored up. We can avoid them easy."

Seth nodded. "Give the ones inside just a few more minutes to get drunker and get down to the serious bargaining. Then we'll move. Any sign of Trilby?"

Plummer shook his head. "I didn't see anybody but the one guard."

"It's a bird's nest on the ground," Kinney insisted. "You two papooses go on home and wipe your snot lockers, I'll take care of these yacks."

"Remember," Seth told them, "no shooting unless they resist. If we do bust caps, no shots toward the hut unless you know all the Cheyennes are out."

He fell silent and the three men waited in the darkness, the sand still warm beneath them. Seth hoped Robert Trilby showed up tonight. As commander of the Indian-fighting elite in this territory, Seth had heard one exaggerated story after another about the murderous renegade Jemez Grayeyes and his fellow Apache marauders. True enough, the Apache menace was real, and Seth had seen proof of their attacks on innocent settlers. But he was independent enough to quickly recognize the corruption and greed behind the Tucson Committee's claim that the Army lacked the courage to handle Apaches as red-blooded Arizonans advocated.

Thinking about the committee made him smile in the darkness. Some time ago a thick envelope had shown up in his pigeonhole back at Fort Grant—thick with new hundred-dollar bills wrapped in a sheet of stationery, on which had been printed the single word OPPORTUNITY. Knowing who it must have come from, and knowing his gesture would infuriate the merchants, Seth had made a great public show of donating every dollar of it to an Indian-assistance agency run by the Quakers back East.

His smile now, as he recalled these things, was short-lived, however. For the thought of Trilby and the Tucson Committee also made him think about Hays Munro and Kathleen Barton. He had read Nat Bischoff's account of the murder-abduction and knew for a fact it was a pack of lies. For one thing, he knew that Jemez Grayeyes and his band had been harassing Longstreet's miners in the Sierritas on the day Munro's head was found protruding from a stake on the Mater Dolorosa reservation.

He's not as black as he's painted, Kathleen had told him about Jemez. Yet she harbored obvious animosity for this cavalry soldier whom she saw as a much-ballyhooed Indian persecutor; nonetheless, her beauty and frank honesty had begun to penetrate the hard bark left on Seth after the tragedy of the Sunday Stroll massacre. He had no tangible proof that Trilby and Charles Longstreet were behind Munro's murder and Kathleen's disappearance. But he had spotted Trilby in Tucson two days afterward, and Seth was sure those deep claw marks on Trilby's face hadn't been left there by a cat. Kathleen had put up a good fight. But was she dead or alive? And if alive, where the hell was she? Seth planned to put those questions to Trilby himself.

Now, because she had disappeared so soon after contacting him about the Comancheros, because he had visited the reservation and openly insulted the Tucson Committee out of spite, it was back: that all-too-familiar feeling of gnawing guilt. Had his carelessness killed or endangered yet another young woman who instead should have been under his protection?

"All right," he said abruptly to his companions, anxious to scuttle such thoughts with the immediate danger of action. "Let's go take care of those horses."

His blood humming with elation, Jemez slowly began to withdraw from his position near the Comancheros. He had indeed been fortunate. Liquor had oiled the Comancheros' tongues, and he had learned all of it: that his brother and sister had been sold to Enrique Padilla, a wealthy *hacendado* in Chihuahua's Valle del Lago Azul, that Kathleen Barton, too, was now Padilla's property.

Jemez realized that all the waiting had come down to this. It was time to hide in a safe place and kill Aragon, who would most likely depart alone, leading the string of Cheyenne prisoners and heading north back to Tucson.

Jemez had finally crawled back far enough to stand up and go after his pony. He was about to round the far side of the mesa when his keen sense of smell detected a familiar sheared-copper odor on the night wind: blood, and plenty of it.

He swerved toward the place where the Comancheros had left their horses. He heard no snuffling, no hooves stamping the ground or loose bits clinking. In the darkness he almost stumbled over the dead herd guard. Then a rag of clouds blew away from the moon, and the Coyotero felt his heart slam into his ribs when he realized every last animal had been silently, expertly throat-slashed to prevent the men's escape.

The fine hairs on his nape stiffened. Jemez glanced behind a hummock on his right and saw Seth Carlson watching him.

Two men flanked Carlson, their carbines trained on Jemez. For a long moment the two frontier legends stared at each other. Each knew full well why the other was there. And Jemez, officially a hostile who had gotten lucky once before in a land where luck was scarce, now assumed that this time he was bound to die, since surrender was out of the question.

"Both of these men are sharpshooters," Carlson said quietly. "You could prob'ly get that Remington pointed. But you'd be sucking wind before you could snap off a round."

And since no one else cared, Jemez thought, with his death would die the last chance for Socorro and Miguelito.

Something else occurred to him.

"You plan to arrest Aragon?"

"Or kill him."

"No," Jemez said, more forcefully than his options allowed. Realizing this, he made his tone less strident. "I told you about this thing tonight because I want to help you. But when I sent the message, I did not expect to kill Aragon this night. And I never thought about you killing him. But understand, this Aragon, he led Mexican butchers to my sleeping family. He is a piece of maggot-riddled shit who killed my family, then sold their scalps. He sold my brother and sister. I mean to kill him. Don't make me die without doing that."

Swinging the cylinder of the Remington out and emptying the bullets into his hand, Jemez approached the three soldiers. He stopped a few feet away from Carlson.

"Last time we met," he said, "I talked the he-bear talk about killing you. So now I won't even try to change your mind about killing me. Just grant me my final request. Let me have Aragon first."

From Kathleen, Seth had learned the role Trilby and his lackey Aragon had played in the massacre of Grayeyes's family. He also knew there was no justice to be had from a white man's jury, that Aragon would never answer for any crimes against the red man.

"This Aragon is a cockroach," the soldier answered. "But I need him."

"No, you don't. I know where Kathleen Barton is. The same place where he sold my brother and sister: a hacienda called La Esperanza in Chihuahua, owned by Enrique Padilla."

Seth said nothing. Abruptly, a shaft of light spread out across the desert as the door of the hut was flung open.

Figures emerged in the darkness, cheerful voices raised in drunken camaraderie.

"Load your pistol," Seth told the Apache, "and stand beside us."

"Aragon is mine?"

"If we have to burn powder, he's yours."

"With this bunch, you'll have to fight."

"I know. Look, don't ask me who you can kill, all right? Do what you have to."

The sudden irritation in the white man's voice told Jemez he had hit a sore place. But this was no time to wonder at it, not with the Comancheros moving closer as they passed flasks of liquor around. The women moved in a tight bunch behind them, tied at the ankles so they were forced to take little shambling steps.

Seth waited until the first Comanchero had discovered the dead guard and horses. Then he shouted, "Freeze! U.S. Army! Drop your weapons. One stupid move by anyone, you're all stew meat. You men at the rear, step away from those women. *Now*, goddamnit!"

"*Arriban las manos!*" Plummer added in Spanish.

In the initial confusion, fearing they might be surrounded, the Comancheros did as told. Seth breathed a bit easier when the frightened but battle-savvy Cheyennes moved farther out of the line of fire. Then a voice rang out:

"*Chingales! Hay solamente cuatro!*"

"Shit, they're pulling down on us!" Plummer said. "Here it comes!"

"Fire!" Seth bellowed, even as the first Comanchero guns spat flames into the night.

The deadly calm mountain troopers focused down to one task and returned unerring fire, and in the space of a few heartbeats the Comancheros lay dead or dying. Jemez, too, had emptied his Remington into the enemy with impressive control of his shots. But he never lost sight of the fact that Aragon had bolted toward the mesa as the firing broke out. In the first second after his hammer clicked on an empty chamber, Jemez's bayonet was in his hand and he ran hard toward the mesa. He caught Aragon by his shoulder scabbard, tugged, spun him around fast, collapsed on top of him in a rolling, tangled confusion. Then he had him pinned and met the mixed-blood's terrified eyes in the weak moonlight.

"Take this face with you forever, cousin," he told him in Apache, knowing Aragon understood the language well. "The face of the man who is now going to spill your guts for eternity."

Jemez flexed hard and drove the heavy point of his bayonet into Aragon's crotch, opening him up like a deer from rump to throat. Aragon's scream was short, ending in a rattling flutter the moment Jemez's blade severed his voice box.

When Jemez stood, Carlson was at his side. The two men watched each other for a long moment. That freighted silence sealed an unspoken agreement between them. It marked the beginning of a shaky cooperation in a private war against a common enemy.

"Why are you still here?" Seth finally said.

"I'm not," Jemez replied, and a moment later he wasn't.

"I sent for you, Corey," Lieutenant General Nelson Trapp said, "because it's time to send the commander-in-chief my official recommendation for the Apacheria campaign. Seeing as how you've become such an assiduous student of military history and the Apaches these late months, I'd appreciate it enormously if you'd take a look at it now and tell me if you think it passes muster."

"I'd be honored, sir," Corey replied, accepting the neatly handwritten sheets Trapp proffered across his desk. The linen-finish paper bore the official seal of the War Department, Operations and Planning Section.

Serving as General Ablehard's aide-de-camp was mostly a make-work position and left Corey with plenty of time on his hands. In addition to regular riding and target practice, he had indeed been boning up on the increasingly more urgent Apache question. Not only did he study every newspaper, magazine, or military journal article he could find on the subject; he had even taken to matching drinks, in the Saber Club, with veteran campaigners of the Southwest Indian conflicts. At General Trapp's request, he had written up brief "speculative reports" on various aspects of a projected campaign. Now, as he read the general's official recommendation, Corey was thrilled and flattered to recognize much of his own language informing this key document intended for the president's eyes.

He glanced up and saw Trapp smiling slyly at him. The sickly sweet, cloying smell of the general's violet throat pastilles made Corey curl his toes. But he grinned back with barely restrained enthusiasm.

"Suit you so far, shavetail?"

"Right down to the ground, sir!"

Corey resumed his reading, nodding more and more vigorously in his gathering excitement.

"*This* part is jim-dandy, sir. 'Raiding is an essential aspect of the Apache social structure. One cannot eliminate the one without the other. It is not effective long-range strategy to simply marshal troops around Ojo Caliente and other passes into Mexico, merely forcing the aboriginals to detour a bit and cross elsewhere. Rather, a bold double strategy is needed, enthusiastic implementation of General Crook's recent tactics. Apaches must be enlisted in greater numbers to assist the Army. Only they can easily pinpoint the hidden strongholds in the Superstition, Mohawk, and numerous other mountain ranges. Once these strongholds are mapped out, a smoothly coordinated hammer-and-anvil approach would supply the coup d'etat: Head the renegades toward the open Sonoran Desert in the southwest portion of the territory. The Mexican army would hold the border when the aboriginals attempted to flee south. Once flushed from the mountains, cut off from flight into Mexico, they would be forced to fight on our terms, not theirs. And, I submit, the fight would be brief.' "

Corey looked up again. "This last point is quite sound, sir. On *our* terms, not theirs. Unfortunately, when you fight like an Indian, you begin to *think* like an Indian. Some of the recent reports on the First Mountain Company prove that."

"You mean Seth Carlson, I take it?"

Corey nodded. It was July now, six months since Carlson's Raiders first took on the Red Peril, and Nat Bischoff had begun to effect a sea change in America's attitude toward her favorite Indian hunter. As if, Corey thought bitterly, they were finally beginning to understand that Seth Carlson grew so tall only by standing on the graves of dead women.

"It's not easy, sir," Corey said, his manner hesitant, reluctant, "to speak out against a good soldier and a man I trained with at the Point. But that donation he made a while back to the Quakers, that proved it to me: Poor Seth has gone battle simple. He's gotten too damn close to the Indians, and now he's gone soft on them. He's got to be replaced, and his way of fighting has got to be replaced. We've got to operate the way the most successful general in the world operated: Genghis Khan's men would fan out wide, flush out all the enemy like game, then drive them before them in an ever-tightening circle. He never lost a battle, sir. Not one."

Trapp nodded. He pushed the pastille around one cheek with the tip of his tongue. "We're of one mind on this, Corey. And I can assure you now: Ferris Ablehard has already told me he's confident he can wrangle a brevet promotion for you, enough rank to command at least a company if not a battalion. Whatever President Grant finally authorizes, you'll be playing a big part in the field."

Trapp folded the letter and slipped it inside an envelope. Then he pulled a stub of candle out of a drawer and lit the wick with a lucifer. He held a nubbin of sealing wax over the flap of the envelope and touched the candle flame to it until liquid pooled all over the flap. Then he pressed the seal of his ring into it.

"The Mexicans have made friendly overtures lately," he said. "I've got a man on his way down there now to sell Juarez on it. I think they'll be cooperative. It's up to the president now. If he approves it, we have a bold new policy directive in place—thanks, in large measure, to you. All Apaches must report to their appropriate reservations by November first, a bit over three months distant. After that date, the Mexican and American militaries will conduct a joint sweep. *Any* Apaches who haven't reported will be killed on sight. It's a matter of time now, Corey, and the will to get a nasty job behind us."

PART FOUR

Chapter 34

"If it would please you, Miss Barton, will you step outside with me? I would like to show you something diverting."

Enrique Padilla's English was stiff and formal, at times the phrasing as odd as the man himself, Kathleen thought. He had insisted on speaking English since her arrival. The *hacendado* had greeted her briefly in Spanish when the Comancheros delivered her. When she failed to respond, he assumed she did not speak that language well. His assumption was made easier by an inordinate zeal to practice his English at every possible opportunity. Kathleen had noticed by now that he really wanted an audience for his soliloquies, not an opportunity to sharpen his dialogue skills. That was fine by her. It was easier to feign attention than to force a conversation. Nor did she plan to let him or anyone else at this pretty-and-polite hacienda prison know that she spoke Spanish.

Without a word she rose from a high-backed chair upholstered in damask and accompanied him through the drawing room of the *casa grande*.

"I consider it the good fortune indeed to have you at La Esperanza as our tutor. I have long desired to provide the instruction in English and other subjects for my daughter, Isabel. Also for some of our young ladies on the—how does one put it?—on the domestic staff."

Kathleen bit back a reply at this urbane show of hypocrisy. "Domestic staff" indeed! Every last one of them was a slave, though most of them seemed content with their lot. Not, thank God, Socorro Grayeyes—her eyes still bore that lidded look of defiance. Fortunately, both Kathleen and the Apache girl had enough presence of mind to quickly disguise their first shock at seeing each other again when Kathleen arrived three days earlier.

Now the *hacendado* watched her face closely as they passed under the white-plastered Moorish arch over the front entrance. Judging from his next remark, he must have seen something in it that didn't please him.

"Would you like to leave us now? Go back to your country?"

She glanced at him quickly. But the tight, smug set of his lips warned her to say nothing. Padilla led her toward the corrals and stables. A gunshot split the late afternoon peacefulness, and she flinched. But Padilla ignored it.

"As you have discovered already, no one at La Esperanza is locked up or kept under guard. If you truly wish to leave, I will whistle for the *mozo* in this very moment. I will direct him to saddle a horse for you. But permit me to also remind you of the many dangers out there, the many—how does one put it?—risks between here and the Rio Bravo to the north. Especially for a beautiful young woman riding alone through this lawless and savage land."

Another gunshot followed, then another; several in rapid succession, an explosion of cheers and whistles, and then Kathleen heard the rapid drumming of hooves. Padilla gave a fastidious little tug to the silk handkerchief protruding from his sleeve.

"Between here and the Rio Bravo," he repeated, "one

could expect to encounter various tribes of godless savages. Maricopas, Karankawas, Apaches. Then there are the savages rumored to have souls: Benito's *rurales*, the Seguridades Publicas, who are the bandits and scalp hunters that form the private army of the Governor of Chihuahua. Also, the roving bands of human refuse who once pretended to belong to armies, but no longer require a flag to justify their killing and looting."

His obscure dark eyes fixated on her wheat-colored hair, drawn tight into a chignon. "And truly, even a . . . Christian man might forget himself in the presence of such a beautiful woman."

His glance felt like slugs squirming against her bare skin. She shuddered but refused to look away. Padilla smiled, baring tiny and perfect teeth.

The gunshots grew louder now as the two passed stone buildings marking the dairy. Kathleen heard men shouting and whistling, more rapid hoofbeats, more shots, a sudden cheer.

"Of course," Padilla resumed, nodding toward a small, walled complex behind the chapel, "every hacienda has its *cárcel*, a legacy of times even more savage than our own. A *cárcel* which, at very tense moments, can also serve as a fort."

He stopped, refusing to walk farther until she had looked. Kathleen saw that the outer walls were narrow-ported for rifle fire. Jagged cusps of broken glass protruded from the masonry along the top of the walls. Padilla's voice took on an ironic edge.

"There was a time when it was necessary to hold many prisoners. It is rarely used these days, of course, now that the proud and humble Benito has finally brought the peace and the prosperity to our noble country. Soon, our streets, too, will be paved in gold just as they are in America, it is true?"

Kathleen had no doubt that all of this flowery sarcasm was a thinly veiled threat. Padilla was reminding her that the *cárcel* could easily be put to use again, should there be any trouble. But such intimidation was wasted on her. Perhaps the fear would come later. But for now, since watching Hays die, there was no soft place left in her for fear. There would indeed be trouble, it was merely a matter of watching, learning, waiting. Never mind these complacent *indio* slaves who could not miss a freedom they had never possessed. It was Hays who had always insisted that passively letting evil happen was evil in itself. Jemez had been right, too, his words about the reservation eerily relevant to La Esperanza: *You're here, this place has you, and now you're part of the trouble.* She would fight. Somehow, some way, she'd live to see this arrogant and cruel monster answer the same God whose power he usurped.

"Ahh," Padilla said, "here we are."

Kathleen saw a huge corral with a long stone watering trough at the far end. Men, some of them the roughest-looking characters she'd ever seen in her life, lined the top poles of the corral on two sides. They shot quick, sidelong glances at her, out of respect for the fact that she was with *el patrón* and thus could not be stared at. Inside the corral she saw the man named Jesus Gallegos. He wore tight trousers, a frogged jacket, a low shako hat made of leather. He stood in front of the water trough, a pistol in his hand. At the far end of the corral the *mozo* raced about on horseback swinging a long braided reata over his head.

"Watch the very tip of the reata," Padilla told her. "Watch it closely."

The *mozo* made another pass, Gallegos fanned his hammer and shot three times. Kathleen watched braided knots fly from the reata, one for each bullet, the tip constantly growing one knot closer to the *mozo*'s hand even as he whirled the leather rope. Again the men cheered and whistled. Gallegos spotted Kathleen and performed a formal bow from the waist, then pivoted neatly to salute his *patrón*. Padilla nodded back.

"An impressive demonstration, true?"

"I suppose so," she told him. She was reluctant, as always, to say anything to him. "I'm not an enthusiast of firearms."

Padilla smiled, revealing those miniature teeth. "Of course not. The rose blooms far away from the thorns. But both are part of the same bush. The amazing aspect about the being wealthy is this fact that one can be strong by paying for the strength of others. For example, my *segundo*'s deadly skill is now *my* deadly skill. The wealthy man is only as strong as whatever he can buy, it is true?"

"No doubt. But one can never buy everything he lacks."

"Perhaps not. But the luckiest among us can buy everything they *want*."

By now they were walking back toward the *casa grande*. Padilla added, "It is not the firearms in themselves, Miss Barton, that are so important to us men. It is the skill at using them which matters, and the men who excel in their use. For they are death merchants, and ours is a tragic nation obsessed with death. One philosopher has called death 'an eternal movelessness.' A comforting thought, it is true? I have always believed that death and suffering ennoble the soul."

In spite of herself, Kathleen let his remarks trigger an image of Hays, of his severed head lying in the bloodstained Arizona sand. The horror was tempered only by her deep, bitter rage.

"There's nothing romantic about death," she said coldly. "Nor suffering, either. If those who are so free to inflict pain had to taste it once in a while, they'd never call it romantic."

"I understand," he said, injecting even more politeness into his tone. "An example of that famous Yankee pragmatism one hears about so often."

While he spoke, Padilla had watched the sun ignite various hues in her light hair. She shuddered when he reached one slim, soft, white hand forward and twined a mass of her hair around it.

"*Qué maravilloso,*" he said in a voice almost hushed to a whisper.

They stood in the shadow of a yellow-flowered tamarind tree. She pulled back when he stroked her hair again. His nostrils flared as his breathing grew deeper. Lust thickened his voice when he spoke.

"Beauty affects me deeply. Sometimes, inside of me, there is this great and pure need. . . ."

"There is little inside you," she told him calmly, "except

base, vulgar lust and cowardice. If you ever met a true man, you couldn't look him in the eye."

This was so far from whatever Padilla expected that he could only gape in astonishment until the rage sent color to his pale cheeks. But before he could express his anger, a voice called out:

"Don Enrique?"

Kathleen whirled to confront the servant named Gabriela. The old woman ignored her as if Kathleen were no more than a dray animal.

"Don Enrique, the senora has been asking for you," Gabriela said, speaking in Spanish and still studiously ignoring Kathleen. "She is up in her room."

Kathleen thought she detected a warning tone in these last words. She watched Padilla glance up toward a second-story balcony on the west side of the main house, as if determining whether this spot where he presently stood could be seen from there.

"Also," the old servant added, "the *cuarto* is ready for this evening."

"All right," he said impatiently, dismissing her with his manner. "Tell Morela to be there at the usual time."

Padilla switched back to English, never suspecting that Kathleen had easily understood their exchange, despite his strong Castilian accent.

"I no longer have an official *mayordomo* at La Esperanza," he said apologetically. "Gabriela fills in. She once worked for my father and is very useful to me."

Kathleen was beginning to understand why. But before she could escape to her own room for a few hours, a vestige of Padilla's rage returned. He had a final bit of advice before he parted from her.

"I am told that you worked to help those less fortunate than yourself, that you taught *indios* how to read and—how do you phrase it?—cipher. You can stay, keep your tongue civil, and perhaps make life more pleasant for the *indios* here. Or, you can run and die. The choice is yours. But I must warn you now with the utmost sincerity. Insult my manhood one more time, and my great sensitivity to beauty will not stop me from killing you with my own hand."

• • •

"Our ten-penny soldier has gone too far this time," Charles Longstreet declared. "We won't have to lift a finger against him, the Army itself is going to cashier his Indian-loving ass."

Trilby nodded. He, Longstreet, and Nat Bischoff were seated around a deal table in the Three Sisters Saloon. The August day was hot as a sun-baked kiva, the afternoon air listless and stagnant. Trilby occupied his usual chair, with his back to the wall and a clear view of the entrance. His eyes instantly looked toward the bat-wings every time they swung open.

"The Army is moving to oust him," he agreed. "But they'll have to be careful, do it slow and put the best face on it. Carlson doesn't lack for friends, even with all the newspaper ink that's been spilled against him lately. Jemez Grayeyes is safe so long as Carlson's left on duty hereabouts. So what I'm wondering is, will they send the soldier packing in time?"

"In time for what?" Longstreet said.

"He means before the Apache has time to kill *us*," Bischoff said.

"For a man who issues so many threats, Bob, you sure seem nervous lately."

"If you had the brains God gave a pissant," Trilby told Longstreet, "you'd see this thing for what it is. I found Aragon's body at that jacal, and it was Grayeyes's work. But he sure's hell didn't kill all those Comancheros by himself. They were dead to the last man. Not a limb wound on one of them, all shot plumb in their lights. Don't you see? Carlson ain't just *tolerating* Grayeyes, they're cooperating."

"Bob's right," Bischoff said. "And once again Carlson didn't even bother to sugarcoat his actions, didn't offer one explanation to appease anyone."

As a result, Trilby thought, scathing editorials had declared the strike against the slavers "the basest form of vigilante gun law" and "criminal meddling in Arizona's affairs." Formal protests had been lodged at Fort Grant.

Longstreet lit a cheroot and tossed the match onto the

sawdust-covered dance floor. He pointed at Trilby with the cigar as he spoke.

"All right, so *now* you worry about it. You shooting your chin off at him during that reception didn't help. You practically dared him to make our lives miserable."

"Simmer down," Bischoff threw in. Evidently the reporter had grown tired of his Mexican cowboy look. Now, wearing a duster to protect his brushed black coat and shirt of finespun linen, Trilby recognized the *New York Herald* writer who had first come out West to check the frontier pulse. "That hick rail-splitter has actually done you a favor. If your contact at Fort Grant is reliable, Carlson's actions have helped to precipitate plans for a major military influx."

"He's reliable. He claims there'll be five thousand troopers mustering in New Mexico, eventually to be garrisoned here —with plenty of horses that'll be needing grain and hay."

"Well, then. Those contracts'll go to you and your friends on the committee."

"He nudged it too damn far," Longstreet said, "when he donated our goodwill payment to the Quakers. He's a reckless sonofabitch who goes too far to insult a man. I hope he enjoyed his little josh."

"It's only a matter of time," Bischoff insisted. "Most of the expansionists are distancing themselves from him now. The Army will follow suit."

Trilby shook his head. "It's no good to count on others to get the job done for us. It's our game and we call the stakes. I'm telling you, it's not just Carlson, it's Jemez Grayeyes, too. It was *him* killed Aragon, and Carlson had to've let it happen."

"Well, this time I'm ahead of you both," Longstreet said. "It'll be months before the Army is in the field. I can't afford to wait that long. It used to be Grayeyes never bothered with gold shipments. All of a sudden, that savage is keen for gold. I've already talked to my associates on the committee about this."

He looked at Trilby.

"Speaking of the Army. My acquaintance at Fort Grant asked me if I know how to get a reliable map of some of the Apache hideouts. I gave him your name. They'll be sending a soldier from the New Mexico Territory to pay you a visit. You'll be paid for your time."

Trilby nodded. "That's all I ever ask."

"One more thing," Longstreet said. "There's still a two-thousand-dollar bounty on the Apache. The committee has authorized me to put the word out discreetly: There's now a matching bounty on Seth Carlson."

Chapter 35

Shortly after the Bureau of Indian Affairs sent an interim agent to replace Hays Munro at Mater Dolorosa, Seth Carlson and Charlie Plummer visited the reservation to talk with the Apache youth named Victorio.

By tacit agreement he had become the communications link between Carlson and Jemez Grayeyes. Victorio was fanatically loyal to Jemez, a leader who sat behind few men in council. So when the Apache battle chief declared Carlson an honorable warrior who could be trusted, the youth obediently excluded him from his hatred against the hair-face soldiers who were slaughtering his people. Thus, Seth found out what Jemez had recently learned through the moccasin telegraph: that his head was now worth the same as Grayeyes's own, two thousand dollars in double-eagle gold pieces.

"Hell," Sergeant Major Jay Kinney said when Seth reported this latest news. "Best way to kill a snake is to catch it in its own hole."

Seth agreed. The idea of the committee setting a price on his plew nettled him almost as much as it did his men. Leaving the rest of the First Mountain Company bivouacked south of the Gila River, he, Kinney, Walt Mackenzie, and Charlie Plummer gave their mounts a good graze, then pointed their bridles toward Tucson.

" 'Pears to me," Plummer remarked to Seth soon after they passed the wagon-road way station at Red Rock, "it ain't just that bunch in Tucson that's giving you the rough side of their tongues lately. I read the newspapers when we stopped back there at Red Rock. I recall when them newspaper boys couldn't stick their noses up your hinder far enough. Now some of 'em's calling you an Indian lover."

"They're sayin' he's gone battle simple, too," Mackenzie threw in. "Goddamn plug uglies who write lies for whiskey."

Seth took his hat off and clapped it over his heart. "Boys, I'm cut plumb to the quick. When a man's lost the respect and loyalty of the newspapers, what the hell's left?"

"Ahh, fuck the newspapers," Kinney said. "Buncha white-livered scribblers. I'm more worried about whatever Corey Bryce is s'posed to be up to. Nothing white about *his* liver."

Seth kept his eyes on the sawtooth pattern ahead where the Santa Catalina Mountains north of Tucson thrust granite peaks into the sky. He, too, had heard the intimations of danger gathering like the mutter of thunder on the horizon —in the newspapers and by way of channels at Fort Grant: word that a new Indian-fighting ideology was gaining favor. Though careful to avoid any direct criticism of Seth, Corey and the other spokesmen nonetheless emphasized the need for massive, concerted action against the Apaches once they had been routed out of their strongholds and herded into the open. This new November first deadline approved by President Grant, they insisted, would not be ignored as the others had been—not by the Army, certainly. The Apaches would either report to the reservations or face an extermination drive the likes of which they had never seen before. The fact was, no one really expected them to heed the deadline. Indeed, the Army was making no effort to get the word to the Indians.

But thinking about Corey was hard, and Seth dropped it quick. He was actually relieved that his newspaper popularity was finally on the wane. The only thing he didn't want to lose was this independence, this total immersion in a hard task that occupied his mind constantly and kept it from wandering places where it shouldn't go.

And lately those places didn't just include Corey and Jeanette. They also included Kathleen Barton.

It had been growing in him since her disappearance: the aching in his gut, the need to help her despite the fact that he had no legal jurisdiction to do so. What had happened to Jeanette—nothing, not prayers, nor regrets, nor raging fits, could undo that. But Kathleen might well still be alive. He had made initial inquiries, based on what Jemez Grayeyes told him. The chrysalis of a plan had already formed.

That plan required meeting again with Jemez Grayeyes. Seth had already sent word to him. Such a meeting was inevitable, anyway. For Seth had noticed the same thing that members of the Tucson Committee were fretting about lately—the point of Jemez Grayeyes's latest raids was to accumulate gold. Why, when he had never valued it before?

But first things first, he told himself. For now it was time to stir up things in Tucson.

The four companions rode abreast down the wagon-seamed main thoroughfare of Silver Street. Seth let his gaze scan the board-front stores, the green canvas awning in front of Longstreet's Mercantile, the odd-job cowboys in broken-heeled boots, the dirty young vendors with their trundle carts.

"Eyes right," Kinney said.

Seth glanced that way and saw they were in luck. Charles Longstreet, Nat Bischoff, and Robert Trilby were just then emerging through the bat-wings of the Three Sisters.

"Timely met," Seth remarked, tugging on one rein and guiding his sorrel toward the tie pole in front of the saloon. The four soldiers dismounted and stood in a line across the oncoming path of the three men.

"Well now," Trilby said when the three civilians were forced to halt. "This looks like a confrontation."

"*This* is a confrontation," Seth replied quietly, raking upward at a forty-five-degree angle with his open right hand. He squared away his shoulders, lowered his center of gravity, swung straight from his heels. He put cold will and hard muscle behind the effort. The heel of his palm caught flush under the point of Trilby's square jaw and snapped his head back hard. The big man's feet almost lifted up from the street, and then he slacked and went down flat on his back.

"Good God a-gorry!" Walt exclaimed, as surprised as Trilby's companions.

Trilby lay among the wagon ruts, wincing at the pain in his sprained neck. Unable to turn his head, he slowly rose to his feet. One hand brushed the dust off his corduroy breeches. He held the other behind his thigh.

Plummer called out, "Watch'm, Seth, he's got a hideout piece!"

"No he ain't," Mackenzie said. "Not in his hand. He's wearing drinking jewelry! Them's horseshoe nails bent over his knuckles!"

"He needs 'em. He makes his brags in front of scared wimin. He's a dry-gulching coward like his Mex buddy Aragon," Kinney said while the two combatants circled each other crabwise, Trilby still favoring his neck. "He's got runny yolks for balls."

"Top, stow it," Seth told him calmly.

Seth suddenly sprang straight up, high as his saddle-hardened legs would take him, and drop-kicked Trilby hard in the chest. This time Trilby flew back several feet, lost his footing and went down again. Before he could rise a second time, Seth moved forward quick and kicked him hard in the face. His boot heel struck with a flat, solid impact and split both lips open deep.

"My God, the man's gone insane!" Bischoff said, and backed away a few steps, his face pale as new plaster.

"That's right, you little quill-nibblin' sissy," Kinney growled. "He'll bite your berries off and feed 'em to your asshole."

Longstreet was nearly as pale as Bischoff, though a desperate defiance showed in his eyes. He spotted Fargo Danford approaching on horseback. He flashed a quick high sign, and the deputy chucked up his mare, hurrying to join them.

A seven-shot Winchester repeater was halfway out of its scabbard when Charlie Plummer snatched the dragoon pistol from his belt. He pointed it, there was a deafening explosion, and Danford's horse dropped dead with a fluttery little sigh that seemed almost peaceful.

Plummer stared first at Kinney, then Walt, feigning shocked amazement. "Son of a *bitch*, boys, I'll be dinged! Guess I disremembered how touchy this ol' gal's trigger is! I only meant to point 'er. Might be I filed it down too close."

One bore of the formidable old pistol was still loaded with its huge conical ball. Acting blithely ignorant of the fact, Plummer held it pointed at the supine Danford while he spoke to his companions. Danford had miraculously escaped a broken leg when his horse collapsed. Now he scuttled first one way, then the other, like a man trying to douse flaming clothes. But each time he moved, Plummer turned in the same direction with his muzzle tracking the deputy as if by sheer accident.

"Whoa!" Danford protested. "Whoa, I ain't in no funning mood just cuz you are. Now *stop* it, goddamnit, afore that ol' hog leg goes off agin!"

"Piss on him, Charlie," Kinney said. "He never bought none of us a beer. You done for his horse, now kill the star man, too."

Walt had grabbed the Winchester when the horse went down. He jacked the rounds out onto the ground and flung the rifle into the nearest alley.

Trilby, clearly in agony, made no further effort to rise from the street. Seth stared at Longstreet.

"I braced him because he's your donkey worker. Next time it'll be you. Now you lissenup. Word has it there's a bounty on my head. I don't like that. I'm waiting three days to see if word's been put out to cancel it. If not . . ."

Seth nodded toward his men. "I got forty sharpshooters breathing fire behind me. *I* can put out a bounty, too. Unofficially, of course. And if my men find me with an airshaft in my head, well, they'd be hard to console. Right, Top?"

Kinney's face went pious and sincere. "T'would be a harsh blow, sir, my hand to God. I'm afraid there'd be some nuts lopped off in what they call cold retribution."

"You take my meaning clear?" Seth asked Longstreet. The businessman swallowed hard, watching Plummer charge the empty bore of his dragoon pistol and then cap it.

"Clear," Longstreet replied tersely.

Trilby was still groaning in the street. Kinney dropped into a squat beside him. "You'd best go find a wash-up, boyo. You're *all* bunged up."

"All right," Seth called to his men. "Let's cinch up."

Jemez Grayeyes had heard certain rumors, vague talk about a huge new trouble storm brewing in the East. But truly, there was always a new storm rising from that direction. And although he understood the white man's winter count, the concept of a strict November first deadline meant little to him. It meant even less to those Apaches who knew nothing of calendars, and still called November the Moon When the Ponies Grow Coats.

He explained all this to Seth Carlson, speaking in simple but good English, when the white-eye battle chief asked what he had heard. The two men had met—alone, palms held up in peace—at the base of Apache Rock, a monolith of wind-eroded sandstone rising nearly a thousand feet above the desert floor northeast of Tucson.

"These rumors," Grayeyes said, voice raised to counter the shriek of a stiff wind, "you, too, have heard them?"

"You're behind the times. They're not rumors. Plenty of soldiers are coming."

"Plenty have already come. I am still here. So are Cochise, Mangas Coloradas, Geronimo."

Seth thought about that and nodded. "You've fought well. But it's a matter of time, and you'll all be killed or captured."

"Any Apache can be killed," Grayeyes conceded. "Even Geronimo. Is it true what I hear—they mean to herd us down into the Sonoran Desert?"

Seth nodded. "So they say. Troop movements seem to bear it out."

Amusement glinted in the Apache's eyes. For a moment

he recalled the long slope he once pointed out to Victorio—the remote desert stretch of southwest Arizona known as the Devil's Floor, and carefully avoided by local Indians. It was still only a vague idea, not a plan. But Jemez resolved to make a close study of these new white-skin stirrings and to alert the other clan leaders.

"Anyway," Seth said, "soldiers aren't all I came to talk about."

The Apache's expressive mouth widened in a grin. Despite his headband, the wind wrapped his long black hair around his neck like a scarf. "Of course not. We Dineh have a name for you: Nantan Maño. The Sly One. You have come to ask why my band has begun stealing the yellow rocks?"

Seth nodded. "Are you using it to buy guns?"

"We steal our guns. I am hoarding yellow rocks now because I plan to buy my brother, sister, and the other Apache children taken from the reservation. Buy them from Padilla in Chihuahua. It is only just that Longstreet's money buy them back."

"What about Kathleen Barton?"

Jemez watched him a long time, his nimbus-gray eyes shrewd with amusement. "Well? What about her? Perhaps you have noticed how the sunlight gets trapped in her hair?"

"Do you plan to buy her, too?"

Jemez nodded. "If this thing can be done. Perhaps Padilla may not sell any of them."

"What then?"

"I chose this way with the gold because I know it would be very dangerous to take my band into Old Mexico to fight. But my band have pledged themselves. If Padilla will not sell our children, we will attack in force. Either we secure our children or we die in the attempt."

Seth shook his head. "It'd never work. You know damn good and well that Chihuahua is wide-open country in the north. It's also heavily patrolled nowadays. It's one thing to slip just across the border at night and steal some cattle. But this hacienda is more than two hundred miles deep into Mexico. A large war party is bound to be spotted. Nor could I lead my men down. U.S. relations with Mexico are touchy right now, and the Army is watching for unauthorized border crossings by American troops."

Jemez watched him closely. "Truly," he said, "I have been waiting for you to demand the gold back. You have said nothing about it."

"Keep Longstreet's gold. Try to buy them with it."

A grin wasn't enough this time—Jemez laughed outright. "Nantan Maño," he repeated, a trace of grudging respect creeping into his voice. "He *does* want the sun-haired beauty back. However, you just said—"

"Try to buy them back. But leave your band where they are."

"And go myself?"

"No. We'll mount a small strike force to take the gold down. Four of us. I pick my best warrior, you pick yours. Four of us, with a string of ponies for the kids—and Kathleen. A small band can move faster, is less likely to be spotted in that terrain, and can mount a lightning assault on the hacienda."

"You have given this thing much thought. Perhaps you love this Kathleen Barton?"

"Perhaps that's none of your damn mix."

Grayeyes laughed again. In an eye blink his face was all business again. "When do we go?"

"From all the bellyaching I've heard, you should have enough gold by now. Can you be ready within five sleeps?"

"Within one."

"Make it three. I have to ride back to join my men first."

Jemez nodded. "One thing more, blue-blouse. Do you know who killed the one who was once the agent at Mater Dolorosa?"

"A machete could have taken his head off. I'd say it was Aragon, accompanied by Trilby."

Jemez winced slightly when Seth directly named Aragon, a dead man. For a moment Jemez felt hot pressure behind his eyes as he recalled those blood-encrusted wicker cradles— witnesses swore that Robert Trilby was one of the men who had run from the cavern slaughter.

"I killed the half-breed who was Trilby's *segundo*," Jemez said, "and I plan to kill Trilby."

"So why tell me? It's your business."

"I only want you to know that I hope to kill him. But if you must do it, may Ussen guide your bullets."

"Just so he's killed. See you in three days?"

Jemez nodded once. "In three days. And then we ride south, Nantan Maño."

Chapter 36

"These little puppies spit out over a thousand rounds a minute, Captain. When they was first phased in, they only fired three hundred fifty. But they've added more barrels and a better magazine hopper that feeds the rounds in quicker'n scat."

Corey Bryce nodded, paying close attention as the enlisted armorer pointed out the improved features of this latest version of Richard Gatling's gun. It was late in August, the height of the dog days in the Southwest, and the influx of troops and equipment for the Apache campaign had begun in earnest. Ten more Gatlings, shrouded in canvas in their clumsy wooden carriages, were lined up in the desert sand behind the two men. Nearby sat flatbed wagons loaded with racks of artillery rifles and rockets. Beyond the stockpile of weapons, rows of new tents were springing up along the west flank of Fort Bates, New Mexico Territory.

The armorer mopped his sweaty brow with a shirtsleeve.

"Good gun, sir. I've fired and maintained every model. But what I can't rightly figure out is how the Army plans to get the 'Paches to ride in front of 'em. They're ign'ant, but they ain't stupid."

Corey stepped closer and cranked the barrels around their stationary spindle, checking the action. "They'll ride close enough," he said, "once they're flushed out and forced down into the open country. It's a simple question of getting control and keeping it, the same as when you drover beeves."

The armorer didn't appear convinced, but wisely held his counsel. The next moment he snapped to attention and saluted. Corey turned and saw General Ablehard approaching.

"Morning, sir."

"Morning, Captain Bryce. Corporal. As you were. Bryce, those railroad tracks look mighty fine on your blouse."

"Thank you, General. I'm fond of 'em, too."

"It's a brevet now, pony soldier, but that rank can be made permanent if you bury some Indians in Arizona dirt. How's the staging operation going?"

"She's humming right along so far, sir. Some of these troops are mighty green, though. I've got the NCOs drilling them."

Ablehard nodded. "Good man. They'll shape up. Everytime there's a new war, us old salts carp about how the sorry new recruits'll never be able to cut it. Somehow, they always do. You can't tell who the heroes are when they're digging latrines. Takes a good battle to show you what kind of *cojones* a man packs."

Ablehard's last comment caused Corey to fall silent. Against his will, he recalled a time when he had indeed witnessed how battle could prove a man's mettle—and cost another man his wife.

Ablehard noticed Corey's troubled frown. The general removed his campaign hat and patted his sallow face with a handkerchief. He lowered his voice.

"Must be a bit hard on you, m'boy, coming back here to Fort Bates. How long's it been since . . . ?"

"Almost a year, sir."

"Ahh, a year. Well. Only a little over two months and that November first deadline expires. Even before that we'll be on the march out of here. I was sure's hell surprised when the president put me in charge of the Apache campaign—I guess he *did* like that strategy recommendation we gave him. Tell you the truth, I've had all the glory I want. I'd as soon be hog ranching back in the capital with a little strumpet named Marlene. But as long as I'm stuck in this godforsaken scorpion pit, I'm going to enjoy watching you turn that company I gave you into front-line Indian fighters."

"They'll be ready, sir."

"That I don't doubt, Captain. And speaking of being ready, I've got a little temporary duty for you. Sort of an advance scout to gather reconnaissance. Only, you won't need your horse. You'll be riding the train."

"Sir?"

"Bill Wentworth, the C.O. at Fort Grant in Arizona, is a good friend of mine from the old days. He reports good progress in hiring new Apache scouts to search out and pinpoint the hiding places. He's working with a civilian named Longstreet in Tucson to procure us a reliable map of the hideouts. This Longstreet, he's a generous contributor to Americans United for Survival. I'd like you to meet with him and his people before this campaign starts. Apparently, one of his men knows the Apache tribe well. Milk him. You'll be outfitted at Fort Grant. Scout the territory a little, get a feel for the terrain you'll be fighting on."

"By all means, General."

Corey welcomed the assignment. It would get him closer to the action and occupy him until the November first deadline.

"We're gaining more information every day," Ablehard said. "We won't need to shove pitchforks into every haystack in creation, we'll know right where to go. They'll either die in the mountains or down on the flats. They will *not* escape into Mexico, not this time."

In the final week of August 1870, Seth Carlson, Charlie Plummer, Jemez Grayeyes, and a Navajo named Armijo eluded patrolling soldiers and slipped across the border near Agua Prieta, bearing southeast through Sonora toward the neighboring state of Chihuahua.

They traveled light, packing all their gear on their own ponies and leading a string of unburdened remounts—unburdened except for one, to which was lashed the hindquarters of an antelope they killed and butchered before entering Mexico. In this scalding heat the meat would putrefy quickly. But the hollowed-out hindquarters offered a good place to stash the thousands of dollars in gold coins and dust Jemez had brought with him. They would kill and butcher fresher replacements as opportunities arose.

At first they were dangerously exposed as they crossed barren pumice plains, the vast silence occasionally broken by the underground rumble of thermal springs, the hissing of sulfurous gas vents. They were forced to deplete their meager grain rations when the niggardly terrain offered nothing but dry sotols for the horses to forage. They collected dry buffalo chips for fuel at night. Every hour, they dismounted and walked for ten minutes to rest their horses without stopping completely—a complete stop left the animals unwilling to move out again in the stifling heat.

Occasionally, riding through basalt canyons or around natural water holes, they came across massacre sights: entire Indian villages where the Mexican army or gangs of scalp hunters had passed through, leaving heaps of charred bones. High in the sierras they rode through deserted old towns made of solid stone, no adobe anywhere. Sometimes the churches still stood, though the old Spanish bells were always missing, having been melted down to make bullets. From these desolate civic graveyards they would descend into fertile river valleys choked by thick bamboo brakes and fragrant tamarind groves.

Not all of the towns were deserted. Sometimes they rode through little whitewashed pueblos conspicuously devoid of young, healthy men—they'd been either rounded up for the army or already killed in one of Mexico's seemingly endless wars or revolts. In such towns the riders enjoyed a welcome diversion, slowing down for a few moments to watch the old men gathered in the *plaza mayor*, drinking wine from goatskins, the young women selling *ristras* of bright red peppers and shaping clay roofing tiles on their thighs. The bigger pueblos featured central *mercados* where the exotic wares included brightly colored macaws and tiny howler monkeys.

On their third day inside Mexico they stopped at a cold-water spring in the Sierra del Nido to water their horses. Seth consulted an Army map of the region.

"According to this, we should reach Valle del Lago Azul sometime tomorrow."

"Word could travel to Padilla fast now," Plummer said. "We'd best skirt all the towns from here on out, or we could end up in the *calabozo.*"

Seth nodded. Twice they had spotted S.P.'s, Chihuahua's Seguridades Publicas, transporting prisoners in double chains. Jemez translated their plans for Armijo, who spoke little English. The Navajo had not so far impressed either white man as a formidable warrior. He was small, pudgy turning to fat, and constantly wore a foolish, toothless grin that made Seth suspect he was soft in the brain.

Plummer stripped to bathe in the cool mountain water. He suddenly startled Seth by bursting out laughing.

"Christ! I like to died at the look on that tinhorn deputy's face when his hoss dropped out from under him!"

A grin worked its way through the grime on Seth's face. " 'Guess I disremembered how touchy this ol' gal's trigger is.' You bullshit artist."

" 'My God, the man's gone insane!' " Charlie shot back, imitating Nat Bischoff's wide-eyed fear.

Both men laughed so hard they dropped into the grass. When Plummer finally recovered from his paroxysms of laughter, he saw Armijo staring at his naked body—staring hard in utter fascination.

"The hell's *he* looking at?" Plummer demanded of Jemez.

"Your tattoo. He has never seen one. He wants to know if he can touch it."

Charlie looked down at the rattlesnake tattooed across his chest, its head coiled around his left nipple. "Hell no he can't touch it. Crazy bastard."

But later that day Armijo proved that he was sane enough when it mattered. They were crossing the final plain before reaching the vast Valle del Lago Azul. Soon it became apparent, from dust puffs on the horizon, that someone was following. Plummer broke out his field glasses and studied the horizon behind them for a long time, separating what was really there from the shimmering heat mirages.

"Gray uniforms," he said finally. "*Rurales*. And they're after us."

This news, Seth realized, couldn't have come at a worse time. They had just started across the plain, with hours of riding ahead. They'd been pushing hard, and even the re-mounts were tired. Yet neither was there any place to shelter.

"Much as I hate to, we'll have to rabbit," he decided.

"Bad plan," Jemez said. He turned and said something to Armijo. The Navajo, his foolish grin seemingly carved into his face, swung down from his pony. He landed awkwardly, almost losing his balance, and Seth and Plummer exchanged skeptical glances.

Armijo slid an old octagonal-barreled Hawken .53 from his scabbard. The two white men exchanged another look when the easygoing Navajo pulled a folding bipod from his pannier and screwed it onto the barrel. He leveled a spot overlooking the approaching *rurales*, then threw a handful of paper cartridges near the weapon. Seth watched him chew the ends off of two cartridges, pouring the black powder into the gun's chamber before seating a ball behind the loading gate.

"He's using a double charge," Seth told Plummer. "Two hundred grains of powder."

"Double charge will give him range, sure, but he'll lose accuracy. He can't hit them from here with that old mountain-man relic. Hell, all you can see is their dust."

Armijo capped the Hawken, then grunted in protest as he sprawled out behind it. Charlie stood behind him with field glasses in hand. The Navajo eased back his trigger until the weapon fired with a solid report.

"Shit-oh-dear!" Plummer exclaimed. "A horse went down!"

Armijo reloaded, aimed, squeezed off his second shot.

"Target!" Charlie lowered the glasses and looked at Seth, grinning.

A third shot, a fourth.

"You done it, John!" Plummer shouted, adding a whoop.

"That's holdin' and squeezin', *kemosabe*. Them bean eaters just reversed course. They're gettin' the hell out!"

"Have him drop another one just to keep them worried," Seth told Jemez.

A few minutes later, while he packed away his bipod, Armijo called out something to Jemez. The Apache looked at Plummer.

"He wants to know if he can touch your tattoo now."

Plummer looked at Seth, then shrugged. "Crazy bastard," he said again. He reached up to unbutton his shirt. "Long as he don't kiss me."

"Don't worry," Jemez said. He grabbed a handful of mane and swung up onto his pony. "Indians don't waste time kissing."

From the narrow, vaulted windows of the library, Kathleen could look out onto the big kitchen garden at the side of the *casa grande*. It was noon, and Socorro was picking vegetables with the Mayan girl named Morela.

Kathleen had just finished another difficult lesson with Isabel Padilla. At sixteen, the daughter of the house was a sullen, spoiled only child who resented these lessons in English. But at least Kathleen was permitted free run of the library, her favorite part of the hacienda. The tall walls were lined with the gilt-lettered spines of books, with displays of small Spanish fist shields and thin sabers of fine-tempered Toledo steel.

Heart thumping fast, Kathleen hurried across to the handsome walnut doors with their carved brass knobs. She pushed one open and made sure no one was approaching. Then she moved swiftly to the spot where several volumes of *Summa Theologica* protruded about an inch beyond the surrounding books. She pulled them out and carefully felt behind them until her fingers encountered cool steel.

Kathleen pulled out a butcher knife with a twelve-inch serrated blade. She crossed to the open window again. She was about to call Socorro's name, then suddenly checked herself and held the knife behind her back: Padilla's wife was strolling across the yard, a rosary of semiprecious stones twined through her fingers. Clearly, she was returning from the mass she attended each morning. But where was Jesus Gallegos, her constant shadow?

Doña Elena glanced toward the library and met Kathleen's eyes. She wore a simple black dress with cream lace cuffs, her jet hair pinned and netted beneath a crocheted snood. The malevolent look she gave Kathleen left little doubt that Elena knew full well why her husband had acquired this beautiful blond "tutor."

Doña Elena finally rounded the back corner of the main house. Again Kathleen opened her mouth to call Socorro. The Apache girl was the only other person who knew where the weapons were being cached.

Just then a faint breeze caressed Kathleen's nape. A moment later she heard a sharp, familiar whacking sound that made her cry out in fright. She whirled around. The old housekeeper, Gabriela, stood in the doorway just behind Jesus Gallegos.

"See?" Gabriela screeched. "See? *Con las manos en la masa!* I told you knives were disappearing. The gringa *puta* plans to kill all of us!"

Again Gallegos whacked his boot with his quirt. The wide-brimmed shako left most of his face in shadow. "I like a woman with spirit. But Don Enrique?" Gallegos shook his head. "He is going to be very angry. Disloyalty hurts him deeply. It may go hard for you, *rubia.*"

He started slowly toward her, his right hand extended. "Give me the knife," he said. "And show me where you have hidden the rest of the weapons."

Chapter 37

On the morning after Armijo's long distance marksmanship turned back the *rurales*, Seth's small raiding party descended from the sierra rimrock to the brim of Valle del Lago Azul. Below them, still shrouded in pockets of mist, lay a vast and lush green patchwork of forests, fields, and glades crisscrossed by pristine rivers and streams. Thousands of tiny rills and streamlets covered the opposite slope. They cascaded steeply down into larger waterfalls that set up a steady, sissing murmur and then crashed down into the boiling foam and mist of a lake at the bottom.

"Katy Christ," Charlie Plummer said. "No wonder Coronado and the rest of them fish eaters from Spain thought there must be cities of gold hereabouts. A man with a stake down there couldn't die poor if he tried to."

"Maybe." Seth pressured his mount with his knees, easing around a spur of rock, and moved up beside Plummer. "But I'll bet he'd have a good chance at dying young."

The trail downward was narrow and steep, switchbacking from shelf to shelf as it descended. Armijo and Jemez rode the most experienced mountain ponies. They eased around the two white-skins and led the descent. Plummer rode drag, leading their remuda.

Seth was third, following the blood bay Jemez rode. He saw Armijo emerge from a switchback down below and to his right. The Navajo glanced back up at him, his foolish grin easily visible from here.

A moment later Seth flinched violently as an arrow abruptly penetrated Armijo's right ear, its shaft sinking hard enough to drive the point out the left temple.

Even as Armijo slid off his pony and slacked dead to the ground, even before Seth reacted, he felt it again: that horrible, cold shock of helpless realization, the awful understanding that everything could go to hell more quickly than a man could believe—just as it had on that bloody Sunday near Santa Fe. Now here it was again, and again his limbs felt like dead stones, his muscles warm and weak as mush.

But any action would have been futile. Unleashing shrill cries, Indians emerged on foot from the thick cover, four or five surrounding each rider and grabbing his mount. Seth's pony reared and spun around as if to break back up the trail. He was just in time to watch Plummer kick one of the attackers down, then fall off the back of his horse when an Indian struck him on the head with a wooden war club. Then Seth, too, was on the ground, a horde of Indians kicking and shoving him, tying his wrists and ankles with braided-horsehair ropes.

Seth heard commands shouted in Spanish, felt rough hands throwing him back across his horse. He was jostled hard down the trail, a brief ride bringing them to a hollow in the trees near a river. The Indians had hobbled their own mounts here before the attack. Seth was pulled roughly off his horse again and propped up sitting with his back to a yew tree.

So far he hadn't been badly hurt, and Jemez—tied up right next to him—looked all right, too, except for a few cuts and bruises. But the back of Plummer's head was matted with blood, and the man appeared only half conscious. For the moment the marauders ignored their prisoners while they rifled through the contents of saddlebags and panniers.

"Karankawas?" Seth guessed, just loud enough for Jemez to hear him.

The Apache nodded. "Mostly. There's a few Yavapais and Maricopas, too."

Seth knew nothing about these last two tribes except that the Maricopas had a reservation somewhere in the southwestern Arizona Territory near the Papago and Pima reservations. But he had encountered Karankawas briefly while pursuing Eagle on His Journey and his Kiowa band into Mexico. The Karankawas had once ranged the long eastern coast of Texas and northern Mexico, rivaling the dreaded Comanches as brutal raiders and marauders. They had been driven deeper inland into Mexico by a combination of the U.S. Army, Texas Rangers, and various private militias and scalp-hunting expeditions. All of which told Seth his little band was up against it now. Jemez's next remark confirmed his fear.

"If it was just renegade Maricopas and Yavapais, they'd exact tribute and let us go after throwing a scare into us—*if* they don't know about the bounty on us. But this band plans to take everything we have and torture us before they kill us. Watch me and do like I do. Whatever you do, don't let them see any fear in your face, and *don't* beg them for mercy. Their leader is a Karankawa, and that tribe makes much of bluffing and making brags. We might stand a chance if they decide we're crazy-brave and don't give a damn."

Seth counted about twenty of them. Some wore modern machine-made clothing, some only ragged hides and worn-out moccasins. Their weapons were as motley as their horses and their garb: He spotted rawhide-wrapped rocks, a flintlock shotgun, various handguns, a few modern carbines. Seth identified the leader. He was small, burned to a deep copper, and wore his hair just long enough to part exactly in the center and comb behind his ears. The lower half of his right ear was missing, and judging from the ragged-leather edge on the remaining portion, it had been slowly chewed off.

He crossed toward the two conscious prisoners, ignoring Plummer.

"*Cuál de ustedes habla español?*" he demanded.

"I do," Jemez said, though by now Seth, too, had picked up a little Spanish.

"I am called Matazal. This valley is mine. And now I see an Apache and a yellow-eyes on the ground before me. You share blood with the mighty Geronimo and yet play the dog for yellow-eyes?"

Jemez left his gaze unfocused and said nothing. The Karankawa had called Seth and Plummer yellow-eyes because the first white men his tribe ever saw were lost mountain men with severe jaundice. The name had stuck.

"Where is your money?"

"What money?"

"*Vaya!* You have money. Or *they* do. Somewhere. Nearby if not with you. No yellow-eyes come this far without it."

"Unless," Jemez said, "they arrive poor but plan to *leave* with money."

Seth had followed most of this. Matazal smiled slightly, clearly tucking that bit of information away for later. Seth repeated a little prayer to himself and hoped Jemez could pull this off.

"All I see you packing now is putrid meat. What kind of *barbaros* eat maggoty meat in a land of plenty?"

Jemez shrugged. "Maggoty meat is better than none. We are moving quickly, and we did not come for the game. Besides, maggots make a good soup."

Seth watched the renegade glance toward the packhorse laden with the moldering antelope. He gave a command, and a man, turning his face away from the stink, approached the horse. He glanced quickly under the meat, lifted one leg and took a swift glance inside before ducking away with his face wrinkled in distaste. Seth realized that, in his hurry, he had not spotted the gold stuffed inside a length of large intestine and shoved to the back of the hollowed-out hindquarters. He shook his head at his leader. Nothing.

"The Apache wants to play with us," Matazal said. "A playful Apache. A *ver!* Let's see how playful he is."

He called out a command in his own language, and several braves quickly untied and stripped the two prisoners. Using rawhide thongs and pointed sticks, they staked both men out spread-eagle. A fire was quickly built, rocks rolled into the flames until they were glowing.

"Don't cooperate," Jemez told Seth quietly in English. "They'll just kill us. Bluff. Do what they don't expect. It can't hurt."

"*Callate!*" Matazal screamed, and kicked Jemez hard in the lower ribs. "Shut up! Speak only Spanish."

By now the rest of Matazal's band had gathered around. All Indians, north or south of the Rio Bravo, dearly loved a group entertainment. Jemez was banking on this. When he got his breath back after the sharp kick, he told Matazal, "I think I know you."

Matazal raised an eyebrow. He used a long stick to roll one of the heated rocks out of the fire. His tone was amused, patronizing. "How so, Apache?"

"Yes, I am sure I know you," Jemez said slowly. "Yes, truly, she was the one."

Matazal used two sticks to pick up one of the rocks. "I cannot place your words in my parfleche, Apache. Speak straight or I cut out your tongue. How do you know me? Who is *she*?"

"Your mother. I mounted her and bulled her, and she howled like a dog in the hot moons."

Most of Matazal's men understood enough Spanish to follow this. Several laughed outright and translated for the others. The men crowded closer, realizing a fine entertainment indeed was shaping up. Matazal knew the rules and showed no feeling. He simply parted the sticks and dropped the smoking rock on Jemez's bare chest.

The Apache's back arched so hard at the pain that he bucked the rock off. But not before the acrid stench of scorched flesh assailed Seth's nostrils. Jemez, though breathless and panting from the pain and the shock to his system, did not cry out. While Matazal rolled another rock out of the fire, Jemez said weakly:

"Your mother was truly frightened when she saw how big I am. Used only to Karankawa men, she was not prepared for such size on a man."

This outrageous effrontery made many of the men howl in utter disbelief. Several looked at the supine Apache with open curiosity, even admiration. By now a huge red welt colored his chest. Nor had they failed to notice the scars on the white man's naked body, clearly left by arrow points and bullets.

This time Matazal dropped the next rock just above Jemez's navel and held it there with his sticks so the Apache couldn't buck it off. Seth almost retched at the prolonged stink of seared flesh. Jemez's ragged breathing told him how bad the pain must be. Seth was incredulous when, only moments after Matazal pushed the rock off, Jemez managed yet another insult.

"Your mother also confessed to me that her own boy tops her often, though he is not man enough to satisfy her as I do. 'Matazal is like a daughter to me,' your mother said fondly."

By now the thoroughly impressed men were clapping and cheering. Matazal, crafty enough to give in before he lost face in a serious confrontation, grinned himself at this reckless prisoner who defied belief.

"Apache, I say it now: you are an *hombre de veras*. But this yellow-eyes, has *he* topped my mother, too?"

He crossed to Seth, sliding a Colt Navy pistol from his sash.

"Listen, Nantan Maño," Jemez told Seth quickly in English, "the pain is a bright red ball. Understand? First you feel it, then you can see it, and then you can pick it up and throw it outside of you."

Matazal ignored Jemez this time, just as he ignored the rocks because he knew his men liked variety. He knelt beside Seth's head, cocked his Colt, laid it flush alongside the prisoner's cheek and fired it. The bullet thumped harmlessly into the base of a tree, but the jarring explosion inside Seth's skull pierced his eardrums like sharp needles. Muzzle flash scorched his scalp, and the spent cartridge flew out hard and raked a hot gash over his left eye.

Seth felt cold dread, sure his hearing was permanently damaged. The explosive ringing, the sudden overloading of his senses, left him too rattled to issue cool insults as Jemez had. But nonetheless he took his cue from the Apache. Whereas normally he would have endured this in stoic silence, now he determined to participate in the ritual. Realistically, all he could hope to earn would be a quick death. But that was better than saying good-bye to his senses one by one before he died miserably anyway.

"More," he begged, ears ringing so hard he could barely hear his own voice. "Give me some more, little squaw-man."

"El quiere mas," Jemez translated, grinning in spite of the pain wracking his chest and stomach. "And he suggests that you belong in your tribe's sewing lodge, not out here leading men."

Matazal called one of his men over and spoke to him briefly. The man crossed to a pony and rummaged in a pannier, returning with a brass-lidded fruit jar. Holes had been poked in the lid. Matazal made sure Seth got a good look inside. A half-dozen scorpions clung to the glass.

Jemez lost his grin as he watched Matazal unscrew the lid and shake all the scorpions onto Seth's naked body. He knew that normally, unless provoked, they would nip with their front pair of claws only and reserve the curved and poisonous stinger at the end of their tails for attacks. But these would be angry from being cooped up in the jar. The least flinch might set them off, and if one attacked, all would. The bite of one was rarely fatal to a man, but six would surely be.

"Tell your friend I am curious to know how he enjoyed my mother," Matazal said.

But Seth was afraid to speak and earn a scorpion bite for the effort. His entire body recoiled at the scaly prickles moving all over his skin. The strong front claws hurt as they pierced his flesh. He tried to flatten himself under them and lessen the contact. Sweat beaded along his scalp, tickling before the drops seeped out onto his forehead and, salt-stinging, into his eyes. If pain was a red ball, so was fear, and now he concentrated on putting it outside of him.

By now Plummer was conscious. Seth heard Plummer taunting the Indians in Spanish in an attempt to divert them from him. Matazal refused to rise to the bait. He used one of his sticks to guide a scorpion lower on Seth's belly, lower yet, until the captive recoiled when the scaly prickle reached his sex.

"Translate this," the Karankawa ordered Jemez. "Tell him to be careful. If he gets hard, it will bite him."

The Indians erupted in hoots and laughter. But before Jemez could translate, Seth spoke up in Spanish: "No, *you* will, *maricón*."

Surprised silence before more laughter erupted, led by Matazal.

"I like you," he told both of the prisoners, adding for the benefit of the spectators, "but not *that* much." More shouts, and someone shot his pistol in the air. "Untie them," he ordered a brave, sweeping the scorpions off of Seth. He picked one up and held it closer. The renegade winked at the pale-as-moonstone Anglo.

"They have no stingers, *compadre*. See? They can easily be pulled out. But of course, how could you know? And still, you did not piss yourself as they usually do."

He turned to Jemez. "You, Apache. You cannot pay a peace price now, but you say you intend to leave rich. Since you must pass through my territory again to leave, I have ears for your words. Now speak, and hope I like what I hear. If not, I kill all three of you. Clean, quick, for you are men and deserve a good death. But your life will be over, and that is always an important thing to consider."

About a half hour before sunset the copper mine shut down for the day. From their position in the scrub oak above the head frame, the three intruders watched a huge Mexican *jefe* herd the youngest of his crew of boys into a mule-drawn buckboard. The biggest youths—none beyond his early teens —walked along beside the buckboard as they made the one-mile trip to the hacienda.

Jemez held his face impassive when he spotted Miguelito clambering into the conveyance. But Seth noticed how his eyes never left the boy.

"Your brother?" he said. His own words still seemed dim to him, still made an echolike aftersound in his ears. But he thanked God he could still hear the other two clearly.

Jemez nodded. His tone hinted at the hatred his face refused to show. "White-skins sent him to the reservation to learn a trade. Now he has one."

"Shame he'll have to learn another."

"Assuming we get out of here with our topknots in place,"

Plummer groused. "I been coshed on the *cabeza* once by that red trash under Matazal. Now Jemez feeds 'em a line of bull about how we come to rob Padilla. They'll be wantin' color before they let us by again, and there's no other way past them—not in a hurry, anyhow."

"It just means we make sure Padilla doesn't get ours," Seth told him. "Anyway, you're too far ahead of the game. Jemez had to offer something or it would've got ugly in a hurry. Matazal had to get a good offer to save face. Worry about him if we get the hell out of here. There's plenty of battle-savvy *jefes* down there, and I saw at least one packing a shotgun."

Seth looked at his companions. "Let's move closer and get the lay of the place."

Jemez and Plummer nodded. They had picketed their mounts on the opposite slope of the mountain. The three men fanned out, Jemez forming the point in deference to his superior skill at concealed movement. He had made a paste from moss and aloe vera and packed it around his burns. But his speed and agility were down, and sometimes the red ball of pain in his mind's eye was too big to throw outside of himself.

They leapfrogged from bush to tree to rock. The three men avoided trails and paths, leaving cover only to move rapidly forward to the next position. They were soon close enough to keep a good eye on the main house and the surrounding buildings. Night had descended, but light spilled from the many windows, and glowing orange fires dotted the grounds. By now Jemez had spotted Socorro and another Indian girl. They came out of the kitchen, both carrying empty baskets, and walked back to one of the numerous rock-and-adobe shelters behind the main house.

Seth and Plummer moved up beside him. "Seen the woman? Kathleen Barton? Or the other two Apache kids?"

Jemez said, "Not the woman. I saw my brother and sister, and the boy named Kato was with the mining crew. I think I know where my sister is staying. When it's darker, I'll go down."

"You dang well better be careful," Plummer said. "I

counted more'n a dozen greasers with guns. There's dogs down there, too. If we're wishful of keeping our hides, we best stay frosty and shoot plumb if we got to."

"Sure, but this could be easier than we dreamed," Seth added. "If we can locate all five of them, we might be able to sneak them out without even contacting Padilla to negotiate. We could have a good start before they even start looking for them. Then, if we have to, we'll have gold to pay Matazal's tribute."

"Easy, my sweet aunt," Plummer said. "One thing I've learned from riding with you, amigo—don't nothing come without busting my hump."

"Make a man out of you," Seth assured him.

" 'Sides, we don't owe Matazal squat after he killed—"

"Never mind a certain person," Jemez cut in sharply.

"Sorry," Plummer said.

When Jemez had trouble seeing his hand in front of his face, it was dark enough to move in closer. But first he turned to Seth.

"Nantan Maño. I have a request."

Seth could barely discern his companion's shape in the still darkness. But Jemez's formal manner made him curious. "I'm listening."

"I do not care if I am killed. But do not let these Mexican devils take me prisoner."

Seth understood immediately. Mexicans, too, commonly employed hanging as punishment. Indeed, it was Mexicans who hanged Jemez's father, not even bothering with a tree. Seth had already learned—from Goes Ahead—about this Apache's legendary dread of the noose, a fear that Indians throughout Apacheria knew and respected.

"You've got my word."

Despite the darkness, Plummer could feel Jemez's question hanging in the air.

"You got my word, too, buck."

A moment later Jemez was gone.

It was the dinner hour now for both the domestic servants and the field and mine workers. Warm aromas drifted from a cook house behind the *casa grande*. Workers, most of them

still children, filed past two women who loaded their plates
with beans, meat, and corn tortillas. Most ate their meal
outdoors around huge bonfires, then drifted back toward the
line of shelters. Jemez did not see his brother and sister. But
he had made a good map in his mind of the hut he had seen
Socorro enter earlier.

Using the big kitchen garden for cover, he slipped past the
main house and through a grassy area dotted with marble
statues. As he emerged from the open yard into the un-
tended grass behind the huts, one of the bonfires silhouetted
an armed guard. He strolled slowly up and down between the
huts, clearly bored, his *escopeta* tucked under his right arm.

Jemez avoided him easily, ducking behind a row of flowering frangipani bushes, then an abandoned carriage house,
emerging well behind the huts now. He stopped at the fifth
one and squatted on his heels beneath the only window. A
light shone inside.

Jemez imitated the fast clicking sound of a gecko lizard—
the signal that a friend was at hand. He heard nothing from
inside. Maybe Socorro was gone now. Maybe she didn't stay
here. Maybe—

Jemez opened his mouth to make the sound again when
Socorro nearly bumped into him in the dark.

For a long time neither of them said a thing. Jemez
reached out, touched her face, felt the hot tears spilling from
her eyes.

"Jemez. You came."

"Did I not say I would come for you, little sister? Has a
Grayeyes ever lied to his own?"

"Only to Mexicans and white-eyes," she said proudly,
tears choking her voice. "Miguelito is here, too. And Kato
and Rosario. Also, Tanta Kathleen from the reservation. She
is a slave here, too, only she tried to help us. They caught
her. Now she is locked up in the *cárcel*."

That news set Jemez back on his heels. Like Seth, he had
already decided that he would not leave without the woman,
too. They dared not remove any of the children just yet—
that would alert Padilla and his men, making it impossible to
save Kathleen.

"Now tell me things, sister," Jemez said gently, again

touching Socorro's face. "Tell me everything you know about this place. About Padilla, about his habits, when he comes and goes. Only three of us are here to do this, so you will have to fight with us and make it four. We will need to know as much as we can. Or else it will go hard for all of us."

Chapter 38

Corey Bryce rested his head back in the leather wing chair, uncomfortable under the curious and unrelenting scrutiny of the other three men. But he met their gazes frankly. He was civil without returning the easy camaraderie they had offered ever since he arrived in Tucson to gather reconnaissance for the Apache campaign.

"Of course," Longstreet said, "even Bob and his men haven't located all of their hideouts. But the maps and information we're providing you will be the best available. Besides that, we've got local redskins looking for more camps right now. By the time the Army is ready to move, you'll be able to coordinate individual strike teams in a massive sweep."

Corey had other priorities than these men did. But he knew damn good and well they didn't want—or expect—this campaign to eliminate the Apache threat. But whatever their motivations, they were, after all, allies of sorts.

"I assure you," he told them, "the Army greatly appreciates the assistance, gentlemen. We mean to get the job done right this time."

Robert Trilby had so far been content to let the other men talk. He occupied the other wing chair at the opposite corner of Longstreet's huge scrollwork desk. The big man was forced to rotate his entire body to look at this young blond soldier with his hat on his knee. Trilby had refused to go to a doctor after Carlson beat him and left him lying in the wagon ruts of Silver Street. He figured it was humiliating enough that Longstreet and Bischoff had witnessed the scene. A doctor would talk it all over town fresh. In an attempt to immobilize his sprained neck, he had taken to wearing a stiff leather military cravat that fastened around his neck with a buckle.

"You'll have the most trouble with Jemez Grayeyes," Trilby said. "He's mostly a loner and he's got a pattern. He raids hot and heavy with some ragtag band, then he always separates himself and holes up in the sierras to the south. There's a 'Pache kid rides from the rez at Mater Dolorosa to Grayeyes's hideout to bring him messages. One of my men managed to trail him last time he went, so we know where that cave is now. Grayeyes still uses it, he left food stores. He'll go back sooner or later."

"Unless he's killed first," Nat Bischoff put in. The journalist stood near the shelf behind Longstreet's desk, the Apache skulls a pair of grinning bookends behind him. "But at any rate, I beg to differ with you, Bob. Grayeyes is a serious problem, granted. But after observing the man close up, I think Captain Bryce's worst obstacle of this upcoming campaign is going to be Seth Carlson."

Corey stiffened slightly, but his face maintained its civil composure. "How do you mean, Mr. Bischoff? Surely you're not suggesting Colonel Carlson will fight on the side of the Apaches?"

"Well, he won't lead them into battle carrying the medicine shield, no. But the man is unstable. He could abet them in his own way. He no longer serves any commander but himself. He's a wind that bloweth where it listeth. Seth Carlson answers to no man, especially when he's got forty loyal guns behind him."

"Definitely unstable," Longstreet chimed in. "And his

men are obviously as crazy as he is. Probably his influence. Last time we ran into him? He beat my man here"—Longstreet pointed his cigar at Trilby—"senseless. And he threatened to kill all three of us. Understand this. He let Jemez Grayeyes ride free when he could have killed him, then turns around and threatens to kill *us*."

Corey glanced at Trilby with new interest. "Colonel Carlson did that to a man your size?"

Anger flushed Trilby's bluff face. But Corey focused his attention on Bischoff. He had asked plenty of questions up at Fort Grant, had kept his eyes wide open here in Tucson. For some time now he had begun to understand something that deeply surprised him: Nat Bischoff, the man who had created the national legend of Seth Carlson, in fact hated the object of his eloquent attention. And judging from spiteful remarks Bischoff had made, Seth despised him right back. For a moment it even occurred to Corey that Bischoff had used Seth to further his own interests. Interests that seemed curiously linked to those of the Tucson Committee.

"I'm just wondering, Mr. Bischoff," he said slowly. "I'm not in the newspaper business. But it seems to me you get most of your information right here in town. Yet you've set yourself up as an expert on the goings-on in this entire territory."

"*He* stays in town, Captain," Trilby said. "But he knows some who leave now and then."

Corey nodded. "You, I take it. A scout's useful, if you can trust him."

"Trust?" Bischoff shrugged. "I trust any man to do what's in his own best interest. That does not preclude a certain amount of cooperation among friends."

Corey didn't consider one man here his friend. They were in it to win—for themselves—and so was he. But he needed their help. It was one thing to suspect that Bischoff had used Seth ruthlessly, as perhaps Bischoff was even using him now, that he was just one more greedy scoundrel splitting the swag with Trilby and Longstreet, patriotic rhetoric be damned. It was another thing altogether to recall that image of Jeanette crumpling dead to the ground, Seth's .44 still smoking behind her. The morality of this situation in Tucson gnawed at

Corey, but the hurt of Jeanette's death still felt like a fresh knife wound. And it was the hurt that guided him now.

He gauged the growing hostility in the room and decided to back off before he lost valuable cooperation.

"You've got a point there, Mr. Bischoff. The white men in this territory have to close ranks and stand together, no matter the differences between them. We can squabble amongst ourselves after we've whipped the Apaches."

"*That's* the gait," Longstreet agreed enthusiastically. "Teamwork, eh? Let Carlson ride his own way. Don't forget the name of the organization we've both joined, lad: Americans *United* for Survival. Gentlemen, I'm a Hoosier by birth, but I despised that Black Republican Lincoln and voted for Douglas. Still, African Abe preached pure gospel when he said a divided house cannot endure."

"Stand," Bischoff corrected him. "A house divided against itself cannot *stand.*"

"Whichever," Longstreet said impatiently. "You take my meaning."

Trilby didn't care two jackstraws about divided houses or "respectable" businessmen like Longstreet—he still planned to one day drive every member of the committee into either a grave or a debtor's prison. Toward that end he had kept careful documentation of their activities. But his first priority now, as urgent as an abscess, was to kill Jemez Grayeyes and Seth Carlson before they killed him.

"Less than two months," Longstreet said to Corey. "Your old friend Seth Carlson will be out of work, and with a bit of luck, Jemez Grayeyes will be picking lead out of his red ass."

Kathleen held it as long as she possibly could, until the pain wound tight inside her and ached all the way out to her hair roots. Then she knew she would soil herself if she didn't act quickly.

She'd been locked up in one of several narrow stone cells, all currently uninhabited except for her, the lice, and the cockroaches. The only objects in the room were a leather water pail and a thin straw shakedown. The horse blanket covering the shakedown was scaly with old stains whose origins she didn't even want to think about.

For the relief of bodily functions, a shallow straddle trench had been scooped out of the floor and drained under one corner of the *cárcel*. Kathleen hated it. It might be convenient for men, but even with her numerous undergarments removed, it forced her into undignified contortions. She made sure there was water in the pail, then gathered her skirt up around her and squatted awkwardly over the trench.

She had just begun to void her urine when a faint noise to her left—the low whistle of excited nostril breathing—claimed her attention.

Padilla stood outside the iron grate of the cell door, watching her with the single-minded fascination of a bird mesmerized by a snake.

She cried out and turned her face away in a warm rush of anger and embarrassment. She had no choice but to finish, her bladder ached so. Nor would she give him the satisfaction of rattling her. Kathleen splashed water into the clay trough, still not looking toward the grate. Weak sunlight slanted through the small window in the back wall, the anemic yellow rays telling her the morning was still young. From here she could see a portion of the narrow-ported outer wall, cusps of broken glass visible along the top.

"Watching you in this moment," Padilla said in English, his voice oddly husky, "your hair a halo around you, so angelic—and yet with you squatting to do your business like the lowest animal—it made me think of a line from one of your English poets. 'If gold will rust, what then will iron do?' It is a compelling thought, is it not, this notion that a beautiful woman destroys the possibility of immortality when she gives proof that she, too, succumbs to base bodily needs?"

She refused to grace this sickness with a response. Padilla laughed. "The haughty *rubia* is too proud to answer."

"What's the point of talking with someone like you? You can't see anything, you create your own reality and nothing else touches it. You think I don't answer you because I'm proud? I'm not particularly proud. I just don't *like* you."

"You do not think I am a man, do you?"

"Clearly you're a man."

"But not a *man*?"

"A good man? No."

"Good men are weak—and thus poor. The world is super-fluous with your *good* men. A good man is no man at all."

"You talk brave now, here, to me. I think you are not so brave with your wife, or when putting on a pious face for the priest."

"Again you insult my manhood?"

"No. I insult your honesty. You strike a brave pose when you're alone with your helpless victims. But most of this pose is a pathetic attempt to justify your unspeakable behavior."

"What behavior is that, Miss Barton?"

"As I said, it's unspeakable. And in any event, you know it better than I."

"Of course. But I want to hear you talk about it—just as I like to hear you make water. It . . . excites me, it—"

"I have no interest in the details of your sickness. I refuse to talk about it. Some actions defy words."

He laughed, jangling the keys in his hand as if to unlock her door and come inside. She stood her ground, the defiance in her face making it clear he was in for a fight. Padilla stayed where he was.

"All right. Talk about the other and I will set you free. Tell me where the rest of the weapons are and who else is plotting with you."

But Kathleen had neither fear nor patience left. The image of Hays's death, the image of Trilby grunting and heaving on top of her—for surely it had been Trilby behind that bandanna—returned and filled her with resolution where perhaps only fear ought to be.

"Tell me," he insisted. "Who plotted with you to destroy the happiness of Los Bendigados?"

"Los Bendigados! Don't make me laugh. Nothing associated with you or this place could ever be blessed."

"Tell me who else, animal that pisses on the floor."

"Go to hell," she told him. "You sick, weak, cowardly piece of trash."

Despite his coolly cultivated Latin equanimity, these words suffused his face with dark rage. The austerely hand-some features crumpled into a mask of vindictive need.

"By what right do you judge your betters? Do the 'men' in your country tolerate such emasculating talk from their women? I am a proud and sensitive Castilian who feels the beauty and pain of this world more acutely than most men, who has needs more refined and rare than those of the 'men' common to your experience. This was God's will, not mine, and I am sure God does not make mistakes. However, the fact that I must point out my own superiority to you proves only that you have a common mind despite your uncommon beauty. I say again, you are indeed proud—far too proud for your station and experience. But I have seen you piss, woman! It is always the proud ones who break the hardest."

Among the useful information Socorro imparted to Jemez was the fact that Doña Elena was, by all accounts, a very religious woman. Almost every morning she joined other devout Catholics from throughout the valley for a sunrise prayer service at the chapel in the nearby pueblo of Rio Lindo. A narrow but picturesque lane led from La Esperanza to Rio Lindo, a pleasant three-mile drive through tamarind groves, orchards, multicolored profusions of wildflowers, and the lush pastures of the hacienda.

On the morning after Jemez spoke with his sister, the three interlopers from Arizona scouted out a large deadfall about two miles from the *casa grande*. They led their mounts behind the thick wall of dead undergrowth and muzzled them with belts and hobbles. Then they waited while a new day's sun began to burn off the surrounding dew.

"I wouldn't mind some hot grub," Plummer told Seth. "Riding with you newspaper heroes plays hell on a man's stomach. Got anything to gnaw on besides plug?"

"Got a cold biscuit in my saddlebag."

"Trot it out, *'mano*." A moment later he added, "Christ, it's hard as a rock."

Plummer gnawed on the biscuit, still complaining, while Jemez kept an eye down the trail and Seth thought about Kathleen Barton. According to Socorro, Tanta Kathleen had been locked up for hatching an escape plot. The woman had sand, he had to admit that—good looks *and* a full ration of courage. But from the little he'd heard about Padilla, she might already be paying a steep price for her brazen plan.

And again he couldn't help wondering if his own carelessness in visiting her and Hays had landed her here.

"Somebody coming," Jemez said.

The steady jangle of tug chains grew louder, then a black-lacquered landau rose from behind a nearby hill, hood up, two handsome white stallions in the traces. A quick glimpse of a lace mantilla, a low shako hat. The three men ducked, staying well back from the lane until the conveyance had passed. Then, riding in single file, they debouched from their cover and took up the trail behind the landau. Socorro had warned Jemez about the trick shooting of Jesus Gallegos, so the pursuers stayed on his blind side and stuck to the trees as much as possible.

However, they'd no sooner begun following it when the landau abruptly jutted left, jostling over uneven ground to a well-sheltered copse about thirty feet away from the lane.

"What the hell?" Plummer said. "They spot us?"

Seth shook his head. "I don't think so."

A grin slowly touched his lips. Plummer saw it, then grinned himself. "Well now, looks like Jesus has risen. Let's go peek at some titties, gen'l'men."

They waited a few minutes before moving again. Seth's hunch proved right: Even before they drew close to the landau, they saw it start to rock madly on its braces. They hobbled their mounts, drew their weapons, moved closer.

Seth heard the feminine keening: "*Ay, Dios! Ay, Dios mío! Eso es, sí! Otra vez! Ay, Dios mío . . . !*"

Plummer shoved a fist into his mouth to keep from laughing out loud. Jemez looked at him and had to fight down his own mirth. Seth, grinning himself in spite of his nervousness, moved up closer to the rocking vehicle. Now he could hear their fervid panting, the athletic sounds of sex.

At a nod from Seth, all three men stepped into view and pressed cold steel into Gallegos.

Doña Elena screamed. Gallegos froze in mid-stroke, his ass bare to the sky, as a gun muzzle filled each ear and another coldly kissed the nape of his neck. Doña Elena's legs rose out on either side of him like slender white drumsticks. The *segundo*'s skintight trousers were now tangled below his knees, his coin-studded *cinturón* dangling down among the reins.

"*Qué . . . qué quieren?*" In view of his present circumstances, the show of manly indignation was ludicrous.

Plummer ignored him and spoke to his companions in English. "I think I'll fuck her, too. I like a woman who talks to God while she's being trimmed."

"Translate, Charlie," Seth said. "Tell him to get off her. She goes with us."

Plummer did as told. Jemez had already moved closer and pulled the *segundo*'s .38 from its holster. When Gallegos was slow to move, Seth grabbed the reins and lashed him across the buttocks. "*De prisa!*"

Gallegos scrambled, pulling his tight trousers up as rapidly as he could. Doña Elena's face drained white with fear after the first flush of shame. Then she gathered herself together.

"Tell him to take our terms to Padilla. Within the next hour, he puts Kathleen Barton and the Apache kids named Socorro, Miguelito, Kato, and Rosario into a buckboard. He drives it himself, no one else comes with him. He drives it to the place just before here where the road crosses through that big open pasture with the stone walls. He waits for us there. We take the prisoners, he gets his wife."

Charlie translated this while Gallegos, having donned his courage with his clothing, scowled darkly.

"Tell him," Seth added, "no tricks or we kill her. Padilla brings the prisoners alone. From that pasture we can see anybody else as soon as they leave the yard. We'll also be watching close. They post any outriders, we kill the woman and run."

Gallegos looked straight at Seth when he answered through Plummer.

"*Perfumado* here says he'll kill you himself if you touch the woman."

"He will, huh? Damn, I respect a gallant man."

Seth pulled Padilla's wife down from the seat. "Tell him one more time, Charlie. Within the next hour. All five prisoners, or Padilla's wife—*his* whore—sleeps with the worms."

• • •

They moved closer and waited, keeping a close eye on the *casa grande* to make sure no messengers were dispatched for help nor riders sent out. They watched the mining crew scatter out on the mountainside for their morning break. Mexican hands worked green horses in a corral near the house, *indio* girls worked the cotton and cornfields as usual. The allotted hour came and went, and then Seth started to suspect a trap was being set.

"He doesn't come soon," he decided, "we assume we're being four-flushed and we clear out."

They had gathered behind the stone wall at the far edge of a vast pasture. Plummer pointed at Doña Elena. She sat on a flat-topped boulder, her face locked in a sulking pout.

"What about her?"

"We'll take her with us."

"*Hell* yes." Plummer grinned. "Nobody misses a hunk off a cut pie."

Jemez nodded toward the trail. "Here comes the buckboard."

"Aww, hell," Plummer groused.

Seth squatted and removed the hobbles from his horse. "You both know what to do. Draw your weapons and keep your eyes peeled. Charlie, tell her to ride up with Jemez. In front."

Doña Elena's face crumpled in distaste at the prospect of riding with an *indio*. But the gun muzzle prodding her stomach was highly persuasive. The three men rode out slowly to meet the buckboard, Jemez slightly forward, the woman in front of him as a shield.

The wagon jounced steadily forward, a team of lazy mules switching their tails at the flies. Seth saw Kathleen on the plank seat to Padilla's right, the four Apache children behind her.

"Careful now," he told his companions quietly. "Could be a man or two lying down in the bed. Tell him to stop."

Plummer shouted, and the *hacendado* spoke to the team and threw the brake forward awkwardly, clearly unused to such manual tasks. Seth took in a pale, slope-shouldered man in a richly embroidered military tunic.

"Those are the children?" Seth asked Jemez.

The Apache nodded.

"All right. Tell him—"

With a quick, springing thud, a hatless Jesus Gallegos rolled out from a body harness that had been hastily rigged beneath the wagon. He tucked and rolled, came up fanning the hammer of his Volcanic. Seth watched Charlie Plummer's jaw drop open in betrayed astonishment as a bullet pierced his heart and took the last breath from his nostrils even before his feet left the stirrups.

Seth fired, fired again, but each time the lithe Gallegos crow-hopped just ahead of the bullet. Gallegos got a bead on Jemez just as the Apache managed to turn his horse hard, and the next shot caught Doña Elena in the ribs. She screamed, and Jesus hesitated, shocked for a moment too long by his mistake. Seth levered his carbine one more time and blew the *segundo*'s jaw off. His next shot caught him flush in the chest, and he was dead.

It all happened in only a few seconds. At the first shots, Padilla had frozen. But by the time Seth planted his second slug in Gallegos, Padilla had gained a purchase on his wits. He pulled a magazine pistol from under the seat and pointed it at Seth, but before he could squeeze the trigger, Socorro loosed a banshee wail and flung herself on him. He screamed as her claws raked into his eyes, the mules surged forward, and Kathleen reached around Socorro and pried the gun from Padilla. He had just gotten Socorro's neck in a good grip when Kathleen held the muzzle to his perfumed hair and—her eyes shut tight—fired. There was an explosion of blood through his perfect hair, and his body pitched down in front of the wheels. A moment later the buckboard lurched hard when it rolled over him.

"Here they come!" Socorro shouted, pointing back toward the hacienda. At least a dozen riders had emerged from readiness behind outbuildings. Jemez slowed them with several carefully placed shots from his Sharps while Seth and Kathleen hustled the children onto the remounts.

Seth didn't look at Charlie Plummer. The body had to lay where it fell, or they were all dead. In a sudden flash of hot rage, he turned and joined Jemez in the slaughter of the approaching horses. In less than a minute they had dropped half the mounts and sent the others retreating.

"All right!" he shouted to Jemez. "That bought us all the time we're likely to get. Let's vamoose!"

Chapter 39

"I don't like him," Robert Trilby said. "He's a sanctimonious sonofabitch just like Carlson."

"He's a rulebook commander," Longstreet agreed. "All the young West Point types are. But Corey Bryce will do to stir things up."

Trilby had to agree on that score. The deep hurt, the brooding rage he had seen in those eyes, bode ill for someone.

"Besides, it's not a question of liking him," Nat Bischoff told Trilby. "The man can't be trusted. You're right, in his own way he's as hair-trigger as Carlson. They've *both* been unstrung by that Santa Fe incident. I say it's best to avoid both of them. Especially Carlson. The word from Fort Grant is he'll be relieved of his command, anyway, once the sweep begins. That's only three weeks away."

That wasn't good enough, Trilby told himself again. Carlson had cold-cocked him, publicly humiliated him. Trilby suffered humiliation from no man—not over the long haul. A man might insult him and walk away. But Trilby didn't sleep nights until such past-due accounts were set straight.

"Avoid him? Best way to avoid a man is to kill him," he said. "I plan to avoid Seth Carlson, all right."

"Right there's the problem with you," Bischoff said. "You get all sidetracked with personal revenge. Your priorities are wrong. Just look at us. Forced to meet here in secret now like common pig thieves. We've got bigger troubles than a grudge against Carlson."

Trilby felt heat rise into his face. "I don't like your tone," he told Bischoff. "Ever since Carlson blind-sided me, you been barking like a full-grown dog."

"Blind-sided? He was looking you right in the eye," Bischoff parried, doing the same himself.

"Gentlemen," Longstreet said impatiently, "the way things have been going lately, we can't afford to be at each other's throats."

Events had forced the three men to avoid the usual meeting places, and, as a last resort, meet in Trilby's quarters on Copper Street. He rented a dingy little two-room walk-up over a harness shop. Trilby had taken secret delight in the other two men's shock when they first laid eyes on his filthy, unfurnished hovel. A shuck mattress on the floor, covered with a mildewed buffalo hide, a strap-and-iron trunk, several nail kegs for chairs—these comprised the furnishings. A fetid stink wafted from the pottery slop jar beside the mattress. The shriveled husks of dead roaches crunched under their soles on the uncarpeted plank floor. Clearly, both Bischoff and Longstreet thought, no matter how neatly he dressed himself for business purposes, this was a man whom domestication had never even breathed upon, much less touched.

"You've got different 'priorities' than me, Nat," Trilby said, his anger passing. "Sorry if the accommodations are a bit crude for you family gents. But I don't have a wife to give my life the soft, feminine touch."

"A bunkhouse is cleaner than this," Longstreet threw in. "Smells better, too. But the accommodations be hanged." He looked awkward and foolish teetering on the edge of a keg, trousers bunched up at the knees to protect his creases.

"I knew Hays Munro had family with money. But the pressure from the investigation of his death is more than I ever banked on. That U.S. Marshal who questioned you, Bob—he'll be back. And next time he'll want to talk to me."

"The Bureau of Indian Affairs is harassing my editor, too," Bischoff chimed in. "I've received my last remittance payment, they're calling me back. With Kathleen Barton back and raising hell, this thing could turn ugly on us. One thing newspaper publishers hate is a scandal from inside the Sacred Bastion of Truth. We have some loose ends to tie up before I leave."

"Yeah," Trilby agreed. "And since I'm the one does the knot-tying, one of them is going to be Seth Carlson. Sounds to me like you two are harping on my ass for wanting to kill him out of revenge. What do you care why it's done, so long as he gets sent under?"

"Well, then," Longstreet said, "I can side with you that far. The man's unpredictability makes him a serious risk. All of your men out there, scattered all over to hell and back, and nobody even saw him go into Mexico. Yet here's Padilla and his wife killed and Kathleen Barton back. She's named Aragon as one of her abductors and the murderer of Hays Munro. She swears the other one looked like you. Carlson must know the whole story."

"So? *He* can't go to the law. He'll have trouble enough explaining why one of his men turned up dead in Chihuahua. She named Aragon as the actual killer, and hell, he's dead now. It was dark, she was scared and my face was covered. Without another witness, she's shit out of luck. Believe me, the starman ain't all that worried about it."

"Maybe," Longstreet conceded. "Lawmen are poor, they can be bought. Still, I'd rest easier if I knew what the hell Carlson is up to. Grayeyes, too. I don't like it when those two drop out of sight for so long."

"Carlson hasn't dropped out of sight," Trilby said. "He's just not fighting 'Paches anymore. According to Dennis Moats, Carlson's men haven't requisitioned ammo in weeks. He's been going around making contact with the bands. But no fighting. He warns them to report to the rezes by the first.

Not that it's doing much good so far, only one or two bands have come in."

"What about Grayeyes?" Bischoff said.

Trilby shrugged one beefy shoulder. His neck had finally mended enough to dispense with the leather brace.

"I wonder about that, too. Nobody's seen him. Prob'ly went back to his cave in the south country. He's safe there, for now. But we finally know where it is. I know, the Army knows. He ain't Geronimo, there's no big magic protecting *his* ass. If he survives the fighting coming up, that's where he'll go. Either way, he's nearing the end of his tether. So is Carlson."

"Carlson? You've said that before," Bischoff reminded him. "But like the Apache, he has proven to be very resilient."

"That he has, that he has."

"I don't like that grin, Bob. I'm telling you and Charlie both, you resort to killing too often and too quickly. It's best now to let it go. There's better ways to cover ourselves. Especially with the woman having taken up the letter-writing campaign where Hays Munro left off."

Longstreet said, "You don't think the marshal poking around has anything to do with her letters, do you?"

"I don't. But you saw that story in the *Rocky Mountain News* about the two contractors in Denver who were successfully prosecuted by government lawyers for fraud against the Lakota Sioux. That sets a dangerous legal precedent. Why run extra risk when Carlson is due to be posted out of here soon, anyway? One more suspicious death won't help us, not with a marshal already nosing around. Just let the fever run its course."

Trilby shook his head. "Slice it anyway you want. The Army will be shipping him out, all right. But if things work out the way I want, he won't be noticing the scenery."

"Do you have any choice about it?" Kathleen said.

Seth held both arms out while she piled them high with stove lengths of newly cut pinyon wood. Behind them, beyond the barren gravel yard of the schoolhouse, stretched the flat and wind-scoured expanse of the Mater Dolorosa Reservation. Here and there a cluster of mesquite-branch huts marked a clan circle. The westering sun backlit the sierras and turned them into dark cinders piled up haphazardly on the horizon.

"I could protest the orders. Or refuse them and resign my commission. Which I've been thinking about doing anyway."

"I thought instructor's duty at West Point was an honor?"

"I s'pose it is."

"I should think so, assuming the man who teaches there is honorable. In this case it's definitely an honor."

Seth shifted the load slightly so he could peek around it and look at her. "I'll take that as a compliment. Especially coming from a woman who told me not to assume I had any importance in her life."

Kathleen flushed and threw the next stove length into his arms a little harder than necessary. Seth had to move adroitly to save the entire stack.

"*That* was several visits ago, Colonel. And anyway," she added, deliberately changing the subject, "I'll skin that Victorio alive when I see him. He knows he's responsible for keeping the schoolrooms supplied with wood."

"Where'd he go?"

"Where else?"

"Jemez?"

"Jemez."

"Why?"

"Who knows? Victorio tells me what he wants to. Careful —a little more to the left."

Seth managed to cross the threshold without losing the stack. The schoolhouse was a low adobe-and-log building divided into two classrooms connected by a dogtrot. The new puncheon floor had been polished by inviting the Apaches to dance on top of corn siftings. It was early October now, cooler toward evening, and Kathleen had taken to wearing an extra crinoline for warmth.

"This new agent," Seth said. He knelt, dropped the wood next to the clay-baked hearth. "This Roger Maitland. What's he like?"

"Frankly? As an agent, he's well-mannered, moderately

well-intended, and completely inoffensive. Also, I'm afraid, completely ineffectual. I think that's why he was sent. The BIA is constantly warring with the War Department. I think Roger represents a compromise. No lackey for the Indian Ring, but no Indian-loving Quaker, either. Unfortunately, this place needs more than a compromise. But I'm an optimist. He's only interim agent, his replacement might be better."

"How's he feel about your letters to the newspapers and magazines, naming names and leveling charges?"

"He disapproves, but he's already told me he won't stop me from writing them unless the bureau makes him do it. Seth?"

"Hmm?"

"These new orders of yours. Why do they go into effect the very day this new Indian campaign starts?"

"That's easy enough. The Army isn't known for being subtle. It's their way of telling me they're not happy with the way I've handled the Apache problem."

"That's not fair."

"Sure it is, from where they sit. After all, I've not only protested this new sweep strategy in writing. I predicted it will end in disaster for the Army."

Seth didn't mention another problem that nettled him. Since the return from Mexico, he had kept a ten-man detail bivouacked at Mater Dolorosa to protect Kathleen and the others. With Carlson's Raiders officially disbanded as of November first, Kathleen would be vulnerable. Vulnerable to Robert Trilby, among others who saw her as a serious threat.

"Have many bands been listening to your warning about the deadline?"

"Listening, sure. Thanks to Jemez putting out the word, they treat me good. I'm Nantan Maño, saver of the children. I even get invited to sit at their councils. But you can tell they're just listening to be polite."

Kathleen said, "What about Jemez? Will he help?"

"He won't have any part of it, and I can't blame him. It would ruin him in his people's eyes, turn him into a white-eyes messenger boy. Besides, he hates the reservations and everything they stand for."

"Yes," Kathleen said, musing. "I don't suppose it helped when Miguelito actually broke out *crying* about coming back here. At least he was eating well in Mexico."

"The girl sure didn't cry. At least, not until Jemez left again."

Kathleen felt a cool, numbing prickle move up her spine as she recalled that lice-infested *cárcel*, the sick urgency in Padilla's tone as he tried to convince her his sickness was a rare and beautiful thing, a gift of God. "No, Socorro didn't cry because she is old enough to know what she faced down there."

Seth watched the storm clouds move into Kathleen's eyes, but he said nothing. The same thing happened every time she heard Trilby's name. This was his third visit, in the weeks since they had returned from Mexico, but seldom had she alluded to that nightmare escape out of Chihuahua. At first luck had been with them. Matazal's renegade band did indeed waylay them on the way out of the valley. But true to his word, Matazal accepted Longstreet's gold in tribute and let them flee—even assisting these two crazy-brave friends by ambushing the posse from La Esperanza.

Thanks, however, to the upheavals in the Provincias Internas, they were hounded all the way to the Rio Bravo. The grueling pace across waterless expanses killed two already weak ponies. They themselves would have died of thirst had Jemez not shot an elk that had recently been to water. They slit the stomach and lived on the contents until they reached a water hole. But the shortage of ponies forced them to take turns riding and left the Apache children barely able to hobble on scald feet, brought on by too much walking in sweat-soaked moccasins. Even now, Socorro still limped.

"Do you think about Charlie Plummer often?"

Her question took him by surprise. Again he felt the little gut wrench that hearing Charlie's name still caused.

"I do," he admitted. "All the deaths are hard, but it's even worse when you can't retrieve the body. It hit Walt and the rest of the men hard. It's little enough consolation, but I keep telling them *and* myself that at least he died quick."

"So did Hays, but as you say, it's precious little consolation."

That made her think of Trilby again. A mask of pure hate settled over her features, and now Seth knew it for sure. Like her, he had little doubt who the man behind the bandanna had been.

"He raped you," he blurted out, not taking time to think about it and not making it a question.

The words jarred her with the force of slaps. But she met his eyes, not looking away, confirming his guess.

"Well?" Kathleen finally demanded after trying to read some of the conflicting thoughts in his face and failing miserably.

"Well what?"

"Well, how do you feel about me? After what Trilby did?"

"Trilby is dirt, and dirt washes off."

Seth framed her face in both hands and pulled her gently into the kiss. Her lips parted for his, surprised but readily yielding, warm and soft and moist. He kissed her mouth, her cheeks, bussed the tissue-thin skin of her eyelids, tasted the clean tang of her hair. She shuddered under his touch, the need for this gentle, passionate warmth roiling her insides as it did his. Afterward they stood quietly for a full minute, neither one trusting their voices.

When she looked at him, her eyes glittered like bits of bright crystal despite the dying light outside. "Seth? Sometimes you just have to make up your mind that you're going to be happy."

"Can a man make up his mind but still not have what he wants?"

"Yes, but isn't he a fool to want what he can't have?"

"Maybe."

With Kathleen safely delivered in the U.S. again, Seth had begun to realize that rescuing her had, by some moral scale he sensed more than understood, partially redeemed him for the death of Jeanette Bryce. After killing her, a door inside him had closed tightly on all his hopes for love and the future, on any sense of self-respect as a man. Now Kathleen had opened that door again, at least jarred it a crack.

But if Kathleen had proven the door could still open, the thought of Corey Bryce could jamb it shut again. *That* was the great unspoken issue of Seth's existence. Not the dead, but the living haunted him. Yes, he could love Kathleen; but so long as the great wrong done to Corey Bryce hung over him, he would never believe in his right to have her. The thought of ever looking Corey in the eye again—that was indeed hanging over him. Seth felt their inevitable meeting looming. He was in touch with Fort Grant and knew about Corey's role in this new campaign, knew his old friend had in fact been here on a reconnaissance mission. He felt the wheel of fortune was about to complete another cycle and cross their destinies again.

Seth pulled Kathleen close, felt the warmth of her, felt her heart ticking out the vitality that even now quickened to its full intensity in his arms. He had felt that vitality before—and then he'd killed it, silenced the vital pulse forever.

"Seth, what's going to happen? With the Apaches—with us?"

He kissed her hair, traced her delicate cheekbones with exploring fingers. But the image of Corey's grief-ravaged face pressed like a cruel tax on his happiness.

"I don't know, lady," he told her honestly. He was sorry for the paltry words, angry at himself that he couldn't do better. "I just don't know."

Something felt wrong.

Long before Victorio rode in with his news, Jemez felt trouble and had stepped outside of his cave. He had gazed carefully down the steep talus slopes where once he watched Mexican soldiers sitting around naked while they boiled their clothing. He glanced all around at the surrounding shelves of traprock. Seeing nothing out of the ordinary, he had crossed to the slight depression near the recessed entrance. The huge boulder, fatter than a well-fed pony, was still prevented from hurtling downward only by the smaller rocks he had left wedged in place at its base. Nothing had been touched.

Still . . . someone had been here.

"I saw three hair-face camps," Victorio said. "Plenty of soldiers with the big-thundering guns. Other patrols have been spotted riding up into the mountains."

Jemez nodded. The two Apaches now sat just inside the

entrance to his cave. "The Sly One told me some things, too. This is their latest battle plan."

"What do we do, Jemez? The soldiers are coming in swarms."

The older Apache smiled as he ground a piece of dry bark into kindling with his fingers and dropped the fragments into the cold ashes of the fire pit.

"Settle down, little brother. It is a stupid plan. But stupid or not, it is going to work. At least, at first."

Most of the last Apache strongholds were located south and west of the Mogollon Rim, a long escarpment extending diagonally from the central Arizona Territory to the southwest New Mexico Territory. Clearly, the small bluecoat strike teams were being positioned to sweep through the smaller ranges southwest of the rim: the Pinaleno, Chiricahua, Huachuca, Santa Rita, Santa Catalina, and Mohawk Mountains. They meant to flush the Apaches, who would then be slaughtered by Mexican soldiers to the south or, if they fled west, American soldiers waiting in the Sonoran Desert.

The plan was so stupid that Jemez liked it. Especially the part about waiting in the Sonoran Desert. The white-skins knew precious little about that country. Jemez, in contrast, had roamed it all his life and knew its features and distinctions well. The desert itself could be used against the soldiers with more effect than bullets. Especially one uncharted stretch known as Devil's Floor, a dangerously unstable, treacherous expanse formed by a wide and porous rock shelf and covered by a thick carpet of drift sand. With solid ground anywhere between one and three feet beneath the shelf, the "false floor" would support small animals. But anything much heavier than a coyote—tricked by the seemingly normal expanse of sand—would eventually crash through the weak rock layer. A similar geological freak in southern Utah had mired an entire emigrant train.

"Spread the word, Victorio. Play along with the white pony soldiers. Let them drive us like cattle and make us converge on the desert as the long knives hope we will."

Victorio's eyes bulged like huge, wet marbles. "But Jemez! We cannot fight them down there."

"No? You will see it, buck. The red warriors of Apacheria will turn these crowing roosters into cowering capons."

But Victorio had told him about more than just the soldiers. After the boy rode out, Jemez thought about Robert Trilby and this new treachery. Now, once again, Jemez would soon have to ride north to Riverbend.

Again he felt it, a chill itching at his skin like dead bunch-grass. In the glow of the fire, Jemez stared toward the middle of the cave and the bladder bag filled with water which hung there from a braided-horsehair rope. It might have been a subterranean air current or a trick of the dancing flames, but the bag seemed to sway back and forth a few times. Watching it, Jemez felt his limbs go weak with a cold, numbing fear.

Chapter 40

"It's no use, Cap'n. She's bogged down to the hubs."

"Christ! Even with four horses pulling the carriage?"

" 'Fraid so, sir. The sumbitches're heavy and the wheels're too skinny for all this deep sand."

Corey cursed again. He glanced up at the long double column. It would take too damn long to harness more horses to the team.

"Last two sets of four to the rear!" he bellowed. "Get this gun carriage moving again, let's go, four swinging peeders on each wheel. Get the lead out, troopers, or we're going to miss this war!"

A private lashed the straining team while the troopers, dripping sweat in a late October heat wave, heaved at the clumsy Gatling carriage. Corey tried not to let the annoyance show in his face, but the effort was getting harder as this expedition ground on. His company had deployed from Fort Bates, Department of New Mexico, sixteen days earlier.

Their final objective was to rendezvous at the reinforced staging area in the Sonoran Desert southeast of Tucson. They set out following Cooke's Wagon Route south, paralleling the Rio Grande until the route swerved west at Deming. By now they should have reached Fort Huachuca—instead they were still well east of Bisbee.

Everything that could go wrong had. Unrelenting sandstorms cut visibility to practically zero and forced them to shelter at midday. The Gatling carriages constantly bogged down and had to be greased several times a day. And the troopers themselves—most of them were green and undisciplined, and thus morale was low. The NCOs had drilled them the best they could, some even respecting Corey's order that brutality and severe hazing were forbidden. But almost half of the new troopers received little or no recruit training and showed up for duty not even knowing whom to salute.

Still, Corey kept consoling himself, his NCOs were battle vets, and NCOs were the backbone of the fighting Army. His troops were well fed, adequately supplied, and sheer numbers alone should prove daunting to the heavily outnumbered Apaches. But fleeing south would not save the savages this time. The Mexican army, in a rare show of cooperation inspired by their hatred for Apaches, was deployed in numerous roving patrols, linked by a series of American observation posts between Tubac and Yuma. It was predicted, however, that the Apaches would opt for the Sonoran escape route to the west—running smack into the American "pointed anvil" of which Corey's company was to be the apex. General Ablehard, unencumbered by heavy equipment, had gone ahead of Corey leading the main body of troops.

Now, as Corey watched his men struggle with the cumbersome gun, his mind worked its way back to that meeting in Tucson with Longstreet, Trilby, and Bischoff. Again he recalled their contempt for Seth Carlson. Corey disliked all three men, and every instinct as a soldier told him Seth was a better man than all three of them put together. But instincts couldn't influence the raw, cankering, conscious hurt—a hurt that had been caused by Seth Carlson.

Corey looked thin and worn, a man depleted of energy and

pressing on only because of his urgent purpose. The drinking, the careless eating habits, the long nights back in Washington spent studying up on the Apaches and military tactics —all of this had left a gaunt, haunted cast to his eyes, which had aged lately and always appeared to focus farther away than they needed to, as if Corey were on a perpetual search for something beyond human ken. It had been especially noticeable during the first few days of the expedition—when the present route traced the exact steps Corey's troop had followed a little over a year ago, just before Jeanette was killed.

The gun carriage finally shuddered free. Corey rode to the head of the columns and gave the signal to advance. All around the men the desert groped toward infinity, broken only by scattered buttes and mesas on the far horizon. Greasy creosote, dull chaparral, mile after mile of purple sage —all of it dwarfed a man, dwarfed humanity. Corey shook his head against the immensity of it all and forced his mind back to the urgent reminder at the center of his universe: *one week*.

One week, and the largest Indian-fighting force ever mounted by the U.S. Army would be unleashed. And if those damned guns bogged down too many more times, he wouldn't have his men in place for the battle he helped design.

One week, a little luck, and then all this hurt and rage fermenting inside him, a liquor distilled from pure hate, would explode in the release of raw action.

One week, and if he could not kill Seth Carlson, he could kill the next best thing—Indians.

"The hell you whining about?" Seth asked Sergeant Major Jay Kinney. "You're the one's always screaming about how there's no glory in peace. Now we're short-timers and you want to sit around the fire swapping war stories."

Kinney pulled his feet from the stirrups and lifted them to keep his trousers dry as the detail crossed a shallow ford of the Santa Cruz River. Seth, Kinney, Walt Mackenzie, and five other men had crossed well upriver from Tucson and Riverbend. There was about an hour of daylight left.

"Swap war stories my fat arse, Colonel. I just ain't too keen on puttin' my bacon in the fire for goddamn Innuns. So what if they're turned into hoors? I never met a squaw yet wouldn't point her heels to the sky for a pretty mirror or a daub of toilet water. Hell, I caught the drip from a sixteen-year-old Mandan gal."

"Atop of that," Walt said, "it could all be a trap. Maybe all you heard was scuttlebutt."

"Maybe. But there *were* Southern Arapaho girls taken during a raid up in Oklahoma two weeks ago," Seth reminded them. "Indian scouts from Fort Grant confirmed that."

"Yessir. But that's always going on. Even if there is a deal tonight and we stop it, won't be but a drop of piss in a cesspool."

"Not if Trilby dies. Trilby dies, the cesspool level goes way down around here."

"*That* shines," Kinney agreed. "Man could enjoy setting Trilby free from his soul."

"True enough," Walt said, understanding things a little better now. Everybody in the unit knew damn well that it wasn't just official duty that attracted their C.O. to Mater Dolorosa these days. "Might mean less trouble for them out on the rez, too."

Seth met his eyes. "It just might, at that."

Walt grinned, bad teeth flashing through his sparse beard. "Well, god*damn*it, then! What're we frettin' and steamin' about? Let's go kill him."

"Augh! Steal their horses and fuck their women!" Kinney growled.

"*You* better learn which is which, Top!" somebody behind them yelled.

"My hand to God, constable," Kinney retorted, "I was only helping that sheep over the fence."

The fording completed, Carlson's Raiders pointed their bridles south toward Tucson. It was Mackenzie who next broke the silence.

"Sir? You heard how Captain Moats was sent into the mountains with his unit?"

Seth nodded. "He's part of the sweep."

"Pardon me all to hell for saying this about an officer in

front of you, Colonel, but Moats is a stupid gazaboo. He's bragging it all over, about how this time the Army will get shut of the Apaches, that *he* won't be letting them go like you did."

"If brains were horseshit, Moats would have a clean corral."

"Sir?"

"Yeah?"

"In a week this unit is officially disbanded. What happens then?"

"You men are no longer under my command, that's what happens. According to the orders, you return to your former units 'at the first opportunity and in the most expedient manner, relying on government transport when feasible.' I get that right, Top?"

"Right as rain, sir."

Walt looked at Kinney, then at his C.O. again. "What are *you* going to do, sir?"

"I might graze around here for a while, see how this brilliant Apache campaign works out."

"That's about what we figured," Kinney put in. "So we all talked it over. The men have decided they'll cut their pickets when you do."

"You can't. You'll risk being listed as U.A."

"Oh, *no* sir!" Kinney looked shocked. "Not if it's loyal troopers such as ourselves, all swearing to the last man we was delayed by an unexpected Indian attack? God spare America's finest from such a gross injustice."

Seth shook his head, grinning. "Why do I bother giving any orders around here?"

Kinney winked. "You're young, you don't know any better."

"All right. But let's worry about next week when it gets here. We might be cracking caps tonight."

The river twisted its way around a cottonwood thicket, and the first lights of Tucson winked into view. .

Twilight was rapidly giving way to nighttime shadows when Jemez hobbled his pony in the cottonwoods surrounding Riverbend.

It was a cloudy, moonless night, the worst kind, he thought, for this kind of business. To his right he could make out the dim outline of Trilby's bear-baiting pit. He was downwind of it and caught a whiff of the bat-board jakes near the pit.

Dead ahead, the familiar group of mud hovels that catered to the denizens of Riverbend. His eyes picked out the largest hut of all, the adobe structure with its rawhide door hanging askew. Several horses were hitched to the tie pole out front, including Trilby's dark cream. So far, though, he had seen no sign of Seth or his men.

Nor of Robert Trilby. But Jemez was convinced by now that Trilby wasn't inside that hovel. There had not been the usual signs of a Comanchero deal. This was a trap, and Nantan Maño was meant to get pinched in it. Jemez had suspected it as soon as Victorio rode south with the news.

But if Trilby wasn't inside, the problem remained of figuring out where he was.

Again Jemez cursed the shape-changing, shadowy darkness. But even his sharp eyes were useless this night, without help from even a few glittering stars.

He would have to give himself an advantage or nothing would get done. Hoping he had enough time, Jemez untied his flannel headband and pulled it over his eyes, retying it tight. He lay down, turned his face into the dead cottonwood leaves, covered his head with them. Now in total darkness, he trusted to his ears and settled in for the wait.

Seth, like Walt Mackenzie, was suspicious of a trap. The first thing he had the men do, after picketing their mounts and infiltrating the cottonwood thickets, was thoroughly search the branch corral out behind the hovel. But Trilby had no men in hiding anywhere near the building.

"All right," he said when the last man had reported back to their position in the trees out front of the clearing before the hovel. "The rest of you wait here. I'm moving up for a closer look. If I give the signal, move in."

"You hog all the fun, sir," Mackenzie said. "Let me go."

"Rank has its privileges. Wait here."

"Could be a trap."

"Like you said, I hog all the fun."

Seth moved out, ending the debate. He shunted from tree to tree, waiting for the soughing wind to cover his noises. Occasionally, a shadowy figure passed by, and he pressed closer into the trees. As he approached a hide-covered window on the near side of the building, he heard voices speaking in rapid Spanish, drunken curses and laughter. It sure as hell *sounded* like Comanchero business going on inside. He began to suspect that Trilby really was conducting a slave deal.

He waited for the next gust of wind, then covered the last open stretch to the hovel. He crouched beneath the window, making sure he hadn't been heard.

Nothing unusual about the commotion from inside. Slowly, he raised one hand to feel the hide flap. It wasn't nailed in place at the bottom. For a moment he paused as a cold tremor passed through his limbs. Some voice inside warned him. He paused to search the shadows all around him, but nothing suspicious turned up.

Carefully, very slowly, he raised one small corner of the hide so he could peek inside.

Jemez waited as long as he dared, preparing his eyes for maximum night vision. Then he lifted his head from the pile of leaves and untied the flannel wrapped around his eyes.

The difference was remarkable. It was as if he had peeled a couple of hours off the night. Where before he had only seen the general shape of trees, now he could make out even the smaller branches at the tips of limbs. He could differentiate bushes, detect movements he couldn't spot before. So of course he easily spotted the Sly One, about to peek into that hovel.

Desperate but methodical, his Sharps clutched tight, Jemez scanned the undergrowth, the alleys between structures. Still there was no sign of Trilby or any other hidden marksman.

Nonetheless, Jemez was convinced this was a trap. Trilby was out there. Once again his finger eased inside his trigger guard and he carefully searched the surrounding area, urging himself to hurry, damnit, *hurry*. . . .

·   ·   ·

A tiny, slanting ray of light leaked out the window as Carlson lifted the flap aside. Trilby silently thanked his prey for providing illumination for his own death.

He leaned one cheek along the stock of his carbine as he held it locked into the hollow of his shoulder. He laid the bead sight square between Carlson's shoulder blades.

Brass, he reminded himself. He'd get only one shot off, and it had to count.

Breathe.

Relax.

Aim.

Take up the *slack.*

Squeeeze the trigger . . .

Where is he? Jemez thought desperately. Trilby was out there, he had to be. If—

Now Jemez noted something with his night-conditioned vision: Two angry jays kept diving at a limb of that huge cottonwood located catty-cornered from the hovel—a tree that provided a clear shot at the hut's only window and door.

He looked closer, squinting, and made out a dark shape that didn't look quite like a limb. But he had no shot at it from here.

Suddenly convinced, clutching his Sharps at a high port, Jemez broke from cover and ran toward the cottonwood.

The moment was perfect, and Trilby had just begun to take up the slack when he stopped himself.

Trilby's contrary nature always made him most leery when things seemed to be going too well. Now, suddenly apprehensive, he lowered his carbine for a moment and turned to look behind him. Nothing. Cursing himself for a fool, he turned back around to sight on Carlson again, then felt ice water in his veins as he saw Jemez Grayeyes just below, aiming a rifle toward him.

At first, glancing through the small opening, Seth was further convinced that slave-trading was indeed going on here tonight. He spotted several men in Saltillo blankets and straw sombreros, young Indian women in buckskin dresses adorned with elk teeth.

But there was no sign of Trilby. Then he looked a little closer and noticed something else. Those Indian women, their faces were familiar. Familiar because . . . because he had seen them around town before, they were already working here as whores. And Trilby, he must be missing because . . .

In a heartbeat Seth understood. This was a trap.

A rifle shot split the silence, Seth leaped, and there was a surprised grunt followed by a crashing thud, a loud snap like a green limb breaking. Suddenly, pandemonium was unleashed. The inhabitants of the hovel fled into the night, and Seth's men converged on the window. And now, tearing the hide flap away from the window, he sent out enough light to spot Jemez, squatting beside somebody on the ground.

The shot didn't kill Trilby. Jemez barely got the round off, and the bullet had lodged near his left hip. But the fall onto a nearby stump had broken his spine. He lay grotesquely contorted on the stump, saliva bubbling in his throat as he fought for a breath of the wind that had been knocked out of him.

Seth put it all together in a moment. He met Jemez's eyes and recalled the Apache's confession about his fear of hanging. And he realized what this trip to Riverbend had meant in terms of risk to Jemez.

Trilby finally managed a breath. "Trunk," he gasped. "My room."

He coughed up a gob of pink lather, twitched hard, fought for another breath.

"Hope—Hope you all die of the runny shits," he added, and a second later he was dead himself.

They found the ledger when they broke open the strap-and-iron trunk in Trilby's quarters. It was all spelled out in meticulous detail: names of individual members of the Tucson Committee with dates and particulars of the numerous frauds they had committed, the names of soldiers and politicians who had conspired with them. Recent entries also covered Nat Bischoff's involvement in detail.

"Jesus Christ with a wooden dick," Kinney said, reading over Seth's shoulder. "Trilby planned to hang every one of 'em."

"This stuff cut any ice in court?" Walt said.

Seth shook his head. "It'd be a long shot, I'd wager. If it was just crimes against Indians, probably not. But plenty of these were schemes against the Army, too."

He glanced around the depressing and filthy hole, wondering how a man could live this way by choice and still call himself human. At any rate, long shot or no, Seth was still officially able—until November first—to initiate an investigation with this ledger. Win, lose, or draw in court, Trilby was dead, and thus the greatest immediate threat to Kathleen's safety was removed.

Oddly, though, he felt very little relief, perhaps because he sensed the moment was looming when he would have to confront an ordeal more harrowing than any danger he had survived so far: He would have to face Corey Bryce.

Chapter 41

The Apache bands were rich in horses this year, the result of successful raids into Mexico and against the vast herds of the Kiowa-Comanche reservation up north. At the beginning of the Moon When the Ponies Grow Coats, they thundered down out of the sierras of southern Arizona, dogged white-skin pony soldiers prodding them hard.

The U.S. Army sweep had been brilliantly coordinated. Caught up in the blood-singing exhilaration of the chase, the triumphant soldiers failed to pay due attention to two suspicious clues: Not only had the Apaches been much more accommodating than usual in giving up their mountain strongholds, but they—not their pursuers—were subtly controlling the direction of their supposedly headlong flight.

They fled the mountains, funneled closer together like headwaters forming a river, and escaped through the vast Green Valley, just as the white-eye battle plan had envisioned. But soon after crossing the Southern Pacific Railroad tracks south of Tucson, they bore gradually northwest again, veering a bit more than expected. However, the pursuing soldiers knew the main force waiting out on the desert flat could adjust its position accordingly. Signals flashed between mirror stations kept the waiting force posted.

Jemez Grayeyes joined a Coyotero band from the Gila, now forming the spearhead of the Apache flight. He carried the medicine shield for the battle, and he knew that the outcome of the upcoming confrontation depended upon how skillfully he controlled those pursuing soldiers—and the main force waiting in the Sonoran Desert. Without suspecting what was happening, they had to be channeled into that one narrow, unstable strip of desert for this plan to work. If the white-skins swerved too far north or south, they would escape harm and the Apaches would be forced to flee into open desert with no place to shelter or hide.

Not usually a very religious man, Jemez prayed to Great Ussen that the white-skins had no advance scouting reports on the little-known desert region he was drawing them toward. For everything depended on their charging across that one place he once pointed out to Victorio: a long slope between two red-rock headlands, known to local Pimas as the Devil's Floor.

But Jemez knew that if the white-skins passed by that shelf, the Apaches would be chased down and slaughtered. And even if the deception worked, it would not incapacitate the entire white-skin force. If it came down to it, Jemez was ready to die with the rest.

On the second day after the War Department disbanded the First Mountain Company, Carlson's Raiders rode out from their bivouac near the Gila River, now officially renegades themselves. With Goes Ahead constantly scouting their left flank to report the whereabouts of the fleeing Apaches, they headed toward the projected contact point.

Sergeant Major Kinney nudged his paint up beside Seth at the head of the columns. "You never said if we're in this fight," he said bluntly.

"I didn't, did I?"

"You going to?"

"Technically, you're all on your own. I can't give you any orders pertaining to combat. The rules of engagement allow any soldier the right to defend himself if attacked."

Kinney hawked up a pellet of phlegm and spat it into the sand. "Ahh, to hell with that. We in the fight, sir?"

Seth grinned in spite of the nervous anticipation causing a loss-of-gravity tickle in his stomach.

"If it's up to me, the First is going to fade back this time and watch the show. I'll ask no soldier to fight in a battle he's not duty-bound to join, nor to refuse aid to a fellow soldier. So pass the word: if the spirit moves any man, he's free to put at the enemy."

Kinney gave him a puzzle-headed look. "That's for the men. How about you?"

"The Army has made it clear they don't like my handling of the Apache situation."

"That's as obvious as a third tit. So why the hell are you marking time around this shithole, Colonel? Ain't you seen enough huggin' matches with redskins?"

Again Seth felt that apprehensive tickle in his gut. Even now, Corey Bryce should be waiting down there on that Sonoran flatland. Seth had no plan, was guided wordlessly south like a migrating bird prodded by instinct.

"Top, what does America do when there's Injun trouble?"

Kinney shot his commander a look full of suspicion. "I'm damned if I'm the boy for riddles, sir."

"Riddle your numb skull, Paddy. Don't you read the God-almighty newspapers? When America fears Injuns, they *send Seth*."

Kinney stole a good look at the deep, scheming furrow between Seth's eyes, the dangerous recklessness in his look. Here was trouble on the hoof. Kinney's face split in a wide smile of anticipation.

"Augh! And by the bleedin' Jesus, looks like they're gonna *get* their Seth. Blood, guts, deception, and death! It's a soldier's life for *this* child."

Several times during the past forty-eight hours, General Ferris Ablehard's "pointed anvil" force had relocated northward, adjusting their position to match the flight of the onrushing enemy. Finally, toward late morning on the fourth of November, a huge yellow dust cloud boiled up on the eastern horizon, and the waiting soldiers knew the fight was finally coming to them.

Corey's company formed the crux of a long, curving skirmish line. As the pursuing soldiers closed with their waiting comrades, the lines would converge like pincers snapping shut. If it was timed right, pursuit into the desert wouldn't even prove necessary. The Apaches would be annihilated in a frenetic cross fire of lead.

Ablehard's command post was set up behind reinforced breastworks directly to the rear of Corey's position. When the general's regimental bugler sounded the charge, Corey's men were to lead the assault.

Corey glanced both ways down the curving line. Officers had unsheathed their sabers, preparing to rally their men. Horses, sensing the tension, had to be restrained from bolting forward. As far as the eye could see, mounted soldiers performed final rifle and equipment inspections. Some prayed silently, others scrawled last minute letters to loved ones, pressing the paper against their pommels while they wrote. By regimental custom, the letters were always tucked into their mess pans, to be sent later by comrades in the event of the writer's death.

Corey had patrolled hostile country in New Mexico, and his men had chased off the renegade force that attacked the Sunday Stroll. But this was to be his first all-out battle, and the nervousness left a sharp tension in the pit of his stomach. But even more intense was the need to unleash this pent-up pain and rage and frustration, to litter the desert floor with Indian corpses. Surviving this fight hardly mattered—he only wanted to get his fair share of kills before a merciful bullet blew his light out forever.

The yellow dust cloud boiled closer, now the ground began to thrum and pulsate from the pounding hooves. Corey drew his saber and made the final on-line inspection of his men, his black charger fighting him harder and harder as the enemy rode closer.

A private from Ablehard's command post rode forward and saluted, handing Corey a folded slip of paper.

Good luck, pony soldier, Ablehard had written. *Next time I see you, we'll toast your first scalp.*

Unlike white-skin soldiers, Indian warriors held no battle formations. Nor did they depend on unit discipline in battle as hair-face soldiers did; rather, they counted on individual acts of reckless courage to sway a battle and inspire their comrades. Thus the medicine shield was always given to a warrior known not for his standing in council, but for acting boldly in the face of danger.

Jemez thrust the red-and-black-painted rawhide shield aloft, inciting the warriors behind him to yipping war cries as they galloped closer to the waiting enemy force. Now and then a carbine spoke its piece as the pursuing soldiers snapped off a round in their direction.

Jemez felt light-headed, having fasted before this battle to induce the trance state that made Indian courage second nature in combat. He could see the soldiers massed below, felt the pursuing force shifting slightly as they set up for the final pincers movement. It had all come down to this moment. The force below was poised on the very brink of the Devil's Floor. Now Jemez had to make the first, perfectly timed movement that would trap both white-skin forces on the unsteady expanse, while leading the Apaches safely along the northern edge. With luck, that should trim the remaining soldiers down to a number the Apaches could face in a hard fight.

He abruptly tugged the reins hard right, heading at a sharply oblique angle across the face of the second headland, the bluff marking the northern border of the sand-carpeted shelf. The waiting force was marshalled on the ridge of the southern border—they would have to plunge straight across the unstable expanse.

Or so he thought. Only a minute after sharply altering the Apache course, Jemez felt his heart sink: A bluecoat officer was instead leading the force *west*, evidently planning to intercept them beyond the bluff—thus avoiding the Devil's Floor completely. Did that mean they knew about it?

If so, the end was at hand for the Apaches. And suddenly,

Jemez no longer felt like a battle chief. He was merely the lead bull taking his trusting herd over a cliff.

"The hell them crazy red niggers up to?" Kinney said. "They can't get away by crossing that bluff—sumbitch ends in cliffs."

Seth nodded, wondering himself. He had spotted Jemez in the lead and immediately suspected the Apache had made more than a bad move. Seth had also recognized Corey leading the waiting force below.

His suspicion about Jemez was confirmed seconds later when Corey abruptly terminated the westward charge and instead veered north across what appeared to be a broad sand blight.

The men of the former First Mountain Company couldn't believe their eyes. One moment, amidst inspiring bugle notes and ferocious kill cries, the waiting force from the south and the pursuing soldiers from the east were thundering to close for the attack. The next, the world literally dropped out from under them.

Seth's jaw fell open in pure astonishment. Horses collapsed by the dozens, throwing their riders hard; wagons and gun carriages lurched to a stop, axles snapping; confused, panicked men tried to cross the sand, but kept breaking through the surface as if it were an ice crust. Men who had been hurt in the fall from their horses hollered piteously, many of them trapped like flies in hot tar.

"Good God a-gorry!" Mackenzie exclaimed. Nor were the mostly inexperienced troopers behind the fallen soldiers paying adequate attention; wave after wave of dragoons egressed onto the sand and crashed through it.

"Well, kiss my Irish ass!" Kinney said in pure astonishment.

The charge was effectively broken. Officers and NCOs tried desperately to regain order, but their commands were lost in the confusing din of curses and nickering, the cries of the injured, the triumphant taunts and jeers from the Apaches up on the headland. But Seth saw that one soldier had managed to avoid the blight, having gone far enough west to skirt the unstable ground. Now, heedless of the con-

sequences of such a foolish move, Corey Bryce singlehand-
edly attacked the gathered Indians, his saber raised in
defiance as he charged up the bluff.

As Corey's charger rapidly closed the gap, Seth watched
Jemez lower his streamered lance and peel away from the rest
to meet the attack. It happened so quickly, Seth could do
nothing. Neither Corey nor Jemez drew firearms. As their
horses made the first pass, Corey leaned sideways in the
saddle and slashed at Jemez, missing; the Apache, left off
balance, nonetheless managed a glancing sideways sweep
with his lance, hitting just hard enough to bump Corey from
the saddle.

"Shit!" Seth whirled to a trooper named Dannon, a good
marksman who also served as unit bugler. "Sound reveille!"

"Sir?"

"Oh, sir your ass, soldier! Blow reveille!"

"Yes, sir!"

Jemez had turned his pony as Corey recovered his senses
and unsnapped his .44 from its holster. The Apache threw
his lance into the ground and slid the Sharps from his scabbard. He had just settled the butt plate into his shoulder
socket when the rousing bugle notes—coming from behind
—made him turn and stare.

Now it was the Indian's turn to gape in amazed disbelief.
Seth Carlson bore down toward him, white truce flag snapping.

"No, Jemez!" he shouted. "No! Just back out of range,
don't kill him!"

Jemez looked at Nantan Maño, then at the soldier with his
.44 drawn. But neither soldier was paying any attention to
the Apache—their eyes locked on each other, aware of nothing or no one else. In that attenuated moment, all other
noise and action ceased. The soldiers below, baffled by the
sudden appearance of this officer bearing a truce flag, fell
still and silent—likewise the Apaches, taking their cue from
Jemez. The moment had a strange, ceremonial importance
that subdued both sides.

Abruptly, Jemez fell back, joining the rest of the Indians.
The only sound now was the crying of injured horses below.
Seth rode farther, halted his mount, swung to the ground.

He closed the final few yards silently, his eyes never leaving Corey's face.

Neither man flinched from a close scrutiny of the other. After a long and wordless stare, Corey was the first to speak. But Seth didn't recognize this tone, nor the mask of hatred from which it emanated.

"So here's the big hero at last. Kills my wife, then saves me. You did it backward, Carlson."

Seth could say nothing, his throat had pinched shut so hard. Corey held his .44 along his trouser seam. Now, slowly, he raised it and pointed it at his old friend.

Jemez went for his Sharps; farther up the bluff, Kinney swore and raised his carbine. But there was no time. Seth made no move to defend himself, his eyes never once leaving his old friend's as it came down to this, and he waited for the Great Thing at last, the blood atonement he was too spirit-weary to protest. But then Seth read Corey's real intention in those desperate, hurting eyes, and he leaped at him even as Corey lifted the muzzle to his own mouth.

"*No!*"

Seth's forearm struck Corey's wrist an eye blink before the weapon discharged, and the slug raked a gobbet of meat out of Corey's left cheek before the .44 thumped into the sand. Then the two men were down, snarling, grappling, tearing into each other hard.

The ferocity of the two-man contest in the sand held the day's great battle at a standstill. The Apaches sat their horses in wonder, the soldiers stood with equal fascination and disbelief. Below, on the south flank of the unstable expanse, Ferris Ablehard emerged from his command post and walked slowly toward the bluff. Like his men, he was intrigued. This was too brazen to call mere insubordination—these two soldiers had just interrupted a major campaign to settle a personal score. Earlier, the ground literally fell out from under Ablehard's attack. The whole damn day had turned into a circus—and a lively one, at that.

"You *killed* her, you *killed* her, you *killed* her, you sonofabitch!"

Each emphatic word was accompanied by a hard jab to the gut and ribs as Corey's weight trapped Seth beneath him.

But Seth's legs and back were strong from the saddle, and he braced them hard to throw Corey clear.

In a moment Seth was on him, pounding Corey's head into the sand. Corey howled with adrenaline rage, threw him, and then the two men rolled hard and fast down the rock-strewn bluff, spooking Seth's horse. They fought with fists and elbows and knees, gouged at each other's eyes, struggled for choke holds.

"You sonofabitch, Seth, you *killed* her!"

"I did my duty, you stupid bastard!"

"You *killed* her, goddamn your stinking, glory-seeking soul to hell, you *killed* my Jenny!"

"Glory? You—You stupid jackass, I did my goddamn stinking mother-rutting Army duty, you thick-headed asshole!"

"No! You *killed* her!"

Farther up the bluff, keeping a wary eye on the spellbound soldiers who were still in disarray, Jemez watched other Apaches exchange brief glances and comments, puzzled nods—truly these white-skins were an unfathomable people.

Both combatants were badly bruised and bloodied now, their breathing ragged and loud—great, wracking breaths like the dying gasps of some fallen beast. There was no energy left in them for words. They fought with grim and silent determination, battering their knuckles raw against each other's skulls. The force of the blows gradually diminished, the movements slowed; their chests heaved as if they would burst from the exertion.

It wasn't clear to the observers which of them finally collapsed first. They simply went down in a heap together, a jumble of confused limbs, then lay side by side, chests heaving.

Seth lost track of time and place and pain, drifting in and out of a delirious fog. Then he was aware that Corey had lifted his head up to look at him. For a moment, his head spinning, Seth confused memory with the present, and the two friends were cadets at West Point again. But when Corey spoke, the raw pain of his tone jolted Seth back to the moment. If ever a voice spoke to him from the heart of human misery, Corey's voice did now.

"Seth? Seth boy, you loved her, too. Why did we have to lose her?"

Out of the throbbing center of his physical hurt, a sob jolted Seth's entire body. It tore at his throat, hurt him coming out, and for a moment he felt the release of hot tears wash the blood from his face. But when he finally answered, his voice was strong and steady and sure. It was the right answer and it was the only answer, and when Seth spoke it, he settled the question as far as men on earth ever could, and both blooded officers knew it.

"Because I did my duty, soldier, that's why."

Jemez saw the star chief below staring up at the Apaches. The show was over. Nantan Maño had stolen the battle and provided a fight just as memorable. But now it was time to flee back into the sierras before the pony soldiers below could regroup.

He took one last, long look at the two young officers lying exhausted and battered in the sand. He thought about the legend of the invincible warrior who had been forced to kill a woman. Jemez understood who this sun-haired young captain must be. And he understood, especially after that bruising battle, what it must mean now as the captain lifted one bloody hand from the ground and gripped Nantan Maño's shoulder.

This thing he had witnessed today—it was somehow holy, like the mountains, and Jemez wanted to think about it, to turn it over with the fingers of his mind and pluck the kernel of meaning from it. The Apache's thin lips parted in a smile. Then, with a last, shrill, yipping shriek of defiance for the Army below, he led his warriors back into the rugged sierras of Apacheria.

Chapter 42

"Gentlemen," George Henning said, "the U.S. government finds itself in a most delicate situation."

Perched on a canvas camp stool in General Ablehard's tent, the civilian administrator for the War Department looked like a jolly elephant balanced on a stump. If anything, Seth thought, the huge man had grown even more mammoth since he had met him at Fort Bates a little more than one year ago. Once again he was dressed in immaculate white linen and a white pith helmet. His military aide, the feckless Lieutenant Worley, hovered in the background, deferential and useless. But no military artist this time, Seth noted. The Army was not so eager to immortalize *this* meeting.

"A very delicate situation," Henning repeated. He looked from Ferris Ablehard to Seth Carlson, then winked. "But I'm a cute old boy. I have a hunch things can be worked out to everyone's mutual benefit."

Outside the closed flap of the tent, a drunken cheer from his men forced Seth to stifle a grin. "*Augh!* I'll outdrink every one of you needle-dick bug fuckers!" Kinney's voice roared, rising above the melee.

"Boisterous lads," Henning said fondly. "They've earned their fun."

Seth occupied a camp stool near the center pole. Ablehard, a glass of bourbon in hand, sat on one corner of an ancient Chinese war chest he insisted on hauling around with him. To Seth, the man looked more like a weary Parisian roué than a general of cavalry. His tent was chockablock with Indian artifacts—many of which Seth recognized as burial-site plunder.

"I was sent here to Fort Grant," Henning resumed in his hearty basso profundo voice, "to see if we can't reach a gentlemen's accord on certain matters."

"George," Ablehard said, "you and I've been covering each other's ass for years now. No need to mince words. Just say it. The Army is worried sick that too many humiliating details about the latest confrontation with the aboriginals will get out. This was supposed to be the battle that broke the Apaches' back. Instead, the 'ignorant savages' played the U.S. Army for a pack of fools."

From outside, another raucous cheer. "Walt Mackenzie brags he'll hump anything that moves!" Kinney bellowed. "But *this* child don't require no motion!"

"Furthermore," Ablehard said, appraising Seth's still-evident bruises, "the War Department does not want the newspapers getting wind of the fight between Corey Bryce and Seth Carlson. That creates the appearance of dissension within the Army. It brings an unhappy ending to the story a whole nation once followed. And costs the Army much of the goodwill it had earned from milking the tragedy."

Seth's opinion of Ablehard went up a notch. He was evidently no great shakes as a general, but at least the man was frank.

Henning smiled, shrewd eyes twinkling. "Just so, Ferris, just so. You have a no-nonsense manner about you that I've always admired."

Henning propped his elbows on his knees, his chin on both fists, and nodded sagaciously. "Well, as for the newspapers . . . I'm happy to say that both of us, Ferris, have good friends in that noble profession. Eventually, of course, men who were there at the battle will talk. But for now, the reports of that recent misadventure have been kind. What people find out later won't mean half so much as what they believe now."

"Kind? I'd say they've been an outright whitewash. Especially that business with all the 'confirmed kills' and how the Army has only to smoke out a few survivors who fled back into the hills."

Henning waved one pudgy hand, as if shooing a fly. "It's all a question of judicious word choice. Would you prefer a less flattering account?"

"Gentlemen," Seth interrupted, "I've had plenty of newspaper types dogging me since they moved into this territory to hear about the great battle. So far, I've made no comment."

The pause after his remark took on layers of meaning. Ablehard watched him with wary curiosity; Henning, in contrast, seemed pleased, as if he had just taught a child a new word.

"And what," he replied slowly, "might encourage you to maintain that policy of silence?"

"Promotions for my men," Seth replied bluntly. "All of them. Meritorious promotions to the next rank. And full combat honors for every man, including Walt Mackenzie and our scout, Goes Ahead. Plus, I want special orders cut giving them enough travel time to cover the delay in reporting to their parent commands. And only half of my troop will return to garrison duty in New Mexico. The other half stays here on temporary duty with me."

"Temporary duty? What temporary duty?"

"I've already been informed that my brevet promotion has been terminated. I'm a lieutenant again, a junior-grade officer. That means I can be reassigned to provost marshal duty—in this case, to form a police force for the Mater Dolorosa Reservation. Only an interim force. Just until

Apaches themselves could organize and train their own police. It's a government installation, and as such, entitled to protection by federal forces if no local protection is available. In my best judgment as an officer, such protection is urgently needed at Mater Dolorosa."

"Reservation police?" Ablehard looked astounded. "Why in God's name would you want to police a bunch of blanket asses?"

"One finds more than Indians on reservations, eh, lad?" Henning put in, grinning. He knew about Kathleen Barton.

"How 'bout it?" Seth persisted. "You got enough pull to arrange all that?"

"Write it down for me. Everything. I like you, stout lad. I'll see to it personally."

" 'Preciate it."

"Nonsense. You've earned it."

Ablehard suddenly laughed. "Why, you young jacksnipe! You and Corey both—interrupting a battle to pull your blouses and fistfight over a woman! *I'd* lock you both in the stockade, make you dig four-holers, except that the War Department would have my resignation."

"They would indeed, Ferris," Henning warned him.

But Ablehard needed no warning. He was a man who often acted without thinking, but he was capable of regret. All this talk of the newspapers reminded him—he and Hupenbecker had gone too far, sticking those magazines and dime novels in Corey Bryce's letter box to agitate him.

"Oh, hell, George, I don't wish the lads any harm. Carlson here has some queer ideas about the red man, but he's earned his right to think what he wants. They're both squared-away soldiers. And by-*God* that was a fight! As I told Corey, too bad it wasn't directed at the Apaches."

"Speaking of Corey, General, where is he?" Seth asked.

"As of this minute, he's in charge of a log-cutting detail in the yellow-pine country to the west. Busywork to make sure you two don't lock horns again. For the near future, his company is part of the force being held here in reserve."

"In reserve for what, if I might ask, sir?"

" 'Until,' " Henning interceded, his voice laced with sarcasm as he quoted official orders he had hastily scrawled himself, " 'such time as the intentions of the remaining hostile escapees can be ascertained.' "

Seth nodded, too lost in reflection to appreciate the irony of the wording. He hadn't seen Corey again since their momentous clash, and he didn't expect to. They had parted under a peace of sorts. Both men finally had one burden off their backs—they had faced each other. But there was so much more Seth wished he could have said, even knowing words were useless now.

Outside, where the whiskey provided by Henning flowed freely, Kinney's mule bray once again forced its way above the other voices:

"Eitey-diety, Christ al-mighty!
Who in the hell are *we?*"

As one, the rest shouted out:

"Wham-bam! Thank ye, ma'am!
We're the *Cav*-al-ree!"

"No question about it," Jim Legget said, looking up from Trilby's secret journal. "This definitely helps. By itself, it'd be little more than hearsay. But if the Territorial Court approves the seizure of financial records to corroborate these charges, it'll be hard evidence to ignore."

Kathleen looked at Seth across the table, smiling encouragement. The three of them had met in the common room of the low adobe building that doubled as chapel and meeting hall at Mater Dolorosa. The saints housed in their niches had been repaired since the attack that killed Father Montoya.

"At first," the young lawyer confided, "when the BIA hired me, I don't think anyone expected an actionable case to come out of this."

Legget nodded at Kathleen. "It was just the reaction to your letters that forced them to it. There was too much pressure, it just couldn't be ignored any longer. Now, though, I sense some support from back East. Don't get me wrong— I'm not naive enough to believe that anybody is going to be punished as they ought to be. But a good case for fraud and conspiracy is shaping up. And no matter if it gets to court or not, business as usual is over for the Tucson Committee. Charles Longstreet, especially, is sweating all this."

"What about Bischoff?" Seth asked.

"On him we have little more than Trilby's say-so, I can't see him being handed an indictment. But if subpoenas go out, he'll be served. There's a good chance he could perjure himself. And as you may know, the publicity alone has already embarrassed his newspaper. The *New York Herald* has let him go. This thing is snowballing. At first, everybody in Tucson closed ranks. But now the rest of the committee have apparently decided to make Longstreet and Trilby the scapegoats. The rest claim they were victimized—they're swearing out depositions all over the place."

"Have they said anything about Hays's death?" Kathleen asked.

"Sorry. On that point they're united to the man. They swear the Tucson Committee had nothing to do with it, and even Trilby wouldn't record a word about that. That case is getting a lot of ink lately, clearly they don't plan to be linked to it. They name that Apache—"

"Jemez Grayeyes?"

"Yes."

"In other words," Seth said, "there's still a warrant out on him for that crime, based on the claims of Bischoff and Longstreet?"

Legget nodded. "That crime among others, as I understand it."

Seth nodded. True to his word, George Henning of the War Department had acted immediately on the young officer's request. Captain Carlson—for Henning had included him in the promotions—was now Acting Provost Marshal and Interim Head of the Mater Dolorosa Reservation Constabulary, which consisted of twenty of his men, including Jay Kinney and Walt Mackenzie. Thus, Seth was aware of increased cavalry patrols throughout the region. He suspected he knew their purpose—as the real details of the much-ballyhooed November showdown with the Apaches began to emerge, the Army wanted to counter the unflattering publicity with news of the capture of notorious Indian criminals. And with Geronimo rumored to be safe far south in Mexico, that left Jemez Grayeyes as the most notorious Apache in this neck of the woods.

Seth's mind surfaced from these gloomy reflections, and he saw Kathleen watching him from across the table. She knew what he was thinking, and her eyes told him she shared his concern.

"Have you ever heard of an Indian winning a case in a white man's court?" Seth asked.

"Tribes, yes, but never an individual."

"So if Grayeyes is arrested for killing Hays Munro, he's as good as dead?"

Legget nodded. " 'Fraid so. Around here a jury wouldn't even bother deliberating. It'd be worse than a drumhead court-martial, it'd be a kangaroo court."

Seth thought again about how Jemez had risked his own life in Riverbend to expose the trap set by Trilby.

Legget watched Kathleen and Seth exchange another troubled look.

"I'm young," he said, "but I've studied plenty of law. Enough to know that law and justice are two different animals. Law is power, justice is truth. It's a constant battle between them."

"Yes," Kathleen said quietly, thinking again of Hays, of his nearsighted but tenaciously held beliefs. She recalled the logo from the *Christian Advocate*, official newspaper of the Methodist Church, wanting desperately to believe the words as she said them: "But 'truth beareth away the victory.' "

Jemez felt his buckskin pony quickening her pace as she sensed the journey was ending.

He gave her her head and let her pick her way through the loose talus. After the aborted blue-blouse attack at the Devil's Floor, Jemez had joined his fellow Coyoteros near the Gila. Now, as was his way when he feared his outlaw status endangered others, he was returning to his remote cave in the south country.

He felt safe for now. He had carefully monitored his back

trail all the way down, had left false sign all along the route. Jemez was sure he was not being followed. Still, that fact seemed odd in itself and bothered him.

At the barranca near his cave he unsaddled his pony, dropped her bridle, and rubbed her down with clumps of sage. Then he turned her loose to graze and picked his way up toward his hideout, saddle slung over his shoulder.

Halfway up he detected a motion in the corner of one eye. He paused to scrutinize the huge rock walls surrounding him. But it was only a lone eagle, soaring against the crags and cliffs.

Jemez climbed the last steep slope leading to the hidden recession that marked the opening of his cave. He stopped just outside, dropped his saddle, took one last, long look all around. Then he bent to pick up his saddle, and his face suddenly prickled with a surge of cold blood.

There, on a flat rock just outside the entrance, was a heel mark of clay—damp clay. The print had only recently been made.

They were waiting for him inside his cave.

Jemez turned to bolt back down the slope. But now at least a dozen soldiers stepped out from cover, blocking the only escape path down this side of the mountain.

He heard a rustling movement from within the cave. Jemez cross drew his Remington and snapped off a round into the cave. Then he bolted up above to the left of the entrance, toward the carefully balanced boulder that was his last desperate defense.

No one was shooting. That made sweat break out on his back. There was only one reason why they would hold their fire: They meant to take him alive.

They meant to hang him.

A face peered out of the cave, and Jemez snapped off another shot. He reached the boulder, but still no one was shooting. Instead, the soldiers from below were closing in on him, scurrying from rock to rock, a net tightening around him. He had only one chance: to create a diversion and hope he could escape in the confusion.

He waited as long as he dared, until the first of the advancing bluecoats were within a stone's toss. Then, working quickly, he wrested loose the last few small rocks restraining the massive boulder. It slid a few inches, grated, scraped, shuddered like a great beast waking up. Jemez put one shoulder into it and heaved. There was a long moment's stubborn resistance, and then the boulder was a hurtling juggernaut crashing down the talus slope.

The crashing din echoed out across the spine of the sierras. The entire mountain trembled as the slide gathered force, pushing more boulders before it. The soldiers below scrambled for cover, two in the lead moving too slow, as an irresistible wave of stone smashed over them. Another screamed hideously as both legs were crushed below the knees, trapped between two boulders. The mountain side still heaved and shifted, men still screamed and ducked, as Jemez, bearing off at an oblique angle to circle the slide, leaped down the steep slope.

"Whatever you do, don't shoot him!" he heard a man shout behind him. "Take the red bastard alive!"

Jemez felt his heart fear-hammering. He jumped from boulder to boulder, reckless, only sparring for time before the soldiers recovered. But he had only begun his escape when, with a jolting tug, a rope encircled his upper body and went tight. His torso flew back, his legs still running, and Jemez fell hard on the talus.

"Good work, Henderson! That's it, keep his arms pinned close so he can't use his gun."

Captain Dennis Moats was flushed with triumph as he and Trooper Henderson picked their way down toward the infamous Jemez Grayeyes. Moats had been provided with the same detailed maps Trilby had given Corey Bryce. He knew the Army wanted Grayeyes bad. This capture would help the government save face in their mostly failed campaign against the Apaches—and prove that Dennis Moats was a better man than the arrogant, Indian-loving Seth Carlson.

Now, as the men in the cave scrambled down to help their comrades who had been trapped in the slide, Moats drew his Colt and cautiously approached Grayeyes. This was no Indian to fool with.

Jemez stared up at him defiantly. But his eyes were those of a trapped animal.

"Truss him up tight," Moats ordered Henderson. "Get his gun and search him good for weapons. Don't let him get near *anything* he could use to kill himself. We're making sure this one gets taken back alive."

Chapter 43

"Sorry. You'll have to leave your gun here," a deputy told the man waiting in front of Seth on the steps of the courthouse.

The man unbuckled his gun belt and handed it to the deputy, who tagged it and handed him back a chit. Seth was next in line. The deputy's bored glance swept over him.

"You on the courtroom security detail, Captain?"

Seth shook his head.

"Testifying?"

"No. Just came to watch."

"Hunh. Seems like half the damn territory has done *that*," the deputy groused, looking at the line still forming behind Seth. "You'd think nobody ever seen an Injun before. Well, since you're an officer, you can keep your weapon."

Seth moved on into the courthouse, a stately fieldstone building with carved marble benches on the lawn. The hallway smelled of beeswax and boasted gleaming walnut wainscotting. The capital of the Arizona Territory had been moved from Prescott to Tucson in 1867, but the Territorial Court remained behind. The territory's all-Anglo bastion, Prescott was a bustling ranching and mining center nestled among ponderosa pines and Douglas firs about two hundred miles northwest of Tucson.

Seth followed the window-lined ell to the courtroom, boot heels drumming on the sanded planks. He heard the hubbub of many voices before he reached the open double doors. Two enlisted guards brought their heels together smartly. Seth returned their salutes, then stepped inside.

It *did* seem like half the territory had turned out for the "trial" of Jemez Grayeyes. The Apache, being neither an American citizen nor a ward of the U.S. government, fell into a crack between jurisdictions. So he was being prosecuted under joint military-territorial law, the Army acting as prosecutor while the Territorial Court actually provided a venue for the case.

Publicity had been heavy, and the spectators' benches were full, as were the rows of chairs set up in the back of the room to accommodate the overflow. Most of the visitors were men, but a few curious women had shown up too. Since it was now standing room only, Seth crowded his way toward the front, letting his uniform clear a hole for him.

The jury was already seated in their box: a dozen white ranchers, miners, and businessmen, many of them clearly uncomfortable in suits and spanking-clean starched shirts. The front row of the spectators' section was dominated by newspaper reporters, notepads open across their knees. Armed soldiers lined both side walls, carbines resting against their right trouser seams. Rumors abounded that Apaches meant to swoop down on the courthouse and free their hero.

Then Seth spotted Jemez, and anger roiled his gut.

The Apache sat by himself, except for a Mexican translator, at the table reserved for the defense. His face was lopsided from swollen bruises. In a gesture of deliberate humiliation, his captors had forced him to wrap himself in a red wool blanket. Some prankster had also stuck a white chicken feather in his headband. But Jemez was in no position to pull it out: His wrists were cuffed behind his back, and "Uncle Sam's watch and chain"—a twenty-five-pound iron ball connected to six feet of chain—had been shackled to his left ankle by a blacksmith.

If he recognized Seth, he gave no sign. The soldier tried to recall when he had seen that vastly remote look on the Apache's face before. Then he remembered. It was when Jemez was being tortured by Matazal and his renegades down in Old Mexico, when he had told Seth how to place the pain outside of himself. Jemez was doing the same now, Seth realized, with his fear.

Seth spotted Ferris Ablehard in the row behind the reporters. The general nodded. Then Seth felt a prickling numbness in his face when he realized the man sitting next to Ablehard was Corey Bryce.

The two young officers met each other's eyes. Corey, too, nodded, and Seth nodded back. Then Seth looked away, unsettled by the unexpected meeting.

After several raps of a gavel, the bailiff's voice rang out, "Oyez, oyez! All rise for the Honorable Judge Cyrus Potter."

There was a clumsy shuffling and scraping of chairs as everyone except Jemez stood up. The judge entered from a door at the front of the room. Potter was a big, florid man in his late fifties. A former Texas Ranger, he conveyed the stern, driven manner of an abolitionist.

Potter took his seat on the raised dais, and the bailiff called out the case currently on the docket: the Territory of Arizona and the U.S. Army versus Jemez Grayeyes. As the charges were read out, Seth realized just what a circus act this was to be. Whereas a white man would be entitled to a separate trial for each major charge, Jemez's reputed crimes were simply catalogued together: the murder of Hays Munro; the murders of two soldiers, and injuries of three more, during his recent capture; the murders of Juan Aragon and Robert Trilby; the murders of various bull whackers and stagecoach drivers and way-station workers. Besides the deaths charged to his hand were numerous woundings, robberies, rapes, cattle raids, and acts of theft and destruction against inhabitants of the territory.

It was a bloody chronicle, and an indignant silence fell over the courtroom when the bailiff finished reading it. Only a veritable fiend could compile such a record of violent infamy. But Seth noticed Corey watching Jemez, a thoughtful frown on his face—perhaps recognizing this Apache as the warrior who spared his life that day the cavalry charge fell apart.

One of the jurors abruptly stood up. "I'm jury foreman, so I.got first dibs on the skull," he called out.

A ripple of laughter. Judge Potter pounded his gavel. "Now goddamnit, Harlan, you shut up. You hear me? This here's a court of law, not a Green River Ronnyvoo."

"Aww, hell, I was just funnin'."

"Like hob you was. You boys want to carve Innun bodies up to sell for trophies, that's your business—though I say it ain't Christian. But this today ain't no business meeting. I oughtn't to even warn you, but I'll give you this one chance. No more sounding off out of turn. Don't rowel me."

"Yes, sir."

But despite the judge's stern warning, Seth soon realized this "trial" was indeed an outright travesty. Not only were there no witnesses for the defense, there was no defense, period. Only a prosecutor. The main reason for even bothering with this show was the journalists down front—their collective reassurance to America that, yes indeed, the authorities were doing their job, and the Apache menace was under control.

Yet Seth soon discovered there was no shortage of witnesses for the prosecution.

Leading the effort against Jemez was a celebrated prosecutor of Indian crimes, Major Jack Lindsey of the Judge Advocate General's Office in Washington. He was intelligent and eloquent, forcefully persuasive, often inducing the audience to vigorous nods of agreement. First he called a string of white witnesses, including Charles Longstreet, in a nonstop litany of the Apache's crimes. Then he surprised the courtroom by summoning an elderly Apache called Popo to the stand.

Speaking through the interpreter, Lindsey said, "Popo, how many winters do you have behind you?"

"Seventy."

"And what is your standing with your people at the San Carlos Reservation?"

"I am Headman of my Broken Lance Clan. I sit behind no man in council."

"I see. A regular big chief."

Lindsey turned to the spectators and winked. Several of them laughed.

"Now tell the people here about the journey you made last June."

"My granddaughter, who is married to a Coyotero Apache, lives at Mater Dolorosa with her husband's clan. She had just given birth to her first child. Despite my years, Ussen has blessed me with health. I made the ride to visit with my granddaughter and the new baby."

"And what did you see on the day you arrived?"

"I saw him"—the old Apache raised a hand gnarled like a peach pit, pointing at Jemez—"arguing with the one who was the agent at Mater Dolorosa."

"You mean Hays Munro, right?"

The old man winced when the name was pronounced. "Him," he agreed, nodding.

"Where was this?"

"Near the agent's house."

"What else did you see?"

"I saw this one strike him many times."

"I see. Then what?"

"I saw the one who was the agent fall to the ground. Then I watched this one raise a battle ax high. It came down hard, and the head of the agent rolled free of its body."

Gasps from the women, angry murmurs from the men. Judge Potter rapped his gavel.

"All right. Then what?"

"This Jemez Grayeyes, he stuck the head on a pointed stake and put it in the ground in front of the house."

More gasps and murmurs. But the courtroom went into collective shock when the prisoner not only spoke up for the first time during his trial, but did so in clear English.

"That old man is a liar. The Broken Lance Clan is all cowards and thieves. He was paid to say these lies."

Potter banged his gavel. "H'ar now! You'll watch yourself in my courtroom, John, and you'll speak only when you're told to."

"Why didn't you inform this court of the fact that you speak English?" the prosecutor demanded.

"Nobody asked. Nobody asked me nothing."

"Gentlemen," Lindsey said, facing the jury box, "if you need further proof of this man's instinctive treachery, now you have it. It was duplicity, and duplicity alone, which drove him to mislead us. And please note this, also: there is absolutely no remorse in his tone *or* his face for anything he has done. He knows right from wrong, he's no animal in the intellectual sense. He simply chooses evil and never once suffers any regret for his actions. I emphasize this point because *actus non facit reum, nisi mens sit rea.* 'The act is not criminal unless the intent is criminal.' Clearly this Apache is capable of both. He's no 'noble savage' defending himself, he's a marauding, murdering, thieving criminal who epitomizes the godless and lawless savagery this great nation is fighting to overcome if it is ever to fulfill its higher destiny."

"Was that your summary, counselor?" Judge Potter demanded. "You spill so damn much chin music, I can't hardly tell."

More laughter. Lindsey threw up his hands, the gesture suggesting that he had done his best to shore up these frontier ruins, and now it was up to men with guts and clear vision to get on with the job.

"I've spoke my piece, Your Honor."

"Good. My stomach's a-growlin'. Harlan, you boys need time to deliberate?"

"What the hell for, Cyrus? He's guilty."

"All right." Judge Potter banged his gavel to quiet the courtroom. "Apache," he said, staring down at Jemez, "the Territorial Court of Arizona has found you guilty. I sentence you to be hanged by the neck until dead. Execution will take place one week from today. I won't bother to add, may God have mercy on your soul. Court adjourned."

As Potter spoke the expected death-by-hanging sentence, Seth watched genuine fear distort Jemez's bruised face for the first time that morning.

Jemez met his eyes, and there was no mistaking the plea in them. Seth looked at all the guards, symbolic of the grossly exaggerated security that would surround this lone Apache until he was executed. Nor would Jemez be given the slightest opportunity to kill himself—this public hanging meant too much to the War Department's Indian-fighting image.

Those in the back of the room started to file out. Two soldiers began to move in Jemez's direction. Seth knew there were only a few seconds left, and then all hope would be lost for this Apache who had saved his life twice, this tough but fair warrior who deserved far better than this outright butchery. And thinking that, Seth knew what he had to do. Perhaps he had even come here to do it, but hadn't let the thought form in his mind until now.

Jemez read the determination in his friend's eyes, and for the first time that morning hope touched the Indian's battered face.

"*Hazlo*, Nantan Maño," he said quietly. "*Do* it."

The people exiting stopped and turned around in surprise when the Apache abruptly began a brief chant in his own tongue. By the time Jemez had finished his death song, Seth's .44 was in his hand and cocked.

Several sentries, caught off guard, started to raise their carbines.

"As you were, troopers!" an authoritative voice barked out.

Seth glanced to his left and saw Corey's service revolver trained on the sentries. However, one of them still continued to raise his weapon.

"I've never been one to bluff, Soldier Blue," Corey warned him, training his weapon on the man.

Corey's voice still echoed in the far corners when Jemez's final defiant shout exploded in the crowded room. Seth's .44 bucked in his fist. The slug caught Jemez flush in the heart and dropped him to the floor, a strange smile of triumph on his face as he defied his enemies in death and once and for all eluded their noose.

In the shocked, timeless silence after it was done, Corey looked at Ablehard as if recollecting something. He swallowed, then announced in a calm voice:

"There it is, ladies and gentlemen. What you just witnessed is the way hardened criminals are handled in Mexico —one of the few things they get right. My name is Corey

Bryce, and that gentleman who just saved you the cost of a hanging is Seth Carlson."

Pronouncing those two names elicited an explosion of surprised voices. Judge Potter was still too startled to call for order. The journalists looked as excited as predators at a feeding frenzy. A few uncertain soldiers held their weapons pointed loosely at the two soldier heroes. They looked to Ablehard for orders, but like everyone else, he felt compelled to see this drama played out.

"Seth and I," Corey went on, one canny eye on the newspaper scribblers, "talked this over real careful. Then we made up our minds to do the right thing. Isn't that so, Seth boy?"

Seth holstered his weapon, nodded. "He's right. We agreed on it as the right thing to do to that murdering savage. Once the sentence was pronounced, of course."

"We're good friends," Corey said. "Two good soldiers, two good Americans."

Corey looked hard at Seth now. "After all," he went on, "it was *Indians* that killed my wife, not Seth. He stood and held and did his duty like a man. It's *Indians* who keep both of us awake nights now while they, ignorant beasts that they are, sleep in blissful peace. They don't have to wake up crying out Jenny's name. But we do, don't we, Seth?"

"That's God's own truth, Corey."

"And now," Corey said, "we'll take what we got coming to us. But you see, folks, Jenny's life has *got* to matter. If the American people want to call us murderers, then so be it. Jenny's life *mattered*, and by-God, what we just did was not the act of vigilantes, but of civilized men.

"Jenny and I were planning to have children someday. Seth here would've been godfather to our firstborn. Those children will never be, thanks to murdering redskins. But I hope all of you folks gathered here today will watch *your* kids grow up in a country where law and decency matter. I hope that. For the sake of Jenny's memory, for the sake of all the other Jennys still alive in this great nation."

By now there wasn't a dry-eyed female in the room, and many of the men were blinking more than usual, visibly moved. The soldiers had lowered their weapons.

Seth aimed a sidelong glance at Judge Potter. The savvy

old frontiersman had not quite fallen for these impromptu histrionics. But he looked down at all the journalists madly scribbling notes, and he chuckled. Potter was a strict man, but he dearly admired men with sand in their craws.

He looked at the prosecutor. "Jack, I could've *swore* that Innun was going for a weapon when he stood up and started that caterwauling."

The Army lawyer nodded, seeing which way the wind set. He, too, looked at the journalists. Any man who tried to protest what those two officers just did would become the scourge of America.

"That's what I thought, too, Cyrus. Captain Carlson was quick to act."

"Ahuh," Potter said, peering at Seth. "Damn quick."

"And even though, as Captain Bryce explained, these two might have *planned* to shoot the Indian—which of course would have been illegal—I think everyone will agree that Captain Carlson instead acted in our defense. Therefore, their illegal plan was never carried out. So there was no crime. I trust the record will reflect that fact."

"I reckon it will, at that," Potter agreed, still staring at Seth.

Seth knew that Corey, too, must appreciate the irony: This time the newspapers were their salvation.

The courtroom killing of Jemez Grayeyes sold more newspapers than had the assassination of Lincoln. A few disgruntled citizens back East deplored it as "base vigilantism." But the vast majority of Americans approved; like a nondenominational prayer, the act was ambiguous enough to please everyone. "Swift justice was meted out in true frontier fashion!" one exuberant editorialist proclaimed, voicing the feeling of the Indian-extermination faction. In contrast, those more sympathetic to Indians saw it as a mercy killing, given Grayeyes's legendary fear of hanging. The Army, meantime, basked in a sudden surge of badly needed military recruitment as thousands of young men volunteered for service, inspired by the romantic tragedy of Seth Carlson and Corey Bryce.

For Seth, Jemez's death was a release, as real as if he'd

been let out of prison. Not only had it bonded him and Corey in a final act of mutual forgiveness, but in his own heart he knew unequivocally that this time he had not "played God" with a human life.

"So what now?" Kathleen asked him two weeks after the incident in Prescott. "Do you accept the teaching post at West Point or resign your commission?"

"That depends."

It was noon, and Seth had visited Kathleen at school. The December day was cool, but clear and sunny, and most of the children were playing a hoop-and-pole game outside.

"Depends on what, Captain?"

Her long hair was knotted tight over the nape of her neck, but sunlight slanted in through the windows and ignited the light streaks. Seth smelled her lavender perfume, the clean scent of soap.

"Well, I can squeeze more time out of the Army by saying the Apache police force isn't yet up to snuff. How long you plan on staying around here?"

Kathleen sat at her desk, marking a set of compositions her pupils had written that morning. She looked up at Seth, who was perched on one corner of the desk.

"Jim Legget is sure now the case against Longstreet and the Tucson Committee will go to trial. I plan to testify."

"Same here. He asked, and I told him I would. Then what?"

She lay her pen aside. Outside, one of the children shrieked with laughter. "Why do you ask?"

"Because," he said, "I want to know if you'll marry me and move back to New York when I take the West Point position."

Time ticked out a long silence between them. More laughter from outside, the sound of feet scurrying past the building. They watched each other during all this, neither of them moving.

"Well?" Seth finally said.

"What do you think I'll say?"

Seth suddenly grinned. "I think if you were going to say no, you wouldn't've said that. That would be cruel."

"I think you're right."

"So I guess your answer is yes?"

"I'd guess your guess is right. But only if you kiss me now to seal the deal."

He did. When they broke from their long embrace, a lone figure was standing in the doorway.

"Victorio!" Kathleen exclaimed, flushing red to the roots of her hair. "*Qué haces?*"

The youth grinned at both of them. "Nothing," he said with exaggerated innocence, turning away. Then he turned back and added quickly, "*He* told me you two would exchange the squaw-taking vows. I am glad he was right."

They both knew he meant Jemez. News of his sensational death electrified Apacheria—every Apache who heard it knew that Jemez Grayeyes had left them a proud symbol of defiance. But Kathleen and Seth also knew what Victorio still refused to accept, that the days of wide-ranging freedom would soon be over for the Apaches, the last and toughest holdouts of all the American Indians. But for now, at least, the extermination policy had lost momentum with the failed attack at Devil's Floor. There were some signs that the government was moving in good faith to negotiate, though few were stupid enough to think the change of heart was permanent or widely supported.

"Seth?" Kathleen said when Victorio had gone.

"Hmm?"

"You never told me, but I know you loved Jeanette Bryce. Is it all right now? I mean—in your heart, about us, is it all right?"

Seth gazed out the windows, out past the Apache children playing on the windswept gravel flat, clear out to the dark purple, shadowy mass of the sierras on the horizon. Again he saw that confusing plea in Jeanette's eyes right before he squeezed the trigger—and then, over the image of her eyes, was superimposed the trapped-deer gaze of Jemez, begging him to free him from the only hell he believed in.

"Yes, lady," Seth replied, taking her hand in his and holding the palm against his cheek. And as he spoke the words, he knew he finally believed them. "It's all right."

ABOUT THE AUTHOR

Raised in Monroe County, Michigan, JOHN ED-
WARD AMES has lived in the West for many years, in
both Colorado and New Mexico. A former newspaper
reporter, construction worker, and drug rehabilitation
counselor, Ames has also taught writing at several uni-
versities. *The Unwritten Order* is his first work of his-
torical fiction. Ames currently lives and works in New
Orleans, Louisiana.

THE AMERICAN CHRONICLES
by Robert Vaughan

In this magnificent saga, award-winning author Robert Vaughan tells the riveting story of America's golden age: a century of achievement and adventure in which a young nation ascends to world power.

❑ **OVER THERE** 29661-2 $4.99/$5.99 in Canada
The *Titanic* goes down; millions pass through Ellis Island; a bloody revolution in Russia; and a single shot in Sarajevo explodes into a world war. This is a decade full of danger, turmoil, and blazing desire.

❑ **THE LOST GENERATION** 29680-9 $4.99/$5.99 in Canada
Gangland wars blaze across Prohibition Chicago, a conquered Germany follows a dark destiny, and ominous rumblings on Wall Street fill this decade with passion, promise, and explosive conflict.

❑ **PORTALS OF HELL** 29276-5 $5.50/$6.50 in Canada
Japan's surprise attack plunges America into World War II. Hitler ravages Europe with death camps and terror, and an explosion in Los Alamos rocks the world into a nuclear age. These pivotal years will forever change the course of history.

❑ **THE IRON CURTAIN** 56510-9 $5.50/$7.99 in Canada
The atomic age is ushered in at a place called Hiroshima; a defeated Germany pays the price at Nuremberg; and a Red scare sweeps across America. It is a time of exuberant hopes and lingering fears as America realizes her destiny.

Available at your local bookstore or use this page to order.
Send to: Bantam Books, Dept. DO 11
          2451 S. Wolf Road
          Des Plaines, IL 60018
Please send me the items I have checked above. I am enclosing $_____ (please add $2.50 to cover postage and handling). Send check or money order, no cash or C.O.D.'s, please.

Mr./Ms._____

Address_____

City/State_____Zip_____
Please allow four to six weeks for delivery.
Prices and availability subject to change without notice. DO 11 1/95

NEW! From Dana Fuller Ross

WAGONS WEST: THE FRONTIER TRILOGY

*THE FIRST HOLTS. The incredible beginning of
America's favorite pioneer saga*

Dana Fuller Ross tells the early story of the Holts, men and
women living through the most rugged era of American
exploration, following the wide Missouri, crossing the high
Rockies, and fighting for the future they claimed as theirs.

❏ **WESTWARD!** 29402-4 $5.50/$6.50 in Canada
In the fertile Ohio Valley, brothers Clay and Jefferson
strike out for a new territory of fierce violence and
breathtaking wonders. The Holts will need all their
fighting prowess to stay alive...and to found the
pioneer family that will become an American legend.

❏ **EXPEDITION!** 29403-2 $5.50/$6.50 in Canada
In the heart of this majestic land, Clary and his Sioux
wife lead a perilous expedition up the Yellowstone
River while Jeff heads back east on a treacherous
quest. With courage and spirit, the intrepid Holts fight
to shape the destiny of a nation and to build an
American dynasty.

❏ **OUTPOST!** 29400-8 $5.50/$6.50 in Canada
Clay heads to Canada to bring a longtime enemy to
justice, while in far-off North Carolina, Jeff is stalked by a
ruthless killer determined to destroy his family. As war
cries fill the air, the Holts must fight once more for their
home and the dynasty that will live forever in the pages
of history.

Available at your local bookstore or use this page to order.
Send to: Bantam Books, Dept. DO 34
2451 S. Wolf Road
Des Plaines, IL 60018
Please send me the items I have checked above. I am enclosing
$_____ (please add $2.50 to cover postage and handling).
Send check or money order, no cash or C.O.D.'s, please.

Mr./Ms._____

Address_____

City/State_____ Zip_____
Please allow four to six weeks for delivery.
Prices and availability subject to change without notice.   DO 34 6/93

THE EXCITING FRONTIER SERIES CONTINUES!

RIVERS WEST

ᴛʜᴇ *HIGH MISSOURI*

A would-be priest looking for adventure, Dylan Campbell signed up with Nor West Company to bring God to the Indians—and to break with his father in Montreal. But as Dylan traveled across the mighty Saskatchewan in the company of a mystical wanderer called the Druid, he learned about love, lust, betrayal, and hate—and what it means to struggle for your life with body and soul.

Discover one of the most thrilling frontier series of our time...tales of mountain men and intrepid women, pioneer families and Native American warriors. Here is the story of North America in all its awesome splendor.

- ❑ The High Missouri, by Win Blevins ....56511-7 $4.99/$5.99 in Canada
- ❑ The Gila River, by Gary McCarthy ....29769-4 $4.99/$5.99 in Canada
- ❑ The Snake River, by Win Blevins ....29770-8 $4.99/$5.99 in Canada
- ❑ The Yellowstone, by Win Blevins ....27401-5 $4.99/$5.99 in Canada
- ❑ The Smoky Hill, by Don Coldsmith ....28012-0 $4.99/$5.99 in Canada
- ❑ The Colorado, by Gary McCarthy ....28451-7 $4.99/$5.99 in Canada
- ❑ The Powder River, by Win Blevins ....28583-1 $4.99/$5.99 in Canada
- ❑ The Russian River, by Gary McCarthy ....28844-X $4.50/$5.50 in Canada
- ❑ The Arkansas River, by Jory Sherman ....29180-7 $4.99/$5.99 in Canada
- ❑ The American River, by Gary McCarthy ..29532-2 $4.99/$5.99 in Canada
- ❑ The Two Medicine River, by Richard S. Wheeler
  29771-6 ....$4.99/$5.99 in Canada

Available at your local bookstore or use this page to order.

Send to: Bantam Books, Dept. DO 40
           2451 S. Wolf Road
           Des Plaines, IL 60018

Please send me the items I have checked above. I am enclosing
$_____ (please add $2.50 to cover postage and handling). Send check or money order, no cash or C.O.D.'s, please.

Mr./Ms._____

Address_____

City/State_____Zip_____

Please allow four to six weeks for delivery.
Prices and availability subject to change without notice.   DO 40 5/94